The
SNOW
GYPSY

ALSO BY LINDSAY JAYNE ASHFORD

The

SNOW GYPSY

LINDSAY JAYNE ASHFORD

LAKE UNION
PUBLISHING

Published by Lake Union Publishing, Seattle

www.apub.com

Amazon, the Amazon logo, and Lake Union are trademarks of Amazon.com, Inc., or its affiliates.

ISBN-13: 9781542040051 (hardcover)
ISBN-10: 1542040051 (hardcover)
ISBN-13: 9781542040044 (paperback)
ISBN-10: 1542040043 (paperback)

Cover design by Faceout Studio, Jeff Miller

Printed in the United States of America

First edition

In memory of my great-grandmother Ann Eliza Fowler,
who never had the chance to learn to read and write.

Chapter 1

Spain: April 18, 1938

The snow has lingered longer than usual this spring. It shrouds the orange and lemon groves in the valley below the village of Capileira and sends fingers of white up the scars in the hillside where the sun never reaches.

The girl sets off in the cold pink dawn, urging the goats out into the street, up the steep path that leads to the mountain pastures. As she climbs higher, a veil of scented smoke drifts up from the fires of rosemary wood being lit in the houses. For a while the only sound is the tinkle of the goats' bells. Then the cries of ravens tear through the morning air. They swoop over the herd, hungry for blood. The girl knows she must be vigilant. They will take a newborn kid if they get the chance.

Her breakfast of bread and cheese is eaten on a moss-covered rock, from which she watches the sun rise over the Mediterranean Sea. If she holds her hand above her eyes, she can make out the misty peaks of Morocco on the other side of the water. The goats tear at the tender new shoots of gorse and thyme, their udders swaying as they roam the landscape.

She is on her way back down when flakes of snow begin to appear. At first, they are soft and sparse, circling like almond blossoms as they fall. Then, as the wind gusts from the glacier on the top of the mountain, they turn into showers of icy splinters that sting her eyes.

A blanket of cloud smudges the sky, and the goats huddle closer, spooked by the sudden change in the weather. Fresh dung showers the path. The smell pinches at her nostrils. But it's not just the flurry of snow. Something else has scared them. Someone is shouting. Angry voices rise from the ravine that separates her from the town far below. The girl can't see over the ridge. But what she hears makes her blood freeze. A voice she knows, rising above the moan of the wind.

When the shots ring out, the goats stop dead. She fights her way through the jam of wet fur and scrambles down the mountainside. Shards of loose rock jab the worn soles of her boots, and thornbushes snag her clothes. She catches her foot in a gorse root and lurches forward, grasping at spiny branches to save herself. But the goats have followed her. They crowd around, a forest of legs blocking her way. By the time she reaches the valley floor, the ravens are already circling overhead.

Snow is falling like feathers on dead faces. Bodies lie where they have fallen. The wind tugs at their clothes, the colors bleaching as the blizzard buries them. She lurches from one lifeless form to another, frantically sweeping eyelids, noses, mouths. She drops to her knees beside two bodies that lie together, letting out a howl of anguish. She cradles their heads, pleading for some sign of life. But their white shrouds are red with blood.

Snow is falling like feathers. Angels coming for departed souls.

Shuddering with sobs, she flings herself down between the woman and the boy. Clasping two cold hands, she closes her eyes, willing the blizzard to go on. If she lies still for long enough, it will take her, too. It won't be a frightening death like theirs. She will simply fall asleep.

But the goats won't leave her alone. They cluster around, nibbling at her boots, pulling off her hat. She kicks out at them and closes her eyes tighter. One of them is making a strange noise. More like a cat than a goat. She wonders if this is the beginning of death—hearing sounds that don't make sense.

The noise grows louder, more urgent. By some instinct she lifts her head. At the outer edge of her vision, something moves. Not downward like the snowflakes, but upward. Pinkish white, streaked with red, like a newly skinned rabbit. It looks like an arm—but it's far too small to belong to the body lying in the snow. She blinks, thinking she must be hallucinating. But it's still there—that desperate, flailing limb. And that thin, insistent cry.

She stumbles to her feet, her legs numb and clumsy. The body is some distance from the others. The wind tugs at a skirt the color of chestnuts. Black hair tumbles from a woolen cap that has fallen sideways. The eyes are open, staring into the sky. And there, in the folds of a shawl patterned with peacocks, is a tiny blood-smeared scrap of life.

The girl reaches out. The fingers that grasp hers remind her of the bunched tentacles of squid in the fish stalls at the village market. She wonders how something so small can feel so strong. Her eyes travel from the hand, along the arm to the body. A girl child. Still attached to its mother by a twist of sinew and veins.

With its frosting of snow, the woman's face is ghostly. A trickle of dark red oozes from a wound at the base of her neck. The girl wonders how the baby can be alive when the person who gave birth to it is dead. But as the thought enters her head, she catches a slight movement—the twitch of a muscle on one side of the mouth. The lips slide apart like melting ice.

"Please . . ." The woman tries to lift her head. The eyelids flutter, blue-veined skin almost translucent. Her voice is a rasping whisper. "Take my baby."

The eyes are cloudy black, like the two halves of a split olive. They hold hers for what seems like eternity, until she feels as if she's falling into the fathomless land behind their dark centers. And then, without a sound, the head falls back into the snow.

The baby gives a piercing wail, as if it knows. The girl stares, bewildered, at its little purple face. She grabs at the shawl, tries to wrap it around the child's body. But the cord gets in the way. Her hand goes to her waist, feeling for her belt. But the leather sheath where she keeps her knife is empty. In the scramble down the mountain, she has lost it.

Her teeth are all she has. The blood is like metal in her mouth. She thinks that she will never forget that taste. Always it will be trapped with the faces of those she loved, in a drift of memory.

She lifts the baby into her arms, tucking it inside her coat. She lowers her head against the blast of the wind, unsteady as she retraces her steps. How can she leave the loved ones lying there? How can she bury them? She sinks to her knees. Offering a prayer is all she can do.

Take my baby.

The goats huddle around as she struggles to her feet. She turns her head toward the mountain, to the fast-disappearing track that winds up to the summit.

Take my baby.

She catches her breath as the cold seeps into her bones.

Take it where?

Chapter 2

England: May 2, 1946

Rose Daniel caught an early train from Waterloo station. It felt good to be getting away from London. Away from the ugliness of the bombed-out buildings and the air of desolation they created. Away from the drabness of the clothes, the shops, the people. There was no color—as if the war had sucked the life out of everything.

Forty minutes into the journey, the train hurtled out of a tunnel into a gully lined with cherry trees. The rush of air sent pink petals tumbling like confetti against the carriages. A few fell through the open window and landed on the gray woolen fabric of her dress. As she brushed them away, the landscape opened out into meadows sprinkled with buttercups, where cows raised curious heads at the clatter of the wheels on the tracks. There was a whiff of farmyards coming through the window—a ripe, wholesome smell, so different from the sour air of the city.

Only another hour and the train would be passing through the wetlands between Chichester and the sea: the place where the Gypsies gathered in springtime to hunt hares and cut willow for making baskets—the place where Rose had once lived in a tent beside a stream for a whole summer and woken each morning to the sound of skylarks.

She slipped her hand inside the pocket of her dress, fingering Nathan's letter. It had been a day like this, nearly ten years ago, when she had last seen him. A day of bright skies and dark shadows. He had come to find her to say goodbye, passing through Chichester on his way to board a ferry at Southampton. He'd said he hadn't had the heart to tell their parents—just left a note on the kitchen table, saying, "Gone to Spain."

The sun slanted into the railway carriage, lighting up the golden fur of Rose's Afghan hound, Gunesh, who lay sleeping at her feet. Her hand went to his head, stroking the soft place between his ears. He had been a puppy—just eight months old—that summer on the Sussex marshes. She remembered how he had growled when Nathan poked his head through the flap of the tent. And how Nathan had tickled him into submission, the two of them wrestling by the stream, clothes and fur covered in sticky emerald beads of goosegrass.

She had cooked breakfast over a little fire of hawthorn twigs and listened to his passionate argument for joining a war in a country he'd never even visited.

"Fascism is the new Satan, Rose," he'd said. "Let Spain fall, and the evil will spread all over Europe."

She had nodded as she slid eggs out of the frying pan onto hunks of brown bread. "You don't need to tell me about fascists. You know the place where I was living last term, in Paddington? It was just down the street from Oswald Mosley's headquarters. His thugs in their black shirts used to march right past our front door, shouting, 'Death to Jews!'"

"Hmm. So that explains why you're living in a tent surrounded by rabbit shit." Nathan had been pulling the petals off a daisy as he spoke. "I did wonder."

"It wasn't only that."

"Oh? Don't tell me—a boy, is it? Who is he? Some farmer's son you locked eyes with while dissecting a dead cat?"

At that point she'd given him a shove, almost sending the eggs slithering off the bread onto the grass. "Listen, Horse, I came here to learn, not to mess around with men! I thought you of all people would understand."

With Rose it was animals in general—dogs in particular—but for Nathan it had always been horses. Even their parents used to call him by the nickname he'd acquired as a child.

"And have you?" He'd given her a sly smile.

"Have I what?"

"Learnt anything?"

"Yes: heaps more than I've picked up in two years at university. Last week I watched a Gypsy man cure a whole litter of sick puppies. They had distemper. He used nothing but herbs gathered from round here. In London they'd all have died. Any vet will tell you there's no hope for a dog in a case like that."

"I wonder what the pet lovers of London will say when you tell them you've picked up everything you know from the Gypsy school of veterinary science?" Nathan was still smiling. "Are you even going to *bother* going back to university in September?"

Rose had clicked her tongue and said, "I suppose I'll have to. They'll never let me practice otherwise. But I hate the way we're taught. Experimenting on live animals is so cruel, the absolute opposite of why I wanted to be a vet. And the drugs we're supposed to use—I'm convinced most of them do more harm than good."

And so they had gone on until it was time for him to leave, talking about *her* life, not his, dodging the stark reality that neither of them could voice: that Nathan might not come back from this war in Spain.

When Rose had kissed him goodbye, she had made herself smile. They had joked about the presents he would bring home. He had promised to buy her castanets so she could learn to dance like a Gypsy.

Over the next two years, there had been a handful of letters, the last one—the one she had in her pocket—was dated March 14, 1938. Then months had gone by with no word from him. When two years had elapsed with no contact from Nathan, their father had set out in search of him. But neither of them had returned. Rose glanced out the train window at a blur of fields and trees. She had promised herself she wouldn't cry. But the faces were always there, behind her eyes. Her father, her mother, and Nathan.

That summer morning when he came to say goodbye seemed like another lifetime. She had loved living alone, happy and free, when she had had a family. How hollow that freedom felt now.

Where are you going, Rose?

Her mother's voice echoed through her head. Standing by the door, her bag packed, Rose had been about to set off in search of her brother. Numb with grief at the death of her father, she felt impelled to follow the trail that he had taken. But she had been hopelessly naive. It was the summer of 1940. Hitler's army had already taken France.

Where are you going?

Six years on, the truth was she didn't know. But she was on her way to find the one person who could point the way.

Chapter 3

Spain: May 2, 1946

In a tavern in the shadow of the Alhambra palace, Lola Aragon lifted her arms above her head. When they could go no higher, she turned the backs of her wrists together, twisting long brown fingers into miniature antlers.

Her eyes were as black as poppy seeds in the glimmering lamplight. She glanced at Cristóbal, who stretched a long-nailed thumb over the strings of his guitar. The three children sitting beside him were watching for the signal. Without even looking at each other, they began clapping out a fast staccato beat. Nieve, the youngest, had hands no bigger than hens' eggs, but she clapped as if the rhythm were a secret language she'd learned in the womb.

Lola moved across the room, her body as slender as esparto grass in a tight-fitting green dress and a shawl the vivid scarlet of pomegranate flowers. Her long dark hair was coiled at the nape of her neck, adorned with sprigs of white jasmine. She snaked her arms, head erect, hips swaying while her feet bombarded the wooden floor.

The people gathered in the tavern had been passing the wine around since the sun had dropped below the terracotta walls of the palace. But they were not too drunk to recognize star quality. Some clapped along with the children, shouting *"¡Olé!"* as each sequence ended. Others just watched, spellbound, their drinks forgotten. There was one man in particular. He followed her with hungry eyes. She could feel them even when she had her back to him.

At the end of the second fandango, the tempo changed. Cristóbal let out the first mournful notes of the *cante jondo*. The deep song. Tortured and passionate, he sang as if blood, not music, were coming from his mouth. Lola's dancing echoed the melancholy sound. Her body told a story of betrayal and lost love. She moved like someone possessed.

When the applause died down, she slipped out the back door to get changed, then hurried back to take the children out into the palace gardens for a late-night picnic of lemonade, cherries, bread, and goat cheese. They sat on blankets under a hazy crescent moon, listening to the crickets making music. Far below them dogs were barking on the banks of the Darro River. The children pinched their noses when the whiff of tainted water drifted up on the breeze.

"It was good tonight." Cristóbal squeezed her arm when he came to join them. "Antonio Lopez couldn't take his eyes off you. He came to talk to me while you were getting changed."

"Please don't tell me it was about marriage again!"

Cristóbal gave a helpless shrug. "What was I supposed to say? He's not a bad man. He has half a dozen mules and a shed full of chickens. You'd never go hungry."

"I never go hungry now!" Lola bit into a cherry and spat out the stone.

"But wouldn't you like a child of your own one day?" He glanced at Nieve, who had fallen asleep on a blanket, one hand still clutching a hunk of bread.

Lola shook her head. "I have a daughter." She reached across to stroke Nieve's hair. "And I have you and Juanita and your kids—that's all the family I need." She tossed the bag of cherries into his lap. "And how could I dance if I was pregnant? It's taken me years to get this far. You know how hard I have to practice. If I stopped for even just a week or two, I'd lose all the energy. Imagine what would happen if I had a baby to look after . . ." She glanced back at him. "Remember, I know what it's like."

"I do understand." He picked out a cherry and studied it for a moment before popping it in his mouth. "But it's not normal for a woman to be without a man."

"Says you!" Lola huffed. "I've never met a man I liked well enough to want to get married. Not here in Granada or back home."

"Well, Antonio asked me to ask you again. I think he's worried you're going to come back from Provence with some French troubadour for a husband."

Lola threw a cherry stone at him. It bounced off his nose and landed in the jug of lemonade. It was eight days until they were due to set off for France, and she couldn't wait. Quite apart from the excitement of performing at the biggest Gypsy fiesta in Europe, it would be pure bliss to escape from all the people who—like Antonio Lopez—kept telling her that a girl of her age had better get married before it was too late.

Sometimes she felt as if she'd crammed a whole lifetime into her twenty-two years. At fourteen she had witnessed something no child should ever see. And she had brought up Nieve on her own, with only a little help from her cousin and his wife. She had been looking out for herself for the past eight years, and she was finally earning good money. If Cristóbal thought she was about to give that up for some dough-faced muleteer, he must be *tonto*. Stupid.

"Come on," she said, arching her back and yawning as she stood up. "We'd better get these children to their beds."

"I might stay for a while," Cristóbal replied. "Juanita won't be waiting up—she's been falling asleep at the dinner table these past few nights."

Lola gave him a hard look. She knew exactly what he had in mind. He would go on drinking into the small hours, pick up a woman, then stagger home to find his pregnant wife on her knees, building a fire to make breakfast.

She lifted the still-sleeping Nieve into her arms and shooed the other two ahead of her. If they hadn't been within earshot, she would have warned their father that he'd better be on his best behavior in Provence. She couldn't bear the thought of having to lie to Juanita about what he might get up to at the fiesta.

Why was it, she wondered, that men were allowed to get away with that kind of thing while she was mocked for not wanting a husband? No one would dream of teasing a nun for choosing not to marry, so why did they curl their lips at her? Was dancing so very different from praying? Flamenco was about surrendering to the *duende*. It was about allowing your body to be taken over by something you couldn't see, only feel. And when you were doing it well, it felt like a religious experience. Sacred and precious.

"Perhaps we *will* find you a husband at the fiesta," Cristóbal called after her. "A big, strong *Húngaro* who'll drag you off and make love to you on a wolf-skin rug!"

"Over my dead body!" Lola whispered the words into the lavender-scented hair of the child in her arms.

Chapter 4

The sun was dipping below the horizon when Rose found Bill Lee. She had first met him the same year that Nathan had set off for Spain—and in the decade since, she had made an annual visit to the place where he could always be found in the months of summer.

His *vardo* was in a different place from the one he usually chose. Its carved front, painted with red and yellow roses, was hidden by a thicket of willow trees. Rose found it only when she spotted one of Bill's dogs—a black-and-white mutt called Bess—roaming along the riverbank. Bess came running up, recognizing the smell of two old friends, and after frolicking in the long marsh grass for a while with Rose's Afghan, she led them straight to her master.

Bill was sitting on the steps of the Gypsy caravan, whittling wood for pegs. A pipe stuck out from his mouth, the smoke curling up from beneath the brim of an ancient felt hat with a peacock feather poked through a tear in the side of it. His long hair, as black as a Gypsy kettle, was tied back with a thin strip of leather. Rose watched him reach down to the pile of wood shavings at his feet and toss a handful onto a smoldering fire. The crackle of the flames stifled the sound of the dog coming through the trees. It was only when Bess leapt up against his legs that he glanced up with wild, dark pony eyes.

The expression in those eyes transported Rose back in time to the day she had first encountered him out on the marshes. It was a look of suspicion mingled with fear. Bill had been out with his three younger sisters, Constance, Patience, and Mercy, collecting watercress to sell at Chichester market. Rose's dog had gone running up to them before she could stop him and overturned one of their baskets. She had apologized for his bad behavior, explaining that he was still just a puppy. And she had caught puzzled looks passing between them as they took in her bare feet, the mud-stained hem of her skirt, and the hazelnut hue of her face and arms.

She looks like us.

Rose had sensed what they were thinking. And it was true. Walking through Chichester, she had often heard people whisper "Gypsy!" as she passed by. The black hair and dark complexion came from her Turkish father. Her French mother had bequeathed the high cheekbones and deep-set gray eyes.

But suspicion had lingered on the faces of Bill and his sisters as they asked what breed of dog Gunesh was and reached out to pat him. Their faces had tightened when she told them she was interested in finding out about the natural remedies Gypsies used for their animals. They had gathered up their baskets and moved on, away down a bend in the river.

A few days later she had spotted Bill on his own, collecting moorhen eggs. She'd had her two goats with her this time as well as Gunesh. Bill had tipped his hat and wished her good morning, but pulled a cloth over his basket, as if he were afraid she would challenge him for taking eggs from the nests of wild birds. Realizing how tactless she had been at that first meeting, she had tried a different way into conversation. She'd asked him if he liked goat cheese—and when he said he'd never tasted it, she'd offered him some as a present.

Before long she had been invited to spend an evening with Bill and his sisters. They had picnicked by the river around a fire of willow branches and eaten soup made of seaweed and snails, followed by elderflower blossoms fried in batter.

Later they'd walked her back to her tent. When they disappeared into the night, she'd had no idea where they were going or how far they would have to walk to wherever they were living. She hadn't asked, because it had dawned on her that the treatment meted out to them by non-Gypsies had made them wary of giving themselves away.

There had been many times, at school and in college, when spiteful words had made her long to deny her Jewish blood. And sometimes she *had* denied it. She sensed that, to get closer to the Lee family, she needed to convey empathy for their way of life. So when she ran into Bill again while picking mushrooms one morning, she started dropping one or two Romany words into the conversation.

"Where did you learn that?" Bill had stared at her, wide eyed, when she'd asked him if she could borrow a *kipsi* to transport the *dinas* she had for him and his sisters. Instead of replying, she'd named the gifts she would put in the basket: *meski* (tea), *foggus* (tobacco), *pobbles* (apples), *pishom* (honey), and *men-werigas* (necklaces).

She had learned these words as a child—from a bewitching Gypsy woman with the fabulous name of Bessarabia, who used to go from house to house, selling wild daffodils. Rose's father, true to his Middle Eastern roots, had strict rules about offering hospitality to people he regarded as being poor, and so the flower seller had been invited in for tea and cake.

Rose had been unable to conceal her fascination. Bessarabia wore a bright-orange skirt and a cloak of purple velvet, peppered gold from the daffodil pollen. Copper rings the size of saucers dangled from her ears, and on her wrist she wore a silver bell tied with a green ribbon.

Keeping her company while she ate, Rose had learned the Romany for objects lying around the kitchen—the words for potatoes, broomstick, kettle, and cake. She wrote them down the way they sounded and added new ones each time the Gypsy called.

Bessarabia had disappeared from her life a few months later when Rose was sent away to school. But the words had lodged themselves in her head. Like a golden key, they had the power to take her into a hidden world. She had watched Bill's face light up when she dredged them from her memory.

"I told my sisters you must have Gypsy blood!" He had taken her hand and run to find Constance, Patience, and Mercy. The sisters had hugged her, pulling out strands of her hair to wrap around their fingers, their eyes shining with relief at no longer having to hide what they called their *kawlo rat*. Their dark blood.

During that summer of 1936, Rose had grown very close to the Lee family. At Chichester market they had introduced her to other Sussex Gypsies. For a packet of tea and a pouch of tobacco, they would tell her how they'd cured a horse or a dog of this or that ailment, where to find the herbs they used for the treatment, and the right way to administer them to the animal.

Bill himself had taught her how to treat a horse with colic by mixing grated gentian root and mint leaves with warm milk and honey. When she went with him searching for herbs, he would take her to hidden places and show her things she'd never seen before, like a beaver's dam and a squirrel's nest. And in return for all that he did for her, Rose had taught Bill how to read.

Now as she waved and ran toward the *vardo*, she thought how little he had changed in the years since that first summer. He was as lithe as the dog that bounded around his feet, and his face, though constantly exposed to the weather, bore no trace of any lines or wrinkles.

"Rosie! *Tatchoavel mi kushti pen!*" Welcome, sweet sister. He bundled her in his arms, lifting her off the grass and waltzing her around the fire.

She kissed his cheek. "Where's Martha? And the *chauvis*?" She reached into her bag. "I've bought them a book of fairy tales—and a shawl for Martha."

"They've gone to visit her mother." Bill smiled at the gifts. "They'll be grieved they missed you!"

Rose held his gaze. Words hung in the air, unspoken. There had always been a slight awkwardness with Martha, the woman Bill had chosen when Rose had turned him down. And seeing their children was always bittersweet, knowing that this was what *she* could have had.

Bill's sisters had revealed his feelings the week before she was due to leave Sussex to resume her veterinary course. Constance, Patience, and Mercy had pulled her inside the *vardo*, giggling, when Bill had set off on a fishing trip.

"He's terrible in love with you," Patience had whispered. "If you marry him, you can live with us—won't that be *kushti!*"

Rose had tried to explain. She'd already told them she was in love with a boy in college.

"But you're not promised to him, are you?" Mercy had given her a sly look.

They hadn't understood when she'd told them she was too young to settle down, that there was so much she wanted to do before getting married and having children. All three Lee sisters had found husbands since that summer. They had eleven children between them.

Now as she looked into Bill's eyes, Rose saw nothing but friendly concern. Whatever romantic feelings he had once harbored toward her were long gone.

A loud bark broke the silence. Gunesh was chasing Bess in and out of the trees, and they had flushed a rabbit from the undergrowth.

"I'll make us a brew, shall I?" Bill hung a kettle on a hook above the fire, then patted the step of the caravan. She settled down beside him, and for a few moments they sat watching the flames rise and fall. He sucked on his pipe and she breathed in the drifting smoke. It smelled of spiced cherries and roasted chestnuts. There was something very soothing about it.

"I've got something to show you." She fished a small package wrapped in brown paper from her bag. "My book."

He unwrapped it, angling the cover to catch the dying rays of the sun. "*Herbal Healing for Animals*." He traced the letters with his fingers. "By Rose Daniel!"

"Look inside."

He flicked through one page, then another. "'For my friend and . . .' What's this word?"

"*Mentor*. It means a special teacher. Someone who guides you."

"'For my friend and *mentor*, Bill Lee.'" His face split into a grin. "Can I keep it?"

"Of course you can!" She grinned back. "It's a *dino*." A gift.

She slipped her arm through his and squeezed it. "The book isn't the only reason I've come."

It was not the first time she had sought him out in a crisis. It was Bill she had run to during the war when her father had suffered a fatal heart attack in France. She thought she would have died of her sadness if she'd not had her Gypsy friend to talk to. Bill had a deep, heartfelt wisdom that went far beyond the well-meaning platitudes she had encountered in London. It was comfort he had given her then. Now she needed his counsel.

He nodded. Patting her hand, he rose to his feet. "Let me make the tea first." He lifted the kettle off the fire with a forked stick.

When the tea was brewed and he was back beside her, she drew in a long breath. "My mother passed away last autumn."

She felt his hand on hers, warm and rough with calluses.

"She never really got over losing Dad. And Nathan." She paused, unable to look at Bill, afraid that if she did, the dam of grief would burst. "That's what I wanted to talk to you about: Nathan. You see, when she was alive, Mum wouldn't hear of me going to look for him. Even when the war ended, she begged me not to go. But now she's . . ."

Rose lifted the teacup to her mouth in a vain attempt to swallow down the lump in her throat.

"You believe he's still living?" Bill's voice was matter of fact. There was no hint of incredulity. Neither was there any trace of false optimism.

"I know it's not likely—but I keep hoping. Today is his birthday. He's—I mean he *would* be—thirty-three."

Bill nodded. "A day like that is bound to be hard. You've grieved for your parents, but you haven't allowed yourself to grieve for him."

"How can I when I don't know for certain that he's . . ." She couldn't say the word.

"A body doesn't have to leave this world to stir up those feelings." He bent to gather a handful of wood shavings. The fire hissed and spat as they landed in the flames. "Grief is living with someone who's not there, who's gone out of your life for one reason or another."

She nodded slowly, slipping her hand inside her pocket. "This is the last letter he sent. It's dated March 1938. He says the war is going badly and he and some of his friends are planning to escape to France. But he'd met a girl in Spain—he doesn't say her name—and she was expecting his baby. Listen to this bit . . ." She screwed up her eyes, struggling to make out the words in the dying light.

I know it's not what Mum and Dad would have wanted, but the war makes you live every day as if it's your last. I'd like to marry her—but they murdered the priest last summer. Even if they hadn't, he would never have sanctioned a Jew marrying a Catholic.

I wish I could tell you her name, but that could put her in danger. All I can say is that I love her very much. We might not have a lifetime to live together, might not have what people are always supposed to have. Living as I do now, I must concentrate it all into the short time that I can have it.

There are Gypsy men fighting alongside us, and they have a different view of death than the rest of us. Their attitude is a calm acceptance. They say simply, "We all must die—no one knows the hour or the trouble and pains we may have to bear before our days are ended. Give thanks to God that we are alive this day and free to breathe the sweet air and hear the brown bird in the tree."

"Gypsy men?" Bill peered over her shoulder at the letter. "Things must have been terrible bad for our folk to fight along *gawjes.*"

Rose nodded. War was an alien concept to people like Bill. Gypsies couldn't understand why anyone would sacrifice themselves over the possession of a piece of land or a dispute over who ruled over it.

"Where was he living when he wrote this letter? Could you go there? Is it safe now?"

"That's the trouble," Rose replied. "I don't have much idea of the location. He said it was south of a city called Granada, in the mountains. The only clue I have is something he said about a village nearby. He was explaining how he met the girl he fell in love with." She scanned the letter until she found the paragraph she was looking for.

We went to buy tobacco one night at a village farther down the mountain. The weather was hot and we were thirsty, so we stopped at a fountain set in the wall of the main street. There's a legend attached to the place: the local people say anyone who drinks the water will find a sweetheart before the next sunrise. We laughed about it while we drank. But the strange thing was, I met my girl that same evening.

20

"It's not much to go on, is it?" Rose folded the letter and slipped it back into her pocket. Bill was staring into the fire, a look of concentration on his face, as if the answer might be found in the poppy glow of the embers.

"Is it a big place, Spain?"

"Very big. Much bigger than England. At least three times the size, I'd say. I found Granada on a map. There are hundreds of miles of mountains to the south. I wouldn't know where to start."

"You need to find someone who knows it, then, don't you?"

"Yes—but how?"

Bill drew on his pipe and breathed out a twisting wreath of smoke. "There's a place you could find Romany folk from Spain without going all the way there. They'd be the ones to ask."

"Is there? Where?"

"A big party in France. The biggest in the whole world. They hold it in Maytime every year in the horse country by the sea."

"Where? Have you been there?"

Bill shook his head. "Can't take the *vardo* over the water. But I've met folk as have been. It's coming soon; you'd have to be quick."

Rose could feel her heart thumping against her ribs. "Do you know the name of it, Bill?"

"The town's named after the two Saint Marys—the ones who first saw Jesus when he rose from the dead. It's in a place called Province, I think."

"Provence?"

"Ah! That's it."

Rose jumped to her feet, unable to sit still. Suddenly there was a glimmer of . . . what? Not hope—that was too strong a word. But Bill had shone a light into the gloom inside her head. It was almost as if he had given her permission to do what she'd wanted to do for so long. But could she really go? Was there any sense in searching when there had been no communication from Nathan for eight years? Her head told her that there was little chance of his being alive, but her heart wouldn't let go. What if he was in prison and unable to write letters? She had to know for certain what had happened to him—one way or another. There would be no rest for her otherwise. Not ever.

"When is it, exactly?"

"It's always the tail end of May."

"I *could* go, couldn't I? There's enough time."

Bill caught the hesitation in her voice. "You're thinking you might not find him." He took her hand in his. "You know, Rose, everything that is lost will be found."

Tears prickled behind her eyes. "Not if a person dies."

"Don't you believe in heaven, Rose?"

"I used to, when I was a little girl. My grandfather bought me a puppy when he came to visit from Turkey. I loved it more than anything. But it got sick and died. I wanted there to be a heaven so I could see it again. But . . ."

"When two creatures pair up—be it people or animals—there has to come a time of parting. Perhaps it began when God separated the earth from the water. Dry land and sea. And the rain that falls on the mountain spends a lifetime finding its way back to the place it belongs." He tapped his pipe against the step and refilled it, his fingers the same leaf brown as the tobacco. When he'd lit it, he said, "What's binding you, Rose?"

"I don't know," she murmured. "There's nothing to prevent me from going. The practice can survive without me for a month or two. And I've got the money from my book to keep me going. It's just . . ." She couldn't put it into words, that sickening fear of what she might actually find.

"Don't be afraid of what you don't know. That kind of fear kills you without you realizing. Like bleeding inside."

Somewhere in the trees a bird began calling, the notes as thin and sharp as icicles in the gathering darkness. It was a sound she recognized from that summer long ago. The plaintive song of a nightingale. She'd heard it the night Nathan had come to say goodbye.

"You're right," she whispered. "I feel like I'm half-dead already."

"So you need to do this. Then you can start living again."

"Yes." She closed her eyes. Now there was only the warmth of the fire, the smell of woodsmoke and tobacco, and the sounds of the night.

Chapter 5

Rose stood by the fireplace, a silver candelabra in her hand. She glanced around the apartment, checking that she had left nothing of her own on the shelves or the windowsills. Tomorrow someone else would be living here: the newly qualified vet who was going to be her stand-in at the practice over the summer. It would save her having to pay rent for the time she planned to be away.

She carried the candelabra over to the cupboard into which she had crammed her books, clothes, and other personal items. Wrapping it in one of her skirts, she wedged it in and locked the cupboard door. The solid-silver menorah was one of a handful of valuable things her mother, Esther, had refused to sell when she was forced to leave the Georgian house in the Cheshire countryside where Rose and her brother had grown up. The seven-branched candlestick had been lit every Friday night before dinner for as long as Rose could remember.

Mother, you haven't been in a synagogue for years—why are you doing that? Nathan's voice drifted out of a corner of her memory. She saw his face, a teasing smile on his lips. A remark such as this would often provoke a heated debate. Rose had always tried to avoid taking sides. At boarding school she had learned about other faiths and developed her own brand of spirituality. But she hadn't wanted to upset her parents by telling them what she believed.

Her hand went to her throat, fingering the pendant her father had brought back from Turkey for her twenty-first birthday. It was a silver-and-gold ḥoshen necklace—a rectangular pendant set with twelve different gemstones, one to represent each of the twelve tribes of Israel. It grieved her to take it off. But it was too precious to wear on her travels. It was going to have to go into the cupboard, too.

Her father's death—just three years after that gift had been given—had brought more than one kind of grief to the family. Within days of the funeral, the bailiffs had arrived, demanding settlement of vast debts Rose and her mother had known nothing about. The house and most of the contents had had to be sold. Esther and Rose had gone to live in a rented cottage in Berkshire, near the place the Royal Veterinary College had moved to when the Blitz began.

By the time Rose had graduated, her mother was seriously ill. There had been no question of applying for jobs. She had cared for her mother and spent what little free time she had writing the book that had been published just before her mother's death.

Rose glanced out the window, across Bloomsbury Square, at the blackened shell of a once-grand house. Coming to live in London had been her way of making a fresh start. She had thought that moving to the city would help her to move on from losing her mother. It had worked—for a while. Her new job had been exhausting but rewarding, and her boss was open minded about the possibility of herbal treatments for animals. But outside working hours she found city life stifling. She longed for greenery and wide-open spaces. On days off she would get as far away from the capital as she could on a train or a bus, taking Gunesh for long walks, whatever the weather. It hadn't helped her put down roots in her new home. Eight months on, there wasn't a single person in London she felt close to.

She walked through to the bedroom, where Gunesh was curled up on the rug next to her rucksack. On the bed lay two maps of Spain—one that showed the whole country and one larger-scale version, of the region of Andalucia. She had spent endless hours poring over these maps in the years since Nathan had left England. The second map was held together with tape, so often had she unfolded it, running her finger along black dots on mountain ranges, wondering which of the hundreds of villages could be the one her brother had described in his letter.

She'd spent whole days in the British Library, going through reference books on Spain, searching for something to go on. But like the inquiries she'd made to the International Red Cross about Nathan, there was nothing. She felt a desperate need to talk to people who knew the terrain and the country personally. But going directly to Spain was not sensible. Andalucia was the size of Ireland. She could end up wandering around for months. She needed a signpost—some clue as to where to start her search. Going to the Gypsy fiesta in France offered the opportunity of talking to people who had lived through the Spanish Civil War and had been on the same side as Nathan. It seemed like her best chance.

She slid the maps into the front pocket of her rucksack. The only things left to pack were the photographs. One of Nathan and one of each of her parents. It was impossible to look at the faces without welling up. Her mother, plump cheeked and smiling, so different from the frail, broken person she had become at the end. Her father, staring boldly at the camera. He had gone to France nine months into the war, believing that his Turkish passport would keep him safe. But he was a Jew first and a Turk second. The neutrality of his native land had not saved him when the Nazis arrived in Paris.

Nathan's picture was very different from her parents' images—not a formal studio shot but a photo Rose had taken herself at the old house in Cheshire. Nathan had been out riding, about to jump off his horse in the stable yard. He looked so young and full of life. It was impossible to believe that he, too, could be dead.

There was another face she had tried to picture in the years since Nathan had been missing. The face of the unborn child he had written about in that last letter. A child who would be seven or eight years old now, if he or she were alive. She couldn't help imagining what it would be like to have a niece or nephew. To be part of a family again. How wonderful that would be.

She slipped the photographs into her wallet, trying to steer her mind toward the practicalities of traveling to France. She mustn't allow herself to fantasize about finding Nathan and his child. She must prepare herself for whatever this search might reveal. To put an end to the not knowing—that was why she had to go on this journey.

Chapter 6

Lola crept out from underneath the sheets. She shivered as her feet found the rough wooden planks of the wagon. The early mornings were chilly in the Pyrenees, even this late in the spring. She could hear a magpie—its mocking rattle competing with Cristóbal's gentle snoring. She glanced at the child. Nieve was still sound asleep, her arms stretched out above her head like a dancer. The peacock shawl was wrapped around her left wrist. It was frayed at the edges now and peppered with moth holes, but the child refused to go to bed without it.

Lola reached across her to retrieve her own woolen shawl that was tangled up in the blanket Nieve had thrown off. She covered up the sleeping child before pulling back the curtain that screened the bed. There was Cristóbal, lying on the pile of sacks that served for a mattress, his mouth open. She thought how innocent he looked when he was asleep.

She made her way to the front end of the wagon, trying not to make it creak. Slipping her bare feet into her boots, she lifted a flap of canvas and eased herself onto the dew-soaked grass. She could see signs of life from the others camped nearby. A wisp of smoke from a fire bought back to life from the night before. A man's shirt and some underclothes hung out to dry on the branches of a hawthorn bush. A gray-muzzled dog cocking its leg against a moss-covered tree stump.

By this evening they would all be in Provence. After ten days on the road, Lola was more than ready. Unlike her fellow travelers, she was not used to the nomadic life. She and Cristóbal had always been house dwellers, not wanderers. In Granada there were both kinds. The Gypsy population waxed and waned like the moon. Cristóbal didn't own a proper *vardo*, like the carved beauties the others in their party possessed—he'd had to fashion one from a wagon borrowed from Antonio Lopez, the mule man. He'd made a roof from bent bamboo and waxed canvas. It leaked a little in the rain, but he'd convinced her it would last for the few weeks they would be away.

She felt the breeze as she stirred up the embers of the fire. Cristóbal would need strong coffee to rouse him from the wine-soaked slumber he had fallen into last night after accompanying her on the guitar. She had danced beneath the stars for the others in the forest clearing, using a wooden board to stamp out the *palos*. It hadn't been easy, performing on a dance floor no wider than her shawl, but it had been good practice for the days ahead.

She wondered what they would be like—these foreign Gypsies. French, Hungarian, Greek, Turkish. Cristóbal, who had been to Les Saintes-Maries back in the thirties, had told her that although they all shared the same *kawlo rat*, she would see many differences between her own people and those from other lands—not just in appearance but in character.

He had said all this as a preamble to advising on the kind of man she should choose as a husband. He seemed obsessed with the business of finding her a mate. It was a side of family life she loathed, this attitude of Gypsy men toward single female relatives of childbearing age. It was so controlling. So patronizing. She reminded him that she had walked across a snow-covered mountain range at fourteen years old with a newborn baby and only a few goats to keep the pair of them from starving to death. If she could survive that, she could survive anything life might throw at her—and she didn't need any man mapping out her future.

"Mama!" Nieve appeared beside her, barefoot and rubbing sleep from her eyes. "What's for breakfast?"

"Mushroom tortilla," Lola replied. "And you're picking the mushrooms." She smiled at Nieve's downturned mouth. "I'll buy you hair ribbons at the fiesta if you can find more than ten."

"How will I know when I get to ten?"

"You can count them on your fingers, like I showed you."

The child examined her hands, a frown wrinkling the smooth skin between her eyebrows.

"One, two, three, four . . . ," Lola began, starting with the thumb of her left hand.

"Five, six . . . ten!" Nieve held up all her fingers at once, a cheeky grin lighting up her face.

Lola rolled her eyes as she handed her a basket. "Put your boots on!" she called out. But Nieve had already vanished, fairylike, into the trees.

A sudden gust of wind rustled the leaves. Lola shivered, pulling her shawl tighter. It wasn't the cold, not really. More like an irrational twinge of foreboding. It was only in the past few months that she had allowed Nieve to go anywhere on her own. Cristóbal's children had been teasing their cousin about being a mama's girl. And Cristóbal himself had told Lola it was high time she gave the child a bit of freedom. But Lola couldn't help the creeping feeling of unease that came over her whenever Nieve went off alone. It was the fear of losing her. Suddenly and without warning. The way she'd lost her brother and her mother.

Rose awoke to the aroma of coffee. A tray had been placed on the minuscule table beneath the train window. The steam from the spout of the silver pot had formed a trickle of moisture on the glass. She wondered how she hadn't heard the steward bring it in—or sensed the change in the light when he'd pulled up the blind. She hadn't expected to sleep so deeply.

She propped herself up on one elbow and craned her neck. Outside was a swirling landscape of lilac, gold, and green. The wind rippling through fields of sunbaked lavender. She retrieved her wristwatch from the narrow shelf beside her bed. In just under an hour, the train would reach Avignon. Then she would board another train for Arles. After that a bus would take her the short distance to Saintes-Maries-de-la-Mer.

She'd never slept on a train before. In years gone by, she would have broken up a journey like this in Paris. But the thought of spending even a single night in the city where her aunt and uncle had lived—and where her father had died—was utterly unbearable.

She'd pulled down the blind as soon as she boarded the train in Calais. It was the only way to avoid glimpses of places that would remind her of happier times, when she and her parents and Nathan would picnic in the Bois de Boulogne or take a boat trip down the Seine on their annual visit to Aunt Isabelle and Uncle Maurice.

From the deck of the ferry, France had looked as gray and ravaged as London. Stepping off the boat onto French soil, she had felt like a mourner arriving at a funeral. She'd climbed onto the train that would take her south, weighed down by the thought of the hundreds of Jewish families who had been forced into cattle wagons to travel in the opposite direction, to the death camps. People like her aunt and uncle. People like herself.

But here in Provence, it was as if the war had never happened. The fields of lavender and sunflowers rolling past the train window were broken only by lines of poplar trees and the odd red-tiled farmhouse.

There were no bombed-out buildings. No sense of decay. It was a land-scape that looked timeless.

Gunesh licked her face all over when she went to fetch him from the guard's van at Avignon, unable to understand why he'd had to spend a night without her. When she'd made a fuss of him, she went to collect her rucksack from the baggage car. It was very heavy. Crammed into the main compartment were a tent, cooking utensils, and a sleeping bag, along with a few basic toiletries and a small assortment of clothes. She had no idea how long this journey would last—or where it would end—but what she had in her rucksack would enable her to stay in Spain for the whole of the summer if she needed to.

She bought food in Arles while she waited for the bus that would take her to the little town where the Gypsy fiesta was being held. She wasn't sure whether there would be many shops in such a place, and she didn't want to arrive without something to offer the people she hoped would help her. If these Gypsies were anything like the ones she had met in England, they would be happy with simple gifts of things they couldn't find or make themselves, such as tobacco, tea, and coffee. She stuffed packets of each of these into the side pockets of her rucksack, along with bread, cheese, and apples for herself.

On the bus she got her first glimpse of the wild landscape called the Camargue. The wetlands bordering the Mediterranean Sea were noth-ing like the Sussex marshes. Sand dunes crowned with pink-blossomed tamarisk trees lined the seashore. Coral-winged flamingos stood knee deep in the brackish water, balancing precariously on one leg, and shy white egrets picked their way across muddy banks to nests concealed in swathes of marsh grass.

Rose caught her breath as she spotted a trio of wild white horses charging through a water meadow, their manes and tails flying out behind them like sea foam. And farther on, she caught a glimpse of a huge black bull lumbering out of a clump of bulrushes, its coat gleam-ing like polished ebony in the sunshine.

As the bus neared its destination, she caught sight of the Gypsy caravans. There were whole fields full of them, a sea of painted wagons with lines of washing strung between them, fluttering in the breeze. She saw naked children kicking up clouds of dust as they chased each other under the *vardos* and out the other side. Dogs snoozed in the shade while women sat on steps, peeling vegetables, plaiting rush baskets, or combing their hair. Men were strumming guitars and saddling up horses. At the edge of one field, she glimpsed two youths, stripped to the waist, fists flying in a bare-knuckle fight.

It was a far bigger gathering than she had imagined. There must be hundreds, possibly thousands of people camped out around the little seaside town. She wondered if it had always been like this or whether the prohibition of such meetings during the war had led to a surge in numbers now that it was over. Where on earth was she going to start searching among such a vast crowd?

The bus dropped her right in the center of Saintes-Maries-de-la-Mer, outside the medieval church. The building towered over the little fishing village like an enormous ship. Its walls were built like a fortress, with arrow-slit windows and castellated turrets. Above the great wooden door was an elegant metal cross whose lower end opened into a heart sitting on an anchor.

She had read about the history of the place in a Baedeker's guide to Provence. According to local legend, two female followers of Jesus—Mary Jacoby and Mary Salome—had fled Israel by boat after the crucifixion. Their servant, a dark-skinned Gypsy girl called Sara, had begged to be taken with them, and when the boat got lost in a storm, it was Sara who had guided the vessel by the stars and brought them safely to the Camargue. She became the Gypsies' very own saint—and they came from all corners of Europe at this time of year to keep a vigil at her shrine in the crypt of the church before carrying her statue in a procession to the sea.

There were queues of people going into the building. A gaggle of young women stopped to buy votive candles from a stall outside the door. They moved like flowers in the wind, their slender bodies swathed in vibrant dresses of taffeta and satin. Some were like carnations, in frilled gowns of bright red or deep pink. Some wore skirts of fluted yellow, like daffodils, while others were wrapped in the sultry purple of orchids.

As they disappeared into the dark interior of the church, a crowd of others came to take their place, all clamoring for candles. Behind them came a group of men, perhaps thirty or forty strong, some playing fiddles or flutes as they walked, others shouting out to the women, calling their names and whistling.

To be surrounded by so many people was dazzling, bewildering. Rose sank onto a bench in the shadow cast by the soaring walls of the church. She had to go and find somewhere to pitch her tent, but the thought of it was daunting. She didn't want to encroach on the fields where the Gypsy caravans were parked. She wanted to keep a respectful distance—and in any case those fields already looked full to bursting. She wondered if she would have to camp on the beach itself. That might be the only available space.

"*Bonjour, mam'zelle!*"

Two Gypsy women with brilliant eyes and thick, shining hair came up to her, half a dozen children following in their wake. One of the women pointed at Rose's rucksack. "*Avez-vous des vêtements?*"

"*Non!*" Rose pulled the bag against her legs. "*Je suis désolée.*" I'm sorry.

They wanted her clothes—but she had packed so frugally she had none to spare. Seeing the women's faces harden, she pulled a paper bag from her jacket pocket. She'd bought sugared almonds at the quayside in Calais, and there were still a few left. She handed them out to the children, telling the mothers how proud they must be to have such handsome sons and daughters. It wasn't empty praise. They were all strikingly beautiful, with the same blue-green eyes and caramel skin as the women.

"*Vous pouvez acheter.*" You can buy. "*Cette fille.*" This girl.

A child of about seven years old, with tumbling curls and a gap-toothed smile, was pushed forward. Before Rose could say a word, the child had climbed onto her lap. Her hair smelled of woodsmoke with a tang of patchouli.

"*Elle est très intelligente.*" All the Gypsy art of persuasiveness was concentrated into the look the mother directed at Rose. For a fleeting moment she allowed herself to imagine taking the little girl. To have a child without the ties of marriage was something she had often fantasized about. But not like this. How could any mother sell her own flesh and blood? And how could anyone *buy* another woman's child? She had never encountered anything like this among the English Gypsies. It was a delicate situation. How was she going to get out of it without offending them?

"*Quel dommage—ce n'est pas possible.*" What a shame—it's not possible.

She kissed the little girl's head and lifted her gently to the ground. Without a backward glance, she clipped Gunesh's lead onto his collar and heaved her rucksack onto her back, closing her ears to the muttered oaths that followed her down the street. The dog, quick to sense the antipathy, turned his head and snarled.

"It's all right, boy," she murmured. "Shush now."

Her colleagues at the veterinary practice in London had looked at her askance when she told them she would be traveling through Europe unaccompanied. To them it was dangerous and foolhardy for a lone woman to contemplate such a journey—especially sleeping in a tent. But she'd never felt afraid with Gunesh at her side. And there was nothing lonely about sleeping out in the open when he was curled up at her feet.

"*Quel beau chien!*" What a handsome dog!

A tall, pale man dressed entirely in black stepped out of the shadows. His dark hair hung down to his neck, and his cheeks sprouted long side whiskers. He stroked the Afghan's neck, bending his knees to a squat so that his head was level with the dog's.

"His name is Gunesh," Rose replied in French.

"Gunesh?" The man glanced up at her, a puzzled look on his face.

"It's Turkish. It means sun—because of his golden hair."

"Ah!" This brought a smile to the pale face. He straightened up and stuck out his hand. "Jean Beau-Marie."

"Rose Daniel."

He cocked his head to one side, searching her face. *"Où habitez-vous? Pas en Turquie?"*

"No. My father was Turkish but I'm from England."

"Gitane?"

She could see that he was really confused now: a girl who looked like a Gypsy but came from England with a dog whose name was Turkish.

"I'm looking for somewhere to camp," she said, sidestepping the question.

He nodded. "I can show you."

He offered to carry her rucksack, but she politely declined. As they walked he told her that he was a Gypsy chief from Alsace-Lorraine in the north of France. Following behind him, she thought what a somber figure he made in his black clothes, walking with his shoulders hunched over like a crow. Despite his friendly manner there was an indefinable sense of sadness about him. She wondered if she should trust him.

He took her to the edge of a field, close to the temporary paddock where the horses that pulled the Gypsy caravans were quartered.

"You don't mind the smell?" He wrinkled his nose, waving a hand at a patch of ground beside the fence. It was just about big enough to take her tent.

"No, I don't mind." She smiled. There was something very wholesome about the smell of horse dung. And it seemed fitting that her search for Nathan had brought her close to the animals he loved so much.

Jean helped her to erect the tent and brought her firewood so that she could boil water. He looked puzzled when she offered him tea, so she brewed coffee for them both instead. He told her that he was the bell ringer in the church for the Gypsy fiesta. "Ring out the bad and the cruel," he said, grim faced. "Ring in something better."

She wondered what had happened to him during the war. The look in his eyes made her wary of asking questions. Instead she told him about her brother and her quest to find out what had become of him.

"There are Spanish folk at the fiesta." He nodded. "There used to be more Spanish than any others, apart from we French." He lifted the tin mug of coffee to his lips, draining the scalding liquid in one go. "Of course, there are less of all of us here than in years gone by."

Rose glanced at the *vardos* parked beyond the paddock. It still seemed like a terrific number to her, so she could only guess at what it must have been like before the Germans invaded. She should have realized, of course. It had been yet another shocking revelation in the harrowing litany of war crimes: that Hitler had destroyed thousands of Gypsies in the same monstrous way he had wiped out Jews.

"Have you spoken to any of the Spaniards yet?" Jean asked.

Rose shook her head. "I haven't had the chance."

"Do you speak Spanish?"

"I learnt it at school, but it's been a while since I spoke it."

"Well, your French is excellent."

"That's because my mother was French. I learnt her language before I learnt English."

"The Spanish Gypsies speak to each other in *kalo*," Jean said. "Do you know that tongue?"

"If it's anything like Romany, then yes, I do—a little."

He nodded. "I think you'll get by. Would you like me to take you to meet some of the Spaniards?"

"Could you? You've already been so kind."

"It's nothing." He held out his hands, palms up. It was then that she noticed the number tattooed on the inside of his left forearm.

He caught her looking before her eyes darted away, back to the fire.

"I was a prisoner. In the place they called Auschwitz. The Nazis killed my family." There was no emotion in his voice. He might have been commenting on the weather. "My mother, my father, and my sister. All gassed. They tried to work me to death in the coal mine, but I wouldn't die." He was staring at the blue ink mark on his arm. "Most days I wish I had."

She drew in a long breath. She had read, of course, about the horrors of the death camps. But to hear about it from the lips of someone who had endured them was utterly heartbreaking. She felt a sudden kinship with this stranger—a need to tell him her own story. "My mother's sister and her husband died in one of the camps. They were Jews, living in Paris."

His eyes searched her face. She had given him the answer to the puzzle of her looks: that she was a member of a race as despised as his own people.

"They were herded onto a train one day and never seen again," she went on. "It was soon after the war started. The summer of 1940. My father was there when it happened. He'd gone to stay with them on the way to search for my brother in Spain. He was rounded up, too. He died of a heart attack, trying to stop the Nazis pushing people onto the train."

Ring out the bad and the cruel. Ring in something better.

She didn't see his lips move. It was as if he'd repeated the words inside his head and somehow transmitted them into hers.

She couldn't bear to think of what Jean must have seen at Auschwitz. The unjust imprisoning and killing of anything had always tormented her. As a student she had been unable to stomach the vivisection practiced on animals. It had been the main reason for her rejection of mainstream veterinary science in favor of herbal treatments for animals. But in Auschwitz, vivisection had been carried out on Jews and Gypsies—some of them women and children. No wonder Jean looked haunted.

"I'll take you now if you like—to find the Spanish folk." She heard his knees crack as he rose to his feet.

She nodded. Lifting the flap of her rucksack, she burrowed inside for the gifts she'd bought in Arles. And for one more thing—the photograph of Nathan. She had taken it what seemed like a hundred years ago, the day she turned eighteen, at the house in Cheshire. Nathan had been out on his favorite horse, Pharaoh, and she'd snapped him with her new camera as he was about to dismount, his face glowing with exertion and his hair blown wild by the wind.

As she followed Jean through the sea of caravans, she pressed the photograph to her heart. She could feel the surge of her own blood, the panic rising in her belly at the thought of what lay ahead. Spain was a big country. What were the chances, really, of anyone from the area Nathan had gone to being here at the fiesta? She'd told herself countless times to be prepared for disappointment—that coming here was clutching at straws. But meeting Jean had fanned the tiny flame of hope in her heart. Despite the brutality he had endured, he had survived. If, as she had sometimes wondered, Nathan had been taken prisoner, there was a chance that like Jean, he was still alive. Maybe he had even managed to escape but was too traumatized to return to his former life.

"Those are Spaniards—over there." Jean was pointing to a group of about twenty people, all eating and laughing around a campfire.

Rose felt her mouth go dry. This was it. There was no turning back.

Chapter 7

Cristóbal picked up his guitar and lowered his legs over the side of the wagon. "Come on," he called over his shoulder, "I want to show you where we'll be performing."

Lola was giving Nieve a wash and brush up. The child had been allowed to run wild these past few days on the road. There was mud under her fingernails and bits of twig in her hair. "We'll catch you up," she called back. "Which way is it?"

"Head for the church," Cristóbal replied. "It's in the square right in front of it."

It took Lola longer than she expected to detangle Nieve's hair. The child wriggled like a worm on a hook and shrieked as if Lola were brandishing a knife, not a comb.

"Shush!" Lola shook her head, exasperated. "People will think I'm murdering you!"

"Well, that's what it feels like!" There was steely defiance in the little face. Nieve's eyes were bright with tears, but she wouldn't let Lola see her cry. She was much too proud for that.

"If you want new ribbons, you have to have tidy hair." Lola held her at arm's length, checking her from head to toe. "Okay—you'll do."

Nieve scrambled out of the wagon ahead of Lola.

"Hey! Wait for me!" Lola was still lacing up her boots. She'd changed out of the dusty skirt and the old shirt of Cristóbal's that she'd worn while they were on the road. Now she wore a fresh white blouse and a skirt of lilac blue. The color was echoed by the cornflowers she had picked from the edge of the field and tucked into her hair.

It was easy to find the place Cristóbal had gone to. The church tower dwarfed the other buildings of Saintes-Maries-de-la-Mer. Lola wondered how such a magnificent structure had come to be erected in what was just a small fishing village. She had thought it was only big cities, like Granada, that had great turreted fortresses. But this place echoed the might of the Alhambra in the way it dominated the landscape around it.

She spotted her cousin in front of the great wooden door, playing his guitar to a group of women. Lola saw one of them giggle softly as he glanced up at her. The others exchanged furtive looks from beneath dark-lashed eyelids. The women were all young—no older than herself—and had clearly taken great care over their appearance. Their dresses made a rainbow of colors—red, orange, yellow, turquoise, violet—and their hair shone blue black where the sun touched it.

"Oh, Cristóbal," Lola muttered under her breath. "You just can't resist, can you?"

"What can't Uncle Cristóbal do?" Nieve tugged at Lola's sleeve.

"Nothing, cariño." Lola took Nieve's hand as she scanned the teeming village square. "Let's go and look for those ribbons, shall we?"

The child nodded eagerly. "And when I've got them on, I want to go and show them to Saint Sara!"

Lola frowned. "She's not a real person—I mean, she was, once upon a time. But now she's . . . well, she's like a doll—a very big doll made of wood."

"I still want to show her my ribbons." Nieve stuck out her bottom lip.

"Yes, of course you can. We've got plenty of time." Lola ushered Nieve past the women simpering over her cousin. "I'm sure Uncle Cristóbal won't mind."

Rose stood in the shadow of one of the *vardos*, waiting for Jean to explain who she was. But Gunesh was not so polite. Perhaps it was the smell of rabbit stew that sent him bounding from her grasp. The Gypsies didn't seem to mind. They clustered around him, clearly taken with his statuesque good looks. As his owner, she commanded their interest even before she'd handed out her gifts of coffee and tobacco.

Jean explained that the people in the group were mainly from northern Spain. Some of the men had fought as partisans during the Spanish Civil War, but none had gone as far south as Granada.

"I'd still like them to see my brother's photograph." She took it from her jacket pocket and handed it to him. "He would have traveled through northern Spain if he managed to get to France."

If Jean thought it was a waste of time, his face didn't show it. He passed the image around and Rose watched the men's faces. There was much scratching of heads and narrowing of eyes. Clearly they wanted to help. But no one recognized Nathan.

One of the men gesticulated at Jean. Rose couldn't tell if he was speaking Spanish or *kalo*, his voice was so gruff.

"He says there's a group from Granada in the next field—he's offering to take us to them."

The gloom that had settled on Rose dissolved in a heartbeat. Murmuring hurried thanks to the others, she grabbed Gunesh by the collar and followed the man through a maze of wagons. To her right she caught glimpses of the sea, glinting amber in the afternoon light. A pair of flamingos glided across the sky, their long bodies silhouetted against the orange orb of the sun. Despite the nearness of the water, Rose couldn't hear the rumble of the waves on the beach. The cacophony in the field drowned out all other sounds. Fires crackled, dogs barked, horses snorted, and babies wailed. Men yelled at dogs, and women screeched at children. Fortune-tellers called out to Rose as she passed by, and flower sellers stepped in her way, thrusting bunches of jasmine and lavender under her nose.

It was a relief when they reached the dirt track that separated the two camping areas. Skirting around the edge of the field, their guide took them straight to the place where the Granada Gypsies had set up home. He indicated a circle of a dozen or so *vardos*, distinguished from the others by bunches of dried pomegranates hung on string from the carved wooden fronts of the wagons. Pointing at the tawny globes rattling together in the breeze, he turned and muttered something to Jean.

"He says the fruit is their symbol," Jean said to Rose. "We hang things up to represent the places we come from. We have cabbages—they have pomegranates."

"Where is everyone?" Rose could see no one on the steps of the wagons or on the patches of land in between them.

"They've only just arrived," Jean replied. "The men are probably sorting out the horses, and the women and children are out fetching water and firewood."

"Oh." Rose tried not to show her frustration. "I suppose I'd better come back later, then? At least I know where they are now."

Their guide was climbing up the steps of one of the *vardos*. He rapped on the wooden door, then put his ear to it. He turned to Rose and Jean and shrugged. *"Lo siento."*

For the first time, Rose understood what he was saying. It meant "I'm sorry."

"De nada," she replied. It's nothing. She made herself smile as she said it. It had been kind of him to take the trouble to bring her here. She mustn't keep him from his family. But she couldn't help feeling that her chances of getting the Granada Gypsies to listen to her would be

severely limited without his presence. She had already parted with all the gifts she had purchased in Arles. An outsider with nothing to offer, she feared instant rejection from these new people.

As she watched him walk away, she heard a shout from the sea side of the field. Through a gap in the wagons, she spotted a group of men with horse tack slung over their shoulders. They were heading toward Rose and Jean. The guide, who had caught sight of them, too, turned back, waving.

Minutes later the men were passing around Nathan's photograph. Unlike the Spaniards she had met earlier, they were asking questions. Which brigade did her brother belong to? What was the name of the mountain range where he was based? Did she know the name of the nearest town?

The first question was easy. She told them that Nathan had been a member of the Fourteenth International Brigade and that he had traveled to the region south of Granada after training in a city called Albacete. But she was unable to answer their other questions. All she could do was repeat the story Nathan had told about the legendary fountain in the village near to where he had lived.

The men looked at one another and shook their heads. Apparently they had never heard of such a place. It must be on the other side of the Sierra Nevada, they said—the side that faced across the water to Africa. It could be in another mountain range entirely: the Contraviesa, perhaps, which ran west to east between the snowcapped peaks south of Granada and the Mediterranean.

Rose stared at her boots. They were trying so hard to help her, but she felt more confused than ever. She asked if there was anyone else in their party who might know of the village Nathan had described. The answer was no. The only other people traveling with them were a guitarist and his cousin, a dancer. Both lived in the city and were house dwellers, not travelers.

Tears blurred Rose's vision as Jean led her back through the field to her tent.

"I have to go now." He took both her hands in his. His eyes, as dark as sea-washed stones, echoed her pain. "We could try again tomorrow. There might be others . . ." He trailed off, looking away, too honest to give her false hope.

She nodded, dropping her hands to release his. "Thank you," she said. "You mustn't worry about me. I knew when I came here that the chances were very slim."

"What will you do?"

"It's a fiesta." She managed a wry smile. "I might as well make the most of it."

"Well, if you need me, I'm over there." He pointed to the side of the field closest to the village.

When he'd gone, she went inside the tent and spent a while just gazing at Nathan's image, as if she could divine the answers to the Gypsies' questions by some sort of telepathy. But it left her feeling more miserable and bereft than ever. What on earth had she thought she was doing, setting off on a trek across Europe, grasping at straws? She leaned across to where her rucksack lay and thrust her arm inside it, burrowing among the clothes. She pulled out a book, its cover stained and creased. It fell open at her favorite page.

"'All shall be well, all shall be well, and all manner of things shall be well.'" She whispered the words to herself like a mantra. They had been written more than six centuries ago by a British nun who'd had herself walled up alive in a cell inside Norwich Cathedral and spent her days giving words of comfort to unseen people in need on the outside, via a window high up in the wall.

Rose had turned to this book countless times over the past few years. Its pages contained a profound, reassuring wisdom that transcended the boundaries of religion. But now, as she stared at the familiar phrase, she failed to feel that reassurance. *How* could all be well? How could she go on with her search for Nathan when she'd failed at the first hurdle?

You know, Rose, everything that is lost will be found . . .

How empty those words of Bill's sounded now.

She reached out her hand to Gunesh, who had settled himself against her legs. Sensing her sadness, he lifted his head and licked her chin. She buried her face in his coat.

"I can't stay here all evening, can I?" She mumbled the words into the silky golden hair. The thought of venturing into the melee outside was daunting. But the idea of being cooped up with her own thoughts was much worse.

The dog thrust out his legs in a long, luxurious stretch, his front paws almost sticking through the tent flap.

"Well, you can stay if you want to. I don't suppose you got much sleep in the guard's van, did you?"

Rose wasn't in the habit of going anywhere without Gunesh if she could help it. But feeling the way she did, there was only one place she could think of going—and it was somewhere dogs were not allowed.

The setting sun had turned the sky into a bonfire. Tiny charcoal clouds drifted across the sea, glowing red where the dying rays touched them. The smell of cooking was everywhere. As Rose made her way across the field, she felt a gnawing in her stomach. All she'd had to eat since leaving the train was an apple and a slice of bread and cheese. She wondered if there might be stalls selling hot food in the village square. Perhaps. But that would have to wait.

The tower of the church cast a long shadow across the road. As she drew near, she saw that people were still standing in line to buy candles. A few yards away there was a man selling pancakes. The scent of frying batter made her mouth water. She thought about buying one but decided instead to save it as a treat for later.

Rose took her place behind an elderly French woman with skin like polished leather who asked her if she would like her palm read while she waited. The word she used—*dukeripen*—was one Rose had often heard when she was among English Gypsies.

"*Merci beaucoup,*" Rose replied. "*Mais non.*" Having her future told at this precise moment seemed like a very bad idea.

"*Ah, je comprends,*" the woman replied. "*Vous êtes très pieuse!*"

Rose didn't try to contradict her. It was too complicated to explain that she was not a Catholic but a Jew—a Jew who belonged to neither synagogue nor church but drew inspiration from the writings of an early Christian mystic. Easier to let this woman think that she was too pious to believe in fortune-telling.

She bought three candles and stepped into the dark interior of the church. The scent of incense and beeswax hung heavy in the air. At the far end of the huge vaulted nave, the shrine of the two Marys glowed with hundreds of tiny lights. As Rose got closer she could make out the flesh-tinted faces of the plaster saints. Lit from beneath, they had an eerily lifelike look.

She wasn't particularly keen on these garishly painted images. From what she'd read in Baedeker's guide, the statue in the crypt down below sounded more appealing, carved out of wood and unadorned. But she didn't feel she could venture down there. It was the Gypsies' special place. Bill Lee had told her that his people would resent anyone who was not of their own blood entering the shrine of the Black Virgin. It was a pity because Sara sounded like just the sort of saint she could relate to: practical, down to earth, and a friend to wanderers who weren't quite sure where they were going.

Rose lingered in the shadows, watching people line up to kiss the feet of the two Marys. She hadn't come here to do that. What had drawn her to the church was a longing to be in a space that felt calm and spiritual. It wasn't that she disliked crowds or music or dancing. That was something she loved about the Gypsy way of life—the ability to conjure up a party at the drop of a hat. But after what had happened this afternoon, it was the last thing she wanted to do. In the tent she had felt trapped, surrounded by so many people enjoying themselves. But in here the atmosphere was very different. She closed her eyes and breathed in the scented air, letting the peace of the place soak into her.

When she opened her eyes, she remembered the three candles she'd stuffed into her pocket. There was less of a crowd around the shrine now. She could go and light them. She walked slowly up to the feet of the statues and took a taper from one of the containers positioned on a ledge in front of the shrine. She placed her candles in a row of others. One for Nathan and one for each of her parents. But when she lit the taper and held it to the wicks, they wouldn't catch. The moment each one flared up, it blew out. Rose glanced over her shoulder. She couldn't feel any draft coming from the door. The other candles in the row were all alight. She tried a second time. Then a third. But flame after flame blew out.

Suddenly Rose felt someone tugging at her arm. She glanced around to see a little girl, no taller than her waist, staring up at her with an earnest expression.

"Ven, intenta encender las velas para Santa Sara." The red ribbons in her dark curls bobbed up and down as she spoke.

"Santa Sara?" Rose smiled at her, puzzled by the foreign words spoken so quickly.

"Av akai!"

This was more familiar. It sounded just like a phrase Bill and his sisters had used when they wanted her to accompany them to some place or another. The child was pointing to the three candles. Rose suddenly grasped what the child was trying to say: she was telling her to take them down to the crypt.

Rose glanced over her shoulder, wondering who the little girl was with. *"¿Tu madre?"* Your mother? She swept a hand at the people gathered around the shrine.

"Abajo." The child jerked her thumb at the floor, then beckoned Rose to follow her.

The hesitation was momentary. This was an invitation from a Gypsy child to enter the inner sanctum of her people. To turn away would be worse than going where she was not supposed to go.

"Soy Nieve," the girl said as they made their way down a narrow flight of stone steps.

"Nyeh-veh." Rose repeated the name as it sounded. It was not one she had ever heard before.

"¿Cómo te llamas?"

"Rose."

"Rose." The child drew out the word, as if trying it for size. *"¿Como Rosa?"*

"Yes, like Rosa." The Spanish was coming more easily to her now. Perhaps it was because with someone so young, she felt less self-conscious.

A hum of whispered voices, like a swarm of bees, was coming from the crypt. When Rose reached the bottom of the stairs, she saw a room that looked like a cave, its rough walls studded with pinpricks of light from the candles placed in every available nook and cranny. The statue of Saint Sara was much smaller than the plaster saints in the main part of the church. The wood from which it was carved looked like ebony, but as Rose got closer, she could see that the dark color had been painted on. The Black Virgin had brown almond-shaped eyes and a mane of dark hair crowned with a circle of white roses. Unlike the Mary saints, who had been dressed for the fiesta in shiny satin robes trimmed with gold lace, Sara wore a simple dress of faded blue cotton.

A Gypsy woman was holding her baby up to the statue, pressing the child's face to the wooden mouth. When she lifted it back down,

Rose could see that Sara's full lips bore faint traces of red pigment, the paint kissed away by generations of worshippers. Two more children were held up in the same way; then the whole group moved toward the steps, leaving Rose and the little girl alone in the crypt.

Nieve pointed to a trough of sand at the saint's feet.

Rose placed the three tallow wands with their blackened wicks alongside others already burning there. To her surprise they kindled immediately. And the flames held when she stepped back. Rose glanced up at the statue. The dark face, tinted gold by the candles, almost looked as if it were smiling.

"Nieve!" A female voice hissed across the chamber. Rose wheeled around to see a young woman hugging the child to her. "I told you to stay close!" The words, spoken in *kalo*, echoed off the walls, clear enough for Rose to understand.

Nieve glanced at Rose, her eyes brimming with tears. Rose stepped forward, wondering how to address the woman. She looked far too young to be Nieve's mother. Hard to believe that such a slim, lithe body had born a child. Perhaps she was an older sister.

"I'm sorry—your . . . she was helping me."

"Her candles wouldn't light, Mama," Nieve said, "so I brought her down here. Her name is Rose."

The woman's expression softened. She tucked a stray wisp of black hair behind her ear and gave Rose something like a smile. Perhaps she was older than she looked. In England it was not unusual for Gypsy girls to be married off at thirteen or fourteen. Maybe Nieve had been born when her mother was that age.

"For my family," Rose said, gesturing at the candles. "This one is for my brother. These are for my mother and my father."

The words kindled something in the woman's eyes. "This one is for *my* brother. My twin." She pointed to a guttering stub of wax in the same trough of sand. "And that one is for my mother." She glanced at

Nieve. "She wanted to light them herself—although she never knew them."

"She's a lovely little girl," Rose said. "And she has such a pretty name. I've never heard it before."

"Oh," the woman replied. "It's like . . ." She raised her hands above her head and brought them down, rippling her long brown fingers. Then she hugged herself and shivered.

"Ah! Snow!" Rose smiled. "And what's your name?"

"Lola." She held out her hand to Rose. "Where do you come from?"

"England."

Lola cocked her head to one side, surveying her through half-closed eyes. "That's very far away, yes?"

"It is." Rose nodded. "What part of Spain do you come from?"

"Granada. But I wasn't born there, and neither was Nieve. We are Alpujarreños."

Now it was Rose's turn to look puzzled.

"From Las Alpujarras—south of Granada." Lola outlined a mountain range with the flat of her hand. "Very high—with lots of snow."

Rose felt her heart shift against her ribs.

"Is something the matter?"

Her face must have betrayed the sudden surge of hope. "I . . ." Rose faltered. She could hear more people coming down the steps. This wasn't the place to start interrogating Nieve's mother. And she had left Nathan's photograph back at the tent. "I'm a little hungry," she said. "There's a stall selling pancakes in the square. I wonder if you and your daughter might like some?"

It was almost dark by the time they'd finished eating. In the twilight it was difficult to read Lola's face. She was listening intently to Rose's story. It was frustrating, not having the photograph to show her. But it would have been difficult for her to see it properly anyway. That was going to have to wait until the morning.

"There was a village near the place where he lived," Rose said. She racked her brain for the word she needed. *Fuente*—that was it. The fountain with the legend. She tried to describe it as best she could. Nathan meeting the girl he wanted to marry the evening he'd drunk from it.

"Yes." It was almost a whisper. Rose could hear Lola drawing in her breath. "I know that place."

"You do?" She felt as if the last bit of pancake had got stuck on its way to her stomach.

"It's only a few miles from where I lived. It's in a village called Pampaneira."

"Pampaneira." Rose breathed the name as if it were a magic charm.

"My mother used to work there—before I was born."

"Nathan said there were Gypsies fighting alongside him—could any of them have come from your family?" Rose regretted the words as soon as she had uttered them. Lola's brother and mother were dead. Thousands of people had been killed in the Spanish Civil War—it was highly likely that they had both been among the victims.

"Not my family." The tremor in Lola's voice was enough to tell Rose that she had guessed right. "My brother was too young to fight. I never knew my father."

"I'm sorry." Rose felt wretched, making her relive what had clearly been a harrowing time in her young life. She glanced at Nieve, who was standing a few yards away, watching a juggler tossing flaming torches. It was just as well she wasn't close enough to hear the conversation.

"It's not your fault," Lola murmured. "I know how it feels, to lose a brother. I understand what you're trying to do." She shifted a little on the low wall they were sitting on. "I didn't know the partisans—but I saw some of them. My brother used to take messages to them when he took the goats out. And my mother let them stay sometimes when they needed to hide. But they—"

"Mama!" Nieve was suddenly beside them, eager eyed. "Uncle Cristóbal says it's time to get ready!"

Lola stood up, her face betraying no hint of what she had been about to reveal. "I can look at your brother's photograph tomorrow," she said, "but tonight, why don't you come and watch me dance?"

Chapter 8

Men were lighting flaming torches in the center of the village square. They cast a golden glow on the faces of the people who had already gathered to get the best view of what was about to take place. There was no stage in the square for Lola to dance on. Like all the other flamenco artists at the fiesta, she was required to perform on wooden boards laid on the paving stones.

"I just have to get changed." Lola turned to Nieve, holding out her hand.

The child shook her head. "I want to take Rose to say hello to Uncle Cristóbal."

Lola glanced across the square. "Where is he? I can't see him."

"He said he was going in there." Nieve pointed to a door with a metal sign hanging above it. The light from the torches caught the lettering of a brand of beer.

"I don't think Rose will want to—"

"It's all right," Rose cut in. "I don't mind."

Lola held her eyes for a moment, as if she were weighing her up. Then, with the slightest movement of her head, she turned away, disappearing into the darkness on the edge of the square.

"Come on." Nieve took Rose's hand. Rose smiled, thinking how strange it was that this little girl had led her to the information she had sought for so long. A child who was the same age that Nathan's son or daughter would be, if he or she were alive.

"Uncle Cristóbal's quite old," Nieve said as they walked toward the door of the tavern. "Much older than Mama."

Rose visualized someone grizzled and possibly toothless, so it came as a surprise when they entered the shadowy room and Nieve pointed to a man who looked no older than midthirties.

He was handsome—Rose could tell that at once, despite the dim light. She studied him as Nieve babbled away to her uncle. His wavy black hair was slicked back from his face, like the glossy coat of a seal. He had a fine, well-shaped nose and intense eyes. He wore a white shirt with a striped neckerchief loosely knotted at his throat. As he lifted his beer glass, Rose saw that he had a leather thong threaded with glass beads tied around his wrist.

"*¡Encantado!*" He took Rose's hand and lifted it to his lips. Then he hoisted Nieve onto his lap and whispered something in her ear. With a giggle, she went scampering off outside.

"Will you have a glass of wine?" He pulled out the chair beside him, moving the guitar that was propped against the backrest.

"Is there time?" Rose glanced toward the door, wondering where Nieve had gone.

"We don't start for another half an hour or so. I sent Nieve to check out the competition. There's a troupe from Portugal on before us."

Rose nodded. She hadn't realized it was a contest.

"My cousin is very nervous. It's her first public performance outside Granada." He motioned to the barman. "You like red wine or white? Or a beer?"

"Red wine would be lovely." Rose couldn't remember the last time she'd tasted wine of either color. In London there were still shortages of everything, despite the war having ended eight months ago. There was always beer to be had in the pubs, but wine was not part of the culture in Britain in the way it was in continental Europe. It had been something her parents found strange—there had always been bottles of claret and champagne in the cellar at her childhood home in Cheshire. But that was another life.

The barman placed a tulip-shaped glass in front of her along with a little dish of black olives.

"¡Salud!" Cristóbal clinked his glass against hers. "So, Nieve told me you come from England. And you look like one of us, but she says you're not. Is it true?" He took hold of the earthenware saucer with a stub of candle in it, holding the flame in front of Rose's face. "Your eyes are gray, aren't they? Not Gypsy black. But they're the same shape as ours—and you have the cheekbones."

Rose felt like a horse being inspected by a wary buyer. There was something rather too familiar about his manner. But the way he looked at her was disarming. She could feel something inside her melting under his gaze.

"I think there must be some Gypsy blood in my family," she said. "On my father's side, probably. He was Turkish—from the port of Smyrna. My grandfather—his father—used to read my hand when he came to visit us: the *dukeripen*—you know?"

Cristóbal smiled, his teeth glinting in the candlelight. "So you know *kalo*, too?"

"I know some Romany words," Rose replied. "That's what they call the Gypsy language in England. But I'm told they're quite alike."

"How did you learn?"

She saw him looking at her left hand. He must be wondering if she was married to a Gypsy. She told him about the summer she'd spent on the Sussex marshes, about the Lee family and her mission to find herbal cures for animals.

"I suppose that's something I might have inherited from my father's side of the family," she said. "I love animals—especially dogs. And my brother, Nathan, has the Gypsy passion for horses." She checked herself, realizing she was talking about him in the present tense. "That's why

I've come here—to try and find out what happened to my brother."
She repeated what she'd told his cousin. "I could hardly believe it when
Lola said she knew the village Nathan talked about in his letter." It suddenly occurred to her that as a relative, Cristóbal might know the place,
too. That he might have been one of the Gypsy partisans Nathan had
mentioned. He was certainly the right age.

Before she could ask, he gave her the answer. "Lola lived in that
part of Spain until she was fourteen," he said. "I've never been there
myself. Her mother was my father's sister, but he left the mountains
before I was born."

Rose tried to conceal her disappointment. "I'm going to show her
Nathan's photograph in the morning," she said.

He didn't reply. He was staring into his glass, rubbing his index
finger around the rim. His nails were long, for a man. But only on that
hand—his guitar-strumming hand, Rose thought. The fingers of the
left hand, spread out on the table, had stubby ends.

"I'm trying not to get my hopes up too much," she went on. "I
mean, it's enough that I know the name of the village. I can go and talk
to the people who still live there."

He looked up, his eyes dark slits in the candlelight. "It might not
be as easy as that."

"Why not?"

"People in Spain don't like to talk about the Civil War. It's like a
family secret, best not spoken about, best hidden in the back of the
drawer and left there until it can do no more harm."

"But it's seven years since the fighting ended. Surely they—"

"That may be true," he cut in. "But the guilt and the shame don't
go away. So many people died. There were atrocities on both sides. And
in the villages, it's worse than in the cities because everyone knows what
their neighbor did. It's like . . ." He paused, his eyes focusing on his
glass again. "It's like waking up with the worst hangover you've ever had,
thinking that the images in your head are from a bad nightmare—then

realizing that it really happened. That you really did those terrible things."

I'd like to marry her—but they murdered the priest last summer.

The sentence from Nathan's letter flashed through Rose's mind. Shocking in its matter-of-fact brevity. It conveyed that a line had been crossed, that this was a place where there were no moral boundaries. How long would it take for a community to talk openly about something like that? A decade? A generation?

"Uncle Cristóbal!" Nieve came charging into the bar like a whirlwind, almost knocking over the table. "They're not very good, those Portuguese! The woman twirled round so fast her skirt got caught in her knickers! Everyone was laughing!"

"Hmm." Cristóbal's face changed in a heartbeat. With a disarming smile he pushed his chair back and rose to his feet. "We'd better go and show them how it *should* be done, then, hadn't we?"

Rose squeezed through the crowd of onlookers, following in Cristóbal's wake. She couldn't help wondering if he had been talking about himself back there in the bar. Had *he* done terrible things during the Civil War? Or had he been using the word *you* in a more general sense?

"Come on." Nieve had a tight hold of her hand. "You can say that you're with us." The child had to raise her voice to make herself heard. "That means you'll be able to sit down instead of standing up."

When they reached the makeshift arena, Rose saw that three bales of straw had been placed at the side of it.

"Those are for us," Nieve said. "Mama won't need hers—you can have that one."

"Are you sure?" Rose glanced at Cristóbal, who sank down on one of the bales and began tuning his guitar. He nodded without looking up.

"Look! Mama's coming!" Nieve pointed to where the crowd was parting. Lola emerged, as exotic as a tiger lily, in a tight-fitting dress of orange-and-black silk. Her hair was studded with marigolds, and a shawl of black lace was draped over her shoulders.

A hush fell over the spectators as she took her place on the wooden board. There was a look of intense concentration on her face. She seemed to be completely oblivious to the crowd pressing in around her. With one foot in front of the other, she raised her arms above her head, stretching her body into a sinuous arc. She held the pose, her eyes fiercely proud, her painted lips unsmiling. Then, with a dramatic sweep of her arms, the dance began.

There was no music for this first sequence. Simply the *palmas*—the rhythmic clapping of hands performed by Cristóbal and Nieve, which kept perfect time with the staccato beat of Lola's feet. The way she moved was magnetic. Every watcher was transfixed. Her body transmitted an ethereal beauty, as if possessed by some otherworldly spirit.

When the dance ended, the applause was thunderous. Nieve flashed a smile at Rose. But other than a slight nod of acknowledgment, Lola remained impassive. She closed her eyes and angled her arms and head, waiting for the next sequence to begin. Cristóbal picked up his guitar, and his fingers rippled across the strings, the notes conjuring a poignant sense of longing. Then, as Lola started to move, he began to sing.

It was the strangest sound: anguished and yet utterly compelling. As if he were leaving a little piece of his soul in each line. Rose couldn't discern the words, but it didn't matter. The song transcended language. It spoke of some primeval pain that drew an echo from the hearts of all who heard it. And Lola gave life to all that emotion. The way she held her head, arched her body, snatched her shawl from her shoulders and whipped the ground—her dancing electrified the air around her.

Rose felt as if all her pent-up grief was suddenly exposed. It made her feel raw, vulnerable—and yet it was somehow cleansing and cathartic.

At the end of the sequence, the crowd went wild. Flowers sailed through the air and landed at Lola's feet. Nieve ran to gather them up, her red ribbons flying out in the breeze as she bobbed up and down. Cristóbal struck up a chord. This time the music was upbeat, not melancholy.

"This one's a *llamada*," Nieve whispered as she laid down long-stemmed carnations of coral, cream, and scarlet on the seat of straw. "Watch her feet!"

Lola looked as though she had slipped into a trance. She swept one arm slowly over her head, turning as she did so, surveying the audience through half-closed eyes as she lifted her skirt to knee height with the other hand. Then, with an explosion of sound, her feet took off in a sequence so fast her shoes became a blur of black against the sun-bleached brown of the wooden board.

Rose watched in awe, wondering how it was possible to keep up such a relentless rhythm. Lola's feet seemed to have taken on a life of their own, rapping out a storm while her upper body remained almost motionless. The only sign of the physical toll the dance was taking was a faint beading of perspiration on her forehead. She finished with a flourish of her shawl, then plucked marigolds from her hair to throw into the crowd, where they were fought over by enraptured fans. Cristóbal rose from his perch on the straw bale to take a bow beside her. What a handsome pair the cousins made, basking in the applause. For some inexplicable reason, a fragment of Cristóbal's warning floated into Rose's head as she watched them:

It's like a family secret, best not spoken about . . .

What had made Lola leave her mountain home at the age of fourteen at the height of the Civil War? Had Nieve been born then? And what had happened to Cristóbal during those years? What dark shadows lurked behind those beaming smiles?

"Say thank you to your mama for me, will you, Nieve? I have to go now." Rose bent to kiss the dark curls between the ribbons, then slipped away into the crowd, not wanting to intrude on whatever celebrations were likely to follow such resounding success.

It wasn't very late, but she needed to feed Gunesh and let him out for a walk. Perhaps after that she could come back to the square and enjoy more of the sights and sounds of the fiesta.

The dog was still fast asleep when she undid the tent flap. He lifted his head lazily as she crawled inside. But when he heard the rustle of her rucksack, he was on his feet like a shot, almost demolishing the tent in his eagerness to get at the food she'd packed in a carefully sealed jar.

When he'd finished eating, she slipped on his collar and lead. They made their way across the field, past the amber glow of dozens of campfires, past faces flushed with heat and the excitement of what the coming night promised. There was music everywhere. Guitars, mandolins, fiddles, flutes. And those who didn't own an instrument improvised: there were drums made from apple boxes and castanets fashioned from wooden spoons.

When they reached the square, she saw that it had been transformed into a vast outdoor ballroom. People of all ages were dancing—from wizened grandmothers to children barely able to walk. They danced in couples, in groups—some even on their own. The music was provided by fiddlers who were standing on the bales of straw that Rose, Nieve, and Cristóbal had vacated.

Rose suddenly spotted a face she recognized. The French Gypsy chief Jean Beau-Marie was dancing near the musicians, executing a complicated routine that involved rapid crossing and uncrossing of the feet. It reminded Rose of the tap-dancing classes she had been sent to as a child. She'd never been able to get the hang of it. If there *was* any Gypsy blood in her veins, it hadn't bestowed the gift for dancing.

"Rose! *Viens par ici!*" Come over here!

Jean bounded toward her, his legs thin but powerful, like a grasshopper. He kissed her on both cheeks. She could smell something stronger than wine on his breath. Brandy, possibly, or some homemade brew.

"I can't dance with you," she said. "What would I do with Gunesh?"

"You can tie him to that fig tree," Jean replied. "He'll be quite safe. We'll be able to watch him while we dance."

Rose hesitated. She did love dancing, even though she wasn't very good at it. "All right," she said. "Just give me a minute."

With Gunesh safely tethered to the tree, she followed Jean into the midst of the dancers. He took her hand in his, raising her arm over her head and twirling her around. Then he lifted her by the waist and spun with her, making her so dizzy she staggered like a drunk when he set her down.

"Jean! Enough!" She laughed, gasping for breath as she leaned on his arm for support. "Can't we just do a normal dance?" She glanced at the Gypsy revelers around them. There was no such thing as normal. This was wilder than anything she'd seen in the Sussex marshes—and it was a world away from the sedate waltzes and foxtrots of London ballrooms.

Jean turned up his hands in a helpless shrug. "Would you like a drink?" He led her back to the tree where Gunesh was tethered, walking a little unsteadily himself. Rose wasn't sure if the dancing or the alcohol was to blame. "We can get wine over there," Jean went on, jerking his head at a stall opposite the church. "But I have something stronger back at the field."

"Wine is fine, thank you. I'll get it." She wasn't sure what to make of him. He had been so quiet and self-effacing earlier on. The drink had changed him. She wondered if it was his way of blotting out the memories that haunted him. Was the invitation to partake of something stronger a veiled attempt to get her into bed? She hoped not.

She left him to fuss over Gunesh while she went to the stall. She was handing out the money for the wine when she felt a hand on her shoulder.

"*¡Rose, pensé que habías ido!*" I thought you'd gone! Cristóbal looked as if he'd just unearthed buried treasure.

"I had to go and feed my dog." She smiled back. "He's over there."

"Looks like someone's trying to steal him . . ." Cristóbal was off before she could stop him.

"It's all right—he's my friend!" Her shout was drowned by the cacophony around her. Grabbing her bottle of wine, she tried to catch up with him, but her way was blocked by a flower seller with a huge basket of carnations.

"Vous voulez acheter?"

"Non, merci." Rose waved away the peppery blooms thrust under her nose.

By the time she reached the fig tree, Jean Beau-Marie had vanished.

"My friend—where did he go?"

"He said he had to do something." Cristóbal shrugged.

Rose scanned the seething mass of people in the square. "But he was going to have some wine."

Cristóbal grinned. "I can help you drink that."

"Where's Lola?"

"She's taken Nieve off to bed. There's another competition tomorrow."

"Another? I thought you'd won!" She shook her head. "It was breathtaking. You had the whole audience under a spell."

"That was just the first round—tomorrow is the final. *Mucho parné.*"

Rose frowned, puzzled by the mixture of Spanish and *kalo.*

"Dinero. Mucho dinero."

"Ah—money!" Rose mimed coins slipping through her fingers.

Cristóbal nodded. "If we win, we get five thousand francs."

Rose did a quick calculation in her head, based on what she'd spent on groceries in Arles. French currency was worth nowhere near as much as before the war, in the days when she'd stayed with her aunt and uncle in Paris. But five thousand francs was still a lot of money. "That's a big prize," she said.

"Yes, it is."

From somewhere behind Cristóbal there came a sudden loud noise, like a thunderclap. Gunesh echoed it with a deafening bark.

"What was that?" Rose swooped down, putting a protective arm around the dog.

"It's the start of the drumming contest—want to go and see?"

Rose shook her head. "It'll scare my dog. I'd better take him back."

Cristóbal watched her untie the lead from the tree. "I'll walk with you."

"You don't have to."

"But I'd like to."

She glanced at his face. The light from the torches gave it a golden glow. His smile was almost angelic. He dropped down to stroke Gunesh, whispering something into his fur. The dog responded by licking him on the nose. It was all the approval Rose needed.

Cristóbal had got the fire going by the time Rose emerged from the tent.

"I'm afraid I don't have any glasses—just these." She held out two tin mugs.

"That's okay." He uncorked the bottle with his teeth. "It'll taste just as good." He settled down on the ground beside Gunesh. "I've never seen a dog like this before. What breed is he?"

"He's an Afghan. From Afghanistan." Rose sat down, the dog between them. "My father was a businessman who traded in rugs and gemstones. He often went on buying trips to Afghanistan. He brought Gunesh back with him. He was only a puppy—just a few weeks old."

Cristóbal nodded. "How old is he now?"

"He's ten." She ran her hand along the length of the dog's back. "Quite an old man now, aren't you?" Gunesh burrowed his nose between his paws.

"Did you always want to be a vet?"

She nodded. "When I was a little girl, my grandfather used to come to visit us from Turkey. He always brought me a pet—sometimes a kitten, other times a lizard or a tortoise. But every time, after a couple of months, the animal would get sick. It would be taken down to the basement, and that would be the last I ever saw of it. My parents never told me my pet had died. I suppose they didn't want to hurt me. But it made me desperate to learn how to cure animals."

"I have a dog, back in Granada," Cristóbal said. "I would have brought him along, but he's not used to traveling. He's a house dog."

Rose had never met a Gypsy who lived in a house. When she told Cristóbal this, he explained that in Spain there were two types of Gypsies—house dwellers and nomads—and that he and Lola belonged to the first group. He told her about the cave houses in Granada that transformed into dance floors by night, where tourists flocked to see flamenco.

"Not all of us are dancers or musicians," he went on. "There are basket makers, cobblers, flower sellers, blacksmiths. My father was a blacksmith—he left the mountains because there was more work to be had in Granada."

Rose sipped her wine, hovering on the edge of asking what had been on her mind all evening. "What was it like in Granada during the Civil War?"

For a long moment Cristóbal was silent, gazing into the crackling flames of the fire. "It was terrible. Unspeakable. Worse than any other city in the whole of Spain. No one knows exactly how many died. It was more than twenty thousand. Not just men—they killed women and children, too. People would denounce their neighbors to settle old scores, and the next thing you knew, the Guardia Civil would arrive on the doorstep. There was no justice—just mass executions."

"What was it like for you?" She held her breath.

"I wasn't there." He brought the tin mug up to his mouth and tipped it back. Then he took the bottle and poured out more wine. "I was in prison."

"Prison?"

"Don't look so worried! I didn't do anything bad—well, not against the law, anyway. My crime was the same as your brother's: I was on the wrong side." He paused, ruffling Gunesh's fur with his fingers. "I was one of the lucky ones. There are hundreds still in prison—men and women. Our esteemed General Franco has a long memory."

Rose closed her eyes, thinking about Nathan, unable to bear the possibility that he might be trapped in such a place. "It must have been . . ." She couldn't finish the sentence.

"It wasn't a party, that's for sure." Cristóbal shrugged. "I was made to work in a quarry, and my right hand got smashed. I thought I'd never be able to play the guitar again."

"Did they release you—when you were injured?"

He gave a grunt of a laugh. "Not a chance. It healed, thank God— but as soon as the bandages were off, they put me back to work. I got lucky, though: one day I managed to slip away from the line. The guards were beating someone up. They didn't see me." He took another swallow of wine. "I found a cave a few miles off and lived there for a few days until I started to go crazy for water. I tried walking south, at night so no one would see me. When the sun came up, I saw farm workers harvesting watermelons. I hid in the back of the truck they were loading them onto to take to market. I got through half a dozen by the time it reached the town." He shook his head. "I don't think anything ever tasted as good—before or since. After that I sang in the streets to get enough money for the train fare to Granada. By the time I got back, the war was over."

He picked up the wine bottle and went to top off her mug, but only a dribble came out. "Sorry!" He gave her a wry smile. "I shouldn't have gone on about the war—it always makes me drink too much."

"It's okay—it's my fault anyway for asking you about it. I'll make us some coffee, shall I?"

While they waited for the water to boil, he asked her why she was traveling alone with only a dog for company. "Is there a man waiting for you back in England?" He gave her a sidelong glance.

"No, there isn't!" She laughed at his impudence.

"Well, a man likes to know these things." He moved away from her, taking a stick from the pile by her tent and prodding the fire to make it blaze more brightly. "Perhaps you're like my cousin. There's a man back in Granada who's desperate to marry her—but she won't have it."

"She won't?" Rose wondered if Lola had been widowed during the war. There had been no mention of Nieve's father when they were standing in front of the candles at the shrine of Saint Sara.

"She says she's not interested in marriage—only dancing."

"So Nieve . . ." Rose trailed off, not wanting to sound as if she was prying.

"She's not Lola's daughter. The woman who gave birth to her died in the war. Lola adopted Nieve when she was a baby."

So that was why Lola looked too young to be a mother, Rose thought. Why had she done that at such a young age? Rose's head was bursting with questions.

"Listen to me, banging on about the war again!" Cristóbal huffed out a sigh and pushed the night air with his hand, as if banishing memories too painful to contemplate. "I want to know about your friends—these English Gypsies. Tell me, do they look like us?"

"Well, some of them do," she replied. "Others have red hair and . . ." She paused, wondering what the Spanish for *freckles* could be. She put her fingers to her face, dotting them over her cheeks.

"They have a disease?" Cristóbal looked horrified.

"No." Rose laughed. "Little brown things—like . . ." She searched for something he might recognize. "Like you get on a quail's egg."

"¡Ah, pecas!" He grinned. "So the sun does shine in England sometimes? I heard it's a very cold place, yet you say they live outdoors. What do they eat?"

She described the meals she had shared with the Lee family—the soups made of snails and seaweed and the elderflowers dipped in batter and fried over the fire. Then he wanted to know about their animals: what breeds of dogs and horses they favored.

"And how do they get money?" He wanted to know. "Do they make baskets like our people?"

"Baskets, yes, but they can only do that in the springtime, when the willow trees make new shoots. The rest of the year they make . . ." She didn't know the Spanish word for *pegs*, so she mimed hanging washing on a line.

"Pinzas para la ropa." He nodded. "We make those, too."

They talked on until the slim waning moon rose beneath the morning star, and the herbs of the Camargue were opening their petals to greet the sun. Rose could see the color of his eyes now—a vivid blue green, like nothing she had ever encountered among English Gypsies. And his skin was the pale golden brown of almond shells.

"I suppose I'd better let you get some sleep. You've got the competition tomorrow—today, actually," Rose said, glancing at her watch.

Cristóbal stretched his arms wide. "I don't think I could sleep now."

"But you should try to rest at least." She smiled at the rueful look on his face. "I'll still be here tomorrow—I'm not going anywhere. Not yet, anyway."

"Promise?" He leaned across Gunesh, who was fast asleep between them, and cupped her face in his hands. "Can I kiss you, *guapa*?"

Guapa. Beautiful. It was a long time since anyone had called her that.

He didn't have to wait for a reply. She closed her eyes and found his mouth with her lips.

Chapter 9

Lola was roused from deep slumber by the sound of someone singing. She lay very still, listening, trying to work out if it was a woman or a man—and wondering if the owner of the voice cared that some people were trying to sleep. Through a small tear in the canvas above her head, she could see the sky. It was pale yellow. Not long after sunrise. Too early to be out of bed yet.

As she pulled up the covers that Nieve had kicked off in the night, she caught sight of the garland of white roses on the hook at the end of the bed. She hadn't dreamed it, then: she really *had* won that first round. Lola drifted back into sleep with a smile on her face.

When she woke again, the garland was gone. And so was Nieve. Lola scrambled out of bed and pulled back the curtain. She had to climb over Cristóbal, who was lying to the left of the pile of sacks he used as a bed. Lola rolled her eyes. From the look of him, he had carried on drinking well after she and Nieve had left the fiesta. She felt like kicking him as she stepped over him. How dare he jeopardize their chances by staying up half the night.

She lifted the flap at the front end of the wagon. There was Nieve in her nightgown, dancing in front of the ashes of last night's fire, as lithe as a salamander, the garland of white roses perched at a lopsided angle on her head. The child didn't see her watching. She had a faraway look in her coal-black eyes—the look of a sleepwalker. But people didn't dance in their sleep. No—this was trance dancing. The kind of dancing Lola always hoped to achieve but couldn't always pull off. It was what happened when the *duende* took possession of your body. It came easily to Nieve because she had been dancing since before she could walk.

Lola sat on the edge of the wagon. Grief came over her unbidden, like a cloud drifting over the sun. Perhaps it was the look of Nieve, all in white, like an angel or a ghost, that brought back that long-ago day on the mountain so sharply. Or maybe it was the garland of roses, reminding her that last night, as she had been crowned winner of the solo dancers, she had longed for her mother and brother to have been there to share the moment.

Nieve danced on, oblivious. Despite the sadness inside, Lola didn't want to break the spell by calling out to her. But a few minutes later, it was broken by someone else: the woman from the next-door *vardo*, clattering pans as she washed them, ready to make breakfast.

"You look very pretty in that," Lola said as Nieve caught sight of her. The child smiled self-consciously as she came back from wherever her soul had flown off to. Her hand went to her head, fingering the garland as if she had forgotten it was there.

Cristóbal's body, golden and naked, was pushing against the soft flesh of Rose's belly. His mouth was moving from her cheek to her neck, covering her with kisses. But she was sliding away from him, down a slippery bank into a dark pool of water.

Her eyes were still closed as she tried to push her way through the membrane of the dream. She could still feel Cristóbal's lips. But that wasn't possible. She hadn't asked him to stay, had she?

It was the smell that snapped her back to consciousness. Dog breath. It was Gunesh licking her face. And in the night, she must have wriggled out of her sleeping bag and rolled across the groundsheet, because her back was now jammed against the tent wall. Condensation had seeped into her nightshirt and left her skin cold and clammy.

She struggled out of the damp cotton and dressed as quickly as she could. She'd had hardly any sleep—but that wasn't the poor dog's fault. He wanted his morning walk.

Outside the tent the festivities of the night before were still going on. She could hear the rhythmic clapping of hands, the notes of a violin, and the plaintive sound of a Gypsy woman singing.

Rose led Gunesh away from the encampment, toward the marshes. The sun lit up the pools of salt water, turning them molten silver. In the distance flamingos were gathered on the margins of a lagoon. Hundreds of them, like drifts of pink-tinged apple blossoms. As Rose paused to admire them, something flashed past her: a kingfisher darted across the surface of the water in a streak of shimmering turquoise.

The air had a tang of seaweed tinged with the scent of thyme and lavender. As she walked on, she caught a whiff of woodsmoke from the fields behind her. She wondered if it was too early to go and find Lola, to show her the photograph of Nathan. Better to have breakfast first, she decided. Lola must have been exhausted after all that dancing—and Cristóbal was sharing the wagon. She didn't want to risk waking him when he'd had so little sleep. The thought of him lying in bed sent a frisson of longing shooting through her. Her mind's eye replayed the dream of their naked bodies entwined. She wondered how he would react when she saw him again. Would he tell his cousin what had happened last night? Her face reddened at the thought.

On her way back to the tent, she paused at the paddock to admire the horses. There were some magnificent ones, including a black stallion with an arched neck and an impressively muscled body. The wind from the sea streamed through his mane and tail, and the sun gave his coat an iridescent sheen, like the plumage of a raven. She couldn't help thinking of how Nathan would have loved such a horse. She could almost see him on the stallion's back, whooping for joy as he rode out onto the marshes.

She was ducking down to get back into the tent when she caught sight of Jean Beau-Marie loping across the field.

"Bonjour!" She waved, trying to catch his attention. Gunesh joined in, barking loudly.

Jean changed direction. But he gave Rose no word of greeting as he reached them—just a curt nod. He glanced from her to the tent and back again. Gunesh jumped up at him, tail wagging. Jean put out his hand, stroking the dog's head absently, as if his mind were a million miles away.

"Where did you disappear to last night?" she asked.

He didn't answer her at first. He bent down to take the Afghan's head in both hands, nuzzling its nose with his. When at last he replied, he didn't look up. "That Spanish guy said he was your boyfriend."

Rose clicked her tongue. "Well, he *isn't*. I don't have a boyfriend— not that it's anything to do with you *or* him!"

"You're right—it's none of my business." He shrugged as he got to his feet. "I'm sorry. That's not why I did what I did yesterday. I wasn't trying to . . ." He met her eyes fleetingly, then turned as if to go.

Rose realized that without meaning to, she had hurt him. She reached out, catching his arm as he moved away from her. "You don't have to apologize. You've done nothing wrong. It's just that I . . ." She hesitated, at a loss to explain how she felt. She'd made it sound as if she didn't like men—which was not true. But there had to be a chemistry—the sort of smoldering desire she had felt when Cristóbal had kissed her last night.

What she had just told Jean was not a lie: Cristóbal could hardly be described as a boyfriend—not after just one kiss. But just remembering it made her burn inside. She knew that if he had lingered a moment longer, it would have turned into something she might have regretted in the cold light of morning.

"I understand," Jean said. The wistful look had turned to one of resignation. "You are grieving, as I am grieving. When your heart is full of sorrow, there's no room left for love."

His words made her feel even worse. To agree with that sentiment would be very wrong, tantamount to using the death of her parents and the disappearance of her brother as excuses for her lack of interest in Jean as a potential lover.

Was there something wrong with her, that she could still be drawn to a man when the loss of her family was so raw? Cristóbal's effect on her was like the pull of the moon on the sea: magnetic, irresistible, and immensely powerful. The urge to kiss him had come from somewhere deep inside—some ancient, instinctive part of her that had blotted out everything for a few magical seconds.

"That man you saw me with last night—he's with the Granada Gypsies," she said. "He has a cousin—the dancer the men spoke about—who knows the village my brother described in his letter."

Jean's face brightened. "So you have something to go on—that's good."

She told him about her plan to show Lola the photograph.

"And if she doesn't recognize him? What will you do?"

"Go and find the village in the mountains. Ask around. Someone there must remember him."

It might not be as easy as that. Cristóbal's warning echoed inside her head.

"You should go to Saint Sara—ask for a blessing."

She nodded. "I already have. That's how I came to meet Lola—we were both in the shrine, lighting candles."

"Then she's smiling down on you. Will you join the procession this afternoon?"

"Yes," Rose said, "I will."

It took Rose a while to find her way back to the wagons with the pome-granates hanging in the doorways. The field seemed even more crowded, as if new arrivals had come during the night and squeezed onto what-ever patch of ground they could maneuver into.

She wasn't sure which of the wagons Lola would be in. She bent over Gunesh, fiddling with his collar, trying not to look as if she was watching the women cooking over campfires and the men weaving bas-kets on the steps. She was hoping to see someone she recognized from the day before, someone who would know who Lola was and where she could be found.

Suddenly she felt something hurtle against the back of her legs, almost knocking her over.

"*¡Tienes un perro!*" You have a dog!

It was Nieve, bright eyed with excitement at the sight of Gunesh—whose head was several inches taller than hers.

"Can I stroke him? Will he bite?"

Rose smiled. "He won't bite—as long as you're gentle with him. His name's Gunesh."

"That's a funny name."

"In a country called Turkey it means sun." Rose pointed to the sky. "It's because he's all golden and shiny."

Nieve nodded. "What's this?" Her fingers, buried in Gunesh's fur, had found the collar of blue beads around his neck. Hanging from it was a silver filigree pendant in the shape of a hand.

"It's a lucky charm from my father's country—it's supposed to keep him safe."

Nieve's face was half-hidden by the dog's body. "You have a father?" There was a note of surprise in her voice, as if Rose had just revealed something quite unusual about herself.

"I used to have," Rose said. "But he died."

"Oh." The small brown hand smoothed the dog's silky coat. "That's the same thing that happened to me. And to Mama."

Rose wondered if Nieve knew that Lola was not her real mother. Cristóbal hadn't said. It was awful to think that the woman who had given birth to her had died when she was still a baby. And just as harrowing to speculate about the manner of her dying—butchered for being on the wrong side or slowly starved in some hellish prison camp. And what about Lola's parents? Something similar must have befallen them for a fourteen-year-old to be left in sole charge of an orphaned baby.

"That's sad for you both." The words sounded pathetically inadequate.

Nieve shrugged. Rose was relieved to see that there was no hint of suffering in the child's eyes. She was too young to remember what it was like to have a father.

"I was looking for your mama," Rose said. "Can you take me to her?"

"She's gone to buy bread," Nieve replied.

"Oh—shall we go and find her?"

The child nodded. "Can I take Gunesh?"

Rose handed the lead to Nieve. "We'd better ask your uncle, though—he'll be wondering where you've gone." The thought of seeing Cristóbal sent a warm tide surging through her stomach.

"No, he won't—he's fast asleep!" Nieve was already on the move. "Come on, *guapo*." She coaxed the dog. "We're going for a walk!"

Rose smiled inside, reminded of the word Cristóbal had used just before he kissed her. It was good that he was asleep: he needed it. She would see him this afternoon. Her hand went to her pocket, fingering the edges of the photograph. The thought of showing it to Lola made her feel queasy with anticipation.

The village square was strewn with the debris of an all-night party. Empty bottles, crushed flowers, and the charred remains of toppled torches littered the paving stones.

They found Lola queuing outside the *boulangerie*. In the bright morning light, she looked even younger. Her face, with last night's dramatic eyeliner and rouge washed away, was fresh and innocent. And there were no flowers or jeweled clasps in her hair—it hung loose down her back, glinting with chestnut highlights where the sun caught it.

Now that the moment had come, Rose was hesitant about showing her the photograph. She joined the queue, pretending that she, too, had come to buy bread. No matter what she'd told herself, she knew she would be crushed if Lola didn't recognize Nathan. Yesterday, when his image was being passed around, she had felt as if a little piece of her was breaking off with every pair of hands that touched it. So now she found herself talking about anything but her brother—about Lola's dancing, her costume, Cristóbal's gifted accompaniment, and Nieve's precocious ability to be part of the performance.

In the end it was Lola who broached the subject of Nathan. They were coming out of the shop, Rose clutching a two-foot-long baguette that she was unlikely to get through before it went hard and stale, when Lola asked about the photograph.

"Oh yes—I have it here." The words came out sounding nonchalant, as if it were a matter of no more importance than buying the bread. But Rose's hand trembled so much as she dug into her pocket that she almost dropped the baguette.

Lola stared at the image for a long moment. Then she angled it to catch the sun. With a little shake of her head, she passed it back to Rose. "I'm very sorry," she said, "but I don't think I ever saw him."

Rose turned away as she took it. Lola and Nieve didn't see her eyes filming over. She called over her shoulder that she had to go and buy food for the dog and would see them later. She dived into a butcher's shop, hoping Nieve wouldn't follow her, knowing that if she had to explain her glum face to the child, the tears would come flooding out.

Gunesh had already had his breakfast—but the process of asking for a bone and waiting for the butcher to wrap it helped Rose to regain her composure. He wouldn't take any money for it, so taken was he with the dog's good looks. Embarrassed by his kindness, Rose asked if she could buy a couple of *saucisses*. She had apples and cheese back at the tent, but she felt a sudden overwhelming need for something fried and comforting.

"Come on! Wake up!" Lola shook Cristóbal roughly by the shoulder. "It's nearly time for the procession! You've been asleep half the day!"

Cristóbal groaned as he opened his eyes. "Is there coffee?"

"Coffee! *¡Cerdo perezoso!*" Lazy pig!

He stretched out his arms, revealing a bare honey-brown torso, the skin smooth and rippled with muscles. Before he could sit up, Lola dumped his clothes on his chest.

"Get dressed! Why do I have to be your mother when you're practically old enough to be my father? What were you up to last night, anyway?"

His eyebrows arched like a hawk taking flight. "Do you really want to know?"

"No, I don't!" She gave him a black look. "You've got half an hour. There's bread in the basket—probably stale by now. We had our breakfast hours ago."

Rose hadn't meant to go back to sleep. She'd climbed back into the tent after cooking the sausages over the fire and closed her eyes, thinking she'd just let her food go down before cleaning the frying pan. But when she opened them again, she could hear trumpets and drums. Struggling to her knees, she opened the flap of the tent. The sound was coming from beyond the paddock, over by the road that led to the village. She crawled out of the tent and stood up, shading her eyes with her hand. She could see something silhouetted against the pale blue of the sky: it looked like a person standing in a boat as it glided over the sea. But the motion was jerky, as if the arms and legs couldn't move. And the sea was in the wrong place.

Suddenly her mind grasped what she was seeing. It was Saint Sara, the Black Virgin, being carried from the church to the beach. The procession was well underway, and she had almost missed it. She grabbed Gunesh's lead and snapped it onto his collar. He pulled in the other direction, unwilling to leave his bone. It took all her strength to make him follow her.

"Sorry, boy. You can have it back in a minute—but this I have to see."

As she hurried across the field, Rose saw that the paddock was empty of horses. Soon she realized why: the procession was being led by them. Snow-white mares and freckled colts trotted along the road, bare of saddles and harnesses, herded like sheep by Gypsy men sitting proud and tall on gleaming stallions.

Behind them were people walking, all in their best clothes. The children were just as elaborately attired as the adults—the little girls in flouncy flamenco dresses, the boys in white shirts and waistcoats and colorful neckerchiefs. Despite their finery, everyone was barefoot.

She wished she'd had time to change into something better than her mud-stained skirt and plain white blouse. But the sight of the statue coming closer drove out such thoughts. Held aloft by a dozen men, Saint Sara looked very different from the simple, unadorned figure Rose had seen in the shrine. She wore a sparkling white cloak over a dress of blue and gold. On her head, a spiky diadem threw out rainbow colors where the sun caught it.

The river of bodies swelled in the wake of the statue. A few yards behind, a second group of men carried a huge cross festooned with fruit and flowers. Behind that was yet another cross—this one a copy of the symbol above the church door, with the heart and anchor entwined at its base. A painted wooden sign beneath it read: *"Pèlerinage des Gitans."* Pilgrimage of the Gypsies.

Rose scanned the press of people, searching for the familiar faces of Lola, Nieve, Cristóbal, or Jean. But it was difficult to pick out individuals in such a crowd. She glanced at Gunesh. She wanted to join in, but she was afraid that all the noise would frighten him. To her surprise, the dog was wagging his tail. She patted his head, wondering what to do with her shoes. After kicking them off, she balanced them in the crook of a branch of one of the tamarisk trees that lined the road. Then she slipped in at the back of the procession, walking alongside an old man strumming a mandolin and a young boy beating a drum.

The tide of pilgrims slowed as it neared the sea. People fanned out along the beach as the men carrying the statue waded waist deep into the water, coming to a stop in front of a fishing boat. Standing in the bow was a bishop robed in white and gold, holding himself steady with a silver crosier. A hush fell over the crowd as he lifted his hand in a benediction. Raising his voice above the rise and fall of the waves, he pronounced a blessing on the sea, on the Camargue, and on the Gypsy pilgrims.

As he lowered his hand, the crowd surged forward, everyone cheering as they waded into the water. Men carried babies above their heads, holding them out for the bishop to touch. Little girls spun around in the waves, laughing as they scooped up the sodden frills of their dresses. Old women gave toothless smiles and theatrical shivers as they stood knee deep in the shallows.

Gunesh bounded into the waves, pulling Rose behind him. Her skirt billowed around her hips. It felt good to be in the water—not just because the waves were doing a good job of getting the mud out of her clothes: it was as if all her doubts and fears about what lay ahead were being washed away, too.

At a sign from the bishop, the men carrying the statue waded out of the water. They passed very close to where Rose was standing. She could see the glass eyes glowing amber in the sunlight and the worn red paint on the lips. Somehow the face seemed more real than it had in the shrine. There was a *Mona Lisa* look about it. Rose could almost believe that the wooden image had come alive, secretly happy to have been freed from the gloomy crypt and allowed to breathe the fresh sea air.

She's smiling down on you.

Jean's words came back to her as the statue moved toward the water's edge. How Rose longed for that to be true. But thus far her journey had brought mixed success. She made a silent prayer for what was to come.

She blinked as the sun bounced off the surface of the water. Black discs bobbed in front of her eyes, blotting out the faces of the people in the sea. It made her feel dizzy. She turned toward the beach, staggering as a strong wave knocked her off balance. She gripped the slippery leather of Gunesh's lead, afraid of losing him. Suddenly she felt a strong pair of hands around her waist, lifting her out of the water.

"¡Ten cuidado!" Be careful! Cristóbal pulled her close as he turned her around. His skin glistened where the salt water had splashed it. She opened her mouth, but his lips stifled the words. She felt a powerful throbbing in her belly as they kissed. When he broke away, it was only to scoop her into his arms and carry her onto dry land.

He set her down among the throng of sandy-limbed people preparing to follow Saint Sara up the beach. Gunesh, who had clambered out after them, shook himself violently, spraying Cristóbal all over.

He spluttered and laughed. "Good job! I'm already wet!" She melted inside as he took her hand. "Shall we finish the pilgrimage? I'm going to need all the blessings I can get to stand a chance in that competition tonight."

Rose looked around, suddenly uncomfortable at the thought of Nieve seeing what had happened in the sea. "Where's Lola?"

"She's gone back," Cristóbal replied. "Nieve has a new dress—she didn't want to get it wet." He rolled his eyes.

Drum beats echoed across the sand, and the crowd pressed in around them. Soon they were being jostled along, away from the sea and back toward the village. Rose could hear the distant peal of church bells above the cacophony of sound around her. No wonder she hadn't spotted Jean among the pilgrims—he must have stayed behind to ring out the saint's return to the shrine.

It was a relief to know that he hadn't seen her kissing Cristóbal. It would have made her seem like a liar after her flat denial that there was anything between them. And she didn't want to hurt Jean by flaunting this newfound . . . She pulled herself up short. What was it, exactly? The warmth of Cristóbal's hand on her skin sent pulses of desire shooting through her body. In the wild, joyful fever of the fiesta, it seemed like the most natural thing in the world to give in to what she was feeling. But should she even contemplate giving herself to a man she'd known for less than twenty-four hours? A man who would be gone for good when the celebrations ended? This wasn't what she was here for. She should be making plans for the journey ahead—looking at maps, consulting train timetables, working out how to get to the place that Lola had put a name to.

The procession came to a sudden halt. They were in the village square, shaded from the baking sun by the great edifice of the church. Rose's skirt, still damp from the sea, hung limply around her legs. She shivered as the bishop raised his hand in the final act of blessing.

"I'd better go and change out of these clothes," she said, breaking away from Cristóbal as the wooden statue disappeared through the doors of the church.

He gave her a lingering look, as if he was about to offer to help her out of them. But he said nothing.

"I suppose you have to get ready for the competition?" She heard herself trying to sound brisk and matter of fact.

He nodded. The change in his expression was subtle, almost imperceptible. "It's not for a couple of hours yet. Why don't you come and eat with us—when you've changed? There's a special meal—seafood paella—do you like that?"

"I've never had it—it sounds delicious." Rose smiled, surprised by how hungry she felt. There was nothing wrong with a last meal with all three of them, was there? It would give her a chance to thank Lola and say goodbye. "I'll have to pack first, though," she said. "The bus leaves for Arles at four o'clock."

"You're not going already?" He spread his hands, palms to the sky. "What difference will another day make? You can't miss tonight—there's going to be a wedding after the competition: music and dancing all night."

"I . . ." She felt her resolve melt away in the white heat of his gaze.

Chapter 10

Lola sat on a threadbare cushion at the edge of the wagon, watching a woman with no teeth throwing mussels into the cauldron of paella. Sitting cross-legged on the hard ground, this matriarch of the Granada clan was cleaning the shells with a knife, which she occasionally wiped on an apron stained red and orange from the paprika and cayenne pepper that had already gone into the pot. Another woman of a similar age was stirring the mixture, her sleeves rolled up to reveal arms as brown and sinewy as tree roots in a dried-up riverbed.

The smell of the raw seafood made Lola want to gag. She was the only woman in the group who had not played some part in preparing the coming feast. Others had peeled the onions and garlic, chopped tomatoes and peppers, gone to the harbor to bargain with the fishermen for prawns and mussels and squid. Lola had learned from bitter experience that it was pointless to offer to help. They didn't want her. She was regarded as an outsider—not just because she lived in a house rather than a *vardo*, but because she wanted no husband.

Every single Gypsy family from the Granada area had a male relative who, during the past five or six years, had come forward with a proposal of marriage. But Lola had rejected them all. She hadn't realized how much the women despised her for it. But they had made their feelings plain on the journey to France. However much she tried, however well she danced, she was tolerated but not wanted.

She sometimes caught these women watching Nieve—waiting for her to misbehave, get food down her clothes, or any other kind of evidence of Lola's shortcomings as a substitute mother. Lola could just imagine what they were saying behind her back. That someone in her position should be grateful to any man who offered marriage; that she had no right to be so fussy; that the child was most likely hers—not adopted but conceived out of wedlock. In Granada she had learned to close her ears to such talk, to ignore the sidelong looks and the upturned noses. But on the road, it had not been so easy.

The woman stirring the paella looked only a few years older than Lola's mother would have been if she had lived. Perhaps the woman would have been a little kinder if she had seen what Lola had seen: a mother and a brother lying cold and bloody in the snow; a dying woman begging for the life of her newborn baby. But no. Granada had seen more bloodshed than any other city in Spain. Who knew what horrors those eyes, staring so intently at the bubbling surface of the cauldron, had seen?

Lola knew she must try not to mind the way these women treated her. But their coldness intensified the pain of not having a mother to confide in. The hardest time of all was when she was about to start performing. That was when she longed for someone to soothe her frazzled nerves. Cristóbal was no good—he was nervous enough himself—and Nieve was too young to understand.

Lola stared into the flames licking around the blackened base of the cauldron. The only person she'd opened her heart to in a long time was the Englishwoman, Rose—a complete stranger. And yet Lola had told her things she'd never revealed to the people in the *vardos*. Why had she done that? Was it just because she and Rose shared the devastating experience of losing a brother? Or was it something else? The feeling that in this outsider, she had found a kindred spirit?

She raked her fingers through her hair. If only she had recognized that face in the photograph. If only she could have softened the pain in Rose's eyes—the look that so perfectly mirrored her own anguish.

Somewhere behind the wagon a dog barked—so loud it made her jump.

Nieve's head appeared through the flap of canvas. "That's Gunesh—I saw him through the hole!" She jumped nimbly over the edge of the wagon and ran around the back. Seconds later she returned, her hand looped through the dog's collar.

"Look who I found!" Cristóbal appeared next. He was looking over his shoulder at Rose, who was a few steps behind him. "Can you believe she's never tasted paella?"

Rose didn't come right up to the wagon. The women by the fire were staring at her. She looked embarrassed, as if she thought Cristóbal shouldn't have invited her without asking the others first.

"Come and sit here." Lola patted the cushion beside her. "Don't worry about them," she whispered as Rose climbed up. "They might look like witches, but they're very good cooks."

"A jalar!" Time to eat! As if on cue the woman with no teeth stood up, scattering the fragments of seaweed caught in her apron.

Rose was on her second helping of paella. She noticed that Lola had hardly touched her food, pushing the little shellfish and the fragments of squid tentacles around her bowl and taking only the odd forkful of rice. Was it because she was worried about keeping that slim dancer's figure? Or was she nervous about the competition?

"This is a big day for you, isn't it?" Rose said. "Cristóbal told me about the prize money."

Lola nodded. "In his head he's already spent it. But there are some very good *flamencas* here. Male and female dancers. From Madrid, from Sevilla, from Barcelona . . ." She trailed off, spearing a prawn.

"You make it look so easy—but I suppose that comes from years of practice?"

"I started when I was younger than Nieve," Lola replied. "I was on an errand for my mother—she'd sent me to buy sugar or something—and I caught sight of some girls in a courtyard. They were learning how to click their toes and heels—the thing we call zapateado. I hid behind a wall so I could watch. The teacher spotted me and asked me if I knew how to dance. I hadn't a clue what I was doing, but I just . . ." She shrugged. "I did it by some instinct, I think. I don't know how long I stayed—I got into terrible trouble when I got back home. But the next week I was back there, taking lessons."

"That was in your village, was it? In the mountains?"

Lola nodded. "In Capileira, yes. I had a good teacher there—but I wouldn't have got to dance for a living if I hadn't moved to Granada." She set her bowl aside, the saffron-colored rice already beginning to desiccate in the heat from the sun. "Will you go there? To the mountains, I mean?"

"Yes, I will. Although your cousin warned me I shouldn't get my hopes up."

Lola's face clouded. "What did he say?"

"That people don't like to talk about what happened during the Civil War. That . . ." Rose hesitated, aware that anything she said might sound like a judgment on whatever had befallen Lola's family.

"It won't be easy, I'm certain of that." Lola turned her face away, gazing into the distance. "It's a beautiful place—I miss it terribly. But I could never go back there." She brought her hand up to her heart and held it there. "Fear remains in the blood."

Rose held her breath for a moment, searching for the right words. "It must have been a terrible time for you," she said at last.

Lola nodded slowly. "When I'm dancing, I stop feeling the pain. Only dance and tears can get rid of it. If I didn't dance, I'd be crying all the time." She closed her eyes as if to shut out images too harrowing to recall.

"I'm sorry to have made you talk about it," Rose said.

Lola shook her head. Opening her eyes, she turned to Rose. "Don't let Cristóbal put you off," she said. "You *have* to go there. We both have pain—yours might be different from mine, but it won't go away, will it? Not knowing if someone is dead or alive is a kind of torture."

Don't be afraid of what you don't know. That kind of fear kills you without you realizing. Like bleeding inside.

Lola's words were an echo of what Bill had said. Two Gypsies, half a continent apart, had given her the same wise advice.

Before Rose could reply, Nieve came bouncing up to the wagon, dragging Gunesh in her wake. "Can I give him Mama's leftovers, Rose? He's been sniffing the paella pan—I think he wants some!"

"Well, yes." Rose smiled. "If your mother has finished."

Lola handed Nieve her bowl. "I can never eat much before I dance," she said to Rose. "I get too nervous."

"Can we take Gunesh for a walk after that?" Nieve flashed a smile at Rose as she held the bowl out to the dog. "I could take you to see Rubio."

"That's our horse," Lola said. "Well, not ours, exactly—we borrowed him for the journey from Granada. He belongs to a friend of Cristóbal's."

"I'll look after Auntie Rose while you get ready."

Rose smiled. No one had ever called her Auntie before. Nieve's expression was very grown-up for an eight-year-old. Rose wondered what it had been like for her, being brought up by someone who was barely out of childhood herself. Probably the two of them were more like sisters than mother and daughter.

"Will you come and see us later?" Lola asked.

"Of course," Rose said. "I'm looking forward it. And Cristóbal said there's going to be a wedding afterward."

"Yes." Lola made a face. "I'm not sure I'll be staying up for that." She jerked her head at Cristóbal, who was standing on the far side of the campfire, deep in conversation with a couple of wizened Gypsy men. "He might try to pair me off with someone. He's been threatening to find me a husband."

"Auntie Rose! Are you coming?" Nieve was tugging at Rose's skirt.

"*¡Bueno éxito!*" Good luck! Rose called over her shoulder as she jumped down from the wagon.

"With the dancing or the husband dodging?" Lola shot her a wry smile. "*Hasta luego.*" See you later.

Rose glanced down at Gunesh, who was curled up at her feet. She was amazed that he could sleep through the whirlwind of sound. Guitars, drums, violins, and castanets. The frenzied stamping of the dancers and the wild applause of the onlookers. There had been four other acts to sit through before Lola and Cristóbal took their turn. All were mixed groups of male and female dancers. There was enormous energy in the performances—the men, especially, were an arresting sight, projecting heartbreak as they hugged their waistcoats to their lithe bodies and desperate bravado as they threw back their heads. But it was difficult to watch when more than one person was dancing in such a small space. Perhaps that would give Lola an advantage over these others.

When the cousins emerged from the shadows at the edge of the square, Rose gave an involuntary gasp. Lola wore a gown of shimmering gold edged with black lace. The tight-fitting bodice gave way to a cascade of fishtail frills that swept the ground as she moved. Cristóbal's costume complemented hers perfectly. He wore a waistcoat of the same fabric as the dress over a crisp white shirt with a *dikló* of black silk loosely knotted at his neck.

Rose followed him with her eyes as he took his seat on the straw bale beside the makeshift stage. The sensation of his lips on hers surged from her memory, quickening her pulse. She saw him reach across to Nieve and give her hand a little squeeze. The child gave him a nervous smile. She looked like a Christmas-card angel, in a white dress trimmed with gold.

A hush came over the crowd as Lola raised her arms and angled her body in that proud, defiant posture that signaled the start of the performance. The moment the *palmas* began, her feet took off in a frenzy of movement. On their walk that afternoon, Nieve had explained some of the dance steps to Rose. The footwork in flamenco was called *escobilla*. *Punta* meant using half a foot; *tacón* was the heel only; *planta* was when the whole foot came down on the ground.

As she watched, Rose wondered how Lola managed not to trip over the golden train of her dress. Somehow, she kept it behind her, sweeping the fabric out in a great arc—an achievement that underlined the skill of her performance because she did it with such effortless grace.

Nieve had outlined the *palos*—the sequence of dances that would make up the competition entry—so Rose knew that this maelstrom of unaccompanied footwork was a prelude to Cristóbal striking up a melody. The name Nieve had given to this was a *llamada*—literally a calling—and that was just how it sounded when Cristóbal opened his mouth. His voice was the plaintive wail of a soul in agony. The drawn-out syllables made the words hard to comprehend, but Nieve had recited the lyrics to Rose. She said it was her uncle's favorite song: a ballad about wanting to die in Granada.

Rose felt the rhythm of the music enter her body like a second heartbeat, drumming against her ribs. Dragging her gaze away from Cristóbal, she saw Lola's fingers sculpting the air as her wrists rotated in a series of intricate movements, like fantail doves rolling in midair.

This time she used her upper body more than her feet to convey the emotion. The combination of her movements and Cristóbal's voice had a transcendent effect on the audience: it was as if they had cast spider threads into the night air to tug at the heartstrings of every man and woman in the vast crowd gathered in the village square.

When the sequence ended, there were shouts of adulation in a dozen different languages. But the performance was not over. With a flick of her wrist, Lola pulled off the fishtail part of her dress to reveal a second layer that hugged her slim body like a silken cocoon. She tossed it toward the straw bales, where Nieve leapt forward to retrieve it. At the same moment, Cristóbal sent a black lace shawl sailing through the air. Lola caught it in one hand, flourishing it like a bullfighter's cape before wrapping it around her shoulders. She smiled at the audience for the first time, signaling that the next number was a happy one.

This time she induced a different kind of enchantment. People were twisting and swaying as if they had itching powder in their shoes. It was impossible not to be carried along by the sheer exuberance of Lola's dancing.

It was not just flowers that showered the arena when the sequence ended. Coins flew through the air, too. Lola held her hand up to her heart as she bowed. Then she gestured to Cristóbal, who rose from his seat to rapturous applause. He, in turn, gestured to Nieve. The little girl was far too busy scooping up the fallen coins to notice—which brought peals of laughter from the crowd.

When eventually the hubbub subsided, Lola, Cristóbal, and Nieve disappeared to await the judges' decision. Rose couldn't have been more nervous if she'd been onstage herself. When the verdict was announced, she clapped her hand to her mouth.

There was no chance of fighting her way through the crowd to congratulate them. The Granada Gypsy men were already there, surrounding them like an honor guard. They hoisted all three onto their shoulders to parade them around the square with Lola at the front. It was like a reprise of the Saint Sara procession—this time with a flesh-and-blood woman instead of a wooden statue.

Rose decided to take Gunesh back to the tent and return when things had died down a bit. She got back to the square just in time to see Lola being crowned with a garland of lilies and Cristóbal taking proud possession of a fat envelope.

She pushed her way to the edge of the arena as they took a final bow. Nieve caught sight of her and gave a small, self-conscious wave. The ceremony at an end, she led her mother and uncle to the place where Rose was standing.

"¡Felicidades, vosostros estuvísteis fantásticos!" Rose hugged each of them in turn.

Cristóbal wrapped his arms around her, pulling her extra close to whisper in her ear. "¿Te veré después?" Will I see you later?

His lips brushed her skin, sending a fizz of desire all the way to her belly. She glanced sideways, aware of how it would look to Lola and Nieve. But they had disappeared into the sea of adoring fans.

Chapter 11

Lola hadn't intended to stay for the wedding. Physically she was spent—but she knew that if she went back to the wagon and lay down, she wouldn't be able to sleep. Euphoria coursed through her body like liquid fire. She'd swapped the gold flamenco costume for an anonymous combination of white blouse and dark-blue skirt. A shawl of the same blue shrouded her face.

"I didn't recognize you," Rose said when Lola touched her arm.

"Good!" Lola grunted a laugh. "I was followed all the way to the changing rooms. Suddenly I seem to be very popular—I suppose five thousand francs does that for a girl."

"I shouldn't think money had anything to do with it," Rose said. "You looked stunning in that dress, and you're the star of the show—no wonder you've got men trailing after you."

"Well, I managed to shake them off, thank goodness."

"Who, Mama?" Nieve piped up.

"No one, *cariño*." Lola stroked the child's hair. "Let's talk about something else, shall we?"

"Oh look!" Rose pointed to a girl of about seventeen who was coming out of the church on the arm of a boy who looked barely old enough to shave, followed by a gaggle of little girls in white dresses. "Is that the bride and groom?"

"It must be," Lola replied. "They're not Spanish. I think they're from Greece. You can tell from her hairstyle."

"How?"

"Can you see how it's all woven with ribbons? They pin it up in a sort of hat shape, then drape a white veil over the top. Only the Greek girls do that. And they have those embroidered velvet jackets, cut off above the waist."

"I can't see!" Nieve was standing on tiptoe. Rose lifted her up and hoisted her onto her shoulders.

"Is that better?"

"Yes—I'm a giant now!"

Rose felt the child stroking her hair.

"I can see everything!" Nieve laughed. "There's Uncle Cristóbal. He's going into that place he went to last night."

"Well, he'd better not spend any of the prize money," Lola muttered.

"Has the wedding ceremony already happened?" Rose was peering out from under the frills of Nieve's dress.

"The church part, yes." Lola nodded. "But the celebrations don't start until they've jumped over the broomstick. Over there." She jerked her head toward the sea side of the village square. "They're going to do it on the beach. They've built a huge bonfire, and they've been roasting an ox for hours—ever since the procession ended. Are you hungry?"

Rose nodded. "I shouldn't be after all that paella—but I am."

"Me too," Nieve chimed in. "Can we go there now?"

They joined the crush of people following the bride and groom. The night air was full of sounds and smells—of musical instruments, singing, and clapping; of tobacco, woodsmoke, and hot human bodies. As they drew near to the quayside, the stink of rotting fish drifted in on the breeze, overlaid with the aroma of roasting meat. Soon the cobblestones underfoot gave way to sand. A fire as tall as a house sent sparks flying into the purple sky and cast a path of shimmering bronze across the rippling ocean.

The wedding guests fanned out, circling the fire as the young couple took their places next to a broomstick lying in the sand. Lola thought how happy they looked, their faces glowing with the heat of the fire and their eyes shining with anticipation. It gave her a wistful feeling. *Would* they be happy? Could they? Was it possible to pledge your life to someone at seventeen and make it last until you died?

"That's going to be quite a jump, isn't it?" Rose's voice broke into her thoughts. The broomstick had been lifted off the sand by two older men, who were holding it at just above knee height.

"Yes," Lola said. "It's not usually that high."

"Why do they have to jump over it?" Nieve frowned.

"It's . . . just what they do." Lola cast a wry look at Rose. "Do you know about this custom of ours?"

"Not really," Rose replied. "I have Gypsy friends who've got married, but I've never been to a wedding."

"They have to jump as high as they can." Lola lowered her voice to a whisper for what she had to say next: "If the girl's skirt touches the broomstick, it signifies that she's not a virgin—or that she's pregnant already. If the boy's trousers touch it, it means he'll betray his bride."

"Poor things," Rose whispered back. "I hope for her sake he's got springs in his legs."

Lola nodded. She couldn't help thinking of Cristóbal's wife. She had a mental image of Juanita bending over a cooking pot, her belly distended. She wondered what her cousin was getting up to back there in the tavern. With a wad of cash in his pocket and the magnetism of being a winner, she feared the worst.

A hush fell on the watchers as the young bride lifted the froth of fabric that covered her legs to the ankle. She was a little dot of a thing— no more than five feet tall. Lola didn't think she had a hope of clearing the broomstick. But she stepped a few paces back and took it at a run, her skirt flying up to her hips as she leapt over the wooden shaft.

There was wild cheering from the crowd. Then it was the boy's turn. With a broad grin he rolled his trousers up to his knees, which brought boos and catcalls from the crowd. But he took no notice and jumped. The trousers stayed up, and he grabbed his bride, picking her up and twirling her around in his arms.

"Clever lad!" Cristóbal's voice took Lola by surprise.

"I thought you'd gone to the tavern?"

"I did—but I wasn't going to miss this. They did well, didn't they?"

"Well, yes—except he cheated." She gave Cristóbal a knowing look, wondering what had happened when he and Juanita had jumped the broomstick. She didn't know, because she hadn't been there. The wedding had taken place fifteen years ago, when she was still living in the mountains.

"Shall I take Nieve?" Cristóbal was talking to Rose now. The child was still on her shoulders—so sleepy that she was swaying sideways.

"It's all right—I'll take her to bed," Lola replied. "You'd better give me that money, though."

"I can carry her back," Rose offered. "You must be worn out."

"No—I'll be fine, honestly." Lola took the wad of money from her cousin and tucked it down the front of her blouse. "It'd be a shame for you to come away now, just when the fun's about to start. I've seen it all before—but you haven't."

"Well, if you're sure."

Lola nodded. She looked around for Cristóbal, but he had already melted into the crowd. She wondered if she should warn Rose about him. But Rose was clearly used to taking care of herself. A woman who traveled alone in a tent with only a dog for company must know how to handle unwanted attention from men.

"Have a good time," Lola said as she took Nieve into her arms. "Will we see you tomorrow?"

Rose nodded. "My bus doesn't leave until four o'clock."

"Come and have something to eat before you go."

"Thank you—I'd like that."

"Oh—and bring your dog." Lola smiled over her shoulder. "Nieve's fallen in love with him. I'm going to have a hard job stopping her from jumping on that bus with you."

Rose was kneeling on the sand, a few yards away from the bonfire, holding a steaming hunk of roast beef out in front of her to stop the juices running onto her clothes. Cristóbal laughed as he sank down beside her.

"We're going to have to go for a swim in the sea after this—just to get clean," he said.

Rose glanced at him, wondering if he was serious. No one would see them in the dark. They wouldn't have to bother about keeping their clothes on. The thought of being naked in the water with him stoked a fire inside that had nothing to do with the hot food she was eating.

"I suppose we could dance first, though, couldn't we?" He tossed a bone through the air. It landed with a small splash in the waves. "Do you like dancing?"

Rose nodded. "I have to warn you—I'm not very graceful. I hate to think what Lola would say if she saw me."

"Well, she won't, because she's safely tucked up in bed." He slid across the space between them, slipping his arm around her waist. "I'm glad you're not skinny, like her," he said. "I love this." He ran his fingers along the curve of her hips. "And this." His hand found the bare flesh in the small of her back where her blouse had come untucked from her skirt. She felt his fingers slip beneath her waistband, setting off a throbbing pulse of lust. When he bent his head to kiss her there, she could smell the sharp citrus fragrance of the oil in his hair. They rolled over onto the sand in a steamy embrace, pulling at each other's clothes.

But there were people everywhere. Rose tried to sit up, struggling to quench the blaze in her belly. "Cristóbal . . . I . . ."

"I know." He placed a finger on her lips. "Not here." He jumped to his feet and helped her up. "There's a place farther along the beach," he said. "No one will see us there."

"But I . . ." She faltered, afraid of what her body was begging her to do.

"Ah! You want to dance first?" His face split into a grin. "That's okay. We can do that."

Hand in hand, they stumbled over the sand to the bonfire, where couples were circling the flames in a wild, galloping waltz. Cristóbal took her by the waist and pulled her close. She could feel the hardness of his body as he pressed against her. There were violins playing, the notes pouring out in a delirious shower of sound. As the music soared he lifted her up, tossing her into the air as if she were no heavier than a piece of driftwood, then catching her under the arms and spinning her around until her legs flew out behind her.

"Enough?" He chuckled as she caught her breath.

"I'm very hot." She fanned herself with her hand. "Shall we go for that swim?"

As they made their way through the tamarisk trees and over the sand dunes, she wondered what on earth she was doing. It had been a long time since she had given herself to a man. The last person she had made love with had been a British fighter pilot called Jim Russell. She hadn't been *in* love with him. She had liked him, admired him. But there hadn't been the primal passion she felt for Cristóbal. She had gone to bed with Jim because he was convinced he was going to die. And he had been right. Three weeks after their first night together, he had been shot down over the English Channel.

That had been more than two years ago. It had left her numb, as if that part of her had gone into hibernation. The shutting down of the physical side of her nature had been compounded by the failing health of her mother. But Cristóbal had suddenly reawakened what had been slumbering inside her. Was it right to let herself go? To surrender her body to someone she was unlikely to see again after tomorrow?

A bird flew overhead, letting out a long, poignant cry. She glanced upward at a sky studded with stars. Was it the romance of it—this Gypsy fiesta with its crazy, exuberant atmosphere, taking place amid the untamed beauty of the Camargue? Was that what was making her throw caution to the wind? Looking at the stars—at the vastness of the universe—made her own actions seem utterly insignificant. Did it really matter what she did tonight?

She could hear the waves gently lapping the sand. Cristóbal was already pulling his shirt over his head. She could see the taut outline of his chest.

"Come on—it's not cold!" He stepped out of his trousers, turning toward the sea as he kicked them onto the sand.

Rose unbuttoned her blouse, throwing it on top of his clothes. Then she wriggled out of her skirt and her underwear, almost tripping in her haste to run after him. The shock as she plunged into the water took her breath away. Her teeth began to rattle, but he pulled her to him, stilling them with the warmth of his lips and tongue. She felt as if she were floating out of time, to a place where nobody but she and he existed.

Locked together, they moved from the sea to the sand. She felt its coarseness against the wet skin of her thighs as their bodies writhed, snakelike, at the water's edge. His mouth was on her neck, traveling down to her breasts. He circled her belly button, licking away the droplets of salt water. She moaned as he edged lower. Then, in a sudden, deft movement, he was on top of her. Inside her. As she climaxed, it flashed across her mind that she might get pregnant. For a fleeting moment she allowed herself to imagine the child they might have—a little girl like Nieve, with Gypsy curls and laughing eyes.

A wave washed over them as he rolled off her. The spray stung her eyes, bringing her sharply back to reality. Broken shells scraped her elbows as she pulled herself up. What was she thinking of? To get pregnant by a man she'd only just met—a man she was unlikely to see again after tomorrow—was a stupid idea. It was one thing to fantasize about having a child without the ties of marriage, but to bring up a baby on her own . . . that would be a monumental struggle, wouldn't it?

But Lola did it.

The thought flashed through her mind as she pulled on her clothes, swiftly followed by the realization that whatever the rights and wrongs, it was too late now.

Gunesh growled at Rose when she pulled back the tent flap. It was as if he knew what she had been up to and disapproved. She rummaged around in the dark and found him a biscuit. Then she rubbed the fur between his ears, murmuring an apology for leaving him for such a long time.

When he'd settled down, she wriggled into her sleeping bag and closed her eyes. Her skin felt tight and gritty from the salt water and sand. Her body ached but her brain was fizzing. Images of Cristóbal flickered on the inside of her eyelids.

He'd tried to make love to her a second time on the way back from the beach. Passing the paddock, they had collapsed onto a pile of straw beside the fence, oblivious to the sharp prickle of the dry stalks on their naked flesh.

"Camelo el olor de tu piel." I love the smell of your skin. He had whispered the words in a mixture of Spanish and *kalo*. And she had murmured a reply that had made him laugh because, in trying to tell him that she loved his body, she had confused the word *cuerpo* with the word *culo*, which meant bottom.

She had felt a delicious sense of freedom. It was so tempting to just let go after suppressing this part of herself for so long. But she'd told him she was afraid of getting pregnant. It hadn't put him off, but in the end they had both fallen asleep, waking an hour or so later to the sound of what the English Gypsies called "horse music"—the neighing, whinnying, and snorting of dozens of animals, made restless by the proximity of slumbering humans.

She had stumbled the few yards to her tent, wondering if he would want to climb in next to her. But he had said good night with a long, lingering kiss before making his way back across the field to his wagon.

The people camped near her tent had gone on singing until the early hours of the morning, making it even harder to get to sleep. But somehow, she must have drifted off, because when she opened her eyes again, it was light outside.

"Rose!"

Still semiconscious, she thought it was Cristóbal calling to her. She fumbled her way out of her sleeping bag.

"Es-tu réveillée?" Are you awake?

The question, spoken in French, penetrated the fug of sleep. It was Jean Beau-Marie, not Cristóbal, trying to rouse her.

She parted the tent flap just enough to see out. "I'm not dressed."

"Sorry—I wanted to say goodbye. My people are leaving now."

"Oh—what time is it?"

"Ten o'clock." He smiled. "Did you have a good time last night? I didn't see you."

"I . . . I was with the Spanish girl I told you about: the dancer." It wasn't a lie. Just not the whole truth.

"Well, I came to give you these." His hand went to the pocket of his jacket. "To wish you luck on your journey." He put a twist of brown paper on the patch of ground in front of the tent flap.

"Oh, Jean—that's . . ." His kindness shamed her. Holding the tent flap with one hand, she slid out her other arm and drew in the little package. Unfolding the paper, she discovered a pair of Gypsy earrings of beaten copper set with stones the color of the kingfisher that had flashed in front of her on her walk across the Camargue marshes.

"Do you like them?"

"They're beautiful, Jean—I . . . I . . ." She faltered, overwhelmed by his unconditional generosity.

"Will you put them on? I'd like to see you wear them."

"Yes, of course—let me get dressed. I'll make us some coffee."

He shook his head. "I can't stay—the horses are already harnessed. Just show me how they look."

She hooked the copper wires through her ears and opened the tent flap wide enough for him to see her head and shoulders. "There! What do you think?"

"They suit you very well." She saw the Adam's apple in his throat rise and fall. "I knew they would. They belonged to my mother—she had eyes just like yours." He stood up. "Take care of yourself, Rose. Perhaps you'll think of me when you wear them."

Tears welled as she waved him goodbye. Her fingers went to the earrings. She didn't deserve them. If he'd known what she'd really been doing last night, he wouldn't even have come to say goodbye, let alone bestowed such a precious gift on her.

The self-loathing persisted as she attempted to clean herself up. She wetted a flannel with the few inches of water she had left in the billy-can, trying to erase all traces of the previous night. Memories that had intoxicated her just a few hours ago resurfaced with the painful clarity of a hangover. She had made love—without taking precautions—with a man she was likely never to see again. What had she been thinking of? How had she allowed herself to get so carried away?

She stuffed her sandy, salt-encrusted clothes into the bottom of her rucksack and pulled on a cotton dress. It was very wrinkled, but at least it was clean. She hoped the creases would fall out as she moved around.

Gunesh tugged at the lead as she fastened up the tent flap.

"I'm coming—be patient," she said. Poor thing. He'd already been patient. He should have been walked hours ago. It was yet another thing to feel guilty about.

She'd only got a few yards from the tent when Nieve darted out from between the caravans.

"I thought you were never coming!" She fell on the dog's neck, laughing when he twisted around to lick her face. "Mama's making tortilla—do you want some?"

"I might, if I knew what it was." Rose hoped the little girl wouldn't see through her brittle smile. The thought of eating breakfast with Cristóbal made her stomach flip over. What if he was as embarrassed as she was? Acted as if nothing had happened? Worse still, what if he had bragged to Lola about last night?

"It's eggs and onions and potato fried in butter," Nieve said, "with other stuff thrown in, like mushrooms or snails. There might be sausage with it today—Mama says we're rich now!"

"That sounds delicious." Rose took the child's outstretched hand. "Is . . . your uncle helping with the cooking?"

Nieve rolled her eyes. "He's much too lazy for that! He never wakes up until the afternoon."

Rose felt her apprehension evaporate. With a bit of luck, she could have a bite to eat and get away before Cristóbal surfaced.

Lola was breaking eggs into an enamel bowl when they reached the wagon. The sausages, already cooked, were keeping warm in a cloth-wrapped metal skillet.

"Can I do anything to help?" Rose asked as Lola spread out a blanket for her to sit on.

"No—you're our guest," Lola replied.

"I don't mind, honestly. I feel guilty being waited on. You're the one who should be taking it easy. Did you find it hard to get to sleep after all that excitement? I'm sure I would have." Rose watched her face, looking for any sign that Lola might know what had taken place after she'd gone off to bed.

"It did take me a while." Lola smiled as she took a head of garlic from a basket. Slipping her hand beneath the waistband of her skirt, she pulled out a wicked-looking knife. "I couldn't help thinking about what I could do with all that money—well, my share of it. Cristóbal will have half, of course." She dug the knife into the garlic and pulled out three cloves. Peeling off the skin, she sliced them into the bowl of eggs. "It means Nieve and I can move to Madrid."

"Oh? Why the big city?"

"It's where España Films is based. That's what I'd really love to do. Be a dancer in the movies."

"That sounds amazing! You'd be perfect, I'm sure."

"It's just a dream, really. I don't know if I stand a chance."

"I'd say that after last night, there's nothing you can't pull off." Rose was watching Lola throw an assortment of torn herbs into the beaten eggs. She could smell parsley, mint, and basil. The mixture hissed as Lola poured it into a frying pan. Rose didn't hear Gunesh come bounding up behind her. He put his paws on her shoulders, almost knocking her over. Nieve followed, out of breath as she hovered on the edge of the blanket.

"I've taught Gunesh to dance! Look!" Nieve clapped her hands twice, and the dog went to her side. She clicked her fingers, moving her hands from side to side in a swaying motion. Gunesh crossed his right paw over his left, then the left over the right.

Rose laughed.

"That's not all," Nieve said. "Watch this." She spun around on the spot, first one way, then the other. Gunesh followed, making circles around her. As a finale, she gestured to the ground with the flat of her hand, and the dog dropped down, rolled onto his back, and waggled all four legs in time to her clapping.

"That's fantastic! How did you teach him all that?"

"With sausage." Nieve shot a sideways look at the covered pan perched on an upturned wooden apple crate. "I only took two." She glanced at Lola, who gave an exasperated sigh.

"Those were supposed to be for us!"

"I know. But you said we were rich now—so I thought it wouldn't matter."

"I don't mind not having any," Rose said quickly. "The tortilla smells absolutely delicious."

A few minutes later, they were eating. Lola had cut the remaining sausages into small chunks so that each of them had some. Rose had a hard job trying to stop Gunesh from snaffling hers.

"He's going to want this for breakfast every day now." She smiled as she pushed his muzzle away from her plate.

"Well, he could if you came with us, couldn't he, Mama?" Nieve gave Lola a crafty look.

"Nieve! You mustn't be a pest!" Lola shook her head. "She's been going on at me all morning—she keeps asking if you can come with us, back to Granada. I told her you have your own plans—that you're going by train—but she won't listen."

"Why can't you come with us, Auntie Rose?" Nieve piped up. "It would be such fun—you could camp beside our wagon, and I could teach Gunesh more tricks!"

"She hasn't got time for that, *cariño*," Lola said. She glanced at Rose with an apologetic smile. "I told her that you have an important job in England that you have to get back to—that you don't have time to travel slowly like us."

Rose looked at Nieve. The child was staring at her with imploring eyes. "Well, I'm not in a terrific hurry," she said. "I've taken the whole summer off, so . . ." She hesitated, the possibilities whirling in her mind. The thought of ambling through Spain with a group of Gypsies was tantalizing. But what about Cristóbal? What would he say if he could hear this conversation? It occurred to her that he might already know about Nieve's suggestion—that he had, perhaps, encouraged her to make it.

"We'd love to have you with us," Lola said. "And we can take you to all the good places in Granada when we get there—it's very beautiful."

"Please come, Auntie Rose." Nieve reached out for Gunesh, who laid his head contentedly in the child's lap.

"When are you leaving?" Rose asked Lola.

"As soon as we've finished this." Lola glanced at her half-empty plate. "We've packed most of our stuff already—we've just got to get Rubio from the paddock."

Rose turned to Nieve. "Want to come and help me take my tent down?"

The little girl nodded eagerly. "Are you really going to come? Do you promise?"

"On one condition." Rose smiled. "I want you to teach *me* how to dance. But no sausages—otherwise I won't fit into any of my clothes by the time we get to Granada!"

It took less than half an hour to pack up the tent and cram everything into the rucksack. Then Rose and Nieve went to lead the horse out of the enclosure. His straw-colored mane tossed as he snorted a protest at leaving all his new friends behind.

"It's all right, boy." Rose patted his gleaming chestnut flank. He reminded her of an animal she'd treated in London—a cart horse who had injured its leg pulling milk wagons. Its owner was going to have it shot, but she had managed to heal the torn tendons with a cold pack of vinegar-soaked seaweed and a diet of sloe flowers mixed with bran and molasses.

They wound their way through the camp, past people busy gathering up pans and blankets and throwing buckets of sand onto smoking fires. As they neared Nieve's wagon, Rose's stomach fluttered at the thought of seeing Cristóbal. She wondered how he had reacted when he heard the news that she was going to be traveling with them. Would he have told his cousin what had happened after the wedding? And if he had, would Lola change her mind about wanting Rose around?

When they got there, Lola was all ready to go. She took the lead rein from Rose and coaxed Rubio into position. She slipped the bridle and collar over his head before fastening the traces to the shafts of the wagon. Then she gestured to Rose and Nieve to climb aboard before jumping up herself.

"Can I take Gunesh inside with me?" Nieve asked.

"Yes," Rose said. "He'll probably be happier in there than out here."

"Ready?" Lola took hold of the reins with one hand, reaching back with the other to grab a long whip that protruded from the canvas flap.

"What about your cousin?" Rose scoured the bare patches of ground in between the few *vardos* that remained. Perhaps he was lingering too long over his goodbyes and Lola had grown tired of waiting.

"Still asleep!" Lola cocked her head backward as the wagon lurched forward. "We'd be here all day if we waited for him to surface."

"So he doesn't know I'm . . ." Rose glanced behind her, trying to see into the gloomy interior of the wagon.

"Don't worry," Lola said. "I'm sure he'll be happy to have an extra pair of hands to help with the chores. He has many talents, my cousin, but he gets away with a lot. His wife spoils him too much."

Rose's mouth went bone dry. "His wife?" Her voice came out high pitched and rasping, like the sound of the wind in the marsh grass.

Chapter 12

It wasn't until they had set up camp for the night that Rose got a chance to speak to Cristóbal alone. After leaving Saintes-Maries-de-la-Mer, the convoy of Spanish Gypsies had traveled west and then south, skirting the city of Montpellier before coming to a stop in a wooded area on the side of a hill. Cristóbal had emerged from the wagon two hours into the journey, rubbing his eyes as he stuck his stubbled chin out into the fresh air. Seeing Rose, he had muttered something she couldn't make out and disappeared again.

She had felt like grabbing her rucksack and jumping off the wagon when Lola dropped the bombshell that he had a wife. But how could she break the promise she'd made to Nieve without a word of explanation?

The long hours on the road had been pure torture, knowing what she knew now. How could she have been so stupid? Why had she not thought to ask him if he was married? He had told her he had a dog back in Granada, but there had been no mention of a wife. He had fooled her into believing he was single by mentioning small details of his home life but leaving out the glaring fact that he was a husband and father.

Lola had unwittingly compounded Rose's misery by chatting about Cristóbal's children as a way of passing the time on the journey. Rose learned that he had a son, Juan, aged twelve, and a ten-year-old daughter called Belén. And Lola had revealed something that made Rose even more wretched: Juanita, Cristóbal's wife, was due to give birth to a third child any day now.

If Lola hadn't been driving the wagon, Rose wouldn't have been able to hide the turmoil she felt inside. The fact that she had slept with another woman's husband was bad enough. But there was something else gnawing away at her as the convoy of Gypsies rolled toward the border with Spain. What if she was pregnant?

When they stopped for the night, she busied herself erecting her tent, choosing a pitch some distance away from the circle of *vardos*. She told Lola that she was tired and needed an early night. Gunesh was with Nieve, so she didn't even have the comfort of his warm body as she crawled inside the tent.

She could hear the crackle of a fire springing into life and the rattle of pans and cutlery. The thought of sharing a meal with Cristóbal made her feel sick. As she lay down and closed her eyes, she wondered what on earth to do. She thought of slipping away in the early hours of the morning when everyone was asleep. She could leave a note, saying that something had happened, and she had to go back to England. But what excuse could she possibly give? How could she have received any news from home while they were on the road? And she had no idea if Lola would even be able to comprehend a written message. None of the British Gypsies she'd encountered had known how to read or write. Most of them thought it an unnecessary waste of effort—completely irrelevant to their lifestyle. Bill Lee was the only one who'd wanted to learn.

Outside, the light was beginning to fade. As she lay there, agonizing over the thought of Cristóbal's heavily pregnant wife, she suddenly heard his voice.

"Rose! Are you awake?" His voice had a harsh urgency.

She lay perfectly still, her eyes tightly shut. She didn't want to talk to him. If she did, she would start crying or screaming at him or both.

"Let me in, won't you?" She heard him pulling at the canvas flap.

"Go away," she hissed.

"Not until I've had a chance to talk to you." The silhouette of his head appeared through the opening. She could smell the bitter orange scent of the oil in his hair.

"What is there to talk about?" She rolled over, pulling the sleeping bag over her head. "Why didn't you tell me about your wife?"

"You didn't ask."

"That's a pathetic answer. You told me about your *dog*, for God's sake! How the hell could you come out with *that* and fail to mention your wife and children?"

"What would have happened if I'd told you?" Cristóbal pulled down the sleeping bag, exposing her head and shoulders. "You were happy last night, weren't you? I was happy. It was beautiful."

"How can you say that?" She yanked the sleeping bag up again. "How could you have done it, knowing your wife's about to give birth to your baby?"

"Because it's natural for a man and a woman to love each other. There's nothing wrong with it. When men and women love, they don't kill or rob: they become givers. They create something magical."

"But it *is* wrong! What would your wife say if she knew? She'd be heartbroken!"

"No, she wouldn't—because she knows I'll never leave her. That's the way we live, Rose. A Gypsy man can have many passing loves—so long as he stays with his wife and children. I thought you knew that. You said you'd lived with Gypsies."

"Just go, will you!" she hissed.

"All right, I'm going. But you'd better remember that it wasn't my idea for you to travel with us."

She heard him scramble out of the tent. Heard his footsteps receding into the night. Her heart felt as if it had shrunk to the size of a walnut, hard and bitter.

Sleep that night was a patchwork of nightmares. She was back in the building she had lived in as a student, wandering from floor to floor, unable to find her bedroom. She would climb into an elevator and press a button, but the doors would open in a part of the building she didn't recognize. Then she was there, walking along the green-painted corridor to the door of her room. She stood outside, hearing laughter, whispers, and the unmistakable sounds of a man and woman making love.

She startled awake, her heart hammering in her chest. If there was such a thing as hell, she was in it. With harrowing clarity, the nightmare had re-created the day, nine years ago, when she had caught Sam—the boy she was supposed to be marrying after graduation—in bed with Daphne, her best friend. Every detail of the betrayal, every emotion, was there, stored away in her subconscious. And now it had seeped out, like something rotten and decayed, to haunt her in her sleep.

Serves you right.

The voice in her head was Daphne's. She could see her face, a look of cold fury twisting her mouth as she flounced out of the room, her blouse buttoned up wrong and the laces of her boots trailing on the ground.

What did you expect him to do while you were frolicking about with the Gypsies?

How Daphne would crow if she could see her now. It wasn't hard to imagine what she would say. Who did Rose think she was, mixing with people like that? Didn't she have the sense to realize that wildness and freedom were shorthand for promiscuity and infidelity?

She closed her eyes, wishing she could rewind the past forty-eight hours. Instinctively she reached out for Gunesh, seeking the comfort of stroking him. But her fingers found only the dew-damp canvas of the tent wall. As she touched the fabric, something butted against it from the other side, as if an animal was grazing outside. Then she heard a familiar bark.

"Gunesh!"

The tent flap burst open, and the dog leapt on top of her, closely followed by Nieve.

"He couldn't wait to see you—and neither could I!" The little girl snuggled in between Rose and Gunesh. "What shall we do today? Will you sit in the wagon with me? It's so boring when Mama's driving and Uncle Cristóbal's snoring his head off. Can we make something? Or play a game?"

"Well, I . . ." Rose hesitated. "I'm not sure whether I can come all the way to Granada with you. I don't think your . . . I mean . . . your uncle didn't seem very pleased when he found out."

Nieve grabbed Rose's arm and squeezed it tight. "You can't go! You promised!"

Rose saw that her eyes were brimming with tears.

"Yes, I did." She murmured the words more to herself than to Nieve. Here was a child with a face to melt any heart, clinging on to her, begging her to stay. A child who was about the age Nathan's son or daughter would be if he or she were alive. As the thought flitted through her mind, she realized that however used and humiliated she was feeling, she absolutely couldn't react in any way that would hurt this little girl.

"Don't worry—I'm not going anywhere." She hugged Nieve tight, whispering the words into her hair.

Chapter 13

Segovia, north of Madrid, Spain: Eight days later

Rose's tent stood in a field that bordered the ancient wall of a convent. The bells had woken her early, but she didn't mind. After opening the front of the tent, she lay back on her pillow, watching two birds flying in and out of the bell tower. They were storks—the most enormous birds she had ever seen. They carried great bundles of wood in their beaks, building a nest that stuck out untidily from the stonework. There was something prehistoric about the shape of them as they glided through the air—the way she imagined pterodactyls must have looked. She remembered seeing pictures of storks in storybooks as a child, carrying a knotted sheet with a newborn human child inside. No wonder people thought they brought babies. With beaks that size, they could probably transport a small elephant.

The sight of something so symbolic of pregnancy and birth rekindled her guilt about Cristóbal's wife. And the sight of the birds would have triggered further dark thoughts had it not been for her period having come the previous night. She had got down on her knees and murmured a fervent prayer of thanks. That, at least, was one thing she no longer needed to worry about.

Rose wondered if Nieve was awake yet. They had got into a routine of taking Gunesh for a walk before breakfast, then settling down together in the back of the wagon before Cristóbal woke up. While Lola drove Rubio along the dusty Spanish roads, Rose was teaching Nieve how to read and write.

Nieve had sown the seeds of the idea when she found Rose's copy of *Revelations of Divine Love* by Julian of Norwich. On the cover was a medieval painting of the nun, who was pictured stroking a cat. Nieve thought it was one of the Mary saints from the church in Provence— and wanted to know where the cat had been hiding when they had been there. When Rose had explained that the image was an English nun who had chosen to live all alone with only a cat for company, Nieve had wanted the whole story. And when Rose began reading, the child had run her fingers over the letters on the page, mystified by the patterns they made.

Nieve's eyes had brightened when Rose pointed to the word *cat* and translated it. "Can you teach me how to do it? You can teach me that, and I'll teach you how to dance!"

Rose had replied that she'd better ask Lola first. She had learned from her time with the English Gypsies to tread carefully in matters outside their experience. Trying to introduce *gawje* ways was generally regarded with scorn. But Lola had been full of enthusiasm.

"Perhaps you'll teach me as well? We could do it when Nieve's gone to bed."

Spending the evenings reading with Lola by the fire was a welcome distraction from Cristóbal. Once the meal was over, he would slope off to drink and play cards with the other men. Rose wondered if Lola had picked up on the tension between them. It was so hard, trying to make it seem as if nothing had happened. Trying to distance herself from him without making the hostility obvious. It was a constant battle, concealing the anger and humiliation she felt inside.

Now, watching the storks building their nest in the bell tower, she couldn't help but think about Cristóbal's wife. In a day or two they would reach Granada, and for the sake of politeness, Rose would have to stay in the city for a few more days. Lola had promised to show her the Alhambra and the Gypsy cave dwellings of Sacromonte, where there was flamenco dancing every night. But no doubt Lola would also take her to see Juanita and the new baby. The thought of it turned her insides to ice.

Lola left Nieve and Cristóbal asleep in the wagon while she went to buy bread. Walking through the cobbled streets of the old town, she caught far-reaching glimpses of the countryside through gaps between the buildings. She knew that they were not far from Madrid. She had made out the letters on road signs, deciphering the name of the city with the aid of the alphabet she kept tucked in her pocket. Rose had taught her to write numbers as well as letters. She knew that Madrid was not much more than a day's journey from where they were now.

As she stood in line at the bakery, she daydreamed about what it would be like to live in Madrid, to walk through the doors of the studios of España Films, to be dressed in fabulous costumes, to dance in front of a camera, to go to a cinema and see herself in a movie. She was going to have to hold on tight to that dream in the weeks to come. Cristóbal would be furious when she told him of her plans. Not because he would be losing his dancer—there would be other girls more than willing to replace her—but because her leaving would represent a final act of defiance: she would be trumpeting her independence from the rooftops, going off to Madrid with Nieve with no need for any man to support her.

Ever since leaving Provence she had been working out how and when the move could be made. She would have to stay in Granada for a few weeks at least—long enough to see Cristóbal and Juanita's baby christened and to sort out a place to live in Madrid. Rose had offered to help with that. She had advised Lola to buy a newspaper in Segovia because it was close enough to the capital city to carry advertisements for places to rent there. And Rose was going to help her write a letter if they found somewhere suitable.

She would have to hide the newspaper from Cristóbal. No point in making him even grumpier than he already was by flaunting her plans. She'd thought that winning the competition would lift his spirits—but since leaving Provence he seemed to have sunk into a black mood. Perhaps he was more worried about Juanita and the baby than he was letting on. She hoped so. It was about time he started taking his responsibilities as a husband and father more seriously.

While the woman in front of her was being served, Lola's mind drifted back to her own childhood. She wondered what it would have been like to have two parents. Her mother had always told her and Amador that their father had died when they were too young to remember him. Growing up at their grandfather's forge in Capileira, they had been happy enough—until the war came. At twelve years old she was too young to realize that the shooting of her grandfather meant that the writing was on the wall for the whole family. Nor could she have known that the lie her mother had told would be revealed in the most horrific way possible.

"*¿Qué quiere?*" What would you like?

The baker derailed her train of thought. He was looking at her with a crooked smile. No doubt he thought her simple or slightly deranged, standing there at the front of the queue with her head in the clouds.

"*Un pan grande y cuatro galletas,*" she said quickly.

She tucked the loaf of bread and the four biscuits into her bag and set off down the street to find a place to buy a newspaper. The thought of poring over the property section with Rose set off a frisson of excitement. It banished the unbearable thoughts that had descended in the bakery to the dark corner of her mind where they lurked like savage dogs, always trying to escape. The banishment was only temporary, of course. Memories like that could never be held at bay for long. But having a dream helped. A couple of weeks ago, it had seemed no more than a fantasy—but winning the competition had made it less of a dream and more of a tangible reality.

The man in the newspaper shop gave her a withering look when she handed over the money. Was it *that* obvious she was a Gypsy? Clearly he was wondering what a person like her was doing buying a paper. She glanced at the big black letters at the top of the page. *El Correo.* Yes, that was the right name—the one Rose had told her to get.

When she got outside she hurried off down the street. Without speaking a word, the man in the shop had made her feel degraded, humiliated. She sank onto a bench in an ornamental garden with a fountain. Beyond the rainbow splash of the water, she could see the terracotta rooftops of houses and the ancient tower of a church. And beyond that, green rolling hills dotted with poplar trees.

Nieve must never feel the way he made me feel.

The words rang out in her head as if she'd spoken them aloud. Over those hills lay Madrid. A place where she and Nieve could shake off the past. A place where no one would whisper the word *gitanas* when they went into a shop. She glanced at the newspaper on her lap. It wasn't just about moving to a new place. What Rose was teaching them held magical power—the power to give Nieve dreams of her own.

The Gypsy wagons rolled away from Segovia, traveling south through the province of Castilla-La Mancha, across great plains dotted with vineyards, castles, and windmills. The sun beat down on the canvas roof, making it too hot for Rose and Nieve to stay inside. Instead they sat on either side of Lola, where the forward movement of the wagon created a welcome breeze. Rose had made two columns on a piece of paper, writing Spanish words on the right and their equivalent in *kalo* on the left so that Lola and Nieve could see the different patterns the letters made.

"What's *sleep* in your language?" Rose asked.

"*Sobar,*" Nieve replied. "That's Mama's nickname for my uncle—instead of Cristóbal she calls him Cris Sobar."

Rose wrote the word down, concentrating on keeping the pencil steady as they bumped over a pothole in the road. She was past the stage of wincing inside every time his name was mentioned, but she still didn't trust herself to look Nieve or Lola in the eye when it happened.

"So *dormir* in Spanish, *sobar* in *kalo*." She held up the paper for them to see. "Think of another word, Nieve."

"*Chungo,*" Nieve replied.

It was a word Rose had heard Cristóbal mutter under his breath more than once in the past few days. It wasn't like any Romany word she'd ever come across. "What does it mean?"

"*Malo,*" Nieve replied. Bad. She glanced sideways at Rose. It was only a fleeting look, but Rose got the distinct feeling that the child had sensed what was going on and was testing her out.

"Those are very different sounding, aren't they?" Once again, she bent over the paper, hoping her voice wouldn't betray her. The thought that Nieve might have even the slightest suspicion of what had happened was unbearable. She had grown very close to the child during the journey from France. She had even begun to fantasize that Nieve could be the child her brother's fiancée had been expecting.

In all their time together over the past few days, Lola had never spoken about the fact that Nieve was adopted—and Rose hadn't let on that Cristóbal had told her. She longed to know more about Nieve's story, but she sensed that it was buried deep with Lola's painful memories of leaving her mountain home.

The evening of the next day was their last one on the road. They camped a few miles south of the city of Jaén, in a grove of Aleppo pines on the slopes of the Sierra Mágina—the Mountain of Spirits.

Rose pitched her tent on a forest floor dotted with wild orchids. When it was up she and Nieve went off to gather mushrooms for the evening meal.

"There are wolves around here," Nieve whispered. "Bears, too. And a thing called a *lince*."

"What's that?"

Nieve clawed the air and made a growling noise.

"A lion? Ah—a lynx," Rose said.

"And there are bandits as well. Uncle Cristóbal told me. When we stopped here on the way to France, we heard some trying to steal our horses."

"What happened?"

"The men chased them off."

Rose wondered if she should have pitched her tent a little closer to the circle of *vardos*. "I think I'd better have Gunesh in with me tonight in that case," she said.

Nieve's mouth turned down at the edges.

"You can have him to stay with you when we get to Granada," Rose said.

"What about you? Aren't you going to stay with us?"

"I'm going to find a room in an inn. There won't be anywhere to put my tent—and your house is going to be a bit crowded, I think, with you and your mother and your cousins. There'll be a new baby, too, won't there?" Rose felt her stomach contract.

"But you'll come and see us, won't you?"

"Yes, of course." Meeting Cristóbal's wife and children was going to be an ordeal—but she could hardly refuse to visit Nieve and Lola in their own home.

Later, when the meal of rabbit and mushroom stew had been eaten and Nieve was tucked up in bed, Rose sat with Lola by the fire. It was just the two of them. Cristóbal had gone to play his guitar with some of the other men. The plaintive rise and fall of his voice drifted across the woodland clearing. Rose wondered how someone so heartless could produce something so profound, so spiritual.

"It's been lovely for Nieve, having you with us these past few days," Lola said. "Lovely for me, too. You've been such good company." Her eyes told Rose that these were not mere platitudes. She had noticed how the other Gypsy women were with Lola. How they excluded her from their tight-knit group with nothing more than their body language.

"And I haven't had to worry about Nieve wandering off on her own," Lola went on. "She nearly drove me frantic on the way to France. Every time we stopped she seemed to disappear."

"I suppose she's at an age where everything new is exciting," Rose said.

Lola nodded. "I know I should let her explore. Give her more freedom. But . . ." She trailed off, leaning forward to poke the fire back to life. "I'm terrified of losing her—that's the problem. I've lost everyone that I've ever loved—and it's made me overprotective."

"It must have been very hard for you, growing up during the Civil War." Rose held her breath, hoping it didn't sound as if she was prying.

"It was the worst time of my life. I lost my grandfather the month the war started. He was a blacksmith, and we lived with him at his forge in Capileira. The Escuadra Negra came and dragged him away. We never knew where he died. But we found out that more than twenty men from our village were killed that day."

Rose listened in silence, staring into the blue-green flames rising from the pine twigs. The Escuadra Negra. The Black Squad. The very name was sinister. Lola would have been only eleven or twelve years old when the war started. The thought of a child seeing her grandfather dragged off to his death was horrendous.

"The men who were left went into hiding higher up the mountains," Lola went on. "They were joined by people like your brother. They carried out raids on fascist military bases and bombed bridges to cut them off. I told you, didn't I, that my mother used to hide partisans in the house sometimes when they came to the village, and that Amador, my brother, used to take messages to them when he took the goats out to pasture."

Rose nodded. She wanted to ask what had happened to them—but she was afraid of saying anything that might make Lola clam up.

"I told you Amador was my twin, didn't I?" Lola paused. Rose heard her blow out a breath. "We used to take it in turn to go out with the goats each morning. One day I was up on the mountain, and it started to snow. I was on my way down, and I heard shouting in the ravine below the village. I heard my mother's voice. I ran as fast I could, but when I got there . . ."

Rose reached across the space between them. Finding Lola's hand, she closed her fingers around it.

"There were bodies everywhere. All women, except for Amador. My mother was lying beside him, the two of them covered in blood, with the snow falling on top of them. I lay down beside them. I thought the blizzard would take me, too, that I would just fall asleep and never wake up. That's what I wanted. But the goats had followed me down. They wouldn't leave me alone. And then I heard a strange noise, like a cat mewing. But it wasn't a cat. It was a newborn baby. The mother had been shot but not killed outright. She was still alive when I got to her." Lola closed her eyes. "I had to cut the cord with my teeth. She asked me to take her child."

Rose tried to imagine her fourteen-year-old self confronted with something so gruesome. How Lola had had the courage to save that newborn's life in such horrific circumstances was staggering. That she'd even known what to do was astonishing.

"I called her Nieve because of the blizzard," Lola went on. "She's always felt like my daughter, even though I'm not the one who gave birth to her. She knows I'm not her real mother, but she doesn't know what happened. I just told her that her parents died in the war."

"Did you know her—Nieve's mother?" Rose held her breath.

Lola shook her head. "She wasn't from my village." She glanced at Rose, her eyes full of concern. "I know what you're thinking. And the answer is, I don't know. I didn't stay around long enough to find out her name. I knew that if I'd been at home when the men came, they would have killed me, too. So I set off up the mountain and didn't stop until I got to Granada."

"You walked all that way with a baby? Through the snow?"

"It took me two days. Some of the goats came with me. Without the milk, Nieve would probably have died." Lola picked up a bunch of twigs and threw them onto the glowing embers. Sparks flew into the night air, dancing like fireflies. "She's very fond of you, you know. I wish she *was* your brother's child—that would be amazing, wouldn't it? But I don't know how you could ever discover the truth—unless you were to find him, of course."

"Can you remember anything about Nieve's mother? What did she look like?"

"She had black hair, like mine—like nearly everyone in our part of Spain." Lola shrugged. "And dark eyes—very dark, like black olives. She was young—but not as young as me. Early twenties, perhaps. I kept one thing of hers—a shawl with peacocks on it. I wrapped Nieve in it. She still has it—sleeps with it every night, like a comfort blanket."

"Who would I ask? How on earth would I start?" Rose shook her head. It was so little to go on—a young pregnant woman with black hair and a peacock scarf. And Cristóbal had warned her that people would be reluctant to talk.

"You can only try," Lola replied. "I wish I could take you there myself. But like I said, I can never go back."

Rose wondered if that was because of the ghastly memories or because Lola was still afraid, eight years on, of those men with guns. *Fear remains in the blood.* That was what she'd said. Could her life really be in danger if she went back to the Alpujarras? Rose sensed that there was something Lola wasn't telling her.

"I suppose we'd better think about getting some sleep," Lola said. "We've got a long way to go tomorrow if we're going to make it to Granada in daylight."

Rose started to get up, but her right leg prickled with pins and needles.

Lola was already on her feet. She took Rose's arm and helped her up. Rose stamped her foot on the ground to get the circulation going; then she turned to say good night.

"Good night, Rose." The glimmering light of the fire lit up Lola's face. She opened her mouth to say something else, but no words came out.

"What? What is it?"

"It's just . . ." Lola glanced at the wagon.

"What?"

"What if you were to find out that Nieve *was* your brother's child? You'd take her away from me, wouldn't you?"

Rose laid her hands on either side of Lola's shoulders, holding her at arm's length and looking her straight in the eyes. "You don't believe that, do you? *You're* her mother—in every way that matters." She shook her head slowly. "Don't get me wrong—I'd be the happiest woman on earth if Nieve turned out to be my niece—but I'd never, ever, try to take her away from you."

"Thank you," Lola whispered. "I just needed to know."

Chapter 14

Granada, Spain: June 6, 1946

Rose closed the door of the attic room and made her way down the twisting wooden staircase. Mornings were the best time of day at the posada, the walls of the inner courtyard dripping with watered flowers, filling the air with the scent of jasmine and myrtle. The past two nights it had been too hot to sleep. There was a tiny window in her room—but opening it had made little difference to the temperature, and it had allowed an army of mosquitoes to fly in and feast on her exposed flesh.

Breakfast was the only meal provided at the inn. Rose appeared to be the sole guest—she hadn't seen anyone else coming or going since she'd arrived. The innkeeper's daughter—who didn't look much older than Nieve—brought her coffee and a tostada. A long bread roll cut in half lengthways, it was spread with tomato puree and slices of melted manchego cheese. It was delicious—but difficult to eat without showering her clothes with crumbs and smearing the sides of her mouth. She was glad there was no one to see her.

When she had finished she clambered back up the stairs to wash her hands and face. Surveying her reflection in the mottled square of mirror above the basin, she reached for the earrings Jean Beau-Marie had given her. The blue stones caught the sunlight as she hooked them in her ears. In Turkey, where her father came from, blue stones were worn to ward off the evil eye. Perhaps these earrings carried the same power. She hoped so. Because today she was going to need all the help she could get.

The inn was at the top of Calle Guinea, a steeply sloping street in the Albaicin—the ancient Moorish quarter of the city. The air outside smelled of scrubbed stones and wet dung. Rose made her way past shops selling brightly colored rugs and lamps of filigree metal. As she turned into the Camino del Sacromonte, she saw a Gypsy flower seller with a big basket of posies.

"*¡Jazmín, jazmín! ¡Hermoso, fresco!*" Beautiful, fresh jasmine. The woman's shouts echoed off the walls of the buildings.

Rose stopped to buy some posies. She would give them to Juanita, along with the silver bells threaded on silk ribbon that she had bought to hang on the baby boy's cradle.

The house where the family lived was on a road that snaked along the hillside. As Rose climbed higher she caught glimpses of the towering terracotta walls of the Alhambra. Lola had promised to take her there this evening, before her performance at the tavern in the palace grounds. Rose tried to focus on that rather than the ordeal she was about to endure.

She rounded a bend that led her past the first of the cave houses of the Sacromonte district of the city. The fronts of the buildings looked like normal houses, but viewed from the side, it was obvious that they were something quite extraordinary. Lola had described how the Gypsies who first settled there had been cave dwellers, and they had gradually built out from the natural sandstone, enclosing the caves to protect themselves against the burning heat of the sun in summer and the cold winds that blew down from the Sierra Nevada in winter.

Rose's first sight of the snowcapped mountains that formed the backdrop to the city had come when the wagon trundled the last few miles along the road from Jaén, the frozen peaks shimmering red and gold with the dying rays of the sun. Her spirits had soared at the sight—not just because it was so beautiful, but because the answer to all that she was seeking lay on the other side of those gilded slopes.

The thought of Lola crossing that snowy wasteland with a tiny baby and nothing but goat's milk to sustain them was incredible. Her bravery and determination were awe inspiring. No wonder she had become a champion dancer, with qualities like that.

As Rose made her way along the road, she saw a trio of Gypsy girls standing outside a tall metal gate that formed the entrance to a low-slung cave dwelling. They wore aprons over long dresses of flowered cotton. Their glossy blue-black hair was pinned up around faces that shot looks of guarded curiosity as Rose passed by.

No doubt they were used to being ogled by tourists. But Rose didn't look like a tourist. On the journey from France, she had started to dress more like the women she was traveling with. She had bought a shawl in Segovia and two lengths of Indian cotton, one with swirling stripes of blue, mauve, and amber and the other patterned with an abstract design of rainbow-colored feathers. She was wearing one of the skirts she had sewn, and with the sprig of pink bougainvillea she had pinned in her hair, she looked not unlike the women at the roadside.

She slowed her pace, examining each house for the distinguishing features Lola had described. But before she found it, she spotted Nieve and Gunesh walking toward her. The dog gave a joyful yelp and came bounding toward Rose, almost knocking her over as he leapt up to greet her.

"Hello, boy! Have you missed me?"

Gunesh nudged her chin with his nose.

"He's been a good boy this morning," Nieve said. "Rafaelito was crying, and Gunesh licked his face until he stopped. Chico's never done that."

"Who's Chico?"

"Uncle Cristóbal's dog. He doesn't like Gunesh—I think he's jealous."

Rose wondered what Juanita had thought of Gunesh, the interloper, covering her newborn son in slobber.

"Rafaelito's asleep now," Nieve said. "Come and see." She took Rose by the hand and led her toward a blue-painted wooden door in the whitewashed facade of a cave house. Rose could see Juanita, her head bent over a wicker cradle placed on the ground. She was singing to her baby, tucking the blankets in around his tiny body. It was a picture of innocence that sent an arrow of guilt through Rose's heart.

"*Esta es mi amiga—la Tia Rose.*" This is my friend—Auntie Rose. Nieve whispered the words over the top of the cradle.

Juanita looked up. Rose was horrified to see that her eyes were red and puffy, as if she'd been crying.

"What's the matter?" Nieve asked.

"Nothing," Juanita replied. "The wind is full of dust today, that's all. Fetch a glass of lemonade for our guest, will you, Nieve?" There was a blanket spread on the ground beside her, and she gestured to Rose to sit down. "*Bienvenida.*" Welcome.

Gunesh spread himself out between them, and Juanita put out her hand to stroke him. "You have a beautiful dog."

"And you have a beautiful baby." Rose's voice sounded as if it belonged to someone else. High pitched and tremulous. She handed over the flowers and the ribbon of silver bells.

"Thank you—you're very kind."

Rose felt even more wretched. She reached out to touch the tiny fingers. "How old is he?"

"Almost four weeks. He came early—the day after my husband left for France." Juanita gave Rose a wry look. "Typical of a man, eh? To disappear when you need him most?"

Rose felt her insides shrivel. She forced her mouth to turn up at the edges. But she didn't trust herself to say anything in reply. Had Cristóbal confessed to what had happened while he was away? Was that why his wife looked as if she'd been sobbing her heart out? And if he had, did she know that Rose was the one he'd been with?

Juanita reached for something on the other side of the cradle. It was a bunch of garlic heads strung together. Juanita took a knife from her pocket and split one open. The cloves fell into her lap, and she peeled them deftly, exposing the creamy white flesh beneath the papery skin. Lifting the edges of the yellow blanket that covered the baby, she tucked the garlic beneath the mattress so that Rafaelito was encircled by it.

"Why are you doing that?" Rose's curiosity got the better of her. This time her voice was a little steadier.

Juanita glanced at the sky. "The heat of the sun will bring out the smell," she said. "It drives away any snakes that might come near."

Rose nodded. Bill Lee's sisters had talked about using garlic to keep away vampires. And it reminded her of something her aunt Ruth—a cousin of her mother—had told her when she was a little girl. Aunt Ruth's brother, who had been a pearl trader, said the pearl fishers of Aden, in the Persian Gulf, strewed garlic in front of their shacks to keep away the great water serpents. Strange, Rose thought, that this Spanish Gypsy mother was using it in the same way.

Nieve appeared with the lemonade. Following in her wake were Juanita's older children, Juan and Belén. Juan was heartbreakingly like his father. He had the same blue-green eyes. When he smiled Rose had to look away. Belén settled down on the rug next to Gunesh. Rose's skirt was in the way, and as the child lifted the folds of cotton aside, she remarked on how pretty the fabric was.

It was a relief when Lola came out of the house to join them. There was nothing in the way she greeted Rose that suggested she had found out about Cristóbal's dalliance.

A few minutes later the baby woke up and let out a lusty wail. Juanita scooped him up and headed toward the house.

"He's hungry, I expect." Lola watched Juanita disappear through the door. Turning to the children, she said, "Why don't you take Gunesh for a walk?"

When they had gone she said, "Poor Juanita's in a terrible state. We had some awful news this morning. Yesterday a baby girl was taken to be baptized—the daughter of a friend of ours—and she never returned."

Rose shook her head, mystified. "You mean she died? In the church?"

"No, she didn't die—she was taken."

"Taken?" Rose echoed. "By whom?"

"By the authorities, we think. The parents don't know. They weren't there. But that's what people are saying."

"But . . ." Rose trailed off, trying to make sense of it. "How could the parents not have been there—at their child's christening?"

Now it was Lola's turn to look puzzled. "Is that what happens in your country? The mother and father take the baby to church? Well, it's different here. The parents stay at home. The godparents come and collect the baby and bring it back when the ceremony is over. That's what's supposed to happen. But not yesterday. They never brought her back. Juanita says her friends were told they'll never see their daughter again."

"Why would the authorities do that?" Rose wondered if the parents had been accused of some crime. She knew from her time with the English Gypsies that they were always afraid of being accused of any bad thing that might happen in a neighborhood—whether they were responsible or not.

"Because she's a little *gitana*." Lola sucked in a breath. "A *rojo* child."

"A red? Her father fought in the Civil War?"

"No—he was too young. His elder brother was a partisan, I think. But it's not that. Not really. It's about the government taking charge of children they consider to be born into the wrong kind of family. We come into that category. People are saying that General Franco has spies in every city. The church is sending people to call at homes like ours.

They pretend to be interested in our religious beliefs, but really they're nosing around. And the next thing you know, the baby disappears."

Lola gazed into the distance, her eyes narrowing as she took in the honey-colored ramparts of the Alhambra. "The tourists have no idea. They only see the beauty. But Granada is a wicked, sinister place. It was bad enough during the war—but it's getting worse. Much worse."

"Where do they take the babies?" Rose pulled her shawl tight around her. It wasn't cold. But what Lola had described chilled her to the core. She pictured Juanita, tucking cloves of garlic under the mattress of Rafaelito's cradle. Clearly there was something much worse than snakes lurking out there.

"They send them to families the government approves of so they'll grow up as *payos*, not Gypsies. To save the race. That's what General Franco says."

It was horribly familiar. Like Hitler all over again. Rose was only too aware of Franco's Nazi sympathies. But she had never imagined that the evil doctrine of racial purity would outlive Hitler; that in a time of supposed peace, babies would be snatched from their mothers because of their *kawlo rat*. Their dark blood.

"It's not only the babies they're taking." Lola turned to Rose, her eyes full of foreboding. "I heard they took nine-year-old twins while we were in France. They said they were too old to be adopted, so they sent the boy to a monastery and the girl to a convent."

Rose stared back, stunned into silence. So it was not just Rafaelito who was in danger. Juan and Belén could be taken, too. And Nieve. Darling Nieve.

"The sooner we can move away, the better," Lola said. "No one knows us in Madrid. We'll get a place far away from the Gypsy quarter. Nieve will go to school while I look for work."

Rose nodded. No wonder Lola was so keen to swap the taverns of Granada for the film studios of the capital. No wonder she had embraced the idea of learning to read and write with such unbounded enthusiasm. Education was a passport to anonymity, a way of shaking off the tags that marked her out to the authorities.

"What about Cristóbal and Juanita? What will they do?"

Lola shook her head slowly. "Juanita has family in the countryside. She'll take the children if she has to. But Cristóbal will never leave Granada. It's in his soul."

Rose passed through a huge stone gate carved with the same fruit that had hung from the *vardos* of the Granada Gypsies. The Gate of the Pomegranates was the entrance to the hilltop fortress of the Alhambra. She climbed the winding tree-lined path, seeking refuge from the afternoon heat among the pools and fountains of the Jannat al-ʿArīf—the palace gardens she'd read about.

Granada was beguiling but suffocating. Wandering the streets of the city was like being trapped in an enormous oven. She had arranged to meet Lola and Nieve in the gardens after the siesta, but sleep had eluded her in the stuffy room at the posada. And so she had gone for a walk, hoping to find a shady, secluded bench to doze on.

She made her way slowly up the slope, past man-made streams that ran along either side of the path. It was like walking through a forest on the side of a mountain. Towering cedars, sycamores, and cork oaks formed a canopy with their branches, blocking out the burning rays of the sun. Her old life in London seemed terribly unreal and far away. And soon she would be traveling even farther south—beyond the snowcapped peaks of the Sierra Nevada to find the village Nathan had described in his letter. The thought of boarding the bus the day after tomorrow stirred up a feverish sense of anticipation—a mixture of excitement and foreboding.

At the top of the hill, the trees gave way to a carpet of orange, blue, and yellow. Irises, marigolds, and roses were framed in low-trimmed hedges of box and myrtle. Passing through another great gate, she made her way through the old walled city created by the Moorish rulers over a thousand years ago.

Every few yards there were glimpses of the outside world between gaps in the architecture. She saw swifts performing astonishing aerobatics, diving and wheeling across the river valley. And in the distance, the cave houses of Sacromonte, with people the size of ants climbing up the road from the Albaicin.

She walked on, through horseshoe arches decorated with blue-and-white mosaic tiles, past stone walls honeycombed with arabesque carvings, along cobbled paths studded with black and white pebbles in intricate geometric designs. Then she went up a flight of stairs whose handrails were channels of running water. It took her into an avenue of fruit trees growing against terracotta walls—their boughs heavy with ripening peaches and apricots.

A profusion of scent filled her nostrils as she entered the first of a series of gardens. Rambling roses, honeysuckle, and oleander climbed up pillars and pergolas. Lavender, rosemary, candytuft, and agapanthus filled ornamental beds and terracotta pots. And between the beds was an abundance of other trees and bushes: oranges, plums, medlars, and magnolia.

Pools of water, long and narrow, formed the shape of a cross at the center of the garden. At the far end a fountain sent shimmering beads arcing through the air. Rose found a bench beneath a cascade of pale-blue wisteria. Hewn from rock, it looked hard and uncomfortable—but the sun had warmed it. She sat back and closed her eyes, breathing in the fragrance of the flowers, hearing nothing but the birds and the gentle splash of the fountain.

The guidebook said Jannat al-'Arīf was an old Arabic phrase. Scholars argued as to the meaning. It could be translated as "Orchard of the Architect" or "the Gardens of Knowing." It seemed impossible that such a haven of tranquility could have continued to exist through the horrors of what had gone on in the city below just a handful of years ago. And that it would continue to exist, like some parallel universe, while people like Lola and Juanita and Cristóbal lived in fear of what the monster who now ruled Spain might do next.

The Gardens of Knowing.

The words seemed to mock Rose's naïveté. She had allowed herself to believe that she could live the Gypsy life. That she could throw off convention and be free, passionate, alive. But in falling for Cristóbal, she had succumbed to nothing more than a romanticized image. He behaved as if he were free—but he was not free in any real sense of the word.

As she opened her eyes, she saw a swift swoop over one of the pools for a sip of water, skimming the surface so fast it barely caused a ripple, the droplets sliding away as if the feathers were coated in wax. As she watched the bird soar into the sky, it occurred to her that what had happened in France had released something inside her. The impermeable membrane spun around her heart by grief for the loss of her family had been breached. What Cristóbal had done felt like a wound, and it had hurt her—still hurt her—but somehow this new pain had freed her. It had forced her out of the cocoon of numbness. Now she knew she could be something more than she was when she left England. A different person. A better person.

She wasn't sure how much time had elapsed when she got up to leave the garden. She wandered into the harem courtyard—the place where the many wives of the Moorish rulers had lived, only able to glimpse the outside world through the fretwork of stone that enclosed the section of the palace they occupied. Rose wondered what that would have been like. It must have felt like living in a gilded cage. They would have been able to see the river, the streets and houses along its banks, and the distant snowcapped peaks of the Sierra Nevada. But they could never set foot outside the palace walls.

The confined world of women at the Alhambra was echoed in the name of the place she entered next. The Tower of the Captive was stunningly beautiful inside. Intricate mosaics of cobalt blue, emerald, and magenta covered the walls. Rose wondered who had been imprisoned here. The guidebook didn't say. A group of tourists was clicking away with cameras. When they left she was all alone in the cavernous space. The silence was unnerving.

It was a relief to get back into the sunlight. She found herself in another courtyard, walking through a forest of elegant pillars with overhanging wooden eaves, delicately carved, like fringes of lace hanging from the sky. At the center of the courtyard was a fountain of twelve stone lions standing in a circle and facing outward, supporting the bowl of the fountain on their backs. The guidebook said that to the Moors, water was a symbol of hospitality. An inscription carved into the walls said "Whoever should come to me thirsty, I shall lead him to a place where he will find clean, fresh water of the sweetest purity." It might have been a quote from the New Testament.

She glanced again at the book in her hand. Apparently, this part of the Alhambra had been built during a period of tolerance and an exchange of cultural ideas between Christians and Muslims. Rose blew out a breath. That was six hundred years ago. Why couldn't people be more tolerant now? Had human beings learned nothing in more than half a millennium?

"I thought I might find you here."

The voice made her jump. It was Cristóbal, so close behind her that when she whipped around, her hair brushed his face.

"I went to the posada, but they said you'd gone for a walk."

"How did you know I'd come here?" Her heart was thudding treacherously against her ribs. Why did he still have this effect on her?

"The landlady said you'd borrowed the guidebook. And Nieve told me she was meeting you up here later for a picnic. I'll be there, too, of course. It would look odd if I wasn't, with the performance being here tonight. So I thought I'd better get you alone while I had the chance."

"There's nothing else to say, is there?" She made herself look right into the blue-green blaze of his eyes, willing herself not to weaken.

"Isn't there?"

"Please don't say you've told Juanita." The thought of her bending over the baby, her face swollen with tears, piled on fresh agony.

Cristóbal shook his head. "I'm not that stupid. I came to say sorry. To make things right."

"It's a bit late for that, isn't it?"

His face clouded. "You . . . you're not . . . ?"

"No, Cristóbal, I'm not. No thanks to you. What if I had been? What then?"

"You would have managed, I'm sure." He shrugged. "You came all that way to France on your own. You don't need people, really, do you?"

She glared back at him, floored by his casual disregard, this knack he had of always turning the spotlight away from his own shortcomings.

"What were you expecting?" he went on. "Did you think we had any kind of future, you and me? A woman with a university degree and a Gypsy who can't even read music, let alone books?"

"The only thing I was expecting was the truth," she hissed. "If you'd been honest with me at the start, it would never have happened."

"Are you telling me you didn't enjoy it?" His eyes narrowed. "Do you know how long I was in prison? Four miserable, stinking years— four years of my life that I'll never get back. Do you have any idea what that does to a man? It changes you forever, Rose—makes you grab whatever you can, whenever you can."

Her lips parted, ready to launch a biting rebuke. But the words stuck in her throat. What he had said was a garbled echo of the very sentiment Nathan had expressed in his last letter.

We might not have a lifetime to live together, might not have what people are always supposed to have. Living as I do now, I must concentrate it all into the short time that I can have it.

The memory of Nathan's words made her understand Cristóbal a little bit better—but she still wanted nothing to do with his lies.

"You're right," she said coolly. "I have no idea what you went through in prison. I thought I knew you—but I didn't. I won't make that mistake again." Without a backward glance, she swept out of the courtyard, past the unseeing eyes of the stone lions. She didn't stop until she reached the wisteria bower in the Jannat al-'Arīf. She curled herself up on the bench, hiding like a child behind the fronds of blossom.

Chapter 15

Lola stood barefoot on a patch of grass in front of the harem courtyard. She raised her arms above her head, and Rose, who was facing her, mirrored her posture.

"You have to make flowers with your hands. Show her, Nieve."

Nieve took Rose's right hand, moving the fingers into position.

"The wrist movement is most important," Lola went on. "Think of the way water swirls." She jerked her head at the fountain behind her.

Nieve began clapping out a rhythm, and Rose attempted to follow Lola's movements. It was hard to move her arms and wrists gracefully while maintaining the very erect posture Lola displayed. And when the *escobilla* began, Rose tripped over her own feet and fell into a quivering, giggling heap on the grass.

"It's no good," she gasped. "I'll never be able to do it—it's much too hard!"

"You can't expect to get it straightaway." Lola was trying to look stern, but her cheeks were pink with suppressed laughter. "It's taken me years of study and discipline."

"But you said flamenco was spontaneous!" Huffing out a theatrical sigh, Rose propped herself up on one arm. "I thought once you got a few of the moves, you could . . . well . . . sort of make it up as you went along."

"It might look like that but it's not." Lola sank down onto the grass beside her. "If you lived a whole lifetime, you could never learn it all. When you prepare to dance, you ask, What are the emotions we are trying to express? What are the rhythms of this piece? You have a backbone of material, but your imagination is just as important. You have to work out moves to reflect every single word that comes out of the singer's mouth."

Rose shook her head. "That sounds incredibly difficult."

"That's why I have to practice so much. When I came to Granada, it helped that I lived in the same house as Cristóbal. A dancer has to get a feeling for what the singer is going to do before he or she actually does it." She brought her fist up to her chest. "It's in here," she said. "Like a sixth sense. It grows the more you practice. When Cristóbal starts to sing, he's supposed to follow the signals I give with my feet. But he gets so lost in what he's singing that it doesn't always work like that. I have to be ready to change what I've planned in a heartbeat."

"Have you told him yet? About going to Madrid?"

"I had to—we're leaving a week from today." Lola glanced across the grass at the tavern in the shadow of the palace walls. "It's going to be strange, performing in this place for the last time."

"How did he react?"

Lola grunted a laugh. "He said it was a bit drastic, going all the way to Madrid to get away from the husband he's lined up for me." She shook her head. "But when he stopped joking around, he said he wasn't surprised. He knows it's something I've been dreaming about for years. And the prize money will keep him going while he looks for a new dancer."

"What about Nieve? How does she feel about leaving her cousins behind?"

"She's sad, of course." Lola followed the child with her eyes as Nieve chased Gunesh around a magnolia bush. Creamy petals showered down as they careered against the trunk. "But she's excited, too. Thanks to you, she's as mad about reading as she is about dancing. She wants to go to school in a place where no one knows her. If she went here, the other children would tease her. She's a tough little thing, but she doesn't need that. It'll be so much easier for her in Madrid."

"Well, I'm certainly going to miss her," Rose said. "And so is Gunesh."

Lola nodded. "Perhaps we'll get a dog of our own one day. Although I don't know how we'd find one as handsome as him." She turned to Rose with a wistful smile. "It's good that you have him with you. To protect you. There are wolves up there in the mountains." She could have added that there were people there, too—people even more frightening than wild animals. She could have told Rose the other reason why she couldn't go with her on her journey to the Alpujarras. That *he* might still be there. The faceless man who haunted her nightmares.

The performance was about to begin. Rose had taken a seat on one of the low benches that had been pushed against the wall in the back room of the tavern. The place was jam-packed. Word of Lola and Cristóbal's success in Provence had traveled fast.

Lola had gone somewhere to get changed. She had seemed keen to get away the moment they stepped into the tavern. When Rose had asked her what the matter was, Lola had glanced fleetingly at a man who was standing at the bar.

"That's the man Cristóbal wants me to marry," she hissed. "His name's Antonio Lopez. I can't stand him."

Rose had watched the man follow Lola with his eyes as she left the room. There was a furtive hunger in them, like a dog hovering around a dinner table, hoping for scraps. He looked about twenty years older than Lola, and his stomach bulged over the waist of his trousers. His thinning hair was slicked across the top of his head like bedraggled feathers.

She had lost sight of him as people began filing through to the back room, jostling for space on the benches. Nieve had grabbed her hand and led her to a seat. Cristóbal was already there, tuning his guitar. He gave her a brief, hooded look. She pretended not to notice, dropping her hand to the floor to find Gunesh, who had curled up under the bench.

It was hot and stuffy in the room. There was a small window in one wall. Someone had pulled it open. It had narrow-spaced bars on the outside, like the window of a prison cell. Rose was looking at it when something very strange happened. A swift flew straight through the bars, darted across the room, and landed in Rose's lap.

It sat there, its claws digging into the fabric of her skirt, staring up at her with its bright little eyes. She stared back, hypnotized—not quite believing it was real. Swifts had always been her favorite birds. They were so strange and mysterious, with so many legends attached to them. She'd heard the English Gypsies call them devil birds, for their screaming, for their crossbow shape, and for their uncanny ability to do everything on the wing—to eat, drink, preen, and mate without ever touching the earth. According to Bill Lee, swifts didn't sleep in the nests they built in the eaves of houses but soared to the moon at dusk to spend the night there, descending to earth with the dew of the morning.

She felt Gunesh brush the backs of her legs, but she hushed him before he could frighten the bird.

Suddenly Cristóbal was standing in front of her. "The bird must go back outside," he said. "Its kind die quickly if they come out of the sky."

She felt paralyzed. If she tried to grab it, it would struggle. It might die of fright. But if it hopped off her lap, into the crowd, it would be trampled underfoot. She was aware of dozens of pairs of eyes on her. The bird had cast a spellbinding hush on the room.

"Take it!" In one rapid movement she grasped the warm, quivering body and thrust it into Cristóbal's hands. He waded through the sea of bodies, opened the door, and tossed the bird into the starlit sky.

Then all hell broke loose. The Gypsies crowded around her, their faces wild with excitement. They jabbered at her in *kalo*, the words incomprehensible. Nieve fought her way through the forest of legs, popping up at Rose's side to translate.

"They're saying that when a bird comes to you like this, it's very, very lucky," she said. "Now you have to make a wish. Think of something you really, really want—and before a year is up, the wish will come true."

Rose's heart was beating as fast as the wings she'd trapped in her hands. She closed her eyes.

"What are you wishing for?" Nieve was whispering in her ear. Rose could feel the warmth of her breath. "Oh no—you mustn't tell me! It won't come true if you do!"

Was it Nieve's voice that drove thoughts of Nathan from her mind? Was it the tenderness she felt for this little girl that made her long for what she'd warned herself about wanting?

A child. The words flashed across the dark side of her eyes. *I wish for a child.*

It was close to midnight when the dancing ended. Each time Lola had taken a bow, the crowd had gone wild for more. Poor little Nieve had crawled under the bench and fallen asleep with Gunesh for a pillow. Now people were crowding around Lola and Cristóbal, proffering bottles of wine and brandy.

"I'll take Nieve home if you want me to," Rose called out when she managed to get within hailing distance of Lola.

A look of concern crossed Lola's face.

"It's okay—you should stay and enjoy yourself. You deserve it!"

At that moment four of the men grabbed Lola and hoisted her onto their shoulders to whoops of joy from the crowd. She gave Rose a shrug of resignation as they carried her off across the room.

Outside it was very dark. The sky had clouded over, obscuring the moon and the stars. Rose had a flashlight in her bag, which helped them to negotiate the steep descent from the Alhambra, along the winding wooded path that led to the Gate of the Pomegranates. Once she and Nieve were through that, there were gas lamps to light the way. They gave the narrow cobbled streets an eerie yellow glow.

"Will you carry me?" Nieve had stumbled, zombielike, down the hillside, but now she was flagging.

Rose lifted the child into her arms, smelling the lavender scent of her hair as Nieve snuggled into her neck. Gunesh was already a few yards ahead of them. He seemed to know the way back to Sacromonte. As she followed behind him, Rose's thoughts returned to the strange encounter with the swift. Why had she wished for a child? Was her growing closeness to Nieve really making her feel broody? Or was it the half-buried hope that Nieve could be her niece?

Lola was trying to get away from Antonio Lopez, who had her trapped in a corner of the tavern, his arm propped against the wall so she couldn't sidle away from him.

"Have another drink!" He lifted a bottle of red wine, pouring some into his own glass before going to top up hers.

"No, thank you. I've had enough." She tried to catch Cristóbal's eye. He was over by the bar, a glass of brandy in his hand, standing very close to a girl Lola had seen him with before. She lived out of town, in a cave house on the slopes of the Sierra Nevada, and came to Granada to sell fruit from a basket in the streets—strawberries, cherries, apricots, or prickly pear, according to the season. Clearly her cousin was having far too good a time to want to come home anytime soon.

"Come on—what's wrong with you?" Antonio moved closer, sliding his hand around her waist.

"Get off me!" She tried to push him away. Although he was twice her size, she managed to knock him off balance. He staggered slightly, his arms flailing as he braced himself against the wall. The people nearby turned and stared. But not Cristóbal. Either he was too absorbed to notice Lola's pleading looks or he was deliberately ignoring her.

"I need to get home." Still cornered, she ducked under Antonio's arm. The smell of rancid sweat mixed with the whiff of stables almost made her gag.

"I'll walk with you," he said, catching her by the wrist. "It's late—you shouldn't be alone."

"I'll be fine." She pulled away from him. She didn't want to hurl insults, show him up in front of all these people, but if he persisted, she would have no choice.

"If that's what you want." He shrugged and drained his glass. "Mind how you go—it's very dark out there."

It took her a few minutes to pack away her costume, her shoes, and her makeup. She slipped out the back door of the tavern to avoid being held up by any other man, emboldened by drink, who might fancy his chances. That was the trouble with dancing in these places. After a few drinks, men thought the passion was for real—that moving your body like that meant you had only one thing on your mind and it was only natural to try to take advantage. Would they be different in Madrid? Was there any hope of meeting someone who didn't see "whore" or "housewife" tattooed on her forehead when he looked at her?

She stood outside the tavern for a moment, breathing in the cool air. The scent of *galán de noche*—night-flowering jasmine—drifted over the wall from the palace gardens. Apart from the muffled rise and fall of laughter, the only sound she could hear was the rhythmic thrumming of the crickets. Slinging her bag over her shoulder, she set off down the path.

Her boots crunched on the fine, sandy gravel. She couldn't see more than a couple of yards in front of her, but she knew the way well enough not to be fazed by the twists and turns as she made her way down the hill.

An owl flew out of a tree, swooping so low she could feel the rush of air from its wing beats. Then she heard another sound. Not the rustle of a bird in the branches but a sharp snap, like a twig breaking underfoot. She looked in the direction it had come from, trying to make sense of the dark shapes at the edge of the path. Was that the trunk of a tree or the body of a man lurking in the shadows?

She walked on, faster than before. Once she reached the Gate of the Pomegranates, she would be safe in the light of the streetlights. She could smell the city now—the stink of the river rising on the night breeze, mingling with the earthy scents of the woodland. She blew out a breath when she spotted the looming mass of the gate, black against the charcoal gray of the sky. But as she passed under the arch, someone grabbed her from behind, pushing her into the rough stone and pressing hard against her.

She kicked out and tried to scream, but a hand clamped her mouth shut before any sound could escape. She felt his breath through her hair, hot on her scalp, a wave of alcohol tainted with the stink of sweat. And mule shit.

Antonio Lopez.

His grip tightened. She could taste blood, like metal, in her mouth. An image of Nieve swam before her eyes. Naked and defenseless, the cord hanging from her belly. With all her strength Lola jerked her head up, jabbing him under the chin. She heard his teeth crunch. He swore. But it had no more impact than a sparrow pecking a vulture.

She felt him fumbling with her skirt, yanking it up over her buttocks. She jabbed blindly with her elbow, catching him under the ribs. He coughed, momentarily loosening his grip on her mouth. In one lightning movement she twisted sideways, thrust her hand inside her skirt, and pulled her knife from the belt around her waist. As he lunged at her, the knife went in, so fast and clean he hardly made a sound as he fell to the ground. And then she ran. Faster than she had ever run in her life, clattering up the cobbled streets, on and on, until she staggered through the blue-painted door of the cave house.

"Lola! My God!" Rose leapt up from the chair by the fire, catching Lola as she fell to her knees.

"I . . . I th . . . think I've k . . . killed him!" Her teeth rattled as the words spilled out.

"What! Who, Lola? Who?"

"An . . . tonio Lopez. H . . . he t . . ." The words disappeared into a great shuddering sob.

Rose lifted her up, half carried her to the armchair. She laid her gently down, stroking Lola's hair. "Don't try to talk. Let me get you something. Brandy—is there brandy?"

Lola nodded, unable to control her lips. She pointed to a cupboard in the wall.

Rose found the bottle and held it up to Lola's mouth.

"Better?"

"Yes." Lola's voice was a rasping whisper.

"Can you tell me what happened?" Rose knelt beside the chair.

"He was waiting for me. By the G . . . Gate of the Pomegranates." Lola bit her lip, trying to control the trembling. "He jumped on me and tried to . . . but I had m . . . my knife."

Rose sucked in a breath. "You stabbed him?"

Lola nodded.

"Is he . . ."

"I . . . I don't know. I just ran."

Rose scrambled to her feet. "I'd better go and find him. He might be—"

"No!" Lola cut in. "You can't! They'll think it's you who did it!"

"But we can't just leave him!" Rose unhooked her jacket from a peg on the wall.

"Why not? He's a monster! He deserves to die!" She spat out the words with a vehemence that stopped Rose in her tracks. Lola could imagine what she was thinking. And it was true. A portion of her heart had frozen solid that day on the mountain. There was no room in it for mercy.

Chapter 16

Rose was dozing fitfully in front of the embers of the fire, a blanket thrown over her knees. Lola had crawled into bed with Nieve and Gunesh after making Rose promise not to go down to the Gate of the Pomegranates.

It had been far too late to go back to her room at the posada—the place would be locked up. There had been no alternative but to try to get what little sleep she could in the armchair. She had fallen into a whirlpool of graphic nightmares, peopled by ghastly figures covered in blood. And Lola was dancing among them in the orange fishtail dress she had worn that first night at the fiesta, her skirts flying out as she slashed and jabbed at their ravaged bodies.

Rose woke with a start. She could hear a whining sound over by the door. She twisted around in the chair, thinking it was Gunesh wanting to be let out. But it was Cristóbal's dog, Chico, she saw—a skinny black-and-white animal with pointed ears, like the dogs portrayed in Egyptian tombs.

She heard a key twist in the lock. Then Cristóbal's voice. He was muttering something inaudible to the dog, who ran back and jumped into the chair on the other side of the fireplace.

"What are *you* doing here?" He loomed into view, his head silhouetted against the slice of pale-gray sky revealed by the open door. He had a hunk of bread in his hand, and he bit off a big mouthful, swallowing it without chewing.

Rose doubted that he had even noticed her leaving the tavern with Nieve. She didn't want to contemplate what he'd been doing all night. "I wasn't waiting for you, if that's what you're thinking," she said. "It was too late to go back to my room, that's all."

"Where's Lola?"

"In bed."

"What time did she get back?" She could hear the foreboding in his voice.

"I . . . I'm not sure. I was asleep. Why do you ask?"

"A man was knifed to death last night. Antonio Lopez." His eyes searched her face.

Rose held her breath, afraid that anything she said would betray the fact that she knew.

"He wanted to marry Lola—did she tell you that?" Cristóbal shoved his dog off the chair and sank down onto it. "People are saying she had a fight with him in the tavern—pushed him away when he tried to put his arm round her. And half an hour later, he was found under the Gate of the Pomegranates with a knife in his guts."

"That's . . . terrible." She stared at her feet, unable to look at him.

"You say you didn't wake up when she came in? How was that? She must have walked right past you!"

"I . . . I had a lot to drink last night." She'd had only one glass of wine. But he wouldn't know that. "I put Nieve to bed, then just collapsed out here. I vaguely remember Lola coming in—she called good night to me, I think—but I couldn't tell you what time it was."

"Well, she'd better have a good story." Cristóbal grabbed a poker from a hook on the wall and jabbed it into the embers of the fire. "The police are going to be buzzing around here like flies."

As if on cue, Chico started barking. Gunesh came running from the back of the house, and the two set up a racket that brought Juanita stumbling into the room in her nightdress.

"Why are they barking?" She rubbed her eyes, staring at Rose. "What's going on?"

Before either Rose or Cristóbal could reply, there was a loud thump on the door.

Chapter 17

Lola sat shivering in a basement cell in the headquarters of Granada's Guardia Civil. They had taken her in her nightclothes, not even allowing her to grab a shawl to keep out the chill of the subterranean prison they had frog-marched her into.

All she could think of was Nieve. Her pale, frightened little face as she watched the nightmare unfolding. The police hadn't cared that she was there. If Rose hadn't taken Nieve's hand and led her back to the bedroom, the child would have heard every sordid detail of what had happened under the Gate of the Pomegranates.

He tried to rape me.

They hadn't seemed to care about that, either. Perhaps if she had been the daughter of the mayor, or a blonde-haired tourist, they would have believed her story.

Gitana. Puta. Gypsy. Whore. She had heard them muttering the words under their breath—words that, in their minds, were interchangeable. She had killed a man whose only crime was loving her enough to want to marry her. That was how they saw it.

As she stared at the dirty floor, numb with cold and shock, something else occurred to her—something even more terrifying than the prospect of standing trial for murder. They would take Nieve away. The authorities would be told that the Gypsy murderess had a child. There would be no question of Nieve being allowed to stay with Cristóbal and Juanita. She would be whisked away, and Lola would never set eyes on her again.

Rose set off for the police station less than an hour after Lola was arrested. Nieve hadn't wanted her to go. She had clung to Rose's skirt with tears welling, as if she was afraid to let her out of her sight.

"I have to try to help Mama." Rose had wanted her to understand. But how could she explain it to a child? That her mother wouldn't stand a chance of being believed because she was a Gypsy, that she needed someone outside the community to plead her case, someone the Guardia Civil couldn't simply ignore as an illiterate troublemaker.

She had left Nieve sobbing into Gunesh's fur. Juanita had been sitting on the bed with her, the baby in her arms and a bowl of cherries in her free hand. But the child would not be comforted. The sight sent liquid steel shooting through Rose's veins. She would do whatever it took to make them listen.

The desk sergeant looked very young. Not much older than Lola. He eyed her with barely concealed disdain until she took out her passport and shoved it under his nose.

"*¿Es usted británica?*" You are British?

The surprise was clear to see. He had pigeonholed her the moment she walked through the door—the slanting cheekbones, the brightly patterned skirt, the dangling copper earrings.

"*Sí.*" She pointed to the place on the passport where her profession had been written in. It said "Veterinarian," but that was a term he was unlikely to understand. "I'm a doctor," she said, pronouncing the words slowly and clearly in her best Spanish accent. "And I work for the king of England." It wasn't really a lie: during the war the royal vet had brought two of King George's dogs to her after reading about her herbal cure for distemper.

"I want to see Lola Aragon—the woman you arrested this morning." Rose dived straight in with what came out sounding more like an order than a request, hoping he was sufficiently impressed by her qualifications to give way. "I'm also a lawyer," she went on. "I'll be acting on Miss Aragon's behalf—so she has a right to see me." This *was* a lie. But there was no one else to fight in Lola's corner. In the absence of a real lawyer, Rose was going to have to do the best she could: try to get the charge dropped before the case went any further.

"Wait here, please." He disappeared through a door behind the desk, emerging almost immediately with a thickset older man with a mustache whose pointed ends looked like the handlebars of a motorcycle. This second officer eyed her up and down as if he were inspecting a stray dog with rabies. Then without a word to Rose, he turned to his colleague and said, *"Diez minutos."*

Ten minutes. Not very long. Barely long enough to hand over the clothes she had brought and offer a few words of comfort.

She followed the desk sergeant down a twisting flight of steps into an underground corridor that stank of stale urine. Before she was allowed into the cell, she had to be searched. He made her strip down to her underwear and spent several minutes looking her up and down before he allowed her to get dressed again.

By the time he went to unlock the door, Rose felt degraded and humiliated—but it was worth it. When Lola saw her, she let out a high-pitched whimper and threw herself into Rose's arms. Her tears seeped through the thin cotton of Rose's blouse.

Rose stroked her hair, fighting back tears of her own. "It's going to be all right, I promise." She could feel Lola's body trembling. With her free hand she groped inside the bag slung over her shoulder. "I've bought you some warm things to put on."

She guided Lola over to the concrete bench that ran along one wall. "Here—have this." She draped a shawl of heather-colored wool around the shaking shoulders. "You can put the other things on when I've gone. I only have ten minutes—they won't let me stay any longer than that."

Lola's face crumpled.

"I'm going to write letters," Rose went on. "To the chief of the Guardia Civil, to the mayor of Granada, to General Franco himself if I have to. I'll tell them what happened: that what you did was in self-defense. That he was trying to rape you because you'd didn't want to marry him."

Lola stared at the wall, shaking her head.

"What's the matter? Is there something else? Something you haven't told me about him?"

"I . . . it's not that." Lola's voice was barely audible.

"What, then? Whatever it is, you must tell me—they'll be coming any second."

"Please, Rose! Just get Nieve away—before they come and take her!"

"You mean . . ." Rose searched her face, bewildered.

"I want you to take her with you to the mountains. Tell the people there she's yours." Lola's eyes brimmed with fresh tears. "It's the only way to keep her safe!"

"You think she's in danger? Because of this?"

"I know she is!" Lola glanced toward the door. "Go today—as soon as you can!"

"I can't just leave you here!" Rose sank onto the bench. She reached for Lola's hand, enclosing it in both of hers. It felt cold and lifeless. She rubbed the flesh, as if she were trying to revive a stillborn foal or puppy.

"But you have to!" Lola grasped Rose's wrist. "Please, Rose! Take my baby!"

Chapter 18

Las Alpujarras, Spain: June 8, 1946

The bus from Granada was packed with people and animals. The windows were open, but it made little difference. The smell was a suffocating mix of hot unwashed bodies and cigarette smoke. Rose's hand ached from gripping Gunesh's collar. She'd been afraid to let go in case he went for the chickens contained in a fragile-looking wicker basket at the feet of the woman sitting across the aisle. Nieve was lying curled up in the seat with her head in Rose's lap. Worn out from crying, she had fallen asleep within minutes of the bus setting off.

The route had taken them due south, through the mountain pass known as the Moor's Sigh—the place where the last Muslim ruler of Granada had stopped for a mournful look back at the city on his way to exile in the Alpujarras. The bus had skirted the western foothills of the Sierra Nevada, finally turning east, along a road with hairpin bends and terrifying ravines.

Rose hadn't noticed the changing landscape. All she could think about was Lola. She was writing a letter in her head—a letter she wouldn't be able to send until she had a return address. That would be the priority when they reached Pampaneira: finding a room. Living in the tent was no longer an option—not with a child to look after. Money was going to be tight, but she would just have to be careful.

The bus began the descent toward its destination—the town of Órgiva. To reach it they followed a road that wound along the bank of a river swollen with meltwater from the high peaks to the north. Passing through groves of citrus and olives, they came to a stop beside a church whose twin towers stuck up like giant honey-colored fingers against the looming backdrop of the mountains.

It was a pretty little town, with flower-filled balconies and a bustling market in the main square. But there was no time to linger. Rose set about negotiating a price with the muleteers lined up outside the church. The only way to reach the villages higher up the mountains was on muleback. After a few minutes of bartering, Rose agreed to a fee of two pesetas and fifty cents for a guide and a pair of mules to carry Nieve, herself, and their baggage to Pampaneira.

The sun was high in the sky when they set off. Swarms of flies followed the mules, making them twitch their heads and swish their tails. Rose tried to bat the insects away with her straw hat, but it didn't have much effect and almost made her lose her balance.

The flies became less of a problem when they left the road and started up a track that followed the river through a shady, steep-sided gorge. As they climbed above the town, the orange and lemon groves gave way to woodlands of chestnut and pine trees. Gunesh went chasing off after a squirrel, and when he finally came back, Rose had to clip his lead on and tie it to the mule's saddle to keep him from doing it again.

Rounding a bend in the river, they saw a great waterfall tumbling over boulders, sending a rainbow of spray across the track.

"¡Cuídate!" Take care! The mule man tightened his grip on the lead reins of both animals. Rose heard the squelch of the animals' hooves in the mud. Her mule almost lost its footing, tipping her sideways, before it righted itself. She got a dizzying glimpse over the precipice, of the waterfall crashing into the river.

"I'm frightened!" Nieve grabbed Rose's arm, fresh tears welling in her swollen eyes.

"It's all right—we'll be there soon. Look! You can see the village—up there!" She pointed to a chimney just visible above the trees, seeping blue woodsmoke into the still air. It was probably just a forester's cottage, but it did the trick—Nieve's face brightened.

"What will we have to eat there? Can we have *migas*? Mama said she used to have *migas* every day—even for breakfast!"

"Well, that's what we'll have, then." Rose smiled. *Migas* was a dish she'd never heard of before coming to Spain. Breadcrumbs fried in pork fat and garlic, served with whatever else you might have in the larder. She hadn't known it was Nieve's favorite. No doubt there was much else she didn't know about the child. She was going to have to learn fast if she wanted to convince people that Nieve was her daughter.

"Is it where I was born—up there?" Nieve fixed her eyes on the plume of smoke as her mule plodded along the muddy track. "Mama said bad people live there. That's why she had to take me away. Are the bad people still there?"

Rose glanced at the mule man. He was a few feet in front of them, puffing away on a cigarette. She hoped he couldn't hear them above the roar of the waterfall. "That was a long time ago," she said. "I'll tell you what: tonight, when we're tucked up in bed, I'll tell you a story about a little girl who lived in a house in a forest—just like that one up there. Would you like that?"

Nieve nodded. "Is it 'Goldilocks and the Three Bears'?"

"No."

"'Hansel and Gretel'?"

"No."

"What, then?"

"I'll give you a clue: it begins with *L*. Can you guess the next letter?"

The game distracted Nieve for nearly half an hour, by which time they were riding past a mill on the river's edge, with the rooftops of

Pampaneira clearly visible on the opposite bank. The houses looked like a series of boxes piled on top of each other on the slopes. The chimneys were shaped like witches' hats, and the roofs were not tiled but covered with grayish-brown clay.

Rose's throat tightened as they crossed the stone bridge that straddled the gorge. Had Nathan seen this same view? Had he walked among these houses? Was this really the place where he had met a girl and fallen in love?

The mules clattered up a cobbled street with a translucent stream running along the edge of it. Each street they turned into had its own miniature man-made river, with the murmur of water a constant background sound. And there were flowers everywhere—terracotta pots bursting with scarlet geraniums in every nook and cranny of the white-washed walls of the houses.

Rose glanced up an alleyway, captivated by ancient-looking roof terraces jutting out over the street so far that neighbors living opposite each other could almost reach out and shake hands. Hibiscus, vines, and bougainvillea tumbled from trellises. Cobs of maize and strings of red peppers hung under the eaves. Down below, a ginger cat crouched on the cobbles, lapping water from the channel cut into the stones. The mule veered sideways as Gunesh tried to chase the cat, but Rose pulled him back before he could get any farther.

The mule man set them down outside the village post office, which had a closed sign hanging in the window.

"*Gracias.*" Rose handed over the fare and heaved her rucksack onto her back. The first thing she wanted to do was to look for the fountain Nathan had described in his letter. After traveling such a long way, she had to have tangible evidence that this really was the right place.

They came across several springs as they walked through the village. Some were just holes in the wall, dribbling water into troughs that were probably intended for animals to drink from. The most elaborate one was in an arched niche in front of the church in Pampaneira's main square. It had three ornamental spouts surrounded by painted ceramic tiles.

"Fuente de San Antonio." Nieve slowly deciphered the words inscribed on the tiles above the bubbling jets of water. There was a verse underneath—too long and complicated for Nieve to tackle yet. Rose couldn't read all of it, either—it seemed to be written in very archaic Spanish, and parts of it had been obscured by time. But she understood the last two lines:

". . . y soltero que lo bebe con intención de casarse no falla! Pues al instante novia tiene." . . . and a single man who drinks it with the intention of getting married—you cannot fail! You will instantly find a sweetheart.

Rose stared at the words, hardly daring to believe. But there was no doubt. This was it—the place Nathan had stopped on the night he met the girl he fell in love with. In all the darkness of the last few days, this was a little ray of hope. She dug into her rucksack and pulled out her water bottle, emptying the dregs onto the cobbles and refilling it from the central spout of the fountain.

"Are you thirsty?" She offered it to Nieve, who took a swig before passing it back.

"It tastes nice," Nieve said. "Better than the water in Granada."

It did taste good. Fresh and cold, with no taint of chemicals. And the thought that Nathan had drunk it made it all the sweeter.

"Shall we go and get something to eat?" Rose held out her hand.

They walked on through the village until they came to a place with tables and chairs set out under a vine-covered veranda.

"Look!" Nieve pointed at the menu board hanging from a nail. "It says *migas!*"

Rose smiled. Not only was it Nieve's favorite, it was the cheapest thing on offer. When the waiter appeared, she ordered it for them both. But when the food arrived, Nieve wrinkled her nose.

"What's that?" She stuck her fork into the pile of fried breadcrumbs, pulling out the tail of a fish. When she dug deeper, she uncovered a brown, sticky lake beneath the *migas*.

The waiter, who was hovering nearby, stepped forward. *"Es una especialidad de la región."* His lips twitched as if he was trying not to smile. *"Migas con chocolate y sardinas."*

"Ugh!" Nieve grimaced at Rose. "Chocolate and sardines!"

"Hmm. That's an . . . interesting combination." Rose took a forkful of the gooey breadcrumbs, trying to avoid the fishy bit in the middle. "Mmm!" She made an enraptured face. It wasn't as bad as it looked. The taste reminded her of the chocolate biscuits her mother used to buy before the war—only much saltier. She swallowed it down. "I think you'll like it—try eating round the edges."

With a bit of cajoling, Nieve ate nearly half of what was on her plate.

"Shall we give the rest to Gunesh?" Rose knocked the sardines over the side of the table onto the cobbles, where they were swiftly gobbled up. She glanced up and down the street, wondering if any of the houses would have rooms available. It would have to be an apartment of some kind—somewhere they could prepare their own food—otherwise Rose's money was going to run out very quickly.

She explained what they were looking for to the waiter when she paid the bill. He cocked his head to one side, glancing at the remains of the *migas*, as if the food were an indicator of what she might be able to afford.

"There's the mill over the bridge," he said. "She sometimes has rooms. The only other place is the posada—but they don't take dogs."

"Thank you." Rose stood up. "What's the lady's name?"

The waiter shrugged. "Señora Molino." He scooped up the money and headed back inside the building.

Mrs. Mill. Either he didn't know the woman's name or he didn't want to say it. Rose wondered if this was a legacy of the Civil War.

Cristóbal had warned her how it had divided communities—and that in the villages, the bitterness was more palpable than in the cities. She wondered what role the occupants of the mill had played. Had they been on the side of the fascists or the republicans? Had they been involved in the atrocities Lola had spoken about? Was that why the waiter was reluctant to say the family name out loud?

As Rose lifted her rucksack onto her back, she realized that she was going to have to be very cautious if she was going to get any further in her search. How to ask questions without ruffling feathers—that was going to take a lot of thought.

Chapter 19

It was just after three o'clock when Rose and Nieve arrived at the mill. Apart from half a dozen scrawny chickens scratching around in the dirt, there was no sign of life. Rose had forgotten that it was siesta time. Not a good time to go knocking on a stranger's door. The only thing to do was wait. She sank down on the riverbank, glad to be free of the heavy rucksack. Nieve kicked off her boots and went to dip her feet in the rock pools near the water's edge, Gunesh following her like a shadow.

"Don't go any closer!" Rose called after her. The mill wheel—a wooden monster dripping with green weed—was churning around and around just yards from where Nieve stood. If they did manage to get a room here, Rose was going to have to give the child strict instructions about where she could and couldn't play.

The sun made Rose feel drowsy. But she mustn't doze off—that would be asking for trouble. Instead she unlaced her boots and went to join Nieve. She stood ankle deep in the water, letting it soothe her tired feet. It was icy cold. But she'd swum in rivers just as bone chilling as this in England. If it hadn't been for the proximity of the mill, she would have been tempted to strip off and plunge in.

A sudden splash made her whip around. A boy of about Nieve's age was standing by the mill wheel, throwing stones into the river. Gunesh leapt to retrieve them. The boy threw another, narrowly missing the dog's head.

"*¡Detente!*" Rose shouted. "*¡Tú le harás daño!*" Stop! You'll hurt him!

The boy had another stone in his hand, but instead of throwing it he scrambled down the bank. Gunesh gamboled up to him and shook himself violently.

The boy backed away. "*Lo siento, no lo vi. ¿Morderá?*" Sorry—I didn't see him. Will he bite?

Rose yanked the dog away. Gunesh had green slime in his coat, and his breath stank of fish. "He won't bite if you're nice to him," she replied. "Do you live here?" She cocked her head at the mill.

The boy nodded.

"Is your mother there? I've come to ask about a room—but I don't want to disturb her if she's sleeping."

Without a word he loped off toward the mill, disappearing when he reached the top of the riverbank. He reappeared a few minutes later with a hard-faced girl at his side. She looked two or three years older than the boy and had the same hazel eyes and curly black hair.

"*Mi hermano dice que usted quiere una habitación.*" My brother says you want a room. The girl glanced at Rose's muddy feet, then at the rucksack lying on the grass. "*¿Gitana?*"

Feeling in her pocket for her passport, Rose shot a warning glance at Nieve. "*No, inglesa,*" she replied.

The girl took the passport, examining each page until she came to the one with the photograph. Rose wondered if she could read—or was just pretending to. "*Vale, está bien.*" She huffed out a breath. "*Porque no aceptamos gitanos.*" That's good—because we don't allow Gypsies.

Rose felt her insides curl. If there had been any other place to stay, she would have walked away. She didn't dare look at Nieve.

The girl sniffed as she handed back the passport. "*¿Cuánto tiempo estarán?*"

"Er . . ." Rose hesitated. "A couple of weeks—maybe longer," she said.

"*Síganme, por favor.*" Follow me, please.

Her tone was annoyingly superior for one so young. Rose felt the girl's eyes on her as she searched through her rucksack for a towel.

"Nieve—let me dry your feet." The towel wasn't very clean. There hadn't been time to do any washing before they left Granada. As she dried her own feet, she felt exposed, vulnerable under the girl's gaze. No doubt she would report back to her mother that the new guests were a pair of dirty English ragamuffins with a smelly dog.

She led Rose and Nieve around the back of the mill, through a low doorway, and up a flight of bare wooden stairs.

"This is it." She opened the door of a sizeable room with low cane ceilings. There was a double bed, a washstand, a chest of drawers, and a table with two rickety-looking chairs.

"How much is it?" Rose asked.

"Six pesetas a week. Room only—payable in advance."

"Is there somewhere I can cook food?"

The girl pointed to the fireplace. "You can buy wood from us—twenty cents a bundle." She put her hands on her hips. "Well? Do you want the room?"

Rose nodded.

The girl held out her hand.

"There." Rose gave her the coins. "I'll have two bundles of wood, please—and some bread and cheese if you have any."

"The bread's all gone—you'll have to wait till tomorrow for that."

"What about cheese?"

"We might have some." The girl shrugged. "I'll ask my mother when she gets up." She tossed a large iron key onto the bed and walked out of the room without another word.

"Do we have to stay here?" Nieve whispered. She looked as if she was about to start crying again.

"Just for a little while," Rose said. She reached into her rucksack and pulled out a packet of candied chestnuts. "Here—this is for being such a good girl on the bus."

Nieve sat on the bed, crunching sweets while Rose began to unpack. "Who's that?" She pointed at a painting in a battered gilt frame hanging on the opposite wall. It depicted a small boy with a halo, carrying a lamb.

"Well, I suppose it's meant to be Jesus," Rose said. "When he was little."

"No es Jesús." It's not Jesus.

Rose spun around, startled. A woman was standing in the doorway—an older version of the girl who had shown them up to the room.

"Señora Carmona." She stepped across the threshold. "And you are?"

"Rose. Rose Daniel." Rose held out her hand. "And this is Nieve." She stopped short of saying "my daughter." No need to tell the lie unless she was asked a direct question.

"And he is San Juan." The miller's wife gestured to the painting on the wall. "He was a shepherd, you know, before Jesus called him."

"No, I didn't know," Rose replied.

"Like Mama," Nieve piped up. "She looked after goats when she was young."

"Did you?" The woman looked surprised.

Rose smiled to cover the jolt of panic Nieve's innocent remark set off. "Yes. I'm a vet—an animal doctor. I worked on farms when I was a student." It wasn't a lie—but she was going to have to warn Nieve to be more careful with what she said.

"And what brings you here? To Pampaneira?"

This was a question Rose had prepared for. "I'm writing a book," she said. "About animals. I needed somewhere quiet to work." Much easier to say that than to risk alienating the woman by mentioning

Nathan. Until Rose knew which side Señora Carmona and her family were on, it was too risky.

The woman nodded, apparently satisfied. "You asked for cheese," she said. "You can buy it from me if you want. I have honey, too. And there's fruit from the orchard—peaches and figs if you want them."

"Thank you."

"You mustn't go into the orchard yourself—come to the kitchen." She glanced at Gunesh, who was curled up on a rug in front of the fireplace. "And make sure you keep him away from my chickens."

"Yes, of course."

"One more thing: don't open the window. The flies are very bad this year. They're spreading typhus down in Órgiva. If you let them in, you'll never get rid of them." With that she turned and walked out of the room.

"I don't think she likes you." Nieve's remark was addressed to the dog—but Rose felt it applied equally to herself.

"Never mind." Rose crouched down next to Nieve, who had her arms around Gunesh. "We're going to have to be careful what we say to her, though. We have to play that game when other people are around."

"Which game?"

"The one where you pretend I'm your mama."

"I don't like that game." Nieve buried her face in Gunesh's fur.

"I know you don't, _cariño_—neither do I. But your mama asked me to play it. She just wants to keep you safe while she's in . . . that place they took her to." Rose bit her lip. How could she possibly explain it? If she told Nieve the reason for the subterfuge, the poor child would be terrified—as if she didn't have enough to cope with already.

"I want Mama." Nieve's shoulders heaved with sobs. "Where is she?"

Rose wrapped her arms around the child and the dog. "We'll get her back very soon," she whispered. "I know it's hard for you. But if you cry, you'll make Gunesh cry, too."

Nieve peered out from behind the dog's ear, her cheeks wet with tears. "Dogs can't cry—can they?" She moved her head so that she was eyeball-to-eyeball with Gunesh.

"Not like you and me," Rose said. "They cry on the inside. When you're sad, he's sad, too."

The child went silent for a moment. Then she said, "Where's his mama?"

"A long way away—in a place called Afghanistan."

"Farther than Granada?"

"Much farther."

"Don't cry, Gunesh." Nieve ran her hand down the length of his back. "When we've got my mama back, we'll go and find yours."

It was very stuffy in the room at the mill. By the time she had finished unpacking, Rose's clothes were sticking to her body. She washed herself and Nieve and sorted out fresh clothes for them both. Then she sent Nieve down to the kitchen to buy cheese and fruit for their supper and made a start on the letter she hoped would get Lola out of jail.

After three quarters of an hour, Nieve still hadn't come back. Rose peered out the window. She had warned Nieve about the dangers of the mill wheel. But she was a child with more than the usual dose of curiosity. What if she'd gone exploring on her own?

Rose couldn't see the mill wheel from the window. All she could see was a flower-filled terrace bordering the orchard. She pulled on her boots and clattered down the stairs, Gunesh hard on her heels. She ran around the corner of the building, covering the distance to the riverbank in less than a minute. The noise the wheel made was deafening. She stepped closer to the edge and peered down into the churning water, terrified of what she might see.

Gunesh's nose nudged the back of her leg. She heard him bark over the roar of the water.

"What is it, boy?" She dropped to her knees and grabbed his collar. "Where is she? Where's Nieve?"

The dog was looking away from the river. When she let go of him, he bounded to a big wooden door set in the side of the mill. Rose ran after him. There was a rusty iron latch—too high for her to reach.

"Nieve!" She hammered on the door with her fist. "Are you in there?"

There was a squeal of rusty hinges as the door swung open. Nieve was on the other side, a puzzled frown on her face and a white-tipped stick in her hand. Beside her stood the boy who had been throwing stones.

"Nieve! I thought you'd fallen in the river! Where have you been all this time?"

"Playing a game with Alonso," she replied. "Come and see." She took Rose by the hand and led her into the cavernous room where the grain was milled into flour. Sacks were stacked all around the room, and the sunbeams coming through the door lit up ghostly swirls of dust motes. She stopped in front of a wooden trough.

"It's called *tres en raya*." Nieve pointed with her stick to a grid pattern filled with crosses and circles drawn in the snowy white flour that filled the trough. "He won the first three—but I've just beaten him!"

Rose huffed out a breath. She could hardly blame the child for wanting to play after what she'd been through over the past few days. "That's very clever," she said. "But next time just come and tell me, will you? Then I won't get worried."

Before Nieve could reply, a small liquid missile splattered into the flour.

"What was that?" Rose tilted her head back. Whatever it was had come from the rafters high above them.

"It's the swifts," Nieve said. "Can you see the nests?"

"Oh yes, I can!" There were at least half a dozen of them, smooth brown cones of mud tucked into crevices in the roof. The parent birds were flying in and out of the hole in the wall, where an iron shaft the size of a tree trunk linked the grinding stone to the mill wheel outside. Watching them dart back and forth reminded Rose of the strange incident with the swift in the tavern. Her wish had come true almost at once—in a way she would never have wanted. She wondered what Lola was doing at this moment, cooped up all alone in a prison cell, pining for the child she had sent away.

"Alonso says their poo makes the flour taste better." Nieve shot a mischievous look at Rose. It was good to see the child smiling.

"Hmm—I wonder if the baker in the village gets his flour from here," Rose whispered. "I hope not!" She looked over her shoulder for the boy, but he was nowhere to be seen.

"It's Corpus Christi tomorrow. Alonso's in it—can we go and watch?"

"Yes, if you want to. What is it?"

"Don't you have it in England?" Nieve looked back at her, wide eyed. "It's when boys and girls take the bread and wine at church for the first time."

"Ah." Rose nodded. "We do have that in my country, but it's called something different."

"Alonso says he has to wear a white sailor suit—and he hates it. But all the children in his class are in it—so he has no choice. The girls wear white dresses with veils. After church they follow the priest around the village. We have it in Granada—people put flowers and candles and pictures of Jesus outside their houses."

It suddenly occurred to Rose that the children Nieve was talking about would all be about the same age as Nathan's child would have been if he or she had survived. If Nathan had died or been taken prisoner, would his fiancée have stayed in the village? Could his son or daughter be living here?

Perhaps it was too much of a leap of the imagination. The letter had said that Nathan and his girlfriend planned to get out of Spain. Perhaps the discovery that they were expecting a baby had triggered that decision. To be pregnant by a man who had fought on the losing side must have felt like a ticking time bomb. Even if the girl had wanted to stay in the village, it was unlikely to have been an option.

But the Corpus Christi event might be an opportunity to talk to local people. She could start with the mothers of the children in the procession. Watch their faces when she showed them Nathan's photograph. Perhaps she should try out the strategy on the miller's wife. But no—there was something about the woman that made her afraid of exposing the real reason for her presence in Pampaneira. It wasn't just the dismissive way the waiter had talked about her. She had left a cold, unwelcoming feeling in the room—despite only being in it for a matter of minutes. Better to wait, Rose decided. Talking to other people in the village first might give her a clue as to which side the Carmona family had been on.

Rose was woken the next morning by the crowing of the mill's cockerel. She rolled over, wondering if the noise had disturbed Nieve. But the child was still fast asleep, clutching the silk shawl patterned with peacocks that she insisted on taking to bed with her every night. Its edges were frayed and there were several holes in it. But it was hardly surprising she was so attached to it.

The images on the shawl reminded Rose of the feather Bill Lee always wore in his battered brown hat. She had asked him about it once. Why a peacock? Why not a pheasant or a jay—birds whose feathers were surely much easier to come by? He replied that the feather had belonged to his father, who had passed it on to him. He explained that to the Gypsies, the peacock was a symbol of protection and safeguarding.

In Nieve's case, Bill's words seemed bitterly ironic. The images on the shawl had been of no help to her mother that cold, cruel day in the mountains.

A young pregnant woman with black hair and a peacock shawl.

Who was she? Somebody's daughter. Somebody's sister. Were any of her family still alive? Someone in this village must know who she was. Just as someone must know the identity of the person Nathan had fallen in love with. Rose tried to suppress the voice inside her head, enticing her to believe they were one and the same woman.

Rose left Nieve sleeping and went downstairs. She let herself out, shooing away the chickens as they clustered around her legs. There was a bench on the terrace, and she sat down among the flowers, breathing in the cool, scented air. From this vantage point, she could see rows of tomatoes and peppers laid out on the roof of the mill to dry in the sun. They glistened in the morning light, as if they were covered in frost. But it wasn't cold enough at night for that—not even up here in the mountains. Rose guessed that it was salt—probably sprinkled on to keep the flies away.

Behind her she could hear the gurgle of water from a stream that wound its way through the orchard to join the river below. This place was very different from the dry, dusty plains she had traveled through on the way to Granada. The fruit trees, the flowers, the abundance of water were a rarity so far south. Nathan must have thought he'd stumbled on a sort of paradise. How tragic that it was a bitter, bloody war that had brought him here.

She thought of the scene Lola had described—her mother and brother gunned down in an act of mass slaughter. It must have happened within walking distance of this place. What had happened to all those dead people? Had anyone buried them? Or were the bodies simply left where they lay, until the snow melted and flowers sprang from the earth to cover them?

Where are you, Nathan?

She whispered the words into the still morning air. Her head told her that she was summoning a ghost. That in all likelihood her brother had never made it out of these mountains. But if he had died here, she needed to know where. If all she could do was mark the place with a wooden cross or a stone, the journey here would not have been in vain. The *not knowing* would be over.

The smell of baking bread brought her back to reality. It made her stomach rumble. She got up and followed her nose to the kitchen.

"Buenos días."

The miller's wife glanced up at Rose, murmuring something inaudible in reply. She was pounding something in a pestle and mortar.

"I wondered if I could buy some bread?"

"Un momento." Señora Carmona emptied the contents of the mortar into a metal pan and carried it through to the lofty room that housed the grinding equipment. Rose followed, thinking the woman was going to fetch a loaf. But the miller's wife set the concoction she'd been making on the side of one of the flour troughs and took a box of matches from the pocket of her apron.

Rose stood watching as a match was struck and held inside the pan until the contents caught fire. An acrid smell wafted across the room.

"What's that?" Rose coughed as the smoke caught her chest.

"It's for the flies!" The miller's wife swept out her arm. "It always works—they can't stand the smell."

"I'm not surprised," Rose spluttered. "What's in the pan?"

"Crushed garlic and the hottest peppers," the woman replied. "And human hair. I'm going to need more of that to do the rest of the house—perhaps you and your daughter can save me some from your hairbrushes."

Rose thought she'd rather put up with the flies than a smell like that. She glanced up at the rafters, where the swifts were darting around in a crazed aerial ballet.

"What about the birds?" Rose asked. "They have babies in their nests—the smoke might harm them."

"They will die." The woman shrugged. "But the parents can make more." She poked at the pan with a stick, stoking up the flames.

Rose looked away. Clearly life was still cheap in this place that had seen so much human bloodshed. What the miller's wife was doing went against everything Rose believed in. She had spent the whole of her adult life trying to save the lives of animals. To watch this wanton destruction was more than she could bear. The only way to stop herself giving the woman a mouthful of abuse was to leave the room.

"What about your bread?" Señora Carmona called after her.

Rose fought hard to resist the temptation to tell her what she could do with it. But there was no sense in getting herself and Nieve thrown out with nowhere else to go. She was just going to have to bite her tongue.

She dived into the kitchen and scanned the walls. There were jars of honey on one shelf and a row of goat cheeses wrapped in muslin on another. Grabbing one of each, she tossed fifty cents onto the table before running back up the stairs.

At midday Rose and Nieve were waiting outside the Church of Santa Cruz for the procession to begin. The Calle Veronica—the street that led through the town to the main square—was lined with little shrines that had sprung up overnight. The people who lived in the village had made them from tables covered in embroidered cloths, on which were placed towering arrangements of olive branches with white lilies woven into them. Lighted candles sat in jars in front of small statues of the crucified Christ or images of the Virgin Mary painted on wood.

Rose had thought about going to the church service—but she hadn't wanted to leave Gunesh in the room at the mill, which was uncomfortably hot by midmorning. It would have been difficult to get a seat in the church anyway—the whole village seemed to have turned out for what was no doubt a very important day in the life of the community. It was like a mass wedding—with miniature brides and grooms. The little girls had skipped up the steps of the church, with their white dresses trailing in the dust and their veils billowing in the breeze. Behind them the boys had marched stiffly, looking very self-conscious in starched suits embellished with gold braid, like pocket-size admirals.

After watching them go in, Rose and Nieve had taken Gunesh for a walk along the river, then come back for a drink at the fountain outside the church. As Rose filled her bottle with the gushing water, she thought about what she was going to say and do when the procession got underway. The best thing, she had decided, would be to make an admiring comment about the dress or suit of one of the boys or girls. Then once the conversation had progressed, she would say that she had come from England on a working vacation to write a book about animals. That, she hoped, would place her outside any simmering resentment that lingered between different factions of the local population.

"Look—they're coming out!" Nieve's voice broke through her thoughts. "There's Alonso—at the front."

The miller's son glanced this way and that at the people pouring out of the church, looking as if he wished the ground would open and swallow him up. Rose spotted his mother, clad entirely in black, coming down the steps. It was something she had noticed throughout Spain, this somber custom of dress the women had. It seemed that as soon as they reached their midtwenties, they wore only black when they were out in public—whether they were married, widowed, or single. To Rose it seemed very repressive—as if a woman over twenty-five was on the scrap heap and should no longer try to make herself attractive.

The children started to move forward, followed by a priest in richly embroidered robes who was swinging a censer. The perfumed smoke wafted over the parents, grandparents, aunts, and uncles assembled on either side of the street. As Rose watched, she couldn't help remembering what Cristóbal had said about the aftermath of the Civil War in small communities like Pampaneira:

In the villages, it's worse than in the cities because everyone knows what their neighbor did. It's like waking up with the worst hangover you've ever had.

What had these people done to each other? Had any of the men gazing proudly at their sons and daughters been members of the death squad that had raided Lola's house the day Nieve was born? Had any of these families lost mothers or sisters in the massacre that had followed?

It was strange to think that Nieve could be a blood relative of one or more of these people, that the gray-haired woman standing next to the miller's wife could be her grandmother, or the ruddy-faced man in the doorway of the church her uncle.

A young pregnant woman with black hair and a peacock shawl.

There had to be a way to find out the identity of Nieve's mother. But it would require an even greater degree of subtlety than the search for information about Nathan. And it could put Nieve in danger. If people found out the child was not Rose's daughter but an orphan, she could be at even greater risk from the authorities than if she'd remained in Granada. And what if there was a relative still living—someone who might claim her and prevent her going back to Lola?

As the procession wound its way along Calle Veronica, Rose caught sight of another group emerging from the church—strange adult figures robed in white like the children but with their faces obscured by hoods with tall pointed tops. They reminded Rose of grainy newspaper images she had seen of the Ku Klux Klan.

"Who are they?" she asked Nieve.

"The *penitentes*," Nieve replied. "They're people who've done bad things. They need to ask Jesus to forgive them—but they don't want to show their faces, because if they did, everyone would know they were bad."

In light of what had just been going through Rose's mind, the hooded figures looked very sinister indeed. The body shapes beneath the robes were all male. She wondered just how bad a person had to be to take part in this public display of repentance—and whether the sins they were atoning for were recent or historic. Could some of these men have been involved in the slaughter Lola had described?

Behind the *penitentes* came a group of middle-aged women chanting a mournful song. The intense, painful quality of the sound they made reminded Rose of the songs Cristóbal sang. She looked away, raising her head in case Nieve saw the look on her face. A blur flashed across her field of vision. Then another. Swifts were diving over the procession, feasting on the flies attracted by the smell of so many human bodies.

Rose, Nieve, and Gunesh fell into step at the back of the procession. After only a short distance, it came to a stop at the first of the little shrines. The priest sprinkled holy water on the olive boughs woven with lilies, reciting prayers that the children in white dutifully repeated. When they moved on again, Nieve asked if she could take Gunesh to the front to walk behind the children. Rose let her go. After a couple of minutes, the procession stopped at a second shrine. Rose turned to the woman walking alongside her.

"*¿No son encantadores?*" Aren't they lovely?

"*Sí, encantadores,*" the woman replied.

"Which one is yours?"

"That one." The woman pointed to a girl whose white satin frock was embellished with silver sequins at the neck and wrists.

"What a pretty dress." Rose paused for a moment, then she said, "I've never seen anything like this before—I'm visiting from England."

The woman's eyes widened. "What brings you to Pampaneira?"

Rose came out with the line about writing a book. Then she said, "My brother used to live here."

"In the village?"

"No—in the mountains. We . . . lost touch a few years ago. I'm not sure if he's still living around here . . ." She broke off with a shrug.

"How long ago did you last hear from him?"

Rose drew in a breath. There was no way of avoiding a direct answer. "About eight years ago."

The woman's face clouded.

"I have a photograph—perhaps you . . ."

She turned away before Rose could finish, elbowing her way through the crowd until she was hidden from view behind the shrine.

By the time the procession had completed its circuit of the village, Rose had had similar conversations with four other people. She had tried an elderly man, a woman in her fifties, and two young mothers. All four had reacted in the same way, polite interest turning to blank indifference the moment they realized that Nathan had been in the area during the Civil War.

As the crowd dispersed, Rose felt utterly despondent. Cristóbal had been right. It was as if a collective amnesia had fallen upon the inhabitants of Pampaneira. How on earth was she going to find out what had happened to Nathan if no one would even look at his photograph?

A breath of wind gusted through the square, sending a drift of petals from the little shrines. It caught Rose's earrings. She felt the twists of copper wire brush against her neck. She pushed her hair aside, checking that she hadn't lost either one. As her fingers touched the tiny blue beads, she thought of Jean Beau-Marie and what he'd said when he'd given them to her. She thought of what he had endured, seeing his entire family wiped out by the Nazis, and of the daily battle he now faced just to carry on living. It put her own despondency into perspective.

As if to underline the point, the bells of Santa Cruz chimed the hour. *Ring out the bad and the cruel. Ring in something better.*

It was as if Jean were sending her a message through the ether.

The next morning Rose was up and dressed by the time the sun rose over the mountains. She wanted bread for Nieve's breakfast—but she wasn't going to buy it from Señora Carmona. It wasn't just the business with the baby swifts: Rose suspected the woman had gone through her belongings while she and Nieve had been out for a walk the previous evening. There had been an impression on the bed—as if someone had sat on it—and her passport had been in the wrong pocket of her rucksack.

She made her way across the bridge that spanned the rushing water far below. On the opposite bank of the river, goats were being driven out of the houses. They were being taken out to pasture by men whose voices echoed through the cool morning air. She couldn't understand what they were shouting. It sounded like "She-bah! She-bah!" Their cries were accompanied by the musical tinkling of the goats' bells. Rose thought of Lola, doing what these men were doing on that fateful morning eight years ago, embarking on a daily routine with no idea that her life was about to be torn apart. And if it hadn't been her turn to take the goats out that morning—if her brother had gone instead—she wouldn't be alive and neither would Nieve.

When Rose reached the bakery, there was already a line of people out the door. She said good morning to the elderly woman standing in front of her—but got no response apart from an almost imperceptible nod of the head. If the woman was not in the mood to pass the time of day with a stranger, she was unlikely to be interested in Rose's search for Nathan. Perhaps she would have better luck later, when the post office opened. Buying stamps for her letters would be a good opportunity to ask questions.

With a loaf under her arm, Rose hurried back toward the bridge. She needed to get Nieve up and dressed and fed before half past seven if she was going to be in time for school. Although it was only a matter of weeks until classes ended for the summer holidays, Rose thought it would do Nieve good to be with other children.

On the way to Pampaneira, Rose hadn't been sure if Nieve would want to go to school. She thought the trauma of seeing Lola dragged off by the Guardia Civil would make the child too clingy and timid for such a big step. But making friends with Alonso had made all the difference. Now that Nieve already knew one of her classmates, she couldn't wait to go there.

As Rose crossed the bridge, she heard singing. The sound was coming from the river. Looking down, she saw women washing clothes in the stretch of water below the mill. They were singing as they beat the wet clothes on the rocks—the sweet, sad, throbbing chant of flamenco.

Cristóbal's face filled her mind's eye. She wondered what he was doing at this moment. He had talked about getting Juanita and the children away from Granada, to their relatives in the countryside. But Lola had said he wouldn't stay away from his beloved Granada for long. And Lola needed him. There was no one else to go and visit her in that dungeonlike police cell. Remembering the disdainful looks she had received, Rose wondered if Cristóbal would get past the front desk. Without the benefit of a British passport and unable to read and write, he was unlikely to be of much help to Lola.

Rose thought of the letters she had written last night. First she had written to Lola herself—a difficult letter to compose because she knew that it was certain to be read by her jailers. She wanted to convey hope for the future and reassurance about Nieve's well-being but was afraid of saying anything that might give away the fact that Nieve was with her in Pampaneira.

When she had finished that letter, she had written three more: one to the chief of the Guardia Civil, one to the mayor of Granada, and another to the mayor's wife. The last one had been an afterthought. It had occurred to her that the powerful men she was writing to might regard Lola's case in the same chauvinistic way as the arresting officers had—that Antonio Lopez had been guilty of no crime because he had repeatedly offered marriage and had the blessing of Lola's only male relative. But perhaps the mayor's wife would see things in a different light. Rose had no idea what kind of woman she was—all she knew was her last name—but desperate circumstances called for a leap of faith. The letter might not even get to her—but it was worth a try.

Chapter 20

Granada, Spain: The same day

Lola was beginning to lose track of time. There was a tiny window in the cell, too high to see out of. It must be north facing, she thought, because the sun never seemed to be on it. And the glass was so dirty it was impossible to tell if the sky was blue or gray. Was this her fourth morning or her fifth? She couldn't remember.

When she had woken up the previous day, the feeling of hopelessness had been overwhelming. Being locked up was terrifying. The rising panic she experienced every time she opened her eyes and realized where she was made it hard to breathe. But worse than that was the loss of Nieve. In eight years Lola had never spent a single night away from her. The ache in her heart was like a physical pain.

She had lain there on the hard, evil-smelling mattress, wanting to die. Images from her life ran through her mind's eye like a movie reel spinning out of control. She went back in time to the day she had found Nieve, wailing and bloody. She saw herself, moments before, lying down in the snow beside the bodies of her mother and Amador. She had wanted to die then. *Would* have died if she'd carried on lying there. But Nieve had saved her.

Don't die, Mama.

She'd heard the child's voice, so clear she had sat bolt upright on her bed in the cell. *Oh God,* she thought, *I'm losing my mind.*

It was then that her body had taken over, moving trancelike, in the only way she had ever known to obliterate anguish. She got to her feet, unsteady at first, and stood in the center of the tiny room. She stretched out her arms. There was less than a foot between her fingertips and the walls—but that was enough. Then she raised her arms above her head. A naked lightbulb dangled from the ceiling, only an inch or two higher than her hands. But if she was careful, she could avoid hitting it.

She made the shape of bird wings with her fingers. She thrust out her chest and angled her hips, holding her head erect and proud. She didn't need music. It was all there, in her head. With a defiant stamp of her right foot, she launched into the dance sequence she had performed on the last night of the competition in Provence. The one that had won the prize.

She danced with her eyes open for fear of crashing into the walls, but she didn't see the dingy, graffiti-covered bricks or the rusty barred door. What she saw was Nieve's face, glowing with excitement as she clapped out the rhythm.

"What's going on in there? Gypsy whore!"

There was a rattle of metal as the door hatch slid open. She could see a pair of eyes through the slit.

"Nothing," she hissed.

"It didn't sound like nothing," the guard replied. "Sounded like hammering. What have you got hidden away?"

"Nothing," she repeated, holding out her hands. "I was dancing, that's all—there's no law against that, is there?"

"Dancing?" He made a sound like a pig grunting. "Well, there won't be much time for that where you're going! The only dance they do at Málaga prison is the shitters' shuffle!"

Lola stared at him in horrified silence.

"Do you know what they'll do when you get there?" he hissed. "It's the same thing they did to the red whores during the war: First they shave your head. Then they force-feed you with castor oil to clean out all the evil shit inside you. Then they strip you naked and march you through the streets on a mule so everyone can see your disgrace." He huffed out a breath. "You'd be there now, but there's no space. Still, it won't be long—something to look forward to, eh?" He slammed the hatch shut.

Lola slumped on the bed, burying her face in the rough blanket.

Don't cry, Mama. Rose is writing letters. She won't let them do that to you.

"Oh, Nieve," Lola sobbed. "Where are you?"

Chapter 21

The village school was on the northern outskirts of the village, beside a track that led farther up the mountain. Each morning, when Rose, Nieve, and Gunesh made their way there, they passed a fingerpost with three place names carved into it: Órgiva, Trevélez, and Capileira. The last one was Lola's village. According to the sign, it was four miles up the mountain. Rose wondered if she could get there and back by the time Nieve finished school. Given its altitude, the terrain was likely to be even more difficult than the route up from Órgiva had been. It would be foolish to set out without food and water, neither of which she had with her.

Glancing up as she waved goodbye to Nieve, Rose caught sight of a group of women coming down the hillside. They carried big baskets on their heads. As they passed by, Rose could smell the herbs they had been gathering—fennel, wild garlic, mint, and thyme. She recognized the leader of the group as one of the people she'd tried to talk to at the Corpus Christi procession.

The silent treatment meted out that afternoon had been repeated at the post office the next day. Rose was beginning to wonder whether the whole village had been on the side of the fascists. That would explain their antipathy to anyone who had fought on the opposite side. But if that was the case, would Nathan really have risked coming here to buy tobacco? And would a girl from a fascist family have embarked on a relationship with an enemy soldier?

The second scenario was not as unlikely as the first—she'd heard of many instances of British girls marrying German or Italian prisoners of war. But perhaps there was another way of interpreting the villagers' reticence to talk: Could it be that they were still afraid, as Lola was afraid? Were they republican sympathizers, still scared of reprisals? Did General Franco's network of neighborhood spies extend to a place as small as this?

They were questions that she couldn't answer. All she knew was that she had come up against a brick wall. Traveling to Lola's village seemed like the only option left to her. In Capileira at least, Rose knew that there had been people who sided with the partisans—people like Lola's family, who had risked their lives to help men like Nathan. Surely, they couldn't all have been executed? There must be some who had survived the war.

She was still thinking about it as she led Gunesh down the path that led back to the village. The route took them through a meadow covered in wildflowers—chamomile, parsley, sorrel, and goat's rue. And among the creamy whites and pale yellows, swathes of poppies splashed the hillside like bloodstains. It was as if the landscape itself were a silent witness to what had happened in this place.

Rose let Gunesh run free for a while before summoning him back with a shrill whistle. Then they made their way toward the village. Before they reached the houses, they passed a weaving shed with baskets outside, heaped with raw silk. There was a mule tied to a post, and she went to stroke it. But before she could, a surly-looking man emerged from the shed and yanked the animal loose of the rope that tethered it, leading it into the building. Moments later it emerged, its panniers loaded with bales of woven silk. She remembered that today was market day in Pampaneira. No doubt the silk was on its way there.

She wound her way down through Calle Veronica until she reached the main square. The stalls were a riot of color, piled high with peppers, eggplants, onions, and tomatoes. Great flat fillets of salted cod glistened like snow in the sunshine, and fat black sausages dangled from lines of string rigged overhead.

Over by the fountain there was a man selling cherries. Cherries were just right for a trek up the mountain—sweet, moist, and easy to carry.

She felt very conspicuous as she crossed the square. It wasn't just Gunesh that made her stand out from the other women clustered around the stalls—she was the only female over twenty-five not dressed in black.

"Quiero algunas cerezas, por favor." I'd like some cherries, please.

He looked up from what he was doing—picking leaves and the odd shriveled berry from the baskets of glistening fruit. Rose was immediately struck by his warm smile. His eyes were blue—not blue green like Cristóbal's, but a clear, pale shade, like the sky on a frosty morning. He was dressed like a Gypsy, with a red neckerchief and a leather waistcoat. But he didn't have the olive skin. His hair was light brown. And he was the tallest person she had seen since coming to Spain.

"Por supuesto, ¿cuántas quiere?" Of course—how many would you like? He had a different accent from the other people she had spoken to.

Rose hesitated. *"¿Una libra?"* She still hadn't got the hang of the units of weight in Spain. She thought a libra was roughly equivalent to a pound—but she had no real idea how many cherries that would give her.

As the man began scooping them into the scales, a wasp buzzed around her head. Gunesh jumped up, snapping at it. Then she felt it flying into her hair.

"Get off me!" She hissed the words in her own language as she batted it away.

The man hovered over the scales, the scoop in his hand. "It's a little over a libra—is that all right?" He spoke in English.

Rose smiled in surprise. "Your English is very good," she said.

"Thank you." He smiled back. "But it's not nearly as good as my cherries. If it was, it would be excellent." He looked at his stall and shrugged. "I would have brought twice as many as this down from the mountain, but my other mule is unwell."

"What's the matter with him?"

"He has a sore on his back—at the base of the neck—that won't heal. I can't put a saddle or panniers on him."

"What's the sore like? Does it scab over?"

The man shook his head. "It just keeps weeping. I've tried bathing it with iodine, but it doesn't seem to help."

Rose nodded. "It might be something called fistulous withers. It's an infection of a fluid sac near the animal's spine."

His eyes widened. "Really? You sound as if you know what you're talking about."

"I'm a vet." She felt herself blushing. She wasn't sure why. There was something disarming in those blue eyes. "Where do you live?" she asked. "If you could take me to the animal, I might be able to help."

He tipped the cherries into a paper bag and handed them over, leaning across to stroke Gunesh as he did so. "It's kind of you to offer. But it's a mile or so up the mountain—near the old bunkers."

"Bunkers?"

"Where the partisans had their base. Have you been up there?"

Rose caught her breath. For the first time since she'd arrived in this village, someone was talking openly about the Civil War. "I haven't," she said, "but I'd like to."

Rose went back to the cherry stall at two o'clock, when the market traders were packing up for the day. She knew his name now—Zoltan Varga—and the fact that he was a Hungarian Gypsy who had come to Spain as a refugee at the end of the war in Europe. He had listened intently when she had told him about Nathan. He told her he'd found boxes of documents, some of which appeared to be in English, in the abandoned cottage where he was now living.

It had been too difficult to go on talking after that—a queue of customers had formed behind Rose—but he had asked her to come back in the afternoon.

"How did you do today?" she asked as he smiled a greeting.

"Not bad," he replied. "It's going to be an easy ride home."

Rose desperately wanted to go with him. It was tantalizing, knowing that he had papers that could hold some clue to what had happened to her brother. But there was Nieve to consider. She would be coming out of school in an hour's time, tired and hungry. It wouldn't be fair to drag her up the mountain.

"If you don't mind coming down again tomorrow, I could meet you by the school," she said. "Do you have any potatoes at home?"

"Potatoes?" His forehead crinkled.

"For the sick mule. If it *is* fistulous withers, the remedy I'd use is a mixture of potato skins and garlic. If you haven't got any, I can buy some and bring them with me."

"You don't have to do that. I can get them from Maria Andorra—the old woman who supplies the cherries."

Rose nodded. "You'll need to peel about six potatoes and boil the peelings in a big pan of water for an hour. Then add four cloves of garlic and leave them to soak overnight. If you do that, I can get started with the cure right away."

"Okay." He bent over to fasten the buckle that held the panniers in place on the mule's back. "Actually, it might be interesting for you to meet Maria—she used to supply the partisans with food."

"Would she talk to me?" Rose frowned. "No one else around here seems to want to discuss what went on during the war."

"Well, it's a tricky subject. But Maria's not like other people—she's a force of nature. She's not afraid of anyone." He tapped the side of his nose with his finger. "She has friends in high places."

Rose tried hard to suppress the surge of hope his words had set off. But it wasn't easy.

"See you in the morning, then." His lips parted, revealing perfect white teeth. Unusual for a Gypsy. The combination of tobacco smoke and a nomadic lifestyle tended to make the men's mouths their least attractive feature.

"Yes." Rose smiled back. "See you in the morning."

Chapter 22

Zoltan was waiting for Rose a few yards from the school gate when she dropped Nieve off the next day. He tipped his hat to them as they came up the track.

"Who's that?" Nieve whispered.

"It's the man I was telling you about—the one who has the sick mule."

"It doesn't look very sick to me."

"He's got two, that's why!" Rose ruffled Nieve's hair.

"Are you *both* going to ride on that one?" The child gave her a mischievous look.

"Nieve! He's brought it for *me* to ride—though I'm perfectly capable of walking up the mountain." Rose shooed her off to join her classmates.

When she reached Zoltan, Gunesh was already there, jumping up and licking his face.

"Get down, Gunesh!" She grabbed the dog's collar.

"It's all right," Zoltan said. "He's a fine animal, isn't he?" He cocked his head toward the school. "And your little girl is very pretty."

"Thank you." Rose turned to stroke the mule, unable to meet his eye. "Her name is Nieve."

"As in the Spanish for snow?"

"Yes. It was snowing when she was born." To change the subject, she asked him where he'd learned to speak English.

"From the soldiers who liberated the camp I was in."

Rose's hand stopped halfway down the mule's neck. "You were in one of the death camps?"

"Yes." His eyes went to his feet. "I was in a place called Mauthausen. In Austria."

"I'm sorry—I didn't mean to . . ."

"You don't have to apologize." He cupped his hands, making a step to help her to climb onto the mule's back. "I try not to think about it."

"I can understand that." She settled herself into the saddle. "Two of my relatives died in concentration camps."

He looked up at her, blinking as the sun caught his eyes.

"They were Jews living in Paris."

"That's terrible. I . . ." He trailed off, looking away.

Rose wondered if, like Jean Beau-Marie, he had lost family members in the camp. Perhaps, like Jean, he wished he had died alongside them. Clearly it was a part of his life he didn't want to revisit. His awkward silence made her change the subject. "This is a very beautiful part of Spain, isn't it?" she said. "I love all the rivers and wildflowers."

"You've come at the best time." He took the reins and began leading the mule up the track. "It's hard to believe now how cold it was in March—much colder than anywhere else I've lived. I was snowed in for a whole week."

"How did you survive?"

"On chestnuts." He made a wry face. "Luckily I had plenty of firewood—the partisans had left a stack of logs behind. Otherwise I might have frozen to death up there." With his free hand he pointed to the rugged peak of the mountain silhouetted against the sky. "It's higher than the highest peaks of the Pyrenees. Have you heard the name of it?"

Rose shook her head.

"The local people call it the Mulhacén—after the last Moorish ruler of Granada. They say he asked to be buried up there." He looked over his shoulder at the land falling away behind them. "Not a bad place to spend eternity, is it?"

It was just a throwaway remark, but for Rose it conjured an image of Nathan lying alone and abandoned. She drew in a breath and expelled it slowly, trying to dispel the dark thoughts that crowded in. Zoltan was right. If her worst fears were confirmed, she must console herself with the fact that this wild, beautiful landscape was exactly what her brother would have chosen as a final resting place.

She twisted around in the saddle, following Zoltan's gaze. She could see the river gorge and the tiny houses hugging the bank. Beyond them, to the east, was another, lower mountain range. The shadows the sun cast on its spurs and ravines gave it the look of crumpled curtains.

"Oh! I can see the sea!" Rose shaded her eyes with her hand.

"Can you see a dark smudge above the blue?"

"What is it?"

"It's Africa: Morocco. The Rif Mountains."

Rose felt her spirits lifting. How amazing, she thought, to be able to see another continent when you walked out your front door each morning. No wonder Zoltan had chosen to settle in this place. A view like this was balm to the soul.

"Where in the village are you living?" he asked as he guided the mule around an outcrop of weathered limestone.

"At the mill across the bridge. It's the only place that allows dogs."

"How do you like it?"

"The room is okay." She shrugged.

"But the landlady is not so nice?" He shot her a knowing look.

Rose hesitated. "I don't think she likes me very much—I'm not sure why."

"She's not a happy person. Her husband was beaten to death by the men of the village during the Civil War."

"Poor man—what had he done?"

"Well, Maria—the old lady I was telling you about—says he was a spy for the fascists. When people came to buy flour, he used to find out what was going on in the village—who was taking messages to the partisans, who was supplying them with food and ammunition. When they found out who had betrayed them, they dragged him all the way to the village square and clubbed him to death, right in front of the church."

Rose thought of Alonso throwing stones so aggressively into the river, and his sister, hard faced and imperious. Bad enough that they had lost their father—but to know that he had been murdered by the fathers of their classmates must be unbearable.

"Señora Carmona is a very bitter woman," Zoltan went on. "She's always spreading what the Spanish call *mala leche*."

"Bad milk?"

"Yes. She never has a good word to say about anyone. I'd be careful what you tell her."

Rose nodded. "I haven't mentioned my brother to her. I told her I'd come here to write a book about animals."

Zoltan tightened his grip on the lead rein as the path narrowed. Ahead of them was a spectacular waterfall tumbling over moss-covered rocks into a pool of turquoise water.

"It's very dangerous up here," Zoltan said. "It's all the meltwater from the glacier at the top of the mountain."

Rose looked longingly at the pool. It didn't look dangerous. If she had been on her own, she would have been very tempted to strip off and jump in.

"We're almost there now." Zoltan pointed to a clump of trees on the ridge above the waterfall. "The bunkers are just beyond those trees."

She would never have spotted the bunkers if she'd come up the mountain alone. Bushes camouflaged the entrance to the system of tunnels and trenches that had been dug into the hillside. Bees hovered over the golden blossoms of broom. A skylark flew out of a tangle of ripening brambles. The waterfall was nothing more than a distant murmur.

"I found a gun lying down there." Zoltan pointed to a spot just below the bush the bird had emerged from. "It was a big old-fashioned hunting rifle with what looked like a bullet hole right through the barrel."

It was hard to imagine violence in such a place. The thought of Nathan holed up here, ready to shoot enemy troops, made Rose go cold. But he must have been here. It was exactly as he had described it in his letter: a hiding place in the mountains above the village where he had met his fiancée.

A few minutes later Zoltan was leading Rose toward a low stone cottage with a barrel-vaulted roof. As she climbed down from the animal's back, he said, "Go on in while I sort him out. I'll make us some coffee. Then we can go and take a look at the sick one."

Rose pushed open the weathered wooden door of the little house. An enticing smell came wafting out—a savory, salty aroma with a tang of herbs. Fennel and mint and something else she couldn't identify. It was coming from a metal pot suspended over a smoldering log fire at the opposite end of the room. Above the fireplace was a hefty pair of animal horns, and on the stone floor in front of it was an enormous fur rug. Gunesh went straight over to the rug and buried his nose in it, sniffing all around the edges. The texture of the hair and the color of it—gray speckled with black and white—suggested only one animal to Rose: a wolf.

"I hope you're not thinking I was responsible for those." Zoltan gestured to the horns as he came through the door. "I do shoot the odd rabbit for the pot—but I'd never kill a magnificent creature like that."

"What was it?"

"An ibex. They're like goats, only much bigger. I see them sometimes up on the ridge above the house." He dropped to his knees, patting the wolf-skin rug. "As for this fellow, I assume he was making a nuisance of himself. Probably came looking for food, not expecting to run into a bunch of armed men."

"You think some of the partisans were living here?"

"They were certainly coming here." He took a poker from a hook on the wall and prodded the fire back to life. "The bunkers were the focus of activity—I think this place was used for preparing food and stabling animals. I found the boxes of documents under a pile of straw. It looked as if they'd been hidden there by someone who'd had to make a hasty escape." He unhooked the stew pot, hanging a kettle in its place. "Shall I get the boxes? You must be desperate to know if there's anything of your brother's there."

"No—it's okay," Rose replied. "Let's go and see the mule first." The prospect of searching through what Zoltan had found made her stomach flip over. She was almost afraid to look, afraid of building up her hopes only to have them dashed if there was nothing there.

The sight of the sick animal forced her to put all other thoughts aside. It had a weeping sore the size of an apple at the base of its neck. Rose took a closer look while Zoltan held the animal's head.

"Yes," she said, "I can see it's infected—it smells pretty awful, doesn't it?"

Zoltan nodded. "The man in the next stall to mine at the market said I'd have to shoot it. He reckons the thing you said it was is incurable."

"A lot of people think that. But I met Gypsies in England who knew how to cure it—that's where I got the remedy from."

"Hmm. There were people in Hungary like that, on my mother's side of the family. I didn't have much to do with animals, though, when I was living there."

Rose hesitated, wondering if he was going to tell her more about his life before coming to Spain, but he didn't—and she didn't want to press him. "Have you got the potato and garlic water ready?" she asked.

"It's in that bucket over there."

"Okay. He's not going to like it, so hold on tight." Rose took a clean piece of rag from her bag and dipped it in the bucket. "Steady, boy!" Between them they managed to keep the mule from rearing up.

"You're going to need to bathe it four times a day until it stops weeping," Rose said. "It shouldn't be quite so much of a shock to him next time. Do you think you'll manage?"

"I think so."

"You need to starve him for twenty-four hours—nothing but water," she went on. "Then give him bran with a dollop of honey mixed in—and a handful each of these." From her bag she produced two bunches of herbs that she'd picked from the riverbank on the way to Nieve's school.

"Is that watercress?"

"Yes—and wild garlic."

"And that's it? No medicine?"

"That *is* the medicine." She smiled. "He should be as right as rain in a week or so."

The kettle was steaming when they went back into the cottage. Zoltan fetched the boxes from upstairs while the coffee was brewing. Then they both started sifting through the letters, identity papers, photographs, and maps. Rose glanced across the table. Zoltan was unlike any Gypsy she had ever met. He was scanning the documents as if he'd been reading all his life.

"I started looking when I got home yesterday," Zoltan said. "I went through all the envelopes with British stamps on—but I didn't find anything with your brother's name on it."

"Some of the letters aren't in envelopes." Rose held a sheet of thin blue airmail paper up to the light. "Did you look at those?"

Zoltan shook his head. "There are notes scribbled on scraps of cardboard, too. Do you think you'd recognize his handwriting?"

Rose took Nathan's letter from her pocket and laid it out on the table. Then they both fell silent, scanning each item and piling them up beside their coffee cups. The knot in Rose's stomach tightened as she read through heartfelt letters from people just like herself. Women who had brothers, sweethearts, husbands, or sons who had left everything behind to join the war against the fascists. And then there were the photographs—images of women, mostly, smiling out with eager, hopeful eyes. Some had messages written in tiny letters at the bottom of the photo or scribbled on the reverse side. To read them was agonizing. Rose wondered if any of these women had seen their loved ones return home.

Zoltan looked up as she was gazing at a particularly moving image of two little boys in Santa Claus hats, waving at the camera. "Not all of them have names on, do they?" he said. "I'll put any like that over on this side for you to have a look at."

Rose drew in a breath as she laid the image of the children aside. She thought it a slim chance that any of the pictures belonged to Nathan. He had never mentioned a girlfriend back in England, and he had left in such a hurry—and in such high spirits—it was unlikely he would have thought of packing a family photograph in his rucksack.

"This is a strange one." Zoltan's voice broke through her thoughts. "It's dedicated to an animal, not a person."

"An animal?"

"Yes. It's written in Spanish. It says 'To the horse, with all my love.'"

Rose leaned across to look at the snapshot in his hand. His thumb was over the face of a woman with long dark hair. "Can I have a look?"

Al Caballo con todo mi amor, Adelita.

Rose's mouth opened but no sound came out.

"What? What is it?"

"My brother," she whispered. "His nickname was Horse."

Rose was afraid to believe that the photograph belonged to Nathan. She told herself that a nickname like that could be commonplace in Spain—although Zoltan didn't agree. It took them another hour of careful searching to find something that corroborated the theory that the girl in the snapshot was her brother's fiancée. It was a note, written in pencil on the back of a railway timetable. Rose recognized Nathan's distinctive, sloping scrawl. It simply said "Tell Adelita I'll be there for Our Lady of the Snows."

"What does he mean?" Rose pushed the note across the table for Zoltan to see.

"It's a *romería*—a sort of pilgrimage they have here in August," he replied. "There's a little shrine on top of the Mulhacén called the Ermita de la Virgen de las Nieves. It was put there by a traveler who got caught in a summer blizzard sometime last century. The storm was closing in, and the only thing he could do was pray. He begged to be saved, if he was worthy. According to the story, he saw a vision of the Virgin Mary, and he promised to build her a shrine if he came through the storm alive." Zoltan shrugged. "So now, on the anniversary of the storm, people come from all the villages down the valley to climb up to it."

Our Lady of the Snows. The name had an ethereal, magical quality. Rose wondered if it had been in Lola's mind when she named Nieve. Perhaps she had even walked past the shrine on that long, desperate trek over the Sierra Nevada.

"When they get there, the priest performs an outdoor communion service. I went to watch last year. It's very cold up there—even on a sunny day. Sometimes, even in August, it's blowing a gale—but they do the pilgrimage whatever the weather."

"It's strange to think of my brother doing that," Rose said. "He was never interested in religion. I suppose it would have been an opportunity for him to meet Adelita without drawing attention to himself." If Nathan had written that note in August, the relationship would have been going on for at least eight months by the time of his last letter home. If the pregnancy had happened early on, the birth of the baby could have happened as early as April 1938. Rose picked up the photograph, gazing into the big dark eyes. Although the girl was smiling, there was an indefinable sadness about her.

As if she knew.

Knew what? The image began to blur. Rose almost felt that if she stared at it for long enough, the answer would come through some sort of telepathy. She blew out a breath. If only that could be true.

"You said they wanted to get to France," Zoltan said. "Do you know when they were planning to do that?"

Rose shook her head. "He sent this last letter in March 1938. All he said was that things were going badly and they needed to get out."

"This is going to be hard for you to hear." He pressed his hands together, steepling his fingers. "There were people from Spain in the camp I was in. Men like your brother, who managed to cross the border into France, were rounded up by the Germans when they took control of the country. There were women, too. Mauthausen was where all the Spanish prisoners were taken."

Rose's throat felt as if it were closing over. She groped inside her bag for the photograph of Nathan. "This is my brother." Her voice sounded croaky. She watched Zoltan's face intently, terrified of what she might see, but just as afraid of his covering up to spare her feelings.

"No." He looked up, holding her gaze. "I never saw him."

"And what about her?" Rose laid the images side by side on the table.

Zoltan shook his head. "I don't know. The women were in a different part of the camp."

"There would be records, though, wouldn't there? I know her first name and roughly how old she was."

"The Nazis destroyed all the records when they knew the Allies were coming," Zoltan said.

Rose stared at the faces in front of her. Part of her was relieved that Zoltan didn't recognize Nathan. If he wasn't in the camp, there was a chance that he had escaped somewhere else, that he and the girl and their child were still alive. But if that were true, where were they?

"I don't know what to do," she breathed.

"You need to talk to Maria—she knows everyone around here. I'd take you to see her now, but she's gone to Granada to visit her sister." Zoltan stood up. "Let me get you something to eat." He went over to the fire and unhooked the pot that had been hanging there when Rose first entered the cottage. "The Alpujarreños call it *puchero de hinojos*. Fennel stew. Would you like some?"

Rose didn't feel like eating, but it seemed rude to refuse the steaming bowl he set down in front of her. And when she put the spoon to her mouth, the taste was as good as the smell.

"Maria gave me the recipe," he said when she complimented him. "I wasn't much of a cook when I came here—I had to learn fast."

"Why did you choose Spain? When you were liberated, I mean."

"I couldn't go back to Hungary." He stared into his soup, his spoon midway between the bowl and his mouth. "Too many bad memories. I was a partisan, like your brother—we carried out guerrilla raids against the fascists when they took over my country." He huffed out a breath, glancing at the spoon as if he'd forgotten he was holding it. "I wanted a new start—somewhere far away from all that, somewhere far away from people, too, if I'm honest."

"I can understand that," Rose said. "You must have seen the worst things human beings are capable of in Mauthausen."

The muscles of his jaw tightened, as if he'd decided not to let out whatever he might have been about to tell her. Instead he said, "Would you like more coffee?"

Rose watched him as he filled the kettle. Hardly surprising, she thought, if, just like Jean Beau-Marie, he wanted to keep the horror of what had happened in the camp locked up inside. But he wasn't completely like Jean—he didn't have that aura of melancholy following him like a dark cloud.

Gunesh was sprawled on the wolf-skin rug in front of the fire. Zoltan crouched down beside him, rubbing the dog's head. Rose smiled as Gunesh rolled over onto his back, wanting his tummy tickled.

"How long will you stay in Pampaneira?" Zoltan glanced up at her, his fingers half-hidden in Gunesh's fur.

"I . . . I'm not sure."

"Does it depend on what you find out about your brother?"

"Partly, yes." She hesitated, wanting to tell him the truth about Nieve, about the trauma of Lola's arrest and the danger of returning to Granada. It would be such a relief to pour it all out to someone. She pressed her lips shut, reminding herself that she'd known this man for only twenty-four hours. Yes, he'd been kind and helpful—but could she really trust him?

"Well," he said, "I hope you'll still be here at the end of next week."

"Why?"

"It's the night of San Juan—a big fiesta in the villages around here."

"A fiesta?" She echoed his words, her mind suddenly filled with Cristóbal's face. "There seem to be an awful lot of them—what's this one about?"

"It's supposed to mark the beginning of summer," Zoltan replied. "Although it's so hot already you wouldn't know the difference."

The beginning of summer.

It sounded like a promise of something good to come. She reached across the table for the railway timetable with Nathan's scrawled note on the back. To be in a room that Nathan would have known, holding something he had written, was more than she ever could have hoped for. But it was only part of the story. How agonizing to learn that the woman who might know the rest was in the city Rose had left just days ago. Now there was nothing she could do but wait.

Chapter 23

Granada, Spain

Every time Lola heard the cell door rattle, she began to tremble uncontrollably, wondering if this day would be the one they came to drag her off to Málaga prison. She had become acutely aware of the different sounds the door made. Even in the dark she could tell if the rasp of metal on metal signaled the hatch being pulled back for the delivery of food and water or the door being unlocked for someone to come inside.

This time it was not just the scrape of the key in the lock that she heard. There were voices. More than one person had come to her cell. What did that mean? Had they come to get her? Did they think it would take more than one guard to get her from the police station to the truck that would take her to prison?

But when the door opened, it was not a guard she saw but a priest. His face was in shadow, and even when he stepped into the cell, it was difficult to make out his features in the gray light filtering through the window.

"Buenos días, mi niña." Good morning, my child.

His voice sounded young. As she came closer, she heard the door lock behind him.

"Buenos días." Her own voice sounded ancient. They were the first words she had uttered in days. She hadn't asked for a priest. Why was he here? Fearful images crowded her mind. Was this what they did when they were about to take you out and shoot you?

"Please, sit down." He gestured to the bed, which was the only place to sit. "I want to help you if I can."

"Help me?" she echoed. "How can you do that?"

"Do you believe, child?"

Lola glanced up at the window. A week ago, she would have answered yes without a second thought. In her darkest times she had always prayed to God and the saints for help. The day she had lost her mother and brother and found Nieve, she had spent the night at the little shrine at the top of the mountain. She had got down on her knees to beg the Virgin of the Snows to get her and the baby safely across the mountains to Granada. But the horror of being imprisoned, of losing Nieve, of facing a life behind bars for killing a man who had tried to rape her—how could she go on believing? How could a loving God allow that to happen?

"It's hard for you, I know," he said. "But if you keep faith, your burden will be easier to bear."

"How?" There was a defiant edge to her voice. *Easy for him to say,* she thought.

"You must be lonely here. They tell me you have family in Sacromonte. Have they come to visit you?"

"They're Gypsies. You know how the police are with us."

"Ah." He nodded. "That must be very hard for you. You have a child, too, don't you? A little girl?"

Lola's eyes flashed with suspicion. "Who told you that?"

"Someone who knows you and cares about the welfare of the child."

So this was what the visit was all about. Nothing to do with her spiritual welfare—just a ruse to find Nieve and cart her off to a convent. "They were telling lies," she hissed. "I don't have a daughter."

"God knows the secrets of our hearts, my child—you risk eternal damnation if you hide the truth from his servant."

"I don't have a child!" The words echoed off the walls. "Give me a Bible—I'll swear on it!"

She heard him draw in a breath. "That won't be necessary. But let me put this to you: if it were true—if you did have a daughter, and you were able to tell me where to find her—you could expect merciful treatment from the judge when your case comes to court."

Lola closed her eyes. She didn't want him to see the tears she was fighting to contain. Trade Nieve for . . . what? A shorter term in jail? A sentence served in a prison less brutal than Málaga? No. Even if this priest had come to her offering her freedom, she couldn't, wouldn't offer up Nieve as a sacrifice.

Swallowing her tears, she opened her eyes and turned them directly on him. "*If* I had a daughter," she said, slowly and deliberately, "I would warn her about people like you. Tell me, Father, what do you think Jesus would say if he was sitting here with us, listening to what you've just said? Do you think he'd approve of people who call themselves Christians snatching babies and children from their parents?"

The priest said nothing in reply. He stood up, making the sign of the cross in the air. "May God have mercy on your soul," he murmured.

Chapter 24

Pampaneira, Spain

It was three days before Rose went up the mountain again. Now that she knew the way, she told Zoltan she could make the journey alone, on foot. But he asked if he could come and meet her halfway. There was something he wanted to show her—nothing to do with the war, he said—just something he thought she'd like to see.

The sun was already warm on her back when she waved Nieve goodbye and set off up the track. For the first time, the child had run into school without turning back for a last glimpse of Rose. She was making impressive progress with her reading, and she was excited about taking part in a dance display the children were putting on for the San Juan fiesta.

As Rose climbed higher, she turned to look at the valley below. She could see Órgiva, nestled in a bend of the river, and the orange and olive groves she had passed through on her way to Pampaneira. In the far distance was the Contraviesa mountain range, not as high as the Sierra Nevada, wrinkled waves of red and yellow and lilac spreading out in a carpet to the sea.

She walked on, through meadows studded with poppies, daisies, and purple vetch. The only sounds were the babble of running water and the high, piping call of skylarks. It was hard to resist the temptation to stop and gather bunches of the wildflowers growing in such profusion. In England she spent most weekends in spring and summer traveling to the countryside to harvest dozens of different herbs for her veterinary practice. The airing cupboard of her London apartment was so stuffed with drying vegetation that there was no room for sheets and towels.

As she made her way along the bank of a fast-flowing stream, Rose spotted something she hadn't noticed when she'd come this way with Zoltan—a ruined mill of ivy-covered stone half-hidden by chestnut trees. The door had long since fallen into the undergrowth. Stepping over the threshold was like entering an ancient fairy-tale world. Wild violets and blue convolvulus had seeded themselves in the crumbling windowsills, and the floor was covered in a carpet of pale-yellow wood sorrel. In what must once have been the fireplace was the skeleton of a sheep, undisturbed by predators, as if a spell had been cast over the old mill, keeping all other creatures out.

She couldn't help wondering if Nathan had been in this place. Perhaps he and Adelita had had secret rendezvous here, halfway between her village and the bunkers. She could almost see them sitting together on the moss-covered grinding wheel, talking in excited whispers about the baby and planning their escape to France.

"Where are you?"

Her voice sounded very loud. The only answer was the gush of water racing past. She tried to shrug off the sense of hopelessness that enveloped her as she walked away from the ruined building. But it wasn't easy. She'd had a tantalizing glimpse of Nathan's life here—but no clue as to what had happened next. Unless Zoltan's cherry-farming friend had something to tell her, it felt like the end of the road.

Zoltan was waiting for her in the shade of a broom bush whose branches dripped golden blossoms.

"I have to tell you about the mule!" His eyes were alight. "The wound's healed up already!"

"That's wonderful." She smiled. "But don't stop the treatment yet— he needs to be on that bran mixture for at least a week."

He nodded, leading her away from the track, through a thicket of chestnut and maple trees. "How are things at the mill?"

"Just about bearable," Rose replied. "I think she stole something from my room yesterday. It was only a tin of coffee—not worth much in monetary terms—but the tin was one I brought from home. It belonged to my mother. I've no proof that Señora Carmona took it—but I can't find it anywhere."

"Have you asked her about it?"

Rose shook her head. "I'm afraid she'd do something worse if I did. She's always killing things—she'd probably put rat poison in our water jug."

"What a horrible woman. Couldn't you move to one of the other villages?"

"I probably could. But Nieve's settled into the school in Pampaneira. She seems very happy there. I wouldn't want to make her start again somewhere else."

Zoltan nodded. "We're nearly there, by the way. The thing I wanted to show you is just beyond those trees."

"What is it?"

"You'll see in a minute." He smiled. "Better keep a tight hold of Gunesh—he might get a bit spooked."

When they reached the edge of the woodland, he put his fingers to his lips and dropped down to the ground, signaling Rose to do the same. "Can you see? Over there?"

At first, Rose couldn't work out what she was looking at. They were in a clearing, the ground in front of them dry and dusty where the sun had penetrated the trees. Suddenly she saw a flicker of movement—something thin and whiplike flicking out of the parched soil. Then, a foot or so to the left, she caught a glimpse of a brown zigzag pattern arching sideways.

"Snakes!" she whispered. She felt Gunesh straining at the lead and put her hand out to pat him on the shoulder. "What are they doing?"

"It's a sort of love dance," Zoltan whispered back. "Watch!"

Rose gazed, transfixed, as the two creatures reared up, advancing toward each other until they collided, then twining and twisting their slim, supple bodies in a swaying rhythm. She could see the thin tongues extended as the snakes shifted this way and that, their courtship dance stirring ghostly waves of dust up from the ground. The way they moved was as graceful and symmetrical as ripples across a pool when a pebble is thrown in.

"Wow," she breathed. "That must be one of the strangest sights on earth!"

"They're Iberian adders," he said. "This is their favorite spot."

"How did you know where to find them?"

"I come down here for honey—there are beehives on the other side of those trees. I first saw the snakes a couple of weeks ago. It must be the time of year for mating."

As they left the clearing and made their way back to the track, a bird piped up from a branch overhead. Rose recognized the call. It was a haunting sound, a fast succession of rich notes, high and low. She'd heard the same song in the Sussex marshes the night she'd said goodbye to Nathan.

"What do you call that in English?" Zoltan glanced upward.

"A nightingale."

"The Spanish call them *ruiseñores*. They say the birds have pearls and corals in their throats."

"That's a lovely way to describe it," Rose said. "I've never heard them sing in the daytime before."

"It's quite common here—I don't know why. There are a lot of them up at Maria's place. They seem to like mulberry bushes—and she has dozens of them."

Rose remembered the silk-weaving shed she had passed in Pampaneira. She asked Zoltan if his friend farmed silkworms as well as cherries.

He nodded. "She weaves the silk herself. She has goats as well. It's quite a big place. She runs it all on her own—won't accept any help. She makes cheese, and she pretty much lives on that and the fruit and vegetables she grows. Once a week I bring her a couple of loaves of maize bread from the market and some salted cod." He made a face. "Have you tried that?"

"Not yet. I've seen it on sale in the village—it looks like starched underwear."

"It does." He chuckled. "And it doesn't taste much better. I've offered her trout I've caught in the river, but she doesn't seem interested in fresh fish. By the way, don't be alarmed when you see her—she's very old and . . . kind of unusual looking. People say she's a *hechicera*."

"What's that?"

"A witch," he replied. "A white witch—that's what it means. They have another word—*bruja*—for the bad kind. I think you'll like her— she's an expert on herbs. She uses them to dye the silk and to make medicine. I've heard people say she's better than the local doctor at curing people." He paused to swipe away a cloud of flies hovering over his head. "That's why she wasn't punished for collaborating with the partisans—she cured the wife of the *comandante* of the Guardia Civil."

"What was the matter with her?" Rose asked.

"She suffered great pain in her legs. She could hardly walk and hadn't slept properly for weeks. Maria says she turned up at the door of the farmhouse one night begging for help. She hadn't dared tell her husband where she was going, because he was a churchy man." He turned to Rose with a shrug. "During the Civil War the Guardia Civil were hand-in-glove with the Catholic church—still are, actually. Anyway, Maria treated her for a week—with some sort of poultice made from leaves—and by the end of that time, she was completely better: not a trace of pain. From then on she never had any trouble from the police." Zoltan took another swipe at the flies with his hat. "That's Maria's place—down there."

The stone farmhouse was half-hidden by the orchard that surrounded it. As they made their way toward it, Rose spotted quinces, plums, and apricots growing among the cherry trees. Then they passed through a patch of mulberry bushes, which gave way to rows of potatoes, peas, and beans. The land that lay directly in front of the house was given over to a profusion of herbs. Rose could smell rosemary, thyme, and lavender, and she could see marigolds, mallows, comfrey, and southernwood. These were the staples of her own herbal medicine practice. She brightened at the thought of meeting a kindred spirit.

There was a big iron bell hanging outside the door of the farmhouse. Zoltan rang it vigorously, making a terrific din. "She's a bit deaf," he said. "I hope she's not asleep."

He rang again. This time Gunesh joined in, barking loudly and pawing the peeling blue paint on the wooden door.

"Shush!" Rose pulled him away just as the door opened. Standing on the threshold was a woman who looked as if she'd stepped out of the pages of a book by the Brothers Grimm. Her skin was a bloodless gray yellow, and her hair clung to her scalp like wisps of spider thread. When she opened her mouth to greet them, Rose saw that her teeth were black and chipped. But she had fanglike canines that looked strong enough to bite through the shells of almonds. Like all the local women, she was dressed entirely in black.

"*Buenos días, Maria.*" Zoltan stepped forward and kissed her on both cheeks. "This is my friend Rose—the one who cured my mule."

"*Buenos días.*" Rose held out her hand. The woman's skin felt surprisingly soft and warm.

"Ella es muy joven para ser una hechicera." She's very young for a witch. Maria arched bushy gray eyebrows at Zoltan.

"I told you—she's not a witch: she's an animal doctor. She went to university in England."

Maria ran her eyes over Rose, from head to toe. "Well, she looks like a Gypsy to me."

"I've lived among Gypsies," Rose said. "They taught me everything I know about curing animals with herbal medicine."

The old woman stared at her for a moment, her head on one side. "How did you cure the mule?"

"The wound was bathed with an infusion of potato peelings and garlic," Rose replied. "Then he was fed on bran mixed with more garlic and watercress."

Maria nodded. "Sit down over there." She pointed to a wooden bench under a canopy of trailing vines. "I'll bring you something to eat and drink."

She disappeared inside, shutting the door behind her.

"You've passed the test." Zoltan smiled.

"But she didn't invite us in," Rose said.

"She never allows anyone into the house—she likes to maintain the air of mystery." He smiled as he sat down beside Rose on the bench. "The local people say the *hechicera* fly down the mountain at full moon and perch like owls in the poplar trees. I think she likes to play up to that image. She says it makes her laugh if she spots people crossing themselves when they see her."

"How old is she?"

"I've no idea. She could be sixty-five or eighty-five. The women in this part of Spain tend to look old before their time. I think it's a combination of the sun and the way they dress."

Maria emerged from the house with a basket in one hand and a metal bowl in the other. She sat on the bench next to Zoltan and pulled a small ladle from the pocket of her skirt. For each of her guests, including Gunesh, she produced a large chestnut leaf from the basket, onto which she ladled dollops of goat curds. She served the dog first, then garnished the remaining portions with a handful of cherries before handing them out.

Rose wasn't sure whether to hold the leaf up to her mouth and pour the contents in or to scoop up the mixture with her fingers. She glanced at Zoltan, who simply raised the leaf to chin level and bent his head over it.

"Delicious," he mumbled, looking up with a white mustache.

"I laced it with a love potion." Maria flashed a wicked smile.

Zoltan rolled his eyes. "She's joking," he said.

But Rose saw that his cheeks were tinged pink. "It tastes very fresh," she said to Maria, trying to make it look as if she hadn't noticed Zoltan blushing.

"I made it this morning," Maria replied.

"Zoltan told me that you used to supply food for the partisans during the war."

"Yes, I did." Maria spat a cherry stone onto the ground. "What of it?"

"My brother was one of them." Rose laid down the chestnut leaf and took Nathan's picture from her pocket. "This is him. I . . ." She trailed off, her voice threatening to break as she handed the photograph over. "I've come here to try and find out what happened to him."

Maria's face was inscrutable as she studied the image. "Yes, I remember this one." She glanced up at Rose, the lines on her forehead creasing into deep furrows. "They called him *Caballo*."

Rose stared at her, transfixed. Had she heard right? Had she finally found someone who remembered Nathan? The woman's face melted as tears filmed Rose's eyes. Her lips felt swollen and clumsy, as if they'd been injected with anesthetic. She wanted to ask Maria if she knew what had happened to him. But her mouth wouldn't form the words.

"He used to come here when he was going to one of the villages," Maria went on. "He was a good boy—used to bring me tobacco. He and the others had to stay hidden in the daytime, but at night they would go into Capileira or Pampaneira for news and cigarettes.

"Early on in the war, they would stay the night with a peasant and his family. But then they started shooting the families who sheltered the partisans, so that stopped."

"I have a friend who lived in Capileira. Her mother and brother were killed for doing that." Rose heard her own voice, distant, as if in a dream. Why couldn't she bring herself to steer the conversation to what she really wanted to talk about?

"It was a terrible time," Maria replied. "People would denounce their neighbors for all kinds of reasons—not political, just to settle old scores. Is your friend a Gypsy?"

"Yes—how did you know that?"

"The Gypsies got the worst of it. One woman in Pampaneira denounced two young Gypsy girls who, she said, stole the sheets from her washing line. Another Gypsy woman was arrested just for fortune-telling."

"Rose has been asking around in Pampaneira about her brother," Zoltan said, "but no one wants to talk. We were wondering if you knew where he might have gone."

Rose shot him a grateful glance.

Maria dug the ladle into the bowl of curds. "He stopped coming here."

"When?" Rose couldn't see her eyes.

"I don't remember." Maria scooped a generous portion of curds onto the leaf at Gunesh's feet. The dog gobbled it up instantly.

"The last letter I had from him was dated March 1938," Rose said. "Did you see him after that?"

"I don't keep track of months and years," the woman replied. "Up here, they don't matter much."

"Did you hear anything about him?" Rose persisted. "He was planning to go to France. Did any of the others talk to you about that?"

Maria didn't answer. Instead she turned to Zoltan. "Can you come and help me with the billy goat?" She jerked her thumb over her shoulder. "He's got one of his horns stuck in a fence." To Rose she said, "You'd better stay here—he'll get even more worked up if he sees the dog."

Rose watched them disappear behind the house. She didn't believe that Maria hadn't heard her last question. It seemed she'd simply dropped the subject of Nathan as if it were of no more importance than one of her animals.

When Zoltan returned, he was alone. "Maria's gone to have a rest," he said. "It took both of us to free the goat, and she's worn out." He bent down to stroke Gunesh. "Shall I walk you back down to the village?"

"It's okay—you don't need to do that." Her voice came out high and reedy. She wondered if he could tell how close she was to tears.

"It's no trouble—I need to call at the post office."

They walked in silence until they reached the ruined mill. Zoltan asked her if they could sit down for a few minutes. She followed him inside, surprised that he needed to rest when they were going downhill, not up the mountain. He sank down onto the ancient grinding stone and patted the space beside him.

"There's something I have to tell you," he said. "Maria asked me to do it because she couldn't face giving you the news herself."

Rose felt as if an icy hand had gripped her heart. "Nathan's dead, isn't he?"

"I'm so sorry, Rose." Zoltan took her hand, the calluses on his palm rubbing against her fingers.

"H . . . how?" she whispered.

"He was caught up in a mass execution staged by a gang of fascist thugs called the Escuadra Negra."

Rose stared at him, motionless, not even breathing. The Black Squad. The same men who had taken Lola's mother and brother.

211

"Maria said it happened in the spring of '38," he went on. "It must have been soon after he sent that last letter. She remembers that it was snowing, and he'd come to see her, early in the morning, to ask if she wanted anything from the village. An hour or so later, she heard gunfire down in the valley. When some of the other partisans came for food the next day, they told her that your brother had been on his way to his fiancée's house, but the fascists had arrested her and were marching her through the village to be executed. When he tried to rescue her, they killed him, too."

Silent tears coursed down Rose's face. It was what she had known, deep down, all along. But no amount of expectation could soften the blow. Until this moment, there had always been that flicker of hope.

Zoltan wrapped his arms around her, pulling her to him.

"I . . . I'm sorry," she mumbled into his shoulder.

"Shhh." He stroked her hair. "Don't try to talk. We can just stay here for a while."

Rose closed her eyes tight, aware that her tears were making his shirt wet. She could hear the babble of the stream through the gaping windows, the calling of birds in the trees that overhung the tumbledown roof. It seemed wrong that the world outside could just go on, exactly as before, when for her, things would never be the same again.

She could feel the rise and fall of Zoltan's chest, the throb of his heart. It should have been a comforting thing—but all she could think about was Nathan lying on the ground with the life ebbing out of his body.

"Would it be easier if you came to my place instead of going back to the village?" Zoltan whispered the question into her hair. "I could go and fetch your daughter from school and fix us something to eat."

The mention of Nieve tipped Rose over the edge of the precipice of grief and shock. She felt as if the grindstone beneath her were disintegrating, and she were falling into some dark abyss beneath the mountain.

"She's not my daughter." She heard the words, not fully aware that they had come from her own mouth.

Zoltan remained silent for a while. Then he said, "You don't have to explain if you don't want to."

Rose raised her head from his shoulder. His eyes were the clear, pale blue of the meltwater from the mountain glaciers. Something in the way he looked at her made a dam burst in her heart. She began to pour out the story of Lola and the harrowing rescue of the baby from the massacre in the snow.

"Is Lola the friend you mentioned to Maria? The one whose family was shot for sheltering partisans?"

Rose nodded. "She's the one who told me about this place. I only knew Nathan was here because she recognized his description of the fountain in Pampaneira."

"And now she's facing a murder charge?"

"I've written letters to the authorities," Rose said. "I can't think what else to do. I can't go back to Granada." She hesitated, drawing in a breath to keep her voice steady. "I mean, there's no reason for me to stay here now—but it would be too dangerous for Nieve."

"I can believe that," Zoltan replied. "I have a radio in the cottage— I've heard reports of children being taken from their parents and put into monasteries and convents. They call it *trasplante*—transplantation—as if they were vegetables being uprooted from poor soil."

"I haven't known Nieve for long," Rose went on, "but she's very precious to me." She checked herself, aware now that she had already let out far more than she had intended. But she felt compelled to tell him what had been on her mind even before the night in the tavern when the swift had landed in her lap. "I know it sounds fanciful," she said, "but I'd almost allowed myself to believe that she might be Nathan's child."

Zoltan pursed his lips. "It's not impossible, is it? You know she was born near here, at around the same time that your brother died. What if the woman Lola found dying was his fiancée?"

"I thought of that before, but . . ." It was painful to spell out exactly what was going through her mind. "I don't think Lola's mother and brother were killed at the same time as my brother. Lola described exactly what she saw that day. She said her brother was the only male victim. All the others were women. So Nieve couldn't be Nathan's child, could she? If she was, he would have been there, too."

"I don't want to give you false hope," Zoltan said, "but there's a chance your brother was killed before the others. Maria said he died trying to protect his fiancée. She didn't say where he died. Forgive me for being so blunt, but if he was shot in the street, his body wouldn't have been with the others, would it?"

"How can I ever know that?" Fresh tears stung the back of Rose's eyes.

"Someone in Pampaneira must know. And Maria knows who knows."

"But she wouldn't even tell me about Nathan," Rose whispered.

"I know," Zoltan replied. "She might come across as a tough old crow, but actually she's very sensitive. She just couldn't bear the thought of hurting you."

"So you think we should go back there?" Rose gripped the rough edges of the millstone. She wasn't sure she could face it.

"Another day maybe." Zoltan put his hand on hers. "But we *will* find out what happened—I promise you that."

Chapter 25

Rose hadn't intended to stay the night at Zoltan's cottage. She barely remembered the walk back there from the ruined mill. She had nodded off in an armchair, and he had left her while he went to collect Nieve from school, waking her only when the evening meal was ready. And then—the minute they'd finished eating—Nieve had curled up with Gunesh on the wolf-skin rug and fallen fast asleep.

"There's no point disturbing her," Zoltan had said when Rose went to rouse her. "Why don't you stay? We can be up in plenty of time to get her to school." He had offered to give up his bed for them, but Rose had been happy to settle down under a blanket next to Nieve and the dog.

She had lain awake for a while, listening to the night sounds of the mountain. In her bed in the village, the only thing she could hear was the rush of water and the clucking of the chickens. But up here there were wild animals. She'd heard the haunting cry of a fox and the hoot of a hunting eagle owl. There was the snuffling, grunting sound of a wild boar and the distant howl of a wolf. And somewhere close to the cottage there were toads, whose croaking songs had lulled her into unconsciousness even though she hadn't felt particularly tired.

Rose woke at first light. For a while she lay where she was on the rug, gazing at Nieve's sleeping face, searching for traces of the woman whose image had lain hidden in a box in this house for all the years that Nieve had been growing up. Could she be Adelita's child? Were those long dark eyelashes and that perfect little mouth inherited from her or someone else? The longer she looked, the more convinced she became of a resemblance. But as a scientist, Rose knew that it was all too easy to get the answer that you wanted from a few unsubstantiated facts. She was letting her heart rule her head. There was no more evidence that Nieve's looks came from Adelita than that her love of animals came from Nathan.

Rolling silently off the rug, Rose stood up and stretched her aching limbs. Holding a corner of the curtain, she peered through the window to see the mist rolling back from the mountain, like a dancer slowly raising the hem of her skirt. There was a deep-red glow in the eastern horizon. As the sun began to climb, it turned a shoal of high clouds into charcoal embers, red beneath and dark gray on top. Within minutes the great ball of the sun had changed from scarlet to pale yellow, and the clouds skimming the hillside were bleached white.

She let Gunesh out for a walk and watched him run up the side of the mountain, chasing half a dozen wild ibex. But they were too quick for him. When he came back, his coat smelled of the aromatic plants growing on the hillside—mint, fennel, rosemary, and thyme.

Zoltan insisted on accompanying them down to the village despite Rose's protests. He brought bread and cheese for them to eat on the way down, and when Nieve was safely inside school, he bent down to plant a kiss on Rose's forehead.

"You know where to find me." That was all he said. And Rose stood watching until the trees swallowed him up.

"Why do we have to live here?" Nieve threw her bag onto the bed when she got back from school. "Why can't we go and live in Uncle Zoltan's house?"

Rose smiled to herself. She hadn't told the child to call Zoltan uncle. But it had been clear from the moment Nieve walked through the door of the cottage that she was smitten. Perhaps it was because Zoltan had promised to make *migas* for the evening meal. Or maybe it was because he had let her help with feeding and grooming the mules.

"I thought you liked it here," Rose said. "You wouldn't be able to play with Alonso if we moved somewhere else."

Nieve's mouth turned down at the edges. "I don't like him anymore. He pulled my hair on the playground today." She sat down on the bed and pulled off her boots. "I've got a new friend. Her name's Pilar. She says I can sleep at her house on Saturday night."

"Saturday? But that's when you're doing the dancing for San Juan."

Nieve nodded. "She wants me go home with her afterward. There's going to be a big party. All her cousins and aunts and uncles are going to be there."

Rose hesitated. Was it all right to let Nieve go to this house on her own? She told herself she was being overly protective. It was a fiesta—something that Nieve should be allowed to enjoy with her new friend. "Well, yes, of course you can go." Rose hadn't intended it to sound grudging, but Nieve picked up on her mood in a flash.

"Maybe Uncle Zoltan will have a party at his house."

"I don't think so." Rose reached across and gathered her up in a hug. "Don't you worry about me—I'll be just fine with Gunesh."

Later, when Nieve was asleep, Rose sat sewing. The school had given instructions that the girls performing the dances at the San Juan fiesta were to wear blue dresses with white aprons and mantillas of white lace. Nieve didn't possess a blue dress, so Rose was making one from one of her own skirts. The apron she had made from a couple of handkerchiefs. As for the lace, she would have to try and buy some at the market.

When the light grew too dim for sewing, she went outside and spread a blanket on the ground in the orchard. She lay gazing up at the sky, watching the first stars appear as the light faded. She thought of Nathan doing the same thing on summer nights on the mountain. Had he tracked the constellations on those endless nights in the trenches? Had he and Adelita lain together outside on a blanket the night their baby was conceived?

To think of such things was pure torture. There were so many unanswered questions. She had vowed not to leave Spain without at least finding Nathan's grave and marking it in some way. But she didn't know exactly where he had died, and there seemed little chance of finding that out. And then there was the agonizing puzzle of the baby. Was there the slightest possibility that Adelita had been the woman Lola had found in the snow? Rose was desperate to know. It was the one glimmer of hope she was clinging to.

Zoltan had said they should go back to see Maria, but Rose wasn't sure she could face it. How long would it be before she could talk about Nathan's death without crying? There was no answer to that question. But what was the alternative? How long could she stay in this village, seeing people on the street, wondering if this man or that woman held the key to what she ached to know?

Rose was no less confused the next morning. She decided to go for a long walk after she'd dropped Nieve off at school—but not in the direction of Zoltan's cottage or to Maria's farm. She didn't want to pester Zoltan, when he had already given her so much of his time—and she didn't feel mentally strong enough to visit Maria without him. What she needed was some time alone. Walking had always helped her clear her mind.

Before they reached the school, she passed the postman. He had got used to her stopping him each morning to ask if there was anything for her. She didn't trust Señora Carmona to pass on mail that arrived at the mill. But there had been no reply so far to any of the letters she had sent to Granada, and this morning the postman's response was no different.

"Why doesn't Mama send us a letter?" Nieve twisted her head around, following the man with her eyes as they walked on.

"She would if she could. But she can't buy stamps at the place where she's staying." Rose cast about for some means of distracting Nieve. The child hadn't mentioned Lola for a few days. Rose needed to change the subject or Nieve would be going to school in tears. "Oh look," Rose said, "there's that cat again!"

"Which cat?" Nieve spun around.

"The fluffy ginger one that drinks water from the stream running down the street." Rose pointed to the place where she had seen the animal a few days before. The trick worked. Nieve ran on ahead, looking up the alleyways between the houses for the nonexistent cat, and by the time Rose caught up with her, the business of Lola and the stamps was forgotten.

When they reached the school, a tall girl with skinny black plaits came running up to them.

"This is Pilar." Nieve dropped Rose's hand to link arms with her new friend. "Goodbye, Au . . . Mama."

Rose sucked in a breath. Nieve had almost given the game away. It was so hard for a child of only eight years old to keep up such a pretense. But there was no alternative. Rose felt bad enough about having told Zoltan. No one else must be let in on the secret.

She decided to take the right-hand fork in the track up the mountain—the one that led to Capileira. She would try to find the blacksmith's forge where Lola had lived as a child. The route took Rose through a very different landscape from the one she had encountered on the walk to Zoltan's cottage. After a few minutes' walk through sparse woodland, the track wound along the edge of a deep, wide gorge. The river was far below, like a ribbon of turquoise silk. She almost tripped as she looked at it. There were rocks jutting up along the path. After that, she kept her eyes on the ground. Gunesh was more sure-footed, jumping over the rocks without a moment's hesitation.

There was something about the gorge that filled Rose with a sense of foreboding. It wasn't just the thought of tumbling over the edge. The steep, almost vertical cliffs, bare of vegetation apart from the odd clump of thistles, had a stark, harsh look to them. As she climbed higher, it dawned on her that this could be the place Lola had described—the ravine she had scrambled down in the snow. It wasn't difficult to imagine murder on such a scale taking place in a spot like this. People rounded up and herded along the valley like animals, to be slaughtered in a volley of gunfire. The killing would be heard but not seen, the bodies hidden from view by the great outcrops of limestone on the valley sides.

Rose stopped, crouching down to get closer to the edge of the gorge without the danger of losing her balance. The idea of Lola scaling these treacherous rocks in a blizzard was almost beyond comprehension. And how on earth would she have got back up again with a baby in her arms? Perhaps this wasn't the place. And yet . . . the more Rose looked, the more intense the feeling of menace became. It wasn't just her—she could feel the hackles rising on Gunesh's neck.

Capileira was not far away. The sound of shooting would have traveled miles, up beyond the village to the mountain pastures above. It all fit exactly with what Lola had described. And she wouldn't have had to climb back up the side of the gorge with the baby—she could have followed the course of the river up the mountain until she reached a place where the valley was not so deep and the terrain easier to negotiate.

Rose's legs felt stiff as she got up from the crouching position. She walked on, trying to dispel the images that crowded in on her—of Lola lying in the snow between the corpses of her mother and brother, wanting to die alongside them; of Nieve's tiny blood-smeared body, fighting for life, wrapped in her dying mother's peacock shawl.

Adelita.

Rose shook her head. She mustn't allow herself to believe that Nieve's mother was Nathan's fiancée.

But what if she was . . .

The muttering inside her head wouldn't stop.

If she was, Nathan couldn't be far away, could he? Perhaps they didn't shoot him in the street. Perhaps they marched him to the gorge with the others, but he tried to make a break for it and they shot him farther down the valley. That would explain why Lola didn't see his body. His bones might be in the river. What if that river runs into the one beside the mill in Pampaneira?

She clamped her hands over her ears. This must be what it felt like to lose your mind.

It was a relief when the track veered around to the left, away from the ravine and into a broad, gently sloping meadow dotted with scarlet poppies, purple-blue lavender, and amber marigolds. She collapsed onto the grass and lay there with her eyes closed, breathing in the scent of the earth and the wildflowers.

Don't you believe in heaven, Rose?

Now it was Bill Lee's voice she heard. Calm and comforting. She could imagine him walking through a place like this, bending down to pluck a flower with his long brown fingers and threading it through his hatband next to the feather. And he would know the names of all the birds, whose sweet, distant calls drifted across the hillside.

Did she believe in heaven? If there was such a place, she hoped it would be like this. A place where the spirits of the dead glided over perfumed, sunlit meadows to a symphony of birdsong. Yes, she thought, Nathan would be happy here. Wherever his earthly body had been left, his spirit would find a home on this mountain.

She raised herself up on one elbow and reached into her bag. Zoltan had given her more cherries as a parting gift, and there were still some left. The juice moistened her parched mouth. She dug a little hole in the ground when she'd finished eating and dropped one of the stones into it. Could a cherry tree grow this high up? She wasn't sure. But it seemed a fitting way to remember her brother.

After another hour of walking, she spotted the roofs of houses in the distance. Above them she could see the top of the mountain, still dusted with snow around the peak. It seemed incredible that snow could persist in a landscape so far south in the middle of June. She thought of Lola, who would have had to walk right over the top to get to Granada. It would be a difficult challenge in summer—but Lola had crossed the mountains in early April. It was little short of a miracle that she and Nieve had survived.

It wasn't long before Rose passed a wooden sign with pine trees and the name of the village carved into it. Soon she was among people again—women strolling along with shopping bags and men standing on street corners, smoking cigarettes.

Capileira was a slightly larger version of Pampaneira. It had the same steep cobbled streets, with water running from an abundance of springs. There were more shops and cafés and a freshly painted building that bore a sign saying "Hotel," as well as a humbler posada. Rose wondered if she'd made a mistake choosing to stay in Pampaneira rather than here. But she wouldn't have been able to afford hotel prices—and if she had settled on Capileira, she would never have met Zoltan.

The memory of his face, smiling as he'd waved them goodbye yesterday, produced an unexpected warmth in her belly. She smothered the sensation like a Gypsy throwing sand on a fire. The humiliation of what had happened with Cristóbal was still raw. She didn't even want to think about getting involved with another man.

After wandering around for half an hour, she spotted a street sign that led her straight to Lola's old home. Calle Fragua—Forge Street.

Halfway down it, the cobbles gave way to beaten earth peppered with goat droppings. She could hear a hammer striking metal as she approached the building at the far end. There were mules tethered outside and a couple of small naked children kicking up dust as they chased chickens out of an alleyway.

Calle Fragua was on the northern boundary of the village, with sweeping views of the whole valley—an idyllic place for a child to grow up. Rose thought of Lola running around like these children, with no inkling of the horrors that lay ahead. She tried to imagine what it would have been like when the death squad arrived to drag her grandfather away. Probably he would have been working when they arrived, like the man she could hear hammering away now. And she thought of that morning when Lola had gone out with the goats, little knowing that she would never see her mother and brother alive again.

It was hard to reconcile the picturesque scene she was looking at now with the atrocities that had taken place here less than a decade ago. She wondered who had taken over the forge when Lola's family had been killed. She was tempted to go inside and ask questions. But she sensed it would be a fruitless exercise. There was nothing to be gained here by raking up the past.

She walked back into the village as far as the church, stopping at a spring to refill her water bottle and pouring some into the bowl she carried in her bag for Gunesh. The church had a strange name: Nuestra Señora de la Cabeza—Our Lady of the Head. Rose thought it must mean the head of the valley. But it seemed strangely appropriate in view of the mental turmoil she'd been suffering since finding out about Nathan.

The church door was open, and she decided to go inside. It was too hot to leave Gunesh out in the sun, and as there didn't seem to be anyone else around, she told him to lie down on the cool stone floor near the door.

The whitewashed walls were adorned with life-size plaster statues of saints whose lips were rather too red and complexions a little too pink. But near the altar was a black Madonna—very much like the statue of Saint Sara in Saintes-Maries-de-la-Mer. A plaque on the wall explained that the church was dedicated to the miraculous appearance of the Virgin Mary to a Spanish shepherd at a place called Cerro de la Cabeza. She'd come to tell him where to find a painting of herself that had been made by the gospel writer Luke and was hidden in a mountain cave when the Moors conquered Andalucia. This statue, the plaque went on, was a re-creation of the painting.

Rose liked the idea of Saint Luke painting Christ's mother with dark skin. It seemed a much more accurate representation than the innumerable pale-complexioned, blue-eyed images hanging in art galleries. The statue was wearing a white robe embellished with gold thread. The swirls of gold reminded Rose of one of the dresses Lola had worn at the fiesta in Provence. It was strange to think of her coming to this church as a child. Very likely she had been baptized in the stone font by the door. And she would have knelt at the altar to take her first communion, dressed as a little bride like the girls at the Corpus Christi procession in Pampaneira.

There were candles flickering on a wooden stand to the left of the altar. Rose hadn't come here with the intention of lighting a candle, but she suddenly felt impelled to do it. Taking one from the box beneath the stand, she held it to a flame. She murmured a prayer as she placed it with the others—for freedom for Lola.

She hesitated as she delved into her bag for money to put in the box. She could hear Nathan whispering in her ear. *What about me?*

Yes, she should light another one for him. And then two more—for Adelita and her baby.

Have you forgotten us? That was her father. No, of course she hadn't forgotten. One for him and one for her mother.

And maybe you should light one for yourself.

When all seven candles were burning, Rose stood for a while, staring at the flames until they blurred into each other. In that moment the barrage of voices stopped. She felt a calm she hadn't experienced in months. It was a sense of timelessness, of life going on in this place generation after generation. It made her feel very small and insignificant. But not alone.

As she made her way back down the nave, she thought of the book she'd carried with her from England, written by the nun Julian of Norwich. She hadn't picked up the book since the trip from Provence. What had happened with Cristóbal had left her feeling very far away from what she thought of as God. But something in the act of lighting the candles had brought her back.

She considered what had unfolded since the last time she'd stepped inside a church. In a few short weeks, she had found the answer to the question that had been eating away at her for eight years. And while it wasn't the answer she would have wished for, there was a kind of peace in knowing it.

Don't be afraid of what you don't know. That kind of fear kills you without you realizing. Like bleeding inside.

She needed to keep those words of Bill Lee's in her mind. There was still so much she didn't know. But tomorrow she would make herself go back up the mountain by the other path. The one that led to Maria's house.

Chapter 26

Zoltan had already set up his market stall when Rose and Nieve passed through the village square on their way to school the next day. Nieve ran to say hello. After five minutes Rose literally had to drag her away.

"Come on—you'll be late for school!"

"Will you come and see me dancing on Saturday?" Nieve called over her shoulder.

"Yes, of course!" Zoltan called back. He arched his eyebrows at Rose: a look that said, *Are you coming back?*

When she returned to the square, Zoltan was serving a queue of customers. She went to buy some lace for Nieve's dance costume. Then she went to the place where Zoltan had tethered his mules, pleased to see that the sick one had recovered enough to come to market.

"It's healed up completely," he called to her. "You'd never know there'd been a wound there, would you?" He scooped some cherries into a bag and brought them over to her. "It's been busy this morning," he said. "Lots of people getting ready for San Juan. The young men have a custom of hanging cherries on the doors of the girls they're in love with. These are for you, by the way." He smiled, cocking his head at the mule. "From him."

"Thank you."

As she tucked the bag away, he laid his hands on her shoulders, holding her at arm's length as his eyes searched her face.

"I was worried about you yesterday," he said. "I thought you might come—and when you didn't, I . . ." He hesitated, frown lines creasing his forehead. "Are you okay?"

Rose nodded. "I'm sorry you were worried. I just needed some time to take it all in. I went for a long walk—up to Capileira—and it did help. I'm going to go and find Maria now."

"You don't want to wait until tomorrow?" He glanced at the baskets of fruit glistening in the sun.

"It's kind of you to offer—but I need to go there on my own this time." She saw the flicker of uncertainty in his eyes. "I'm prepared for whatever she can tell me, however bad it is. I just need to know—to get it over. Do you understand?"

He nodded. "Just remember I'll be here. If you want to talk."

She raised her hand across her chest, feeling for his fingers on her shoulder. "Thank you." She wanted to kiss his hand but was afraid of sending out the wrong signals. Instead she drew it to her cheek and held it there. His skin felt warm and it smelled of cherries.

Maria Andorra was milking goats when Rose found her. The pungent, earthy smell of the animals hit the back of Rose's throat as she pushed open the door of the shed behind the farmhouse. She held Gunesh's lead tight, afraid that he might break free and cause chaos.

"I thought you'd be back." Maria raised herself stiffly from the low milking stool, rubbing her left hip.

"I'm sorry to disturb you," Rose said. "But I need to know what happened. Where it happened. And when. Otherwise I . . ."

"You can't really believe it?"

Rose nodded.

Maria picked up the pail of milk and covered it with a metal plate. "Come with me," she said.

Rose followed her through rows of potato plants until they reached the stream that ran through the farmland. Maria set the pail down in the shallow water, picking up stones to lay on top to keep the current from dislodging it. Then she eased herself down onto the grassy bank and patted the space beside her.

"It was the day after Easter. The eighteenth day of April. As I said, I don't keep track of the months up here—but that's one date I do always know, because it's my birthday." Maria spread out her hands, turning them over to examine the knotted blue veins that snaked from the wrists to the knuckles. "I turned seventy that year. Your brother brought me a present. Something he'd made himself. A horse, it was."

Rose felt the tightness of threatened tears in her throat. She clenched her jaw, fighting them back.

Maria took a clay pipe from the pocket of her skirt and tapped it against a stone. "It was a lovely thing. He'd carved it out of elder wood." She stuffed a pinch of tobacco into the pipe and held a match to it, sucking in short, sharp breaths. The smell reminded Rose of sitting on the steps of Bill Lee's caravan on that May evening, just weeks ago. If she'd known then what lay ahead, would she have set out on this journey?

Maria took the pipe out of her mouth. "I remember how we laughed when he gave it to me, because he was wearing some old clothes of mine and the sleeves were far too short—you could see his hairy arms. I had to give him a shawl to cover them up. That was how he got away with going to the village in daylight, you see."

"Disguised as a woman?" Rose had a fleeting sense of something drifting up from her subconscious, almost within reach—but too fragile to grasp.

"He told me he had to meet someone in Pampaneira," Maria went on. "It was to do with getting him and his girl out of Spain." Maria sucked on the pipe, casting a wary glance at Rose. "Did you know that she was pregnant?"

"Yes," Rose whispered. She felt as if she couldn't breathe.

"Such a wicked thing to do." Maria blew out a wreath of blue smoke. "They killed twenty-five women from the villages around here that day. Dragged them away from their children—even tore a baby from its mother's breast. The only rule they had—if you can call it that—was that they wouldn't kill a child that was too young to have taken holy communion. They didn't care if a woman was pregnant. In their twisted minds that didn't count."

Rose could hear a bird calling from somewhere in the rushes on the other side of the stream. It sounded very far away, as if it inhabited some other realm. She felt as if she had floated out of her body and was looking down on the shell of herself sitting beside Maria.

"Your brother wasn't with Adelita when they burst into her house—but he saw them marching her through the village with the others they'd rounded up. He slipped into the line next to her and pulled her into an alleyway when they were going past the church. But someone saw them. The guards handcuffed him. He was taken to the ravine with all the others."

Rose was aware of a prickling sensation on her leg. It was a fly crawling over the bare flesh below her knee. She brushed it away. The movement brought her back from the trancelike state that had overcome her. Maria was describing it all in the kind of detail that suggested she had seen it herself. And yet Zoltan had said that she was up here when the shots were fired and had heard only a secondhand account of what happened from the other partisans.

"How do you know?" Rose turned to look at her. "Who saw it?"

Maria brushed a wisp of smoke-stained hair away from her furrowed forehead. "The wife of the *comandante*. I was treating her for pain in her legs. She was sitting in the window of her house the day it happened. And her husband told her the rest." The dark irises of Maria's eyes, ringed blue-white with age, flickered this way and that, as if she were watching it unfolding on a cinema screen. "He told his wife that they'd killed the English partisan they called the Shepherdess. The one who'd evaded them for so long by slipping in and out of the villages dressed as a woman. He said your brother had thrown himself in front of his girlfriend when the shooting started. He couldn't save her, of course. No one survived."

The fragment of memory that had been hovering at the edge of Rose's consciousness suddenly coalesced into a clear image. Bodies in a blizzard. All female, Lola had said, apart from her twin brother. When she had scrambled through the snow, frantically searching for her loved ones, she could have come within inches of Nathan's corpse and mistaken it for the body of a woman.

"He would have been a wonderful father." The lines around Maria's mouth deepened as she puffed on the pipe. "If only they'd got away a few weeks earlier. But Adelita was not strong. He was afraid she wouldn't make it through the mountains. He was waiting for the weather to change."

Rose stared at her, clinging on to hope. Because Maria couldn't know, could she, that a baby had been taken, alive, after the massacre? How could anyone but Lola have known that?

"W . . . what h . . ." She was so choked up she could hardly get the words out. "What happened to their . . . remains?"

Maria held the pipe above her lap, staring at the smoldering tobacco. "They weren't given proper burials. People were too afraid, you see. The church said the *rojos* were so vile that even the earth didn't want them. One man went there a couple of days after the shooting, when the snow had melted. What he saw affected him so badly he died of a heart attack a week later."

"What? What did he see?"

"You don't want to know."

"Believe me, whatever you tell me can't be worse than what I've imagined."

Maria took another lungful of smoke. "He said one of the women must have given birth as she was dying. He saw the cord lying in the snow. But there was no baby. He thought an animal must have taken it."

Rose felt as if her heart had stopped beating. "Adelita?"

Maria shook her head. "Her little one was spared that fate, at least."

Tears burned behind Rose's eyes. With a handful of words, Maria had snatched away the last vestige of hope. Nieve was a stranger's daughter, not Nathan's. The child she had fantasized about was gone forever.

"I'm sorry." Maria placed her pale chicken-claw fingers on Rose's sun-browned arm. "It's such a terrible waste of life."

"Who was she?" Rose murmured. "The mother of the baby?"

"Her name was Heliodora. She was a silk weaver. A Gypsy woman—one of the house-dwelling kind. She was highly skilled—she could create the most amazing patterns in the cloth she made. Her shawls were like paintings, full of flowers, butterflies, and birds." Maria's hand returned to her pipe. Pulling it out of her mouth, she tapped out the ashes and stuffed fresh tobacco into the bowl. "She and her husband came here from Morocco. They hadn't been living in Pampaneira for very long. He was killed in '37, in the backlash that followed the murder of the local priest."

"My brother wrote about that in his letter."

"Did he tell you that they paraded the priest through the village with a horse's bridle round his neck?"

"No, he didn't mention that."

"It was a terrible business. They treated him like an animal, insulting him and blaspheming him. Then they made him drink vinegar, like Jesus on the cross, before killing him. Things were bad enough before, but what was done that day tore the village apart. Anyone who'd even been out on the streets when it happened was rounded up. Heliodora's husband had been taking bales of silk to Órgiva that day, and he got caught up in it. Probably she didn't even know she was pregnant when he died. When she started to show, there were all kinds of rumors flying around. People said the father was the merchant who'd employed her husband. Whether it was true or not, I don't know. But the merchant's wife denounced her. That's why Heliodora was shot."

The tears that Rose had fought so hard to contain spilled out at the thought of Nieve clinging to the peacock shawl in her sleep—her fingers wrapped around the frayed, faded fabric that had very likely been woven by her mother's own hands. Rose felt an overwhelming urge to get up and run from this place, down the mountain to the school, to gather the child up in her arms and bury her face in Nieve's hair.

"I have to go now." Rose jumped to her feet, wiping her hand across her cheeks. "Thank you for . . ." She broke off, unable to say any more.

"Let me give you something first," Maria said. She stood up stiffly, holding her hand to her back. "It's in the house—I won't be a minute."

Rose followed her silently back through the rows of vegetables. It was as if her mind had broken loose from her body. Her limbs were doing exactly what they should, but she felt like an automaton. She stood, rigid, outside the door of the farmhouse while Maria went inside. When the old woman reemerged, she pressed a small, hard object into Rose's hand. "He would have wanted you to have this. You did a brave thing, coming all this way to find him."

Rose opened her fingers. In her palm lay the tiny figure of a horse.

Chapter 27

The early-morning sun slanted through the tree outside the window, casting dappled shadows on the gray woolen blanket that covered the bed. Rose rubbed her eyes. Where was she? This was not her bedroom at the mill. Where was Nieve? And Gunesh?

There was something on her head. She could feel a cold, wet sensation on her scalp. Panic seized her. She tried to scramble out of the bed, but a searing pain shot up her left ankle. Then the bedroom door opened, and Zoltan's face appeared.

"Oh good—you're awake." The worry lines between his eyebrows relaxed a little.

"What happened? How did I get here? Where's Nieve?" The questions tumbled out in a voice that sounded as croaky and ancient as Maria's.

"It's all right." He sat down beside her, stroking her hair. "Nieve's playing outside with Gunesh. I put you in here to get some rest. You must have fallen coming down the mountain. I found you on my way back from the market."

"But I . . . I don't remember . . ."

"Shhh. Don't try to talk. You were out cold—that's why you don't remember. You must have knocked your head on a rock when you fell. There's no wound or anything—just a small lump—but you need to take it easy for a day or two." He reached across to a jug on the windowsill and poured water into a glass. "Here. Drink this. I'm going to take Nieve to school now. I'll make you some breakfast when I get back if you feel up to eating anything."

When he'd gone Rose spotted a familiar object on the bedside table. It was the wooden horse her brother had carved for Maria. She reached out to touch it, running her fingers over the smooth curve of its back. Thank God she hadn't lost it when she fell on the mountain. It was the one thing that connected her with Nathan.

She must have drifted back into sleep soon after that. When she woke up again, Zoltan was standing beside the bed with a tray of coffee and toasted bread spread with apricot jam.

"Thank you." She struggled to raise her head. He slipped his arms behind her shoulders and eased her into a sitting position. "Was Nieve okay going to school?"

"Fine," Zoltan replied. "She loves animals, doesn't she? I think she was born to ride a mule." He set the tray on her lap and poured coffee into an enamel mug. "Oh! Did I hurt you?"

She felt stupid, pathetic, for welling up at the very mention of Nieve's birth. "No," she whispered. "It's just . . . Nieve . . . she . . ."

"You don't have to explain. Maria told me everything. She came over last night with that poultice for your head."

"I thought I could take it." Rose lifted the coffee to her mouth, breathing in the sharp aroma. "I'd told myself a hundred times that it was impossible—that Nieve couldn't be my brother's child—but in here . . ." She clasped her hand to her chest. "I was clinging to it. When you told me that Nathan was dead—well, it was all I had left. And then, when Maria filled in the rest . . . it was like I'd crucified myself on a shadow."

"I wish she hadn't given it to you in such gruesome detail. If I'd been there with you—"

Rose held up her hand. "I made her tell me everything. It was the only way I could know for sure that Nieve wasn't Nathan's daughter."

"You've made a huge difference to that little girl's life, you know." Zoltan pushed the plate of toast across the tray toward her. "She told me she couldn't read or write before she met you."

"She's an easy child to love. Her mother—Lola, I mean—was afraid I might try and take her away if I found out she was my niece. That was before Lola was arrested. I told her that whatever happened, I'd never do that."

"What will you do now? Is there any chance of Lola being released?"

"I don't know. I've written letters to everyone I can think of. But no one's replied. I go cold every time I think about it. She could be locked up for years."

"Would you take Nieve back to England?"

Rose shook her head. "I don't know. She seems happy here, doesn't she?" Glancing at the shape of her foot under the bedclothes, she added, "And I'm not going anywhere in a hurry, am I?"

"Well, not for a couple of days. But it's San Juan tomorrow—remember? I've promised Nieve I'll get you down the mountain on the mule so you can see her in the dance display."

"Oh God—I'd forgotten all about it!"

"Hardly surprising—you've had a bump on the head." Zoltan's lips pressed into a wry smile. "You'd better eat some of that toast. Apricots are good for the brain."

"Are they?" Rose took a big bite and swallowed it down. "I didn't know that."

"Nor did I." Zoltan grinned. "Don't stop eating now, though, will you?"

The sun was low in the sky as the mule made its way through the cobbled streets of Pampaneira. Zoltan walked in front with Gunesh at his heels. He held the lead rein, taking care not to let the mule get too close to the water channels. Rose held tight to the saddle. The swelling in her ankle had gone down, but she was afraid of putting any weight on it, so only her good foot was in a stirrup.

"The houses look pretty," she said. "I can see why you did such brisk business the other day."

"Looks like love is in the air, doesn't it." He smiled over his shoulder as they passed yet another front door festooned with a garland of white roses and jasmine blossom studded with cherries.

Rose wondered if Nathan had hung flowers and cherries on Adelita's door. Very likely they had met and fallen in love in the summer of '37. But it seemed unimaginable that such innocent pleasures as adorning a sweetheart's house with flowers and dancing around a midsummer bonfire could have gone on during the dreadful years of the Civil War.

"That one doesn't look so nice, does it?" Rose pointed to a door on the other side of the street. It had a bunch of thorns and nettles tied to the door knocker.

"That's what they do if they've had a quarrel," Zoltan replied.

"If someone hung something like that on my door, I'd take it down—I wouldn't leave it hanging there for everyone to see."

"They can't—it's bad luck. Anything that's hung on a door must stay there until sunrise tomorrow. If a girl takes it down, they say she'll never marry."

"How do you know all this?"

"Maria told me."

"Is she coming tonight?"

"Oh no—much too dangerous," he said with a wry grin. "They burn an effigy of a witch on the bonfire. She'll be tucked up in bed while the fiesta's going on."

Zoltan led the mule out of the village and across the bridge to the mill. Rose wasn't looking forward to going back there, but she had to pick up Nieve's costume, which she'd left lying on the bed the previous morning.

There was no sign of life when they got there. She gave Zoltan the key, and he disappeared inside while she stayed sitting on the mule. She'd had to ask him to look through her things, to find spare underwear, nightdresses, and a change of clothes for Nieve and herself. It was embarrassing—but there was no way she could get up those stairs herself.

"Oh, you've come back, have you?"

The miller's wife came from behind, startling her so that she nearly lost her balance.

"Buenas noches." Rose twisted around in the saddle. But before she could explain her absence, Señora Carmona let loose a tirade:

"Didn't take you long, did it, to find yourself a man? I've seen him selling his cherries in the market. A dirty Gypsy—that's what he is. I don't know how you could lower yourself. I thought you were an educated person! Writing a book, indeed! Well, you needn't think you're spending another night under *my* roof! Whatever he's gone up there for, you'd better tell him to bring the rest as well. I want you and the kid and that slobbering dog out! Out!"

At that moment, Zoltan appeared in the doorway.

"Señora Carmona, you misunderstand," he said. "Rose injured her foot while walking in the mountains. She only—"

"Don't give me that rubbish!" the woman hissed.

"You're wasting your breath, Zoltan. She took a dislike to me the day I arrived." Rose's voice, quiet and controlled, belied her seething anger. "You're not interested in the truth, are you?" she said, turning to Señora Carmona. "You only want to see the bad in people. And I wouldn't spend another night here if you paid me. I'd rather sleep under a bush!"

"I'm sorry," Rose murmured, stroking the mule's neck as it labored back up the village streets, its panniers bursting with her possessions. "And sorry to you, too," she said to Zoltan. "Looks like you're stuck with us until I can find somewhere else to stay."

"You don't have to do that," he replied. "I like having you and Nieve in the cottage. It gets lonely up there sometimes."

"But we've taken your bed!"

He shrugged. "I'm quite comfortable on the rug. Believe me, it's luxury compared to what I had to sleep on in Mauthausen. I spent two years on a filthy straw mattress crawling with lice."

"Hmm. Well, I'm sorry for reminding you of that. But thank you—you've already done so much for us."

"We'd better speed up a bit if we're going to get that costume to Nieve in time for the performance." Zoltan smiled. "Do you mind if I carry you the rest of the way? It'll make it easier for the mule."

He lifted her from the saddle. Somehow, he managed to hold her with one arm while leading the mule with the other. Her head was over his right shoulder. She could smell the earthy warmth of his skin through his shirt. When they reached the village square, he set her gently down on one of the wooden benches that had been set out in front of the church for the dance performance. Then he tied the mule to a ring in the church wall and set off on foot to deliver Nieve's costume to the school.

As she watched Zoltan go, Rose couldn't help drawing a comparison between him and Cristóbal. Physically, they were very different. Zoltan was much taller and fairer complexioned. Cristóbal had the kind of face that turned heads, while Zoltan's attractiveness came from somewhere deeper. His kindness, consideration, and respect for her put Cristóbal's behavior to shame. She closed her eyes, shutting out images of Cristóbal and summoning the memory of nestling against Zoltan's shoulder. He had made her feel . . . what? Protected. Safe. Not things she'd ever thought she needed from a man—and yet . . .

Instinctively she reached under the bench, feeling for Gunesh. He gave her a reassuring lick as her hand found his head. She let out a long breath. It was impossible to deny the gentle, seductive charm Zoltan exuded. And she was about to move into his home. She was going to have to be very, very careful. Her heart was too fragile, too scarred, to be exposed again.

By the time Zoltan returned, the square was crowded with people. Everyone was in their best clothes, the women in bright frilled dresses and the men with colorful shirts and jaunty hats. Rose wished she'd had time to retrieve something more attractive to wear when they'd stuffed all her belongings into the panniers. She felt very dowdy in her dusty workaday skirt and blouse.

"Did you manage to find Nieve?" Rose shifted her bag to make a space on the bench for Zoltan.

He nodded. "And I brought you something." In his hand he had a rose. It was dark red—so dark that the center was almost black. "They call it *terciopelo*—the Spanish word for velvet. It has a wonderful scent. There's a bush of them growing behind the school."

She took it from him and held it to her nose. The fragrance was heavenly, subtly sweet with a hint of something musky and exotic.

"I thought you could wear it in your hair—for the fiesta."

"Thank you." She smiled as she tucked the stem behind her ear. He seemed to have a knack for sensing how she was feeling. With the simple gift of a flower, he had instantly lifted her spirits.

Zoltan cocked his head toward the fountain, where Señora Carmona was standing, as black and brittle as charcoal, talking to her daughter. "I see the dragon has arrived."

"I suppose she was bound to come," Rose replied. "I've been pretending to read so as not to catch her eye." Rose showed him the piece of paper in her hand. It was a receipt for the bus ticket from Granada to Órgiva. "It was the only thing I could find."

"Well, she'd better not give us any more grief—I might not be able to keep my mouth shut next time."

A hush fell over the square as the children began to troop onto the makeshift stage erected against the wall of the church. Rose had a strange sense of déjà vu as Nieve stood in line with the other little girls and lifted her hands above her head. She looked like a miniature version of Lola. The way she held herself, the curve of her hands and arms, and the proud, defiant angle of her head were just the same. When she began to dance, it was hard to believe that—unlike her classmates—she had been rehearsing for only a matter of days.

"She's very good, isn't she?" Zoltan murmured. "A natural."

"Lola's a professional dancer," Rose whispered back. "It's strange—they're not related, but Nieve seems to have inherited her talent."

As she watched the child switch effortlessly from a graceful *letra* to a fast foot-stamping sequence, she glowed inside with pride. When the audience erupted in applause, Rose felt as if her heart would burst.

After the performance ended, Nieve came hurtling through the throng of people in the square to where Rose was sitting. She leapt onto Rose's lap and wrapped her arms around her neck. Gunesh immediately leapt up, too, licking Nieve's face as his tail wagged back and forth.

"Gunesh!" Nieve wiped her cheek with the back of her hand, pressing her face closer to Rose's. "Did you like me?" she whispered.

"Like you? I *loved* you!" Rose hugged her tight, kissing her through her curls. She was on the verge of adding that Lola would have loved to see it, too, but she bit her tongue. To say such a thing would only upset the child, rob her of this moment of elation.

"What about you, Uncle Zoltan? Did you like me?"

"I think you're the best dancer in the whole school—and I want you to teach me how to do it." He grinned. "You won't make me wear a dress, though, will you?"

"Silly!" She batted at him with her hand, laughing as she jumped off Rose's lap. "I've got to go to Pilar's house now."

"What time will you want to come back tomorrow?" Rose asked. "Did she say?"

Nieve shook her head.

"If it's anything like last year, no one'll be in bed before sunrise," Zoltan said.

"I could walk to the mill easily from Pilar's," Nieve said. "Shall I meet you there?"

Rose and Zoltan exchanged glances. "We're not going to be staying there anymore, actually," Rose began. "Señora Carmona was cross when we went back to get your costume." She glanced across the square to where the woman was deep in conversation with Pampaneira's priest. "She said some nasty things to me. So we're going to stay at Uncle Zoltan's for a while longer."

Nieve beamed, clapped her hands, and ran off toward the stage.

Rose followed her with her eyes until she disappeared, hand in hand with Pilar. Could it be possible to feel closer to a child if they were your own flesh and blood? With sudden clarity Rose realized that it made no difference that Nieve wasn't Nathan's daughter. Nathan had brought this child to her, and she loved her—deeply and unconditionally.

It was almost dark when they got back to Zoltan's cottage. He'd had to unload the panniers and leave them behind the woodpile in the school yard to enable the mule to get Rose up the mountain. She had all that she needed in a bag slung over her shoulder: clean underwear, a nightgown, and her toothbrush. He'd promised to bring everything else when he went to collect Nieve.

"Shall we sit outside for a while?" Zoltan went inside to fetch a blanket and some cushions. He lifted her out of the saddle and laid her down, then went off to feed and water the mule.

Rose lay back on the cushions. Although it was nearly eleven o'clock, the air was still warm. In the pale-indigo sky, she could see the first stars coming out. The trees and bushes were alive with the musical thrumming of the crickets. Then she heard an owl calling. The sound fractured the air, a shrill, mournful cry—like a song for dying souls.

Don't you believe in heaven, Rose?

For a split second she felt Nathan was there beside her, lying on his back, gazing up at the stars.

"You're not asleep, are you?"

Zoltan's voice broke the spell. He'd brought her coffee and a plate of something she couldn't quite make out in the darkness.

"Would you like one of these?"

"What are they?" Rose propped herself up on her elbow.

"They're called *buñuelos*. Sweet fritters—a bit like doughnuts. The bakery only sells them on festival days—I'm not sure why. They're very good."

"Mmm." Rose felt grains of sugar crunch between her teeth as she bit into it.

Scenting food, Gunesh lifted his head from the blanket.

"Can I give him some?" Zoltan asked.

"Well, he shouldn't really have sweet things—but I suppose a little bit won't hurt him."

Zoltan crouched down beside her and broke off a morsel of the *buñuelo*. "Oh look—they've started lighting the bonfires."

Rose straightened her elbow, raising herself a little higher off the blanket. In the dark folds of the valley below were tiny pinpricks of yellow light, each village marking the beginning of summer with its own towering blaze. "Do you think they all have witches on top of them?"

"I don't know. They certainly have some strange customs around here. In one of the villages, they have a procession in winter where they make a huge figure of a fox out of paper and carry it through the streets on the men's shoulders. Someone dressed as a priest follows behind it, reciting all the crimes this fox is supposed to have committed during the previous year. They call it the *Paseo de la Zorra*."

"*Zorra?* Feminine?"

"Yes."

Rose grunted. "Witches, vixens—why is it always the female that gets the blame?"

"I suppose it's been that way since Genesis, hasn't it?" He settled back on a cushion. "There's a vixen living in the copse behind the cottage. Have you heard her?"

"I did—that first night I stayed here."

"She had a litter of cubs a couple of months ago. I used to creep up there first thing in the morning to watch them playing. I tried to sketch them. I'm not much of an artist, but it made me feel good." He huffed out a breath. "That sounds sentimental, I know."

"No, it doesn't. I feel just the same when I'm out picking herbs for my veterinary practice. I get childishly excited when I see a flower I'm not expecting to find—something that's bloomed earlier or later than usual or something that wouldn't normally grow in the place I'm searching in."

"It's the same with the stars," Zoltan went on. "I had no idea of the different constellations until I came to live here." He swept his upturned palm toward the sky. "I don't think I ever noticed them before."

Rose had never met a Gypsy who lacked an intimate knowledge of the night sky. She wondered if Zoltan had lived in a city in Hungary. Perhaps his people had lost the sort of knowledge that caravan dwellers possessed. She longed to ask him about his family, but she was afraid to. He hadn't volunteered more than a scrap of information about his life before the concentration camp, which suggested it was too painful a subject to talk about.

"When you were putting the mule to bed, I was lying like you are now," she said, "imagining my brother looking up at this exact same patch of sky. I find myself doing it all the time. Even before I knew for sure that he'd died, I'd look at a view, a bird, or a meadow full of flowers and think, Nathan must have seen this."

"That's something good to hold on to, isn't? That someone we loved was part of all this incredible beauty."

Rose slid back onto her cushion. For a while they lay in silence, both gazing at the night sky. Then Gunesh began to burrow into the space between them, wriggling this way and that until he'd made himself comfortable.

"Gunesh!" Rose tried to move him farther down the blanket. One of the dog's hind legs was jabbing her neck, and she thought his tail end must be jammed against Zoltan's face.

"Don't move him on my account," Zoltan said. "He's nice and warm—like a hot water bottle."

That was the last thing she remembered him saying. They both must have fallen asleep soon afterward. When she opened her eyes again, the hillside was coral pink with the first rays of the rising sun. She felt the warmth of a body against her back and snuggled into it. But what she felt against the bare strip of flesh between her blouse and the waistband of her skirt was not Gunesh's silky fur. It was the rough cotton of Zoltan's shirt. Sometime in the night the dog must have moved, and the two of them had rolled together on the blanket.

She lay quite still for a moment. Zoltan was still asleep. She could feel the regular rise and fall of his chest. It was a pleasant sensation, the feeling of being cocooned in the folds of his body. But the pleasure was tinged with guilt. She mustn't be lying here when he woke up. Mustn't allow this intimacy to develop any further.

He murmured something in his sleep. Something she couldn't make out. Then his arm snaked across her waist.

It was so tempting to reach out for him, to slide into something joyful, physical, to blot out the pain of the past few days. The wild side of herself—the side that she had allowed total freedom in Provence— was urging her to let go. But the other half of her nature—the part that came from her straitlaced French mother, not her bohemian Turkish father—had the upper hand now. To lose herself in a moment of passion would further complicate an already complicated situation. And for the first time in her life, she had a child to consider. Nieve needed her undivided attention. Rose simply couldn't allow herself to get emotionally entangled.

Inch by inch, she shifted away from him until she felt grass beneath her hand. Her ankle was still sore. She didn't trust herself to try standing up. Instead she crawled across to the cottage on all fours to where Gunesh lay basking in the early sunshine. He licked her face as she pushed open the door and made her way inside. By clinging to the armchair, she was able to pull herself up. Once she was upright, it was relatively easy to hop about on one leg. She managed to light the fire and fill the kettle. By the time Zoltan appeared, rubbing his eyes in the doorway of the cottage, breakfast was almost ready.

"How did you manage that?" He shook his head, his brow creased in puzzlement. "You should have woken me up."

She felt a familiar surge at the sight of him. It was his eyes. Pale and sparkling as meltwater. Curled up with her back to him on the blanket, unable to see those eyes, it had been easier to resist him. She was going to have to try not to get too close. Otherwise she might not be so strong.

Chapter 28

Four days later

By the next market day, Rose's ankle was strong enough to walk on. But she didn't go to the village with Zoltan. They had ridden to Maria's the previous evening to load up the panniers with the last of the season's cherries and the first of the ripe plums, and Maria had asked for a favor. There were wildflowers growing higher up the mountain that she needed for medicines she was making, but her hip was too stiff to allow her to go very far from the farm. She wondered if Rose might go and find them for her.

Over the past few days, Rose had spent a lot of time with Maria. She hated to be idle, and while her ankle was healing, there was only so much she could do in the day-to-day running of Zoltan's tiny cottage. So she had volunteered to help with the milking of Maria's goats and the cheese making—things she knew how to do and could perform while sitting down.

Zoltan had been taking her over there each morning by mule. And while they worked together, the two women had endless conversations about the various herbal cures they had tried—Rose on animals and Maria on humans. Rose had started writing down everything that Maria told her. It had occurred to her that she could follow up her book on natural veterinary remedies with another one about herbal medicine for people. When Maria asked her to go gathering wildflowers on the slopes of the Mulhacén, she was full of enthusiasm. It would be a chance to find new species—herbs she would never find growing in Britain.

"Are you sure you're okay to go walking up the mountain?" Zoltan asked.

"I think it'll do me good," she replied. "I need to strengthen the muscles that I sprained. Don't worry—I'll stop and rest if I think I'm overdoing it."

"Well, if you're sure." He fastened the buckle on the second set of panniers and gathered up the lead reins of the two mules. "Is there anything you want me to get you while I'm in the village?"

"Could you call at the post office again?"

"Do you want me to go to the mill as well, just in case?"

Rose's face clouded. "If anything's gone there, it'll probably be on the fire by now."

"How long is it since you wrote to those people in Granada?"

"Nearly three weeks. If there's nothing waiting for me, I'm going to write more letters. If I keep pestering them, they won't be able to ignore me, will they?"

"I hope not." He glanced at Nieve, who was playing with Gunesh on the grassy bank behind the cottage. "She doesn't talk about Lola, does she? Do you think she's forgotten her?"

Rose shook her head. "When we first arrived, she cried a lot. After she started school, I hardly dared mention Lola for fear of upsetting her so much she wouldn't be able to do the things that normal children do. Talking about it is too traumatic for her. I think she's buried the pain deep inside."

Zoltan nodded. There was a faraway look in his eyes that hinted at pain he, too, had buried. He pulled on the reins, and the mules lumbered forward. "Nieve," he called, "are you ready?"

Rose set off a few minutes after waving them goodbye. She wanted to get up the mountain while it was still early, to get to the flowers before the sun parched them of dew. She had water, fruit, bread, and cheese in her rucksack—enough to keep her going for several hours. And if anything happened—if her ankle gave way again—she would send Gunesh back down to raise the alarm.

She followed the course of a stream, walking beneath trees whose boughs hung over the water. There were maples, junipers, holm oaks, and willows. Elder trees dropped tiny snow-white florets, as delicate as confetti, each time the breeze stirred the branches.

As she climbed higher, the woodland gave way to a region of gray rock and pincushion plants—cacti the size and shape of the Moroccan leather footstools she had often glimpsed in the dark interiors of Spanish houses. Dotted among them were rockroses, with wrinkled pink petals and yellow centers. This flower was on Maria's list. She intended to extract oil from it, which she said was good for nervous complaints, and make a brew of the petals as a gargle for ulcerated throats.

The next plant Rose spotted was a larger cactus—the prickly pear. Maria wanted the flowers that sprouted from the leathery green flesh to make a cure for amoebic dysentery. Picking them was a tricky process. It took nearly an hour to gather enough to fill one of the muslin bags the old woman had given her.

With two out of the five on her list accounted for, Rose decided to take a break. There was a flat rock just above the place where the prickly pear grew. She lowered her rucksack onto it and settled down to take in the breathtaking view of the valley and the sea beyond.

Something on the edge of her field of vision made her look up. A huge bird glided noiselessly over her head. It was bigger than any she'd ever seen—its red-brown wings glinting as the sun caught the feathers. A golden eagle. She watched, mesmerized, as it glided over an outcrop of rocks before soaring up toward the peak of the mountain.

Somewhere up there, where fingers of snow still clung to sunless crevices, was the little shrine Zoltan had described—the one dedicated to the Virgin of the Snows. She wondered how long it would take to reach it from here. Judging by the steepness of the terrain, it was certainly not something to contemplate with a newly mended ankle.

She thought about the story Zoltan had told her, about the traveler caught in a blizzard on top of the mountain, who had prayed for help and seen a vision of the Virgin Mary. What was it Zoltan had said? *He begged to be saved, if he was worthy.* It made her think of Lola, who must have taken the same route as that long-ago traveler to get to Granada. If anyone was worthy of being saved, she was. And yet she was locked up in a ghastly prison cell with no prospect of release.

Rose closed her eyes, summoning up the image of the statue she had seen in the church of Nuestra Señora de la Cabeza, of the Black Virgin in the gold-spangled dress.

Please, God, if you're real, set Lola free.

It was the first time she had prayed since leaving England. She felt as if her faith were hanging by a thread. The sense of peace she had felt in the church at Capileira had been fleeting, swept away the very next day by the grim facts Maria had divulged. Could a few murmured words, however fervent, really alter the course of a human life? Had that traveler been saved from the blizzard because he prayed, or would he have survived anyway? Did the Virgin Mary really appear to him on the mountain, or was he hallucinating as hypothermia began to shut down his brain?

There was no straightforward answer to any of those questions. The scientific rigor that had been drummed into Rose as a student was of no use in pondering such matters. Faith was not about facts or certainties; otherwise it wouldn't *be* faith. Believing was what counted. Even when the odds seemed impossible. Did she believe?

Her mind's eye flashed back to that summer, ten years ago, when she had camped out on the Sussex marshes, waking each morning with joy in her heart at the sound of the birds and the scent of the dew-covered meadow. In those days she had sensed the presence of God in every living thing: the birds, the animals, the trees, and the flowers—and in Bill Lee and his sisters. Was she the sort of person who could believe in a benevolent creator only when things were going well? Was her spirituality the fair-weather kind? Too flimsy and ephemeral to stand against a storm?

She glanced at the cliffs above her head, as if the answer were up there, contained in the little shrine she couldn't reach. Did the pilgrims who climbed up to it each year find answers to *their* questions? Was the journey the key rather than the destination?

She thought of her own journey to Spain—full of unexpected twists and turns, exhilarating highs and miserable lows—ending in nothing but a sense of closure, of something laid to rest. But no—that wasn't the whole story. Because other lives had been affected by this journey. If she had chosen *not* to come to Spain—if she had stayed safely cocooned in London—what would have become of Nieve?

Rose drew in a sharp breath. The sun was high in the sky now—and there were still three more plants to find. With some difficulty she got to her feet. Her ankle felt stiff, and she hobbled the first few steps from the rock to the goat track she'd been following. It was a relief when she spotted two of the wildflowers she was looking for growing just a few yards apart. One was the Sierra Nevada violet—more like a pansy than the violets native to Britain, with pale-pink and yellow petals. Maria said the crushed leaves could be used as a poultice to treat skin cancers and growths. The other herb was called trumpet gentian, with intense blue flowers shaped like the musical instrument it was named after. It was the root of this plant Maria wanted. She used it to neutralize the poison in snakebites and scorpion stings.

Once she had collected enough of each of these, Rose trudged on up the path. She paused to admire a flower she had read about but never seen: *Plantago nivalis*—the star of the snows. It had tiny star-shaped petals covered in fine hairs that looked like frost when the sun caught them. She crouched down to get a closer look, and when she straightened up, she caught sight of the final item on her list. Tall, with a halo of ghostly white petals, the opium poppies sprouted in the shadow of a blackened cactus that looked as if it had been struck by lightning.

Rose had been surprised when Maria had added this plant to the list. "Aren't they dangerous?" she'd asked.

"Of course," Maria had replied. "Many herbs are dangerous unless you know what you're doing. Opium poppies don't cure anything—and they'll kill a man if he takes too much—but they're wonderful for relieving unbearable pain."

Maria had explained that it was the juice of the poppy heads she needed, extracted from the plant before the petals fell off and the seeds inside the pod dried out. Rose picked half a dozen and packed them carefully inside her rucksack. Then she started to make her way back down the track. If anything, going down the mountain was harder than going up. The angle of her foot aggravated the soreness of her ankle. When she came to a place where the path ran past a waterfall, she decided to take off her boots and soak her throbbing muscles.

The water was breathtakingly cold. Even Gunesh, who had lowered his head to take a drink, jumped back in surprise at the icy temperature. But once she got used to it, the effect was very soothing. She sat on a rock, both feet dangling in the gushing pool the meltwater had carved out. The only sound was the splash of the water and the background chorus of cicadas. In such a remote spot, with the sun so hot, she was tempted to throw off her clothes and get right into the pool. But with her ankle still weak, it wouldn't be sensible. The rocks beneath the surface were slimy with weeds. She could end up stuck in the freezing water, unable to clamber out.

She thought about the last time she had been out for a swim—in the sea in Provence with Cristóbal. It made her wither inside to remember the way she had felt that night, the wild, erotic sense of being in love in a place where the night went on forever. This mountain wilderness could hardly be more of a contrast with the frenetic atmosphere at Saintes-Maries-de-la-Mer. As different as Zoltan was from Cristóbal.

She closed her eyes, angry with herself for allowing Cristóbal back into her thoughts. But she couldn't help wondering where he was now—whether he had taken Juanita and the children to the countryside for safety, whether he had stayed there or come back to Granada to try to see Lola.

Thinking of Lola sent the icy sensation in Rose's feet coursing through her whole body. She felt guilty for being in such a beautiful place, for breathing in fresh mountain air and feeling the sun on her skin while Lola was shut away in a gloomy, stinking cell.

As she opened her eyes, she caught a movement on the opposite bank. A flash of black and white. Then another. She blinked as her brain tried to make sense of what her eyes were seeing. A pair of badger cubs, tumbling over each other as they frolicked in the sunshine. Instinctively she reached for Gunesh's collar, afraid that he would jump into the water and try to get at them. But the dog had dozed off in the heat.

She watched, enchanted, as a third cub appeared over the top of the bank. She had never seen badgers in daylight before. Like the golden eagle that had flown over her head, it was magical. Uplifting. A private show for her delight. As if God were saying, *Here I am.*

Chapter 29

Granada, Spain

Lola was on the edge of consciousness when the door of the cell opened. At first, she thought she had died in her sleep, because the figure who came toward her and sat down on the bed looked like an angel. The scant sunshine coming through the window lit up golden hair wound into two thick plaits that encircled the head like a halo. It was a noble head, neither feminine nor masculine, but something in between.

"*Buenos días, Lola.*" The voice was strong but gentle, the Spanish words tinged with a foreign lilt. "My name is Aurora Fernandez. Your friend Rose Daniel wrote to me."

"Rose?" Lola struggled to raise herself up from the bed, muscles that had once been so strong wasted by weeks of meager food and inactivity.

"Yes. She told me what happened—what caused you to do what you did."

"Who . . . how did . . ." Lola faltered, confused.

"I'm sorry—I should have explained." The woman tucked a stray wisp of blonde hair behind her ear. "I'm the wife of the mayor of Granada. I'm English, like your friend—although I don't think she knew that when she wrote to me. She said that she hoped that as a woman, I might understand the unfairness of what had happened to you. She asked me to intercede with my husband. To get the murder charge dropped."

"C . . . can you do that?" Lola's lower jaw trembled with emotion, making her teeth rattle out a staccato rhythm.

"I'm trying. Nothing's certain—not yet. But I wanted to come and see you—to let you know that there is some hope."

"Th . . . thank you, S . . . Señora Fernandez."

"Please—call me Aurora." She reached inside her bag and produced a parcel wrapped in waxed paper. "I brought you this. It's tortilla. And there are plums in here, too." Her hand went back inside the bag. "I would have brought more, but I have to be very careful. The relationship between my husband and the chief of the Guardia Civil is a delicate balancing act. It wouldn't do to take too many liberties."

Lola unwrapped the package. The tortilla was still warm from the oven. She brought it up to her face, breathing in the intoxicating aroma. "Why?" she whispered. "Why are you doing this for me?"

There was a moment of silence. Aurora's eyes searched the wall beneath the window, her irises almost translucent as the light caught them. "I had a friend who went through a similar ordeal as you. It happened during the war. Her name was Freda. We both came to Spain as nurses from England, and we were taken to a field hospital on the Aragon front. It was grim, but for me it had a happy ending: I met my husband when I was treating him for a gunshot wound. But my friend . . ." Aurora paused, closing her eyes. "She went for a walk on her own one night, just to get away from all the horror on the wards, and she was raped by a gang of retreating soldiers. We didn't find her until the following morning. She died of her injuries a few days later."

Lola could find no words. She reached out her hand, but it froze in midair. A woman like this—clean, fragrant, respectable—wouldn't want the touch of a filthy, unkempt creature like herself. But at that moment, Aurora opened her eyes. Seeing the hand suspended above hers, she grasped it firmly.

"I couldn't save Freda," she whispered, "but I'll do everything in my power to save you."

Chapter 30

Pampaneira, Spain

Rose was sitting in the armchair, resting her ankle, when Zoltan and Nieve returned from the village.

"How did you get on?" Zoltan glanced at her foot, which was propped on a stool. "I hope you didn't overdo it."

"It was fine—I found everything Maria wanted. And I saw badger cubs—three of them—playing by a waterfall, just a few yards from where I was sitting."

"Really? I've never seen badgers round here. You must show me."

"I will." Rose smiled. "Hey, Nieve," she called, "where are you going?"

Instead of running up to Rose and kissing her, Nieve had dropped her schoolbag on the kitchen floor and was heading out the door with Gunesh.

"What's the matter with her?" Rose asked.

"Oh, she's grumpy because her friend Pilar wasn't at school today." Zoltan took the kettle from beside the fire and went to fill it. "She says she doesn't want to go tomorrow unless Pilar's back," he called over his shoulder.

"How are we going to know that?"

"We're not." Zoltan shrugged. "I tried bribing her with the promise of *migas* for supper, but she turned her nose up at that. Apparently, someone in her class said *migas* is what poor people eat."

"Probably Alonso, from the mill," Rose replied. "He's a trouble-maker, like his mother." She eased herself out of her chair and went to wash her cup while the kettle was boiling. "Talking of the mill," she said as Zoltan spooned coffee into the pot, "was there anything for me at the post office?"

He shook his head. "Sorry. I bought you some stamps—if you want to write again tonight, I can post them tomorrow."

"Thank you—that was kind of you." The prospect of composing all those letters again—in Spanish—was daunting. She wished she'd kept copies of the ones she'd sent. It would have made it a lot easier. But she had been full of optimism when she'd posted the first batch. It hadn't occurred to her that nearly three weeks on, she wouldn't have received a single reply.

It was such a warm evening that they ate supper outside. Rose had made elderflower fritters from the blossoms she had found overhanging the stream.

"These are really delicious!" Zoltan retrieved a crumb of batter that had landed in his lap and popped it into his mouth.

"Haven't you had them before?"

He shook his head. "I never knew you could eat flowers."

She smiled. For a Gypsy, he seemed to know very little about the nomadic life. But perhaps that was normal in Hungary—to live in a house rather than traveling about.

Nieve was toying with her food, pushing the battered flower heads around her plate.

"Don't you like them?" Zoltan asked.

Nieve didn't reply.

Rose glanced at him over Nieve's head, mouthing the words *Gypsy food* with a wry smile.

But before the meal was over, Nieve said that she didn't feel well.

"Do you want to go to bed?" Rose asked.

Nieve nodded.

"It's very unusual for her to want to go to bed this early," Rose said when she'd tucked her in. "You know what she's usually like—tearing around with Gunesh. She hardly ever goes to bed before I do."

"You don't think she's putting it on, to get out of going to school while Pilar's away?"

Rose shrugged. "She felt quite hot. But it might just be the weather. We'll see how she is when she wakes up."

They went back outside to eat the cheese and plums Maria had given Rose in return for the herbs she had gathered on the mountain. It was almost dark by the time they had finished. They settled back on the blanket to watch the stars come out. Rose couldn't help thinking of the last time they had done this, the night of the fiesta, when they had fallen asleep outside and she had woken the next morning with his body wrapped around hers. A surge of longing rose, unbidden, deep inside. Would it be so wrong to snuggle up to him? She closed her eyes, needing no voice inside her head to tell her the answer. She only had to summon the image of Cristóbal.

"Can you see that one? What's it called?"

She opened her eyes. Zoltan's face was inches from hers. She turned her head toward the sky, aware of the magnetic pull of his eyes.

"In Britain they call it the Plough," she replied, her voice unsteady. "But my Gypsy friends always called it the Great Bear."

"It doesn't look much like a bear to me."

"No, it doesn't." She heard a cricket strike up somewhere behind her head. It sounded very loud in the stillness of the twilight. "Can you see that one over there, shaped like a letter *W*?"

"Yes—what is it?"

"It's called Cassiopeia—named after a queen of Ethiopia who was punished by the gods for being too vain."

"What did she do?"

"She boasted that she was more beautiful than the sea nymphs. So the god Poseidon sent a sea monster to terrorize the coast of Ethiopia. The queen was made to tie up her daughter, Andromeda, on the rocks as a sacrifice to it."

"What happened?"

"Andromeda was saved at the last minute by a hero called Perseus. But Cassiopeia was turned into stone, then put into the sky. As punishment for her vanity, she spends half the year circling the North Star upside down."

"That sounds a bit harsh." She heard him laugh to himself. "No chance of any vanity up here, is there? Not a mirror in the place." He propped himself up on one elbow, his face hovering over hers. "Not that you need one." She could feel his breath on her skin. "You're very beautiful, Rose."

She lay perfectly still, afraid to move, longing to kiss him, but held back by the thought of what it would lead to.

"I've been wanting to tell you that since that first day at the market— I hope you don't mind."

"Oh, Zoltan," she murmured, "you're so lovely. But I'm scared. I don't know how long I'm going to be here. And I've been hurt—in the past."

"I'd never do anything to hurt you."

"I believe you." She reached out, stroking his shoulder with the tips of her fingers. "It's just . . . well, it's not just me, is it? I have Nieve to think about."

"Yes, of course, I understand. You think it's too soon."

"She's had so much to deal with in her short life. I've tried to give her a sense of security, of normality—but if you and I were to . . ." Rose hesitated. She felt awkward, talking about something so heartfelt in such a matter-of-fact way. "I think it would really confuse her."

"I'm sorry—I'm being selfish. You're right, of course. That's one of the things I love about you, Rose: you're so caring. You always put other people first."

His words made her feel hollow inside. If he could have seen her in Provence, sleeping with Cristóbal without bothering to find out that he had a wife and children in Granada, Zoltan probably wouldn't even want her in his house, let alone say something so tender.

He put his finger to his lips, then brushed it over hers. "Could we just lie here together for a while? I won't take any liberties, I promise."

The hesitation was only momentary. She snuggled against him, the warmth of his skin sending delicious pulses through her body. It was pure torture, wanting him so much but needing to hold back. It would be lovely to fall asleep like this. But she mustn't let that happen. Nieve might wake up in the night and wander outside—to witness the very thing Rose was trying to resist.

She opened her eyes wide, gazing up at the stars, willing herself to stay awake until he fell asleep. Then she would tuck the blanket around him and creep off to bed.

When Rose opened her eyes the next morning, she was aware that something was wrong. Nieve's face was so close that her features were blurred, but even without clear vision, Rose could tell that it looked different. Propping herself up on the pillow, she gasped in alarm. Nieve's face was covered in an angry scarlet rash.

"Mama . . ." Nieve murmured the word in her sleep, tossing her head from one side of the bed to the other.

"It's all right," Rose whispered. She laid her hand gently on Nieve's forehead. It was burning hot. "I'm going to fetch something to cool you down—I won't be a minute."

She ran into the kitchen and poured water into a bowl. She was about to carry it back to the bedroom when Zoltan appeared in the doorway. She turned to him, her face creased with worry.

"What's the matter? Is it Nieve?"

"She's burning up—there's a rash all over her face. I think she might have measles—or chicken pox."

Zoltan looked as though he'd seen a ghost.

"What?" Rose stared at him. "Do you know what it is?"

"I didn't want to worry you." He pressed his lips together until they disappeared. "I heard in the village yesterday that there's an outbreak of typhus. A couple of people who work in the silk-weaving shed have gone down with it. I wondered whether Pilar . . ."

"Pilar has typhus?" Panic rose like bile in Rose's throat.

"I don't know." Zoltan sounded wretched. "I should have asked. It . . . didn't occur to me."

"We need a doctor." Rose scoured the cottage with her eyes, ranging over the ibex horns above the fireplace, the wolf-skin rug on the floor, the kettle in the hearth, as if the person they needed were concealed in the walls or under the floorboards.

"Yes—of course. But shall I fetch Maria first?"

"Can she cure typhus?" Rose had never doubted the power of herbs to heal. But would anything Maria had be strong enough for a disease known to kill the weak and vulnerable?

"I don't know. She'll know what to do, though, while I go for the doctor."

Maria's face gave nothing away when Zoltan brought her into the bedroom. She asked Rose to undress Nieve so that she could see the full extent of the rash on her body. The child was barely conscious. She groaned when Rose undid the buttons of her nightdress, as if the slightest touch was painful.

"*Sí,*" Maria muttered under her breath. "*Es tabardillo.*"

"*¿Tabardillo?*" Rose repeated.

Zoltan reached for her hand. "It's what people round here call typhus. Red cloak. Because of the rash."

Maria motioned for them to follow her into the kitchen. She took a bunch of something bundled in brown paper from the bag slung over her shoulder. When she unwrapped it, Rose recognized the plant by the small emerald seed cases beading the creeperlike stems. In Britain it was called goosegrass. She had a vivid memory of Nathan getting covered in the sticky seeds after rolling about with Gunesh the day he came to say goodbye to her in Sussex.

"This is good for all fevers," Maria said. "Take a handful, pound it in a pestle and mortar, then infuse it in warm milk. Give her two tablespoons three times a day if she can take it. If not, use it as a poultice on her forehead and give her water with a little lemon and honey to drink." She turned to Rose, the crow's feet at the corners of her eyes deepening. "Keeping the fever down is all you can hope for. I wish I could do more for her."

Rose didn't trust herself to speak. She felt as if her throat had swollen up and closed over. She glanced at Zoltan, tears brimming.

"The doctor must have something stronger," he said. "Give Nieve some of that while I go and fetch him."

"I'm afraid the doctor won't be able to offer you anything more effective than this," Maria replied. "You're going to have to be very brave, Rose. There's a war raging inside that little body, and the odds are not good."

⋙⋘

It was well past noon by the time Zoltan returned with the doctor. Typhus was spreading its deadly tentacles through Pampaneira. Half a dozen new cases had been reported in the past twenty-four hours, Pilar among them. One of the silk weavers—a woman in her late sixties— had died in the night.

Rose went through the motions of greeting the doctor, but she felt completely numb as she led him through to where Nieve lay. The child was thrashing about on the bed, her eyes wild, as if nightmarish scenes were appearing on the walls. She no longer recognized Rose. The only words she uttered were *Mama* and *agua*. Water was all she could take. The herbal mixture had made her vomit the moment it passed her lips.

The examination took no more than a minute. "She has the severest form of the disease—a strain brought over from Spanish Morocco. The flies are spreading it—they're very bad this year." The doctor tucked his stethoscope back into his bag. Then he said, in quick Spanish to Zoltan, that Nieve was dying and Rose must be prepared for this.

"*¿Cuándo?*" When? Rose spoke the word without looking at him.

"Any hour," he replied in a low, gruff voice. "Three days at the most."

"I won't let her die!" Rose bent over the tiny feverish body, her tears falling onto the livid crimson spots on Nieve's chest. "There must be something you can do!"

"If she was older, I'd try injecting her with penicillin," the doctor said. "That sometimes works. But she's too small. Her heart's laboring too much to take it. All you can do is keep her cool and give her water when she asks for it. Try to resist getting too close to her—otherwise you might catch it, too."

When he had gone, Zoltan gathered Rose up in his arms, stroking her hair while she sobbed into his shirt.

"You haven't eaten all day," he whispered. "Let me get you something."

She shook her head. "I couldn't," she mumbled.

"But you must try, Rose. And you must get some sleep. You need to keep your strength up. We can take it in turns to sit with her." He eased her into the armchair and went to fill the kettle. "Oh, I forgot!" His hand went to the pocket of his trousers. "This came for you." He handed her a crumpled envelope with Spanish stamps. "The postman saw me in the street—he said it arrived this morning."

The nervous anticipation Rose would have felt at finally receiving a letter from Granada was completely extinguished by the grim reality of the sick child in the next room. She opened the envelope with a blank face, hardly able to take in the pomegranate symbol stamped in the top right-hand corner and the words "Oficina del Alcalde" inscribed below it. Her eyes widened as she scanned the handwritten lines. It was in English.

"It's from the mayor's office." She turned it over. The letter was signed Señora Aurora Fernandez. The mayor's wife. She flipped the sheet over again, her heart racing as she read what the woman had written:

> *Dear Miss Daniel,*
> *Thank you for bringing the case of Señorita Lola Aragon to my attention.*
>
> *While there can be no doubt that she is guilty of manslaughter, there is a case to be made that the crime was committed in self-defense.*
>
> *I am writing to let you know that your friend is to be released, with immediate effect, in the light of new evidence about the character of the deceased man and his behavior on the night of the incident. She has asked me to write to inform you of this. She awaits the return of you and your daughter to Granada at the earliest possible opportunity.*

"What?" Zoltan closed the space between them with a single stride.

Rose sat motionless, staring, unblinking, at the letter in her hand. "Lola's been released." They were words she had feared she would never say. If it had arrived a day earlier, she would have been dancing around the room. "She wants me to take Nieve back to Granada. Oh, Zoltan—what on earth am I going to tell her?"

Chapter 31

Granada, Spain: The next day

Lola woke in a panic, sweat beading her forehead. She sat bolt upright in the dark, searching the shadows. The smell was different. The stomach-churning stink of every kind of human waste mixed with the stinging fumes of disinfectant had been replaced by something fragrant and intoxicating. Coffee.

She put out her hand, feeling the smooth, starched texture of a newly laundered sheet instead of the roughness of a prison blanket. "I'm home," she whispered. "I'm home."

She slid her legs over the edge of the bed, feeling with her toes for her shoes. It felt strange and wonderful, being able to walk to the bedroom door and open it. Cristóbal was in the kitchen, pouring coffee into a cup, an unlit cigarette sticking out of the corner of his mouth.

"Sorry—did I wake you?" He put down the pot and struck a match. "I didn't mean to be back late." He gave her a sheepish smile as he lit the cigarette. "You know how these things go on sometimes."

A month ago she would have given him a tongue-lashing. Told him how selfish and ill disciplined he was. But the relief at seeing him—of having the solid familiarity of his face there in front of her—drove all such thoughts from her mind.

"Would you like some?" He reached for another cup.

Lola sat down at the kitchen table, her eyes ranging over the blue-painted chairs, the flower-patterned curtains, the golden-haloed picture of Jesus hanging on the opposite wall. Even in artificial light the room felt vibrant, alive, the objects in it a source of wonder. How could she not have noticed the colors in this little house? How had she ever allowed herself to take things like a table and a cup of coffee for granted?

"Did you get much sleep?" Cristóbal sat down beside her. "I imagine it's pretty hard to adjust after being cooped up in a place like that."

She nodded. "I keep waking up thinking I'm still there. I'm glad you're home. It's reassuring, hearing you moving about. I wouldn't have liked to come back to an empty house." She took a sip of coffee, savoring the sensation on her tongue. "You must be missing Juanita and the children."

He sucked on his cigarette. "I thought I'd go and visit them today. Will you come?"

"I'd like to," Lola replied. "But I'm hoping Rose and Nieve will be here soon. Aurora promised to write the day they released me. Rose should have got the letter yesterday at the latest. With a bit of luck, they'll be on the bus this morning."

"Do you think it's safe—for Nieve to come back here?"

"We won't be staying long."

"You're still planning to go to Madrid?"

"Yes—as soon as I look less like a ghost and more like my old self."

"You need sunshine—and lots of *migas*." He blew out a wreath of smoke. "There never was much of you, was there? We need to fatten you up a bit before you think about dancing again."

"I tried to dance while I was locked up, you know. It was the only way I managed to stay sane. But if the guards heard me, they yelled at me. I had to spread my blanket on the floor and dance on that."

She lifted her cup to her lips. "In the end I was too weak, though. I could only pretend to dance, sitting on the edge of the bed and moving my arms and feet. I used to close my eyes and imagine I was back in Provence."

"That seems like years ago, doesn't it?"

Lola nodded. "And it seems like an eternity since I saw Nieve."

Cristóbal had already left when the telegram arrived. Lola was sitting outside the front door, gazing at the sun lighting up the smudges of snow on the Sierra Nevada. Out of the corner of her eye, she saw a boy in the uniform of the Correos—Spain's postal service—his limbs laboring as he pedaled up the hill. She had seen boys like this before, cycling around the city. But no one she knew had ever received a telegram. Because no one in the cave houses of Sacromonte could read or write.

She wondered where he was going. When he jumped off his bike a few yards from the house, her heart began to thud.

"Señorita Aragon?" The boy came closer, holding out a piece of paper.

Had they changed their minds? Was this a summons? Were they coming to take her to Málaga prison? She wouldn't let them. She'd run away. To Madrid. Anywhere. But what about Nieve? How could she leave without Nieve?

"You have to open it." The boy's eyebrows were so dark and full they met in the middle, the hairs arching over the bridge of his nose as he spoke. "I can't leave until I see you do that." There was no subtlety in his voice. He sounded as though he was taking pleasure in humiliating her. Waiting for her to hand the telegram back for him to decipher.

Her hands shook as she prized it open. She stared at the printed message, confused by all the capital letters. She could feel the boy's eyes on her. The words started to swirl on the page.

Take the letters one at a time.

Rose's voice rang out inside her head.

That one—like two dancers bowing to each other—it's M. *One leg is an* I. *Two legs joined in the middle is* H.

MI HIJA . . . My daughter . . . Lola's stomach lurched as the words emerged. *GRAVEMENTE ENFERMA.* Gravely ill. *VEN A LA FUENTE SIN DEMORA.* Come to the fountain without delay.

Lola had never ridden a bicycle before. She almost came off as she careered down the hill. But it wasn't so very different from dancing—just a matter of poise and balance. She had offered the boy two pesetas, then three. In the end she had handed over five. There wasn't time to haggle. There was only one bus to Órgiva—and no other way she could think of to get to it in time.

She left the bicycle chained to a lamppost outside the Iglesia de Santo Domingo. The bus was revving its engine, ready to go. Breathless and exhausted, she scrambled up the steps and fell into a seat next to a large woman with a basket of figs on her lap.

As they left the city behind, dark thoughts began to crowd in. She didn't notice the orchards and vineyards in the valley below the road. All she could see was an image of Nieve, pale and crying, lying on a bed in some anonymous room in a place whose address she didn't even know.

Gravely ill.

Rose wouldn't have used those words unless the situation was desperate. Lola felt as if claws were tearing at her heart, trying to pull it out of her body. Nieve had always been such a healthy child. Apart from the odd cold and a mild case of chicken pox, she had never really been unwell. If Lola could just get to her. There must be a chance that she would pull through. There had to be. The thought of living without her was unimaginable. Unendurable.

Lola thought fleetingly of the vow she had made—that she would never go back to the Alpujarras. It hadn't occurred to her that circumstances might force her to return. Rose wouldn't have taken the decision to summon her back lightly. She knew what harrowing memories the place held. But Rose couldn't know that there was more. That Lola was scared—terrified, in fact—of what might happen if she went back to the area where she'd grown up. Because the chances were, *he* was still living there: the unknown man who had killed her mother and brother—and would have killed her, too, if he'd had the chance. Because whatever she had done with her life in the past eight years, she would always be the enemy: from a family who had sided with the partisans.

Lola had scant regard for her own safety now that Nieve's life hung in the balance. But the faceless man hovered like a specter at the margins of her mind's eye, refusing to go away.

Chapter 32

Pampaneira, Spain

The streets of the village were deserted. It was siesta time—and so hot that even the cats had retreated to the shadowy recesses of the whitewashed houses that lined Calle Veronica. The only sounds were the chirping of birds in cages set on windowsills and the trickle of running water.

As the mule lumbered along the cobbles, Lola was aware of eyes watching her from the vine-covered balconies that overhung the streets. One woman leaned forward as the mule passed, shading her eyes to get a better look. Even though this wasn't Lola's village, it made her feel conspicuous. If there had been more time, she would have brought something to disguise herself.

She wondered what she was going to do when she reached the fountain. The place where Rose and Nieve were staying must be somewhere close by—close enough for Rose to be able to see her from a window when she arrived. Because leaving Nieve—even for a few minutes—would not be an option.

The muleteer took his money when they reached the main square. She stood for a moment, trying to remember the way to the fountain.

She had been to Pampaneira only a handful of times as a child. Although it was just a few miles from Capileira, there had been few reasons to come down the mountain. She remembered a trip to buy fabric for the dress she had worn for her first communion. Her mother had wanted silk, but they couldn't afford it. In the end they had settled for white cotton with a sash of silk ribbon. It was a bittersweet memory, of a time of innocence and normality, before war ripped the mountain villages apart.

Lola could see a bell tower peeking above the witch's hat chimneys of the houses. She recalled that the fountain had been in front of a church. She had a vivid mental image of the three gushing spouts. She remembered stopping to drink there on the day she and her mother had come shopping for the dress material. She had been fascinated by the patterns of letters on the tiles—but unable to read what they said. Her mother had explained the legend then, and Lola had glanced this way and that, afraid that she might be fated to marry any boy she set eyes on at that moment.

As she set off in the direction of the church, she heard the deep, joyful barking of a dog. Instinctively she knew that it was not just any dog.

"Gunesh!"

He came bounding down the street and launched himself at Lola. She wrapped her arms around his neck, tears pricking her eyes at the familiar feel and smell of him. He licked her cheek as one tear escaped. In her fragile state, it made the tears come faster.

"Lola?" She looked up to see a tall fair-haired man coming across the cobbles. Gunesh stopped licking her and scampered over to him. "I'm a friend of Rose's—Zoltan—she sent me to meet you."

"Oh . . . I . . ." Lola held out her hand, confused.

"They're staying at my house. It's a little way up the mountain. Rose didn't want to leave Nieve."

Lola nodded. "How is she?"

"She's very sick. She's been calling for you—but she doesn't really know where she is."

"What is it? What's wrong with her?"

"It's typhus."

Lola's hand flew to her mouth.

Zoltan laid his hand gently on her arm. "Let me take you to her. I have a mule tethered by the church. It won't take long."

The door of the cottage was open. As they drew near, Zoltan took hold of Gunesh's collar to stop him bounding inside. With his other hand he helped Lola dismount.

"You go on in," he said. "She's in the bedroom—turn right as you go through the door."

Lola's legs almost buckled as her feet touched the ground. She felt light-headed, as if she had no control over her limbs. She stumbled toward the cottage, tufts of lavender and rosemary brushing the bare flesh of her ankles. She took hold of the door handle as she crossed the threshold, steadying herself. The air inside had a tang of lemons. And another smell—like boiled spinach—coming from a pot hanging over the fire.

"Lola!" Rose appeared, ghostlike, in the gloom. Her hair was scraped back from her head, emphasizing the hollows under her eyes. She looked as if she hadn't slept for days.

"Oh, Rose!" Lola's lower lip trembled as she lurched across the room, arms outstretched. The two women hugged each other, silent tears mingling where their faces touched.

Rose led Lola into the bedroom. Nieve was lying on her side, facing the wall. "She's not asleep," Rose whispered. "She has moments when she lies still like that, but most of the time she's tossing and turning with the fever."

As if on cue, Nieve let out a thin, anguished wail and flailed out with her arm. Lola gasped at the sight of her face, peppered with crimson blotches.

"*¡Mama!*" Nieve cried out, her eyes still closed. "*¡Agua!*"

"*¡Cariño!*" Lola dropped down onto the bed and pillowed Nieve's head in her hand.

"There's water in the jug," Rose breathed. "I've been dipping a cloth in it and holding it to her mouth—it's the only way she can drink now."

"How long has she been like this?"

"Since yesterday morning. There was a fiesta in the village. She went to stay the night with a girl in her class at school. I didn't know there was typhus in Pampaneira—I would never have . . ."

Lola reached out, clasping Rose's wrist. She wanted to say that she understood, that she knew Rose would only ever have done her best for the child, but all that came out was a strangled sob.

Zoltan appeared in the doorway. Lola was intent on trying to get Nieve to swallow some water. She didn't look up when she heard him whisper to Rose that she must try to get some rest. Rose said nothing. She hardly made a sound as she tiptoed from the room.

"Can I get you something to eat or drink?" Zoltan crouched down by the bed so that his head was on a level with Lola's.

She shook her head, incapable of uttering a reply.

"I'll leave you for a while," he said. "If you need anything, I'll be in the next room."

Lola heard him shut the door. In the thick silence of the little room, her tears poured out unchecked. She groped in the pocket of her skirt for a handkerchief. As she mopped her face, Nieve opened her eyes. There was a wild, frightened expression in them, as if something monstrous were sitting beside her.

"Nieve—*cariño*—it's me, it's your mama," Lola whispered.

The look of terror turned to one of blank incomprehension. With a rasping sigh, Nieve turned her face to the wall.

Rose didn't think she would be able to sleep. The most she had managed in the past thirty-six hours was a brief, fitful doze in a chair by Nieve's bed. She took a blanket outside and laid it on the grass in the shade of an elder tree whose branches almost touched the wall of the cottage. She lay down and placed the edge of the blanket over her face to keep off the flies. As she closed her eyes, images tumbled around her head like dead leaves in a winter storm.

The sight of Lola had been a shock. Rose knew that her own appearance must be far from normal. She couldn't remember the last time she'd washed her face or brushed her hair. But Lola's time in prison had taken a heavy toll. Her already slim body was almost skeletally thin. Her lovely face with its proud cheekbones was hollow and pallid. The journey from Granada must have drained what little strength she had. And then the trauma of seeing Nieve like that . . . Rose clenched her hands together, digging the nails into the skin. "Oh God," she murmured. "Did I do the right thing?"

Demon voices hissed back at her, telling her that in bringing Lola to this place, she was jeopardizing a life that already hung in the balance. What if Lola caught typhus, too? In her weakened state, she was unlikely to be able to fight it. But what else could Rose have done? Lola would never have forgiven her if she *hadn't* sent that telegram, if she'd left her hanging on in Granada until it was too late . . .

Rose felt as though her brain would burst out of her skull. Was this the beginning of the disease taking hold? Was she becoming delirious? Or was it just exhaustion and distress? She tried to regulate her breathing, tried to drive out all other thoughts as she silently counted in and counted out. She thought of the little book she had brought with her from England, written by a woman who had spent most of her life offering comfort to souls in torment through the high barred window of a hermit's cell.

All shall be well, all shall be well, and all manner of things shall be well.

275

How could she believe that? How could anyone believe it, faced with the imminent death of someone they loved?

Because every individual being, from a flower to a child, is of concern to the creator of life.

Those words, penned nearly a thousand years ago, had been a touchstone for Rose since her student days. The note at the front of the book said that Julian of Norwich had not always been a nun, that there were hints in her writing of an earlier life as a wife and mother, and that she had possibly lost her family in the plague epidemic that had swept through England the year before she had taken her vows.

If that was true, how could she have gone on believing?

Rose opened her eyes, gazing up at the blur of leaves and sky above her head. It hadn't occurred to her until now that this was the same tree whose wood Nathan had used to carve the little wooden horse he had given to Maria. She tried to imagine him sitting beside her now, working away with a knife while he talked to her. What would he say? What would he want to tell her?

She must have drifted into sleep pondering the answer. When she opened her eyes again, the sky had turned from bright blue to indigo, and a sprinkling of stars could be seen through the silhouette of leaves and branches.

The vestige of a dream drifted across the edge of her mind. She tried to catch it before it slipped away. Nathan was in it—she could see him riding across a meadow on Pharaoh, his favorite stallion, laughing as the wind tugged at his clothes. He pulled on the reins suddenly, bringing the horse to a standstill. He jumped off and knelt on the ground, pointing to something white.

What is it? What are you trying to tell me?

But as she grasped at it, the image faded.

A sudden cry had her jumping to her feet. The horribly familiar sound of Nieve calling out in pain had a new intensity—loud enough to penetrate the walls of the cottage. Rose ran inside. Lola and Zoltan were both by the bedside. They looked up with tortured faces.

"I don't know what to do," Lola wailed. "She's in agony."

Rose couldn't reply. The sight of Nieve thrashing around, her eyes wide with terror, was unbearable.

"I've tried to give her some more of that stuff Maria brought," Zoltan said, "but she just spits it out."

Rose nodded. "It's so hot in here." She went to unlatch the window.

"What about the flies?" Zoltan said.

"They don't seem to be so bad at night—and they can't make her any worse than she already is," Rose murmured. "Let's at least get some air into the place." As she pulled the window open, she saw the garden lit up by the rays of the moon, which was just rising. Something caught her eye, glowing white on the edge of the garden, where bare rock rose up from the grass. She had a sudden sense of her mind grasping at something fleeting and elusive—something of potent significance that she couldn't pin down.

"I have to go outside," she said. "I won't be a moment."

As she made her way toward the pale shapes hovering beneath the rocks, a fragment of memory drifted into her mind's eye, merging with what she was looking at. It was an image from the dream of Nathan. Now she knew what he had been pointing at when he jumped off his horse. The ghostly white shapes were the petals of flowers she had never seen growing this close to the cottage—flowers she'd spotted when she had been gathering herbs for Maria high up on the mountain. They were poppies. Opium poppies.

Are you telling me I should give her that?

Rose whispered the words into the night air, as if Nathan were standing there beside her.

But she's just a child.

It was a desperate, dangerous remedy. Not a remedy at all—just a way of easing the pain. But Nieve was dying, slowly and in agony. Surely Rose should do anything in her power to ease that suffering?

She crossed the grass to the rocks, bending over the swaying poppy heads, breathing in their bitter scent. She had written down what Maria had told her. A handful of the gray-green heads brewed in water over the fire. The liquid sweetened with honey and administered on a teaspoon. Reaching out, she dug her nails into one of the slim, pliable stems.

Rose didn't tell Lola what was in the brew she prepared that night. It would only add to the trauma she was already suffering. When Lola asked what it was, Rose simply said it was something to deaden the pain.

Zoltan, who had come into the kitchen as she was stirring the mixture, had simply nodded when she said what was in it. "If it helps in any way, it's got to be worth a try," he said.

When it came to getting the liquid into Nieve's mouth, Rose was afraid she would either spit it out or vomit it up. But to her relief the child did neither. Perhaps it was the honey that did the trick. Rose didn't know. But within minutes of taking the opium mixture, Nieve lay still and peaceful on the pillow, her breathing regular and her skin much cooler to the touch.

Rose managed to persuade Lola to try to get some sleep in the armchair by the fire. Zoltan offered to sit with Nieve, but Rose could see how exhausted he was.

"I'll watch her," she said. "You can take over in the morning."

He gave her a sad, soulful look. Neither of them could say it out loud: that tomorrow would be the third day—the day the doctor had predicted would be Nieve's last.

Rose lost track of the hours as she watched Nieve hover between life and death. She sat on the edge of the bed, gazing at her sleeping face, thinking that she would give anything to swap places, to be the one to die instead of this child who had never had the chance to fulfill the promise her sweet, bright, playful little soul contained.

She repeated a single, silent prayer, over and over, like a mantra. *Please, God, let her live.* It felt hopeless, futile. But praying was all that was left to her now.

The moon could no longer be seen through the window. The poppies, which had stood out so clearly earlier on, were lost in shadow. Rose thought how strange it was that she had never noticed them before. It was as if they had sprung up overnight.

When dawn tinged the sky outside, Rose reached out to touch Nieve's forehead. She felt very cold. The first rays of the rising sun revealed that the ugly red rash had disappeared. Her skin was as white as the petals of the opium poppies. Rose's heart began to race. She bent down low, listening in vain for the whisper of Nieve's breathing. She pressed the tiny wrist with her fingers, desperately feeling for the flutter of a pulse. There was nothing. No beat of life. Just cold, cold flesh.

"Oh, *cariño*, don't leave me!"

Tears spilled down Rose's face. She heard the choking sound of her own sobbing. Impossible to stop.

Don't cry.

Whose voice was that inside her head, tormenting her?

Please don't cry.

She blinked. Saw Nieve's face through the blur of tears. Her eyes were open. And she was smiling.

Half an hour later Nieve was sitting up in bed, feasting on goat cheese and ripe figs.

"Are you sure you can eat all that?" Lola glanced from Nieve to Rose, her eyes glassy with emotion.

"I'm absolutely starving, Mama!" The cheeky grin was the same as ever. The only sign of the illness that had ravaged her body was the pallor in her face and the stringy look of her unwashed, unbrushed hair.

When the meal was finished, Nieve lay back on the pillow and dozed off. Zoltan took the plate into the kitchen, leaving Lola and Rose to gaze in wonder at the sleeping child.

"I still can't quite believe it," Rose whispered. "Can you?"

Lola shook her head slowly. "I thought I was going to lose her." She turned to Rose, tears streaking her face. "As punishment for taking a life."

Rose reached for her hand. "I don't believe God works like that. What about the life you saved? Nieve wouldn't be here at all if it wasn't for you. You put your own life on the line for another woman's child—and gave her all that love. What does a person deserve for *that*?"

Lola shook her head. "I don't know."

"Well, I think I do: a miracle. And you got it."

Zoltan and Rose left Lola with Nieve while they went to tell Maria the good news.

The old woman's eyes widened when she heard what Rose had done. "That was a big risk you took. If the brew was too strong, it would have finished her off. How did you get the right dose?"

"I'd written down what you told me. I figured that if I halved the amount, that would be safe for a child of Nieve's age. It's what I do when I'm treating animals—the dose is always worked out according to the weight, whether it's a horse, a dog, a sheep, or whatever." Rose turned to Zoltan. "I was terrified of giving it to her, though, wasn't I?"

"But seeing her suffer was just as terrifying," he replied.

Rose nodded. "I knew how dangerous it was. And at one point I really thought she'd died. That I'd killed her. She was stone cold and completely still. I couldn't hear her breathing, and there was no pulse."

"You took her to the gates of death," Maria said. "Shut the body down to allow it to heal itself. Sometimes that works—sometimes it doesn't. She must be a strong little thing."

"She is." Rose smiled. "When we left, she was sitting outside on the grass, making a daisy chain for Gunesh. She wouldn't let him come with us—she said she wanted to see him wearing it when it was finished."

"You haven't left her all alone?" The wrinkles gathered on Maria's forehead.

"No—she's with her . . ." Rose checked herself. "She's with the friend I told you about—the one who used to live in Capileira. She lives in Granada now, but she came back to visit." She glanced at Zoltan, wondering if she'd given away too much.

Maria nodded and disappeared into the house.

"She won't tell anyone, if that's what you're worried about," Zoltan said.

"Are you sure?"

He nodded. "She risked her life, providing food for the partisans. She and Lola were on the same side."

Maria came back with something in her hand. It was a gift for Nieve—a silk purse with dried lavender sewn into the lining.

"You must be tired," Zoltan said to Rose as they made their way back through the orchard.

"Not really," she replied. "I should be, I know. But I feel as if I could run a marathon."

He stopped walking, shading his eyes as he scanned the hillside. "We could go for a walk up the mountain if you like. You can show me where you saw those badger cubs."

"Yes, I'd like that."

It felt good to be out in the sunshine after the trauma of the past few days. There was a cooling breeze blowing down from the glacial lake at the top of Mulhacén. It rustled the branches of the trees and sent orange blossoms drifting onto their heads.

"They have names for the wind in Spain," Zoltan said as brushed away a petal that had landed on his nose. "An old boy at the market was reeling them off one day. There's the dry, hot wind that blows from Morocco and covers everything in red dust; the one from the southwest that always brings rain or snow; a cold one from the northeast that kills the almond blossom if it comes too early . . ." He trailed off with a shrug. "Don't ask me to remember their names—there are half a dozen or more."

"You've picked up so much about this country—considering you've only been living here for a year or so." Rose smiled. "Do you think you'll stay?"

Zoltan looked away. "Maybe. I'm not sure. I've heard there are opportunities in Argentina. They speak Spanish there, so I'd be off to a good start."

"That's a long way away." She shivered as the breeze caught the bare skin at the back of her neck. Why did the thought of his leaving make her feel so desolate?

"It's only an idea," he said. "I haven't really thought it through." He brought his hand sharply up to his eyes. "Look! Up there on the ridge. Ibex—can you see?"

She followed his gaze. At first, she saw nothing but rocks. Then a flicker of movement revealed the shape of an animal, its gray-brown body perfectly camouflaged by the landscape. Then she spotted another. And another. They were chasing each other along the edge of an impossibly sheer cliff face, springing from rock to rock like children playing tag.

"They're amazing, aren't they?" Zoltan said. "How they don't fall . . ."

They stood watching until the wild goats disappeared over the top of the ridge.

"It's a good thing Gunesh isn't with us," Rose said. "He'd probably have tried to chase them."

"What did he do when you spotted the badgers?"

"He'd dozed off. There was water between us and them—I don't think he could smell them."

"Was it that stream?" Zoltan pointed to the left. Rose caught a glimmer of silver—the sparkling torrent of a waterfall tumbling over rocks.

"I'm not sure," she replied. "I'll recognize it when I see it. Shall we go and have a look?"

They walked along the banks for a while until they reached the spot Rose remembered. Lying facedown among the reeds, they watched and waited. The sound of the water was soporific. Rose found herself struggling to keep her eyes open. She was almost asleep when she felt the touch of Zoltan's fingers on her wrist. Looking up, she caught a glimpse of white among the vegetation on the opposite bank. A pointed snout with a black button nose emerged from the reeds, glistening with droplets of water.

Zoltan's fingers pressed her skin as they saw another badger cub scrambling down to the water. She heard him catch his breath as a third one joined them. For a few precious seconds, the trio gamboled about in the sunshine. Rose wasn't sure why, but the sight of them brought tears to her eyes. A sob rose in her throat before she could swallow it back.

"Oh, Rose!" Zoltan rolled onto his knees, crouching beside her, cupping her face in his hands.

"I'm sorry—I've frightened them away."

"Come here." He lifted her into a sitting position. "It's no wonder you're feeling fragile. You've been through hell these last few days."

She felt the warmth of his skin on hers as he drew her close. Her head was tucked against his collarbone, her mouth touching his neck. Without really knowing what she was doing, she found herself kissing the soft, pale flesh below his chin. She heard a murmur—a low groan, as if she'd touched a bruise. Then his mouth found hers, hungry and urgent as he eased her back down onto the bed of reeds.

The protective wall she had built around herself was swept away on a flood tide of pent-up emotion. She couldn't remember taking off her clothes or his. But when it was over, they were both naked, lying with their limbs entwined. She snuggled into him, breathing deeply. The scent of him mingled with the sharp fragrance of wild garlic and the earthy smell of the stream. She was afraid to open her eyes because the sky was too blue, the sun too bright. She felt like a dragonfly emerging from the shell of its old body. Tender, vulnerable, but aware of an awesome transformation. Ready to take to the sky after only ever glimpsing it through a tangle of weeds.

Chapter 33

Rose felt as if she had stepped outside the bounds of time and reality into an enchanted realm where there was no past and no future. The days were long and warm, and she was with the people she loved: Zoltan, Lola, and Nieve. She shut her mind to what lay ahead. To decisions about going back to England. And to what Lola was going to do when Nieve was strong enough to travel.

If Lola suspected what was going on with Zoltan, she said nothing. She rarely left Nieve's side. Hardly surprising, Rose thought, after being starved of her company for all that time and then almost losing her. And it was no hardship, taking on the daily tasks of getting food and firewood. It gave Rose and Zoltan the excuse they needed to slip away for an hour or two.

There was no need now to make the daily journey to the village to take Nieve to school. By the time the child had recovered enough to make the trip, classes were over for the summer. Nieve wanted to go and see her friend Pilar, but Rose was afraid to take her. They'd had no news from the village since the doctor's visit almost a week ago. Maria was the only other person they'd seen—and she rarely ventured down the mountain.

"Pilar is still poorly," Rose said, feeling horribly guilty for deceiving Nieve. "Uncle Zoltan's going to market tomorrow—he'll find out if she's well enough for you to visit."

Zoltan glanced at her over the child's head. They were both dreading what he was going to discover when he got to Pampaneira.

"You'll be going to a different school in the autumn, when we move to Madrid," Lola said. "You'll make new friends there—that'll be good, won't it?"

"What about Pilar? Will I still be able to go to her house?"

Lola darted a helpless look at Rose.

"Shall we take Gunesh for a walk?" Rose took Nieve's hand. "He's been so lazy this morning—he doesn't like going out anymore unless you're there throwing sticks for him."

Lola and Rose followed as Nieve scampered off with the dog.

"I'm going to miss her so much." Rose bit her lip, trying hard not to well up. "When are you thinking of going?"

"I thought maybe the day after tomorrow. We'll get the bus to Granada, sort out our things, then head off to Madrid after the weekend."

Rose nodded. The lump in her throat made it hard to speak.

Lola glanced at her, her face taut with emotion. "I feel awful, taking her away from you. You've been like a mother to her. I wish you could come with us."

Rose had a fleeting vision of making a new life in Madrid instead of going back to London. Apart from her job, there was nothing to make her want to return to England. She could speak Spanish well enough now to open a practice in this country if she chose. But what about Zoltan? They hadn't talked about the future. She knew him well enough, though, to be certain he would hate city life. He loved the peace here on the mountain, far removed from the crowded, claustrophobic conditions he had endured in Mauthausen. How could she ask him to leave it all behind to follow her to Madrid?

"Do you have to go so soon?" Rose stared at the ground as she spoke, too churned up to look at Lola. "Couldn't you stay a little longer?"

"I've already stayed longer than I should have."

Rose looked up, aware of something in the way the words were delivered. Not tinged with regret, but something darker. "It must be hard for you," she said, "being back in the place that holds such terrible memories."

Lola nodded. "But it's not just that. I . . ." She hesitated, glancing ahead to where Nieve was holding a stick above her head, making Gunesh dance around her. "I didn't tell you everything, Rose. That day in the ravine, when I heard my mother calling out—it wasn't just screams of terror. There was something else." Lola closed her eyes, as if playing back the moment in her head.

"What? What was it?"

"I heard her shouting at someone. Even through the snow, I heard every word: 'Are you going to shoot him, even though he's your son?' That's what she said."

Rose stared at her, uncomprehending. "Your *father* was in the firing squad?"

"It's beyond belief, isn't it?" Lola breathed. "I told myself it couldn't be true, that I must have heard wrong. But when I got to the bottom of the ravine, there they were, covered in blood." Her eyes narrowed. "My mother always said our father was dead. She told us he'd died of a fever when Amador and I were too young to remember him. I never questioned it—why would I?" Lola's hands scooped the air. "It never occurred to me that she would lie about something like that."

"Do you know who he was?"

Lola shook her head. "They'd all gone by the time I got there. I still have nightmares about him. A man with a gun and no face. A man who would have killed me, too, if I'd been in the house when they came."

"Was he one of the Escuadra Negra?"

"I don't think so. They didn't do the killing—they just rounded people up and handed them over. The Guardia Civil were the executioners."

"The *police*?"

"That's why I'm so afraid." Her eyes darted to the copse of trees on the hillside above them, as if she thought he might be lurking there. "They still arrest people who were part of the resistance, you know. There are hundreds of them—men and women—in prison all over Spain.

"Sometimes, in those nightmares, I'd dream of seeing his name written on a piece of paper. That was before I learned to read. It was just meaningless shapes—like he was taunting me even while I was asleep. And I would wake up covered in sweat, my fists clenched, because I'd been dreaming of punching him, over and over, until he dropped down dead."

"I suppose you *could* find out his name—if you wanted to," Rose said.

"How?" Lola frowned.

"Well, if it was me, I'd go to Maria—the old woman who sent that purse for Nieve. She's lived around here for a long time. She was the one who told me what happened to Nathan."

Lola looked at her, anxiety clouding her eyes. "Does she know who I am? Did you tell her?"

"No—but I think she might have guessed." Rose raked her hair with her hand. "When I was trying to find out about Nathan, I told her I had a friend whose mother and brother had been executed near here. I never imagined then that you'd ever come back. I'm sorry—if I'd known what was going to happen to Nieve . . ." She searched Lola's face. "You mustn't worry, though—she's on your side. She helped the partisans during the war. Zoltan says most of their food came from her farm."

Lola didn't look convinced.

"We could go and see her now if you want to," Rose said. "The farm's not far away—just beyond those trees."

Lola stopped walking. "I . . . I'm not sure."

"Isn't it better to know your enemy's name? Otherwise you're frightened of every shadow."

Nieve hid behind Lola's skirt when Maria emerged with Rose from the shed where the goats were milked. When the old woman had stood over her bed, she had been too delirious with fever to notice her. Even though Nieve's eyes had been open, she had no memory of her.

"This is the lady who sent you that lovely purse," Rose said.

Nieve peeped out, a wary look on her face.

"My, aren't you pretty now?" Maria smiled. "All those nasty spots have gone!" She paused, her head on one side. Rose saw that her eyes were on Lola now. There was a strange expression on the old woman's face. As if she recognized her. Was that possible? Rose wondered.

"This is my friend Lola," Rose said.

Maria nodded. "You're the image of your mother, my dear."

Lola flinched. "You knew her?"

"I used to see her in the market. She worked in Pampaneira as a young girl."

"How did you know she was my mother?"

Maria felt in her pocket for her pipe. She stuffed tobacco into the bowl and put it to her lips without lighting it. "I think we should sit down," she said. "Perhaps the little girl would like to have a go at milking. Will you show her, Rose?"

Lola's hands were trembling as she took the glass of wine Maria brought out for her. She felt as though she were standing against a door, trying to hold back an army with a battering ram. The dark images that had

289

haunted her dreams for the past eight years were fighting to burst into the light.

"Your mother was a maid in one of the houses—did she tell you that?" Maria held a match to her pipe, shielding the bowl with her other hand as the tobacco caught alight.

"Not exactly," Lola replied. "All she used to say was that she worked in Pampaneira before we were born."

"Did she tell you who she worked for?"

Lola shook her head.

"It was the wife of Diego Batista."

A flicker of recognition crossed Lola's face. It was a name she'd heard before. A name that people in her village had spoken in whispers. "The *comandante*?" Lola stared at the wisp of smoke snaking toward her.

"Yes." Maria sucked on the pipe. "He wasn't so high up when your mother worked for his wife. He was just an officer in the Guardia Civil."

Lola's fingers clenched around the glass in her hand. Her tongue felt as if it were glued to the roof of her mouth. She brought the wine up to her lips. It tasted warm and bitter.

"Is he still alive?"

Maria sucked on her pipe before she answered. "Still alive, yes. He lives in one of the big houses now—opposite the Iglesia de la Santa Cruz."

Lola held Maria's gaze through the smoke. Her eyes began to blur, the old woman's face morphing into the spectral image of the man with the gun. "He's my father," Lola whispered. "That's what you're saying, isn't it?"

Maria took the pipe out of her mouth. "That was the rumor when your mother left. People said his wife threw her out when she discovered she was pregnant." She poked at the smoldering tobacco with her thumbnail. "It wasn't your mother's fault. Batista was a brute. His wife told me so when I treated her for a problem with her legs. What he wanted, he took. And your mother was so young."

Lola opened her mouth, her lips trembling. "Are you saying he raped her?"

The tobacco glowed red as Maria inhaled. "I'm sorry. Rose said you needed to know—but this is hard for you to hear."

"Yes, it is," Lola whispered. She heard her mother's voice, crying out through the falling snow. Pleading with a monster who had abused her and abandoned her. A monster who was about to destroy his own flesh and blood. The murderous thoughts that had haunted Lola's dreams surged through her head with dizzying intensity, driving out the fear. He was down there, in the village. She must have passed right by his house. She could find him. And she knew how to kill a man . . .

She tried to stand up, but her legs wouldn't obey her. She staggered forward, spilling wine down her skirt.

"Oh—Lola!"

Rose came running across the yard. Lola crumpled against her like a rag doll.

Chapter 34

It was well after midnight when Rose blew out the candles in the cottage. Lola was asleep in the bedroom, worn out by the emotional turmoil the visit to Maria had caused. Rose crept out the front door and sank down onto the blanket spread over the grass.

She blamed herself for the state Lola was in. Finding out her father's name had unleashed a maelstrom of rage and grief that threatened to tip her over the edge. She had said she wanted to kill him. Moments after tucking Nieve up in bed, she had been pacing the floor of the cottage, fists clenched, ranting about what she would do to him if she got the chance. At one point she had grabbed the knife Zoltan had been using to peel potatoes and made for the door. Zoltan had had to twist her arm behind her back to make her drop it. The shock of that had reduced her to floods of tears. She had lain facedown on the stone floor, beating her knuckles until they bled.

"Thank goodness Nieve didn't see all that," Zoltan said as he came to join Rose on the blanket.

"I'm going to have to watch her like a hawk tomorrow," Rose whispered. "I was going to go with you to market, but I daren't leave her."

"I'll keep my eyes open," he replied. "I know Batista's house. She'd have to walk right past my stall to get to it."

"She told me this morning that she was planning to leave the day after tomorrow. She's going to go and live in Madrid."

Zoltan searched her face in the firelight. "That's going to be hard on you, isn't it? Saying goodbye to Nieve."

Rose pressed her face into his neck, tears prickling her eyes. "I can't imagine not having her here," she murmured. "I was only supposed to be looking after her. But she's become so . . . so much more." She couldn't bring herself to say what she really meant: that Nieve had become the child she had wished for that night in the tavern in Granada—and that she couldn't love her more if she were her own daughter. "Lola said she wished I could go with them to Madrid."

Rose regretted the words as soon as they were out. It sounded as if she were trying to manipulate Zoltan into saying whether he saw a future for the two of them.

"Is that what you want?"

"I'm not sure what I want. I should go back to England. To my job. But . . ." She hesitated, closing her eyes as she felt his breath on her neck.

"I don't want this to end, Rose."

She felt his lips move down to her collarbone, pausing to kiss her there before sliding down her body. "Neither do I," she murmured.

Zoltan had already loaded up the mules and set off for the village when Lola emerged from the bedroom the next morning. Rose was stirring *migas* over the fire. She looked up warily.

"I'm sorry." Lola dropped her head, muttering under her breath. Rose heard the word *loca*. Crazy.

"I don't blame you for wanting to kill him," Rose said. "I could murder him myself."

Lola looked up.

"It's quite possible that he shot my brother as well as your relatives," Rose went on. "But what good would it do, going to his house and confronting him? The chances are we'd be arrested before we got anywhere near him. And even if we did, we'd never get away with it. We'd be killed ourselves. And what would happen to Nieve then?"

"I know you're right, but it's hard to control those feelings." Lola glanced over her shoulder. The door was open a couple of inches. Nieve's head was just visible. "She's still asleep," Lola said. "When she wakes up I'm going to have to tell her that we're leaving. I need to go today, Rose, not tomorrow. I've got to get away from him."

Rose nodded, staring past her at the sleeping form beyond the bedroom door. Her heart felt as if it were being squeezed in an iron fist. "I'll come with you to Órgiva. We can borrow Zoltan's mules. If we go straight after breakfast, I can get them back to him before the market packs up." She went to unhook the pot of *migas* from the fire, not wanting Lola to see the anguish in her face. If they took Zoltan's mules, she would have to return them. There would be no chance of her making a spur-of-the-moment decision to jump on the bus to Granada.

As she doled the contents of the pot onto three plates, she tried to imagine what life was going to be like after Lola and Nieve had gone. It was too early to know if she and Zoltan had any real future together. She could have asked him last night, but after the trauma of the day's events, all she'd wanted was to lose herself in the warmth of his body. The thought of leaving him behind was unbearable.

"You know I'd love it if you came with us." Lola was suddenly beside her. "But I'm not blind, Rose. I've seen the way you and Zoltan look at each other. You've fallen for him, haven't you?"

"I . . ." Rose faltered, the ladle halfway between the pot and the plate. "I don't know what to do—I feel as if I'm being torn apart."

"You don't have to decide now," Lola said. "I'll write to you when we get to Madrid. I'll let you know where we're staying. You can come and visit us, can't you? Even if you decide to stay here."

Rose nodded, pressing her lips together to stem the fresh tide of emotion Lola's words had set off. Yes, she could visit. But it wouldn't be the same. The thought of not seeing Nieve every day, of not watching her grow up, was heartrending.

It took less than half an hour to pack their belongings. Lola had left Granada with nothing but the clothes she was wearing. Nieve's things fit into a small suitcase.

"Where's your rucksack, Auntie Rose?" Nieve asked as they walked through the door of the cottage into the sunshine.

Rose turned away, fiddling with the latch.

"She has to stay behind to help Uncle Zoltan for a while," Lola piped up. "But we'll see her soon—once we've found a place to live in Madrid."

Nieve's eyes brimmed with tears. "What about Gunesh?"

"He has to stay here, too. But we'll get a dog of our own once we're settled—that'll be exciting, won't it?"

Nieve wouldn't be comforted. She sobbed silently as they made their way down the track, her shoulders twitching beneath the thin fabric of her blouse. Rose walked in front of her and Lola, not trusting herself to speak. The three of them trooped down the hillside as if they were on their way to a funeral.

They'd almost reached the ruined mill when a familiar sound came drifting on the breeze—the clump of hooves on sunbaked earth. Someone was coming toward them, hidden from view by the bend in the stream.

"Rose!"

Zoltan came riding out of the trees at a trot, yanking the second mule on a lead rein. His face was pink with exertion.

Rose ran up to him. "What are you doing back so early? Did they close the market?"

"Nothing like that." He was panting for breath. "There was a man asking questions. He wanted to know who was living with me."

"A policeman?" Rose's hand flew to her mouth.

"I don't know. He wasn't in uniform." Zoltan glanced over to where Lola was standing with the suitcase in her hand. "Someone must have seen her when she met me by the fountain."

"What's happened?" Lola had come up beside them. Her face crumpled as Zoltan repeated what he had told Rose. "There was a woman outside one of the houses," she said. "She stared at me as if she knew me." Her eyes went from Zoltan to Rose. "I didn't think anyone in Pampaneira could know me. But Maria said I'm the image of my mother . . ."

"The *comandante*'s wife," Rose breathed. "Could it have been her watching you?"

"Whoever it was, word's obviously spread around the village," Zoltan said. "It's not safe to go there. They'll be watching out for her. Maybe checking the bus in Órgiva as well."

"What can we do?" Rose could hear the panic in her own voice. "If we go back to the cottage, they might come looking."

"We'll go over the mountain." Lola sounded almost unnaturally calm. "I'll take the route I took with Nieve when she was a baby."

"Over the Mulhacén?" Zoltan shook his head.

"Why not? I did it in a blizzard back then—it'll be nothing in weather like this."

"But there are people looking for you now," Rose said. "I can't let you do that on your own—I'm going with you."

"We'll both go with you." Zoltan jumped down from the mule and lifted Nieve into the saddle. "Let's get going—if we unload the panniers at the cottage, you three can ride most of the way."

❦

Rose was carrying one of the baskets of plums into the shed when she glimpsed something that stopped her in her tracks. It was something black and shiny, glinting in the sun as it jerked along the path below the cottage—the three-cornered patent-leather hat of an officer of the Guardia Civil.

She dropped the basket and ran into the cottage.

"There's a policeman coming!"

Zoltan moved like lightning, grabbing the suitcase and herding them all into the bedroom.

"Get under the bed," he hissed. "Don't come out until he's gone."

They lay on their stomachs, squashed together in the semidarkness. Rose could feel Lola trembling.

"Why are we hiding?" Nieve whispered.

"We're just playing a little game," Rose replied. "It's like hide-and-seek. We all must be very quiet. And Gunesh isn't allowed to bark. Shall I show you how to stop him?"

Nieve nodded.

Rose showed her how to encircle the dog's snout with her fingers, applying gentle pressure to the lower jaw. It was something she'd instilled in him as a puppy when they were living in the Sussex marshes—a way to avoid frightening the sheep and any wild animals they might encounter.

Moments later they heard a loud rap on the door. Zoltan must have taken his time answering it, because a fist thumped the wood before the sound of voices reached them.

"*Buenos días, Comandante.* What brings you up the mountain?"

Rose felt Lola clutch her arm.

"I hear you have a couple of women living with you. A regular little harem, eh?"

There was silence for a moment. Then Zoltan said, "Well, I have had one or two girlfriends, yes. A man gets lonely up here. But they don't stay long. It's not much of a place for a woman, is it?"

Rose could picture him, a half smile on his face, spreading his hands, palms up.

"I'm looking for Lola Aragon. She's a fugitive, wanted for war crimes."

"Lola Aragon." Zoltan repeated the name, drawing out the syllables. "There was a Lola a few months back. We don't usually get as far as last names, if you know what I mean."

He sounded so convincing. Rose glanced at Nieve. This wasn't a conversation she should be hearing.

"She might be using a false name—she was seen with you in Pampaneira last Saturday." The policeman's voice had a harder edge now.

Lola's grip on Rose's arm tightened.

"Oh, her!" Zoltan grunted a laugh. "She was a strange one. She went off to Capileira a couple of days ago. I haven't seen her since."

There was another moment of silence. Rose felt Lola squirm, as if she was trying to wriggle out from under the bed. She groped for Lola's hand in the darkness, squeezing it tight as she pulled her back. Then they heard Batista again, his voice even more menacing now:

"I don't have to remind you, do I, that you're a guest in our country? If I find out that you're harboring a collaborator, things could become very difficult for you."

"Are you threatening me?"

"Just reminding you that you're no better than she is."

Rose stiffened. What on earth did he mean by that?

"You won't mind if I look around the place," Batista went on. It was a statement, not a question.

"Be my guest."

The door of the bedroom flew open. It was a heart-stopping moment. Rose clung to Lola, praying she would stay where she was.

"As you can see, there's no one in here." Zoltan sounded so casual. "There's a shed outside, if you want to look in that."

The door clicked shut. The sound of footsteps receded and died.

"Quick!" Rose hissed. "We have to get out while he's in the shed!" She prized herself out, grabbing Gunesh's collar. Nieve wriggled out after her. "Come on!" She bent down. Lola was still under the bed, her head buried in her arms.

Lola muttered something, the words too muffled for Rose to hear. Her body was rigid.

"Please, Lola! It's our only chance! He'll be back in a minute. He's not going to give up until he's searched every inch of this place."

Lola emerged painfully slowly, as if her limbs were cramped. Her face looked gray.

Rose opened the door, scanning the room before running across to the front door, which was still ajar. She pushed it wider, praying that it wouldn't creak. Then she edged along the outside wall of the cottage until she could see around the corner. She spotted a mule tied to the nearby fence post. Then she caught a flash of white—Zoltan's shirtsleeve. He was standing in the doorway of the shed. Batista must be inside.

Rose darted back into the cottage, waving frantically to Lola, who was crouching behind the bedroom door, peering out.

"Come on! We can hide in the woods until he's gone." Rose grabbed Lola's arm and pulled her out. "Don't be afraid—they're still in the shed."

As they got through the front door, Lola doubled up, retching.

"What's the matter, Mama?" Nieve forgot to whisper. "Are you sick?"

Rose crouched down, her face level with Nieve's. "I'll help Mama, cariño—I want you to run up to the copse with Gunesh. Can you think of a good place to hide?"

As the child disappeared with the dog, Rose hooked her arms under Lola's ribcage and pulled her up. Lola stumbled forward, a dead weight.

"Please, Lola—you have to help me!"

They covered the distance to the corner of the cottage at a snail's pace. Then they were in the open. A hundred yards of meadow lay between them and the trees. There was no way they were going to make it before the men emerged from the shed. Not like this. Rose let go of Lola and bent down, taking her by the waist and heaving her over her shoulder. Straightening up, she started to run. Lola was as light and limp as a rag doll.

"*¡Deténgase o dispararé!*" Stop or I'll shoot!

Rose flung herself and Lola to the ground. The impact winded her. As she gasped for breath, she felt Lola struggling free. The sole of a boot scraped the skin of her wrist as Lola hauled herself up from the ground.

"No, Lola!" Rose gasped. "Stay down!"

But it was too late. Lola was already on her feet, her body suddenly energized.

She screamed at the figure pointing the gun, "*¡Usted es malvado! ¡Malvado más de lo imaginable!*" You are wicked! Wicked beyond belief!

Rose lifted her head a couple of inches off the ground, watching in terrified silence as Lola moved toward Batista.

"Stay where you are!" He raised the pistol higher. "Don't make me shoot!"

"Go on, then—do it!" Lola yelled. "You've already killed your own son and the mother of your children! But that's not enough for a bastard like you, is it?" She stopped a few yards from him, her head erect, her hands on her hips. As if she were preparing for a dance, not dicing with death.

"You think you're better than me?" He sneered back. "*You* who are living under the roof of a Nazi!" He waved the gun to where Zoltan was standing. "I don't suppose he told you how many *rojos* he gassed in that death camp?" He jerked his head sideways, launching a gob of spittle into the air. "Oh yes, I know all about that!"

Rose felt as if an invisible hand had punched her in the face. Batista was lying. He had to be.

"Shut up!" Zoltan took a step forward, his face white. "And put that bloody gun down!"

"Don't you threaten me!" Batista wheeled around, brandishing the pistol. "Do you think General Franco's going to let you stay when he hears about this? It was a dumb idea in the first place—giving sanctuary to Nazis—but when he finds out you've been hiding this *rojo* whore . . ."

"*¡Hijo de puta!*" Son of a bitch! Lola ran toward him. But at the same moment, Zoltan hurled himself at Batista, knocking him to the ground. A shot rang out as the gun fell sideways.

"Lola!" Rose screamed.

Zoltan and Batista were wrestling for the gun. The policeman clawed at Zoltan's leg as he tried to stand up. Zoltan kicked out at him. Scrambling to his feet, Zoltan grabbed the pistol and fired two quick shots.

"No!" Rose heard her own voice, muffled and distorted, like someone shouting underwater. She was running, running, but it felt as if the ground were sucking her down. Then she saw that the daisies beneath her feet were spattered scarlet.

Chapter 35

Rose saw Lola fall to her knees, staring at the face of her father. At the furrowed skin, the thinning gray hair, and the pouched, bloodshot eyes. Seeing him clearly for the first time in her life. Dead.

"Get her into the house!" Zoltan didn't shout the words. He didn't even raise his voice. But there was a hard edge in the way he said it. Rose felt as if she were looking at a stranger. "Where's Nieve?" His eyes ranged over the hillside like an eagle looking for prey.

"Sh . . . she's up in the woods," Rose stammered. "I . . . t . . . told her to hide."

"Find her. Get them both ready to go. There's brandy in the cupboard if you need it." He jerked his head at the lifeless body on the ground. "Leave him to me."

Rose moved, trancelike, toward Lola. She helped her up, then guided her toward the door of the cottage.

Lola took the brandy without a word, draining the glass in a couple of swallows.

"You'll have to change out of that skirt," Rose said. "There's blood on it. You can have one of mine—it'll be too big, but we'll just have to make do." It was as if someone else were speaking through her mouth.

How could she be standing there, talking about clothes when a man was lying dead outside?

Can it be true, what he said?

The question hammered inside Rose's head. She told herself that Batista had made it up. That it was just a ruse to distract Lola. But his words had set off a chilling echo, calling forth half-forgotten memories—things that had fleetingly puzzled Rose, like Zoltan's sketchy knowledge of the night sky, his ignorance of Gypsy medicine, and his perfect teeth.

She tried to fight down the panic rising from her stomach. Lola was walking over to the bedroom, unbuttoning her stained skirt.

"Will you be all right if I go and find Nieve?"

Lola nodded. She looked how Rose felt—as if she were trapped in a bad dream, unable to wake up.

It took a while to locate Nieve. She had fallen asleep inside the hollow trunk of a tree. It was only when Gunesh appeared, wagging his tail, that Rose spotted her.

"I heard a noise," Nieve said as they made their way back through the woods.

"What kind of noise?" Rose struggled to keep her voice steady.

"Like a bonfire when it crackles, only louder."

"Probably someone out hunting." Rose glanced down the hill, shielding Nieve as they emerged into the meadow. But there was no sign of Zoltan. The body had vanished.

When they reached the cottage, Lola scooped Nieve up in her arms and hugged her tight. "I've packed food and water for the journey," she said, glancing at Rose over Nieve's head. "I didn't know whether . . ." She paused, biting her lip.

"I have to talk to him," Rose said quickly. "But you two should get going. Wait for me at the top of the mountain—I'll catch you up there."

Her eyes darted to the door. "Could you bear to take Batista's mule? It's still tied up outside."

Lola's eyes widened.

"It makes no sense to leave it here," Rose urged. "It's not the animal's fault that its owner was a monster."

"A monster?" Nieve whipped her head around. "Where?"

"Auntie Rose was just joking." Lola stroked the child's hair. "Come on, *cariño*—there's a special present waiting for us outside."

A bloody trail led across the meadow from the spot where Batista had died. As she began to follow it, she caught a whiff of smoke. She ran to where the ground fell away. Zoltan was stripped to the waist, shoveling earth. A few yards away a heap of clothing smoldered on a wood fire. A flame curled up the shiny leather tricorn hat balanced on top of the pile.

Zoltan didn't hear her until she was standing right behind him.

"Tell me it wasn't true."

He drew his hand across his forehead as he straightened up. "Let me explain, Rose—"

"It *is* true! My God!"

"Listen to me—please!" He went to take her hand, but she snatched it away.

"You made me believe you were a *prisoner* in a concentration camp! Said you were a Gypsy—when all the time you were *killing* Gypsies—women and children like Lola and Nieve! And Jews! People just like *me*."

Zoltan closed his eyes, shaking his head. "I was never a member of the party—I never subscribed to that. We were just part of a state machine. There was no choice about joining the army—you had no say in where you were sent or what you did."

"So you just did nothing?" Rose blew out a breath. "You were *there*, watching all those innocent people being slaughtered!"

He dropped down to a squat, his head in his hands. "Rose, I can't change what I was. I'm ashamed of that person. Ashamed that I was too much of a coward to resist what I was being made to do."

She grabbed his wrist, pushing him, sending him sprawling to the ground. "Are you telling me that you were some lowly camp guard just driven by orders? Do you expect me to believe that Batista would have a file on a person like that?"

He raised himself on his elbow. She saw the muscles in his jaw quiver as he opened his mouth. "No, I don't. All I'm asking you to believe in is forgiveness."

"Forgiveness?" Rose stared into the face that, just hours before, she had been kissing. Into eyes so blue, so soulful. Eyes that had deceived her—and a mouth that had lied to her: not just once but countless times. Even if she could make allowances for that, how could she absolve him of collaborating in the murder of all those helpless people?

"It's not me you should be begging for mercy," she said. "Did it never occur to you, when you were making love to me, that if I'd had the misfortune to be born in occupied Europe, you'd have killed me without a moment's thought?"

Zoltan stared at the mound of earth beyond his feet. "Don't you think I burned inside when you talked about what happened to your relatives? Don't you think I wake up every single morning hating myself for what I did? When you came into my life, it felt as if I'd been given a second chance, that if you could love me, I could somehow learn to love myself."

"I *did* love you," she breathed. "But it wasn't the real you. The person I fell in love with doesn't exist. I don't even know your real name, do I?" She held up her hand. "No—I don't *want* to know!"

"Rose, please!"

She clapped her hands to her ears, stumbling across the grass. To remain in his presence a moment longer was utter misery. She had to get away. Had to find Lola and Nieve. Had to break out of this nightmare.

Lola sat on a sun-warmed rock, watching Nieve chasing Gunesh in and out of the crumbling stone walls that were all that remained of the shrine of the Virgin of the Snows. She had taken shelter inside those walls on that terrifying trek to Granada, huddling against the warm bodies of the goats in a desperate bid to stop herself and the baby in her arms from freezing to death.

She thought about the man whose actions had driven her up the mountain in the teeth of a blizzard. The man who now lay lifeless in the valley below. She had wished him dead that night all those years ago—murderous thoughts interspersed with frantic prayers for her own life and the life of the baby. She'd recalled the story of the traveler stranded in snow, who had prayed to the Virgin for mercy. And she'd tried to convince herself that Christ's mother would surely look kindly on a young girl with a baby. But she hadn't really expected to survive that long, dark night. How could she deserve mercy when her heart was so full of hate?

A short, sharp bark brought Lola back to reality. Gunesh was charging downhill, his tail wagging furiously. Lola scrambled off the rock, shading her eyes. A lone figure was coming up the steep bank of a stream, arms outstretched, hair trailing in the breeze.

"Rose!"

Rose didn't spot her at first. She was too busy making a fuss of Gunesh, who had launched himself like a missile out of the wild thyme bushes cloaking the hillside. Then Nieve, who had gone running after the dog, entered the fray. With a whoop of joy, she wrapped her arms around Rose's legs.

Nieve gave a theatrical sigh when they reached the spot where Lola was standing. "We thought she was never coming, didn't we?"

"You walked?" Lola glanced at Rose's rucksack as she laid it on the ground.

"I couldn't have taken one of his mules, could I?" Rose pressed her lips together. She looked as if she was trying hard not to cry.

"It's true, then," Lola whispered.

Rose nodded, looking away. "I didn't have time to pack much. Just my passport and purse and some underwear. And the little horse that Nathan carved. I left all the rest behind."

"Come and sit down." Lola patted the rock. "Are you hungry? We've had something already." She glanced at Nieve. "Why don't you take him down to the stream, *cariño*? He's probably thirsty."

Lola waited until Nieve was a safe distance away. "What did he say?"

Rose dug her thumbnail into a patch of lichen growing on the rock. "That he was only following orders. That he had no choice about sending people to the gas chambers." She brought her thumb up to her face, staring at the smudge of yellow on her skin. "He said he wasn't that person anymore—but he *is*. He's just killed your . . . *that man* . . . in cold blood. You saw what he did: he took aim and shot him, twice. He could have thrown the gun away, couldn't he? He could easily have overpowered a man of that age—tied him up somewhere while we all got away—but he just killed him."

Lola gazed into the distance, at the blur of blue and gray where land gave way to sea. "I killed a man, too."

"But you were being attacked—that's different." Rose shook her head slowly. "He asked me to forgive him. But how could I do that? How could I go on living with him, knowing he was responsible for killing all those people in the camp—people just like me and you?"

"Do you still love him?"

"I . . ." Rose hesitated. "I don't know. I love the person I *thought* he was—that's not the same, is it?" She scraped off another fragment of lichen. "The Gypsies I knew in England used to say that not to forgive someone is like drinking poison and expecting someone else to die."

"That's how I felt about . . ." Lola clamped her mouth shut. She couldn't, wouldn't, call him "my father."

"How could you possibly have forgiven what he did?"

"I couldn't," Lola whispered. "What does it really mean, anyway, when someone says they forgive a person? Someone who's destroyed their life?"

Rose let out a long breath. "I suppose it's about letting it go—not letting the person off, but refusing to carry them around inside your head any longer."

"I wish I'd never seen him. I don't think I'll ever get that face out of my head."

"You will," Rose murmured.

"Will I? What about Zoltan? Can you erase the memory of him? Do you want to?"

"No . . . yes . . . I don't know." Rose closed her eyes tight.

Chapter 36

Granada, Spain: Three days later

Rose was gazing into the mirrored surface of a pool, watching the reflection of a swift as it swooped low over the water. It was little more than a month since she had sat in this same spot in the perfumed gardens of the Alhambra, trying to put the past behind her, thinking about how Cristóbal had behaved.

Yet again, she had been deceived. Had allowed herself to believe. Which one was worse—Cristóbal or Zoltan? Cristóbal had not actually lied to her—he had simply withheld the facts. But Zoltan had woven a fabric of lies—a whole fake identity—made even more abhorrent by the fact that he had pretended to be one of the very people he was responsible for murdering.

So why did she feel so empty? Why did it feel like a bereavement, losing him?

A body doesn't have to leave this world to stir up those feelings. Bill Lee's words drifted through her mind. That sense of grief, of living with someone who was no longer there, was overwhelming.

She thought how ironic it was that right from the start, it was Zoltan's compassion that had impressed her—the many small acts of kindness and thoughtfulness that had eased the pain of her search for Nathan. She remembered how he had lifted her spirits at the San Juan fiesta with the simple gift of a flower for her hair. How she missed that feeling of being cherished. But that had all been part of the act, hadn't it?

I'd never do anything to hurt you.

She had believed him. Trusted him. How could he have thought there was any kind of future for them when he had broken that trust? Not just broken it—smashed it to smithereens.

Her hand strayed to the side of her face, her fingers finding the beaded copper wire hooked through her ear. This earring had once belonged to Jean Beau-Marie's mother—a woman who had died at the hands of men just like Zoltan. The thought of what Jean would say if he knew that Rose had slept with a Nazi made her feel physically sick.

She got up from the bench and made her way back through the gardens, trying to focus her mind on the future, not the past. This time tomorrow she would be in Madrid. She and Lola would start looking for somewhere to live. And while Lola pursued her dream of getting into films, Rose would need to find work in a veterinary practice. It would take time to build up enough capital to open her own business— perhaps a year or so. It would be quite similar to London, treating the pampered pets of city dwellers, but having Nieve around would make all the difference. Rose pictured her helping after school and on weekends, in her element, surrounded by animals.

The path from the gardens wound down through the trees to the Gate of the Pomegranates. Rose felt her spirits dive again as she approached the towering stone arch. It was impossible to walk through it without remembering what had happened in the shadow of those walls. No wonder Lola was so desperate to leave this city behind.

Rose had left Lola packing up the few remaining things she planned to take with her to Madrid. They had tickets for the afternoon train, which would get them to the capital by early evening. Cristóbal would not be there to see them off. He had left early that morning, on his way to the country to spend some time with Juanita and the children. He had hardly spoken to Rose since she had come back—as if her presence was an uncomfortable reminder of a part of himself he was trying to shake off. Perhaps he was changing. She hoped so.

Nieve and Gunesh came running up to her as she rounded the bend in the Camino del Sacromonte.

"Auntie Rose! The taxi's here!"

"Already?" Rose glanced at her watch. It was more than an hour before the train was due.

"Mama says we should get there early—just in case."

Rose quickened her step. The scant possessions she had brought with her from Zoltan's house were already packed. There was nothing else she needed to do.

Lola was in the hallway, sitting on a suitcase to try and get it shut.

"Here—let me help you." Rose knelt on the floor and pushed down until the catch clicked into place.

"Thank you." Lola cocked her head toward the kitchen. "A letter came for you. Aurora brought it round."

"Aurora?"

"The mayor's wife—the one who got me out of jail."

Rose stared at her, mystified.

"It's from Pampaneira." Lola lowered her eyes.

Rose stumbled to her feet. The letter was lying on the kitchen table. It was addressed to Rose Daniel, care of Aurora Fernandez, Oficina del Alcalde, Granada. With trembling hands, she flipped it over. There was no name or return address on the back. But it could only be from him—sent via the only person who would know where Lola lived.

My darling Rose,

By the time this reaches you, I will be on a boat to Argentina. But I couldn't leave without saying goodbye.

I asked you to believe in forgiveness. That wasn't fair. I destroyed the faith you had in me—and that's something I can never mend. And in my heart, I know that even if you'd never found out about my past, it would have been wrong of me to try to keep you for myself.

Being with you was something rare and wonderful— like watching those badger cubs by the waterfall or the foxes in the woods. Something to be savored, but not owned. Don't ever let anyone try to control your destiny, Rose. You should be free—not tied to any man. Especially not a man you could never look in the eye without feeling pain.

I'll never forget you.

There was no signature. Just a single *X.*

Chapter 37

Madrid, Spain: Two months later

Lola burst into the apartment, her face radiant. "I got it!" She waved a piece of paper over her head. "We start filming next week!"

"Lola! That's fantastic!" Rose jumped up from the table to hug her. "I knew you'd do it! They'd have been mad to turn you down."

"I was worried they'd think I was too thin." Lola glanced down at herself. "I've put on a *bit* of weight these past few weeks, though, haven't I?"

Rose didn't reply. She went back to the table and gathered up the documents spread over it.

"I thought we could go out for a bite of lunch—to celebrate." Lola pulled out a chair. "How about the place across the road from Nieve's school? That always looks busy—it must be good."

Rose nodded without looking up. "I'm not sure I'll be able to eat much—I had all that tortilla for breakfast."

"*All* that tortilla? You didn't eat enough to keep a bird alive!" Lola tipped her head, trying to catch Rose's eye. "You're not feeling ill, are you?"

It was something they had both been afraid of. As well as taking the utmost care of Nieve, they had watched each other for any sign of the disease that had almost claimed her life. By now, Lola thought, they should be out of danger—but Rose's lack of appetite was worrying.

"No, I'm not ill." Rose tucked the pile of papers under her arm and headed toward the bedroom. "I'll just go and get changed."

Lola followed her. "Something's the matter—what is it?"

Rose sank down on the bed, staring at her feet. "I wasn't going to tell you. I . . ."

"What?" Lola knelt on the floor, looking up into a face creased with worry.

"I think I'm pregnant."

Rose was glad the tapas bar was so crowded. The babble of other people's conversations drowned out the incessant whispering inside her head. The voices that taunted her for being so stupid, for throwing caution to the wind despite the lucky escape with Cristóbal. What had possessed her? How had she ever imagined it would be safe to have sex with Zoltan without taking any precautions? Was she so unhinged by the ordeal of Nieve's illness that she believed the simple rules of human biology no longer applied to her?

"You must try to eat something." Lola was looking across the table, her eyes round with concern. "You have to keep your strength up."

"Do I?" Rose pushed the mixture of shrimp and asparagus around her plate. "Why? I'm not going to . . ."

"Don't say that." Lola glanced over her shoulder. "That's not really what you want, is it? To go back to England to find some . . . butcher?"

"No . . . I . . ." Rose heaved out a sigh, pushing the plate away. "I've always longed for a child. You know how I feel about Nieve. But how could I . . ." She trailed off, shaking her head.

Lola dropped her voice to a whisper. "How could you have *his* baby? Is that what you mean?"

"Yes," Rose murmured. "That's exactly what I mean."

"I suppose my mother said the same thing to herself. If there had been any choice, I would never have been born." Lola lifted her glass of wine to her lips. "What matters is how you bring a baby up. What values you can give to him or her—not what kind of person its father was. I hope I'm proof of that."

Across the room someone knocked a plate off the table. It fell onto the tiled floor with a terrific crash. Instinctively Lola turned to the source of the noise. When she looked back at Rose, the chair was empty.

Lola found her crouched on the floor of the bathroom, tears streaming down her face. "Oh, Rose! I'm sorry—I didn't mean to upset you!"

"Y . . . you didn't," Rose mumbled. "Wh . . . what you s . . . said—I . . . I needed to hear it."

It was three weeks later that the letter from Rose's publisher arrived. He had written to say that he loved the idea of a book about herbal remedies for humans. The letter contained an advance that would tide her over until well after the baby was due.

"We're going to be all right, aren't we?" She passed the check to Lola, who passed it on to Nieve.

They beamed at each other as the child read the amount out loud. "What's that funny squiggle in front of the number?" She thrust the check up to Rose's face.

"It's a pound sign—in England we have pounds instead of pesetas."

"How much is it—in pesetas?"

When Rose told her, Nieve gasped. "Just for writing a book?"

"It's going to take me quite a long time." Rose smiled.

"And when she's finished it, she's going to need a rest." Lola scooped Nieve up and sat her on her lap.

"Why?"

"Because next year—in the spring—Auntie Rose is going to have a baby."

Nieve turned to Rose, her mouth open. "Will it be a girl or a boy?"

Rose laughed. "I don't know! We'll have to wait and see."

"Can I choose its name?"

"Well, if it's a girl, yes, you can—but if it's a boy . . ." Rose glanced at Lola. "I already have a boy's name."

"I think I can guess," Lola said. "Nathan."

Rose nodded. "And his middle name will be Joseph, after my father."

Nieve was staring at her. "But the baby won't have a father, will it?"

"No, *cariño*—but it'll have me and you and your mama. It'll have a family."

Chapter 38

Pampaneira, Spain: February 2001

Wild rosemary is in flower along the road that winds up the mountain, the pale lilac petals interspersed with the darker purple hue of lavender and the bright amber of marigolds. Rose smiles as she glances out the window of the car, thinking what a good thing it is that a road now connects the villages of the Alpujarras. At eighty-five, she's a little stiff to go anywhere on the back of a mule. But wild horses would not have prevented her from making this journey—and she knows that Lola feels just the same.

After decades of hiding the past away, the Spanish authorities are finally facing up to what happened during the Civil War. It's the children and the grandchildren of those who died who have campaigned for change. They want answers. They want proper burials for the dead.

Petitions have been sent to the government, and a new law has been passed. And so today, in Pampaneira, people are gathering to see the remains of those who were executed in the ravine laid to rest in proper graves.

As the car rounds a tight hairpin bend, Rose glimpses a field of almond trees whose branches are covered in blossoms. In the wind they look like brides dancing with confetti in their hair. And further on are groves of orange trees, heavy with ripe fruit.

"Are you okay, Mama?" Nathan catches her eye in the rearview mirror. "It's a bit like being on a rollercoaster, isn't it?"

"I'm fine!" Rose smiles back, watching the sun glance off his forehead as the car takes another bend, lighting up the peppering of gray in his hair. He reminds her so much of her brother. And he inherited his uncle's love of horses. Rose's latest home is a cottage on the grounds of the stud farm he has set up in Segovia. It's good to be living close to him. And it means that the grandchildren can pop in to see her whenever they feel like it.

"You know, I don't remember any of this." Nieve is sitting in the passenger seat, craning her neck at the view. She still has curly hair, but it's white now. She's due to retire next year from a long and distinguished career in the law.

"*I* do," Lola replies. She shoots a heartfelt glance at Rose. "I'll never forget that ride up the mountain, the day you sent the telegram. It was the worst day of my life."

Rose thinks how glamorous Lola looks, even though she's dressed for a funeral. In her late seventies, she can still turn heads.

As the car slows down, Rose notices Lola reaching into her handbag for a pair of dark glasses. But it's a futile gesture. The paparazzi are out in force. Rose was expecting a few photographers—for an event of such significance. But word must have got out that Lola Aragon is going be attending. The news hounds are not going to miss the chance to capture an international celebrity coming to pay her respects to the recovered remains of long-dead family members. They still call her "the face of flamenco." Even if she lives to be a hundred, that will never change.

There's a welcome committee standing by to make sure that the photographers and the TV cameras don't intrude on what is supposed to be a private ceremony. The cemetery is cordoned off, and once they're inside the whitewashed walls, the atmosphere becomes more serene.

Nathan takes his mother's arm as they make their way down the few steps to the Garden of Rest. Nieve is just ahead of them, helping Lola. When they are all safely down, Nieve glances at a woman who is standing a few yards away, handing out booklets. "That's Ortiz Chanes," she whispers. "She's from the Granada wing of the Association for the Recovery of Historical Memory."

Rose nods. She has followed reports of this organization in the news. They've been uncovering Civil War mass graves around Spain since the late 1990s. But it's only a few months since legislation has been passed to support those who want to excavate the remains of their loved ones. As a high-court judge, Nieve has been a driving force behind that new law.

Rose, Lola, and Nieve were among the first people in the country to undergo DNA tests to enable their dead relatives to be identified. Burial vaults have now been made ready for Nathan, for Lola's mother, and for her twin, Amador. There's also a grave for Heliodora, Nieve's biological mother. And Rose has asked for Adelita's name to be added to Nathan's gravestone, although there was no means of identifying her remains.

Lola turns to Rose with a wistful smile as Nieve goes to greet the woman who has campaigned alongside her. "When I was growing up, there was an old saying in these mountains—that children fostered by goats grow up to be noble adults."

"You must be so proud of her."

"I am. I don't know how she did it, raising a family and making such a success of herself at the same time."

"Well, she had a pretty good example in you, didn't she?"

"Not to mention her Auntie Rose." Lola's eyebrows arch over the dark glasses. "Are you still getting all those letters from the States?"

"Yes—they've asked me to be the keynote speaker at a convention in Chicago this summer. The American Herbalists Guild. I don't know if I'm up to going all that way."

"Yes, you are!" Lola takes Rose's gloved hand in hers and squeezes it. "Nathan told me you did an emergency caesarean on one of his mares last week—how many vets are still doing *that* in their eighties?"

"I think they're about to start." Nathan has been reading the names on the vaults. Nieve comes back at the same time. They all link arms as the priest begins to recite the words of the committal.

They watch the coffins slide, one by one, into the vaults. When the priest reads out the name of Lola's mother, Rose feels the grip on her arm tighten. Then Amador. Rose hears Lola release a long breath. There is a sense of the past finally being laid to rest.

Next is Heliodora's coffin. How sad for Nieve, Rose thinks, that she has never even seen a photograph of the woman who gave birth to her.

And then it is Nathan's turn. Rose offers up silent thanks that her search for him brought her the family she longed for—in a way she could never have anticipated. And in her heart, she knows that if his spirit is nearby, looking down on them, it won't stay here for long. No. Nathan will be up there on the mountain, his soul gliding through the scented meadow, where the cherry stone she planted all those years ago has grown into a fine, strong tree.

AUTHOR'S NOTE

The Snow Gypsy is a work of fiction inspired by someone who really existed. The character Rose Daniel is based on Juliette de Baïracli Levy (1912–2009), a British-born herbalist and author noted for her pioneering work in holistic veterinary medicine. After training as a vet, she left England to study herbal medicine in Europe and beyond, living with Gypsies and nomadic farmers, from whom she acquired a wide knowledge of herbal lore.

She went to live in Spain's Alpujarras region in the decade following the Second World War with her young son Rafik. Her daughter, Luz, was born there. Nieve's near-death from typhus in *The Snow Gypsy* is based on Juliette's successful treatment of Luz, who almost died as a baby from the disease.

Like the fictional Rose, Juliette had a brother who was killed after enlisting as a soldier. Many other incidents in the novel reflect Juliette's real-life experiences. Those who wish to distinguish fact from fiction might like to read the autobiographical books she wrote. The ones I particularly drew on were *As Gypsies Wander* (1953) and *Spanish Mountain Life* (1955).

In her later years Juliette gave workshops in the United States on herbal medicine and became known there as "the grandmother of the herbal renaissance." Growing interest in her ideas and her unusual life has led to several of her books coming back into print, including *Common Herbs for Natural Health* (originally published in 1974), which provided useful material for *The Snow Gypsy*.

I have Chris Stewart's *Driving Over Lemons* (1999) to thank for bringing Juliette to my attention. When he and his wife took on a remote farm in the Alpujarras in the 1990s, her *Herbal Handbook for Farm and Stable* (1952) was their go-to resource for dealing with sick animals.

In my thinking and writing about Spain, I have been particularly influenced by Giles Tremlett's excellent analysis of Civil War secrets, *Ghosts of Spain* (2006). Gerald Brenan's *South from Granada* (1957) provided fascinating details about the way of life in the Alpujarras in the first half of the last century. Jason Webster's *Duende* (2003) and *Sacred Sierra* (2009) gave me an insight into the world of flamenco and the timeless customs of rural Spain.

ACKNOWLEDGMENTS

I'm grateful to all my friends in Spain for their encouragement during the writing of *The Snow Gypsy* and for the insights they gave into a country that still has so many buried secrets. Particular thanks to Christina Aldridge and Loli Muñoz, who were kind enough to correct my very poor Spanish.

Thank you to Jodi Warshaw and everyone at Lake Union for the wonderful job they do and to my editor, Christina Henry de Tessan, for her perceptive suggestions.

Huge thanks to my friend Janet Thomas for her inspiration, her wise advice, and the many happy lunches we have had over the years.

Finally, I have my close family to thank: Mum and Dad for their unflagging enthusiasm; my children, Ciaran, Ruth, Isabella, and Deri, for making me laugh and helping me negotiate the minefield of modern technology; Steve, my husband, for his constant good humor, even at absurd hours of the morning, and for all the fun we've had exploring Spain together.

ABOUT THE AUTHOR

Raised in Wolverhampton in the United Kingdom, Lindsay Jayne Ashford became the first woman to graduate from Queens' College, Cambridge, in its 550-year history. She earned a degree in criminology and was a reporter for the BBC before becoming a freelance journalist, writing for a number of national magazines and newspapers.

Lindsay began her career as a novelist with a contemporary crime series featuring forensic psychologist Megan Rhys. She moved into historical mystery with *The Mysterious Death of Miss Jane Austen*, and her three most recent books, *Whisper of the Moon Moth*, *The Color of Secrets*, and *The Woman on the Orient Express*, blend fiction with real events of the early twentieth century.

She has four children and divides her time between a house overlooking the sea on the west coast of Wales and a small farmhouse in Spain's Sierra de Los Filabres. When she's not writing, she enjoys volunteering for Save the Children, kayaking, and walking her dogs, Milly and Pablo.